The Woman Who Was Not All There

The
Woman
Who
Was Not
All
There

A NOVEL BY PAULA SHARP

PERENNIAL LIBRARY

Harper & Row, Publishers, New York
Grand Rapids, Philadelphia, St. Louis, San Francisco
London, Singapore, Sydney, Tokyo

"The Man" first appeared in *New England Review Bread Loaf Quarterly.*

A hardcover edition of this book was published in 1988 by Harper & Row, Publishers.

First PERENNIAL LIBRARY edition published 1989.

Library of Congress Cataloging-in-Publication Data

Sharp, Paula.
  The woman who was not all there.

  "Perennial Library."
  I. Title.
PS3569.H3435W6   1989   813'.54   88-3348
ISBN 0-06-091602-8

89 90 91 92 93 FG 10 9 8 7 6 5 4 3 2 1

This book is dedicated with love
and *saudades* to
Ivonete de Souza Betarelli,
who kept me lively and rejoicing while I wrote it,
and to my one and only brother,
E. Sharp.

CONTENTS

ACKNOWLEDGMENTS

Grateful acknowledgment is made to Marjorie Horvitz, Lesley Shark, Sally Waller, and Emily Wheeler for careful readings of this book. For certain essential details, the author is indebted to Lisa Arrington, Andy Fox, Jonathan Poor, Rosemary Sharp, Skeet, Steven B. Wasserman, and various Renaud myths. The author also wishes to thank Gina Maccoby for bringing this book to light; Terry Karten for her editorial suggestions; and the New Jersey State Council on the Arts for generous financial support.

1. Ghosts

THE MAN

Marjorie's husband, Byron Coffin, had misled her for so long that she learned to lean away from life to keep from falling over, like a woman walking a large dog. The week after Marjorie and her husband separated permanently, she quit her job as a nurse's aide and withdrew from the evening nursing classes she had been attending sporadically for years. All month, she sat on the living room couch from morning until night, playing cards with her four small children, reading "Humor in Uniform" in the May 1963 *Reader's Digest,* and watching monster movies on afternoon television.

Marjorie was amazed by the variety of monsters that had developed over the years of her marriage when she had been working and unable to watch much television. There was the Wolfman, whose victims became wolfmen, and Dracula, who turned the ladies he bit into female replicas of himself, pale women with desperate-looking eyes and widow's peaks. There was the Phantom of the Opera, who carried girls into underground sewers, and the old wall lamp in Marjorie's living room had the same smooth, glistening surface as the phantom's face. There were also the monsters who were more modern and appeared in color on late-night television. These arose from scientists toying with human genes, from men overexposed to radioactivity or archaeologists thawing inhuman creatures from icebeds in the Arctic. The more modern monsters could not be stopped by silver bullets or ordinary acts like falling from cathedral tops. They were shapeless forms that grew from the size of molehills into mountains by devouring everything in their path, beginning with the stick that prodded them and the hand that held the stick and then the whole man attached to the hand; or they were men who should have died but could not, their natural deaths having been interfered with by the unnaturally curious.

Sometimes at night Marjorie would wrap herself inside her covers like a mummy, thinking of things that could grab her arms or feet if she let them travel too far from her sides. She would drink a little Johnnie Walker or Jim Beam to put herself to sleep, and then pull her bedspread around her neck, which felt so small and thin and vulnerable. After Marjorie had spent a month of semisleepless nights and restless days keeping to herself in the house, her older sister, Bertha, arrived in Durham driving a red Ford Falcon. Bertha told Marjorie to brush her hair and get out of the house and make something of herself. Bertha, who had no family of her own, insisted that the four children stay with her in New Orleans for a month, and that Marjorie let the two youngest live there for the entire summer. Marjorie agreed, because all through May she had felt out of sorts with her children: she was snappish and impatient. She was afraid of becoming an old shrew.

Before Bertha left with the children, she stayed in North Carolina for two weeks, getting the hospital to rehire Marjorie, enrolling her in a summer nursing program with instructions to get her degree once and for all, and baby-sitting the children. Bertha took money out of her stipend from Tulane, where she was studying for her doctorate in anthropology, and paid two months' back rent on Marjorie's falling-apart house with its small, weedy front yard, which sloped precipitously into the street. When Marjorie complained that she did not want to be stuck with the awful name Mrs. Coffin the rest of her living days, Bertha obtained and processed the papers necessary to change Coffin back to Marjorie's maiden name, LeBlanc. Bertha repaired a dripping faucet in the kitchen sink, shampooed the living room rug, and changed the ancient battery in Marjorie's Oldsmobile.

In June, the day before Marjorie's courses began, Bertha packed her nieces and nephew into the Ford Falcon. A week later, Marjorie received a letter from the children, with their pictures pasted on top. She pinned the letter to the refrigerator and looked at the pictures every morning during breakfast. Above the photographs, Bertha had written:

> I love you once
> I love you twice
> I love you more
> than beans and rice.

Under the pictures, Marjorie's son and daughters had scrawled their names and ages: Carla—6, Karen—7, Sam—8, Ruth—9. They looked like one child in different poses. They all had lantern jaws and malarial complexions and hair that burst from their heads like black milkweek fluff. Byron Coffin had had the same fine hair and underbitten smile.

Marjorie was startled by how little the children had changed after being away from her for the first time, even if only for a week. She had expected them to look like strangers. And then she had been surprised to see how much Ruth and Carla looked like little boys. They had not dressed in clean clothes for the pictures, and they had dark dirt sideburns and red dirt mustaches. Karen appeared to have washed herself, and was wearing a dress, but her mouth hung open as if she had been talking during the picturetaking. Only Sam's face was red with violent scrubbing, and Bertha, probably as a joke, had made Sam wear a clip-on Catholic school tie. The tie hung at a devil-may-care angle and his top button was missing.

All during June, while the children were away, Marjorie experienced sensations of imbalance and drunkenness which abated only when Ruth and Sam returned to live with her.

When Marjorie pictured Ruth and Sam in her mind, she saw them clinging to either arm, anchoring her on both sides and holding her upright. Sometimes, however, Marjorie had moments of missing her two younger children that were so overpowering she felt completely airheaded and weightless, as if a strong wind could lift her up and carry her away.

By July, when Ruth and Sam returned, Marjorie rarely thought of Byron Coffin anymore. She now saw that the best a woman could ever do with a man would be to love that part of him which existed only in her imagination. She could imagine he had loved her as she did him, believe he loved touching her as she had loved touching him. Hope that a warm feeling jumped up his spine just sometimes when he thought of her. But if a woman ever became confused and mistook her imagination for what was real, so that true life took her off guard, something terrible would happen; she would turn into a pillar of salt like Lot's wife.

Marjorie had decided to face the fact that she would never remarry because she had four children and was twenty-nine. She believed that men her age and older were interested in "young things," and she was realistic enough to know that she no longer qualified as a young thing. So she was surprised when loneliness continued to bother her. She did her best to conceal it from Ruth and Sam, but loneliness shadowed Marjorie so constantly that she could only hide it from her children by avoiding them. On weekdays she left early for her work at the hospital and did not return to the house until seven. Marjorie spent all afternoon Sunday and part of each Saturday reclining in a wicker chair on the porch of her friend Rita, drinking gin and tonic or whiskey or, more recently, margaritas.

But even so, loneliness stalked around the house like a hunter, or sat mutely at the supper table with no place mat or chair set for it, and stole food off Sam's and Ruth's plates when they were not looking. It wore big, tobacco-colored shoes to attract attention when it was least wanted—in the evening after school, in the middle of *The Rifleman* on television, or when Ruth and Sam played in the woods behind the house. It had a strong, sweat smell you could not ignore, like a man who has stood all day on a hot corner with his hands in his pockets.

*   *   *   *

On a Saturday morning in August, Sam and Ruth were sitting with their dog on the back steps, watching the pinewoods.

"I saw him," said Ruth. "Right there, next to the garden. Just leaning there against the pine tree, smoking a cigarette."

Marjorie could not tell what her children were talking about. A clump of black hair curled over Sam's narrow forehead. His brown eyes, motionless as two rusted nails, focused steadily on a far pine, trying to conjure a vision into being. Sam wore a moss-green T-shirt and brown pants sawed off at the knee. Ruth had dressed herself identically, in a green T-shirt and mud-colored shorts. When Ruth leaned forward and whispered to Sam, her profile to Marjorie, Marjorie felt as if she were staring at both sides of a coin at once. Since Carla and Karen had stayed behind with their Aunt Bertha, Ruth and Sam had drawn even closer together. They would have been friends except that they were uncertain where one of them began and the other left off.

Marjorie rose on the edge of the garden where it bordered the woods, and walked toward her children. When she reached the porch, her flip-flops slapped the floorboards, making her sound as though she had four feet instead of two. "What're you hooligans doing out here?" she asked. "I thought you were going swimming at the lake."

"We're going," Sam whispered, as if by speaking aloud he would betray Ruth's secret.

For a moment, Marjorie stood silently above her son to see if he would tell her more, but he only raised his eyes and stared at her darker ones. A slipping bun curled against his mother's neck in a black nest. She was wearing a nurse's aide's uniform and carrying a hand-knit pocketbook the color of lichen. Before Sam had gone to live with his aunt, his mother had always carried two long steel knitting needles that stuck out like tusks from her flowered bag. Sam owned twelve sweaters she had made for him. ten of which no longer fit him.

"Well, I'm going to drive down to Fred's Nursery to get some fertilizer for the garden," Marjorie said, bending over to kiss Ruth.

Ruth could smell gin on her mother's breath, a scent stronger than pine needles. "How long you going to be gone?"

"Oh, a few hours. I'm stopping by Rita's on the way home. Want to start the car?" Marjorie held the keys in front of Ruth, who grabbed them and ran across the porch to the Oldsmobile, then slid into the car seat and poked the keys into the ignition. When she had slipped down so that her foot could reach the gas pedal, she stuck her head out the door and yelled, "When you getting back from Rita's?"

"Oh, I don't know. About seven o'clock maybe."

Rita was over thirty and had never married or had children. Whenever Marjorie saw her, Rita was wearing the same blue cotton shift and carrying a tonic bottle with a picture of a volcano on its label. Her eyeglasses were as curved and blue as the bottoms of vermouth bottles, and her dark hair had a bourbon cast to it that reminded Marjorie of Bertha's hair. Rita had not always lived in North Carolina. Her parents had moved to Durham from New York City, and when Rita grew up, she herself had returned to the North and spent five years in Jersey City, where you could not go out in broad daylight without some man jumping on you to kill you or take your money.

Rita ran a laundromat ten blocks from Marjorie's house. Marjorie had met her when cleaning a month's worth of dirty work uniforms, while all the children were away. Rita smelled of borax and clothing softener, and had helped ease Marjorie into the world of manlessness. Rita did not hate men, but they rarely entered her territory and she did not miss them. Once every few weeks Rita would relate to Marjorie that a man had entered the laundromat, an arrogant trespasser, and asked Rita for change.

"A man comes into the mat yesterday and says, 'Hey, Baby, gimme change for a dollar?' And you know what I said?" Rita raised her eyes, greatly magnified by her glasses as if to emphasize her astonishment. "'I ain't no goddamn baby. I'm a human being.' And do you know what he said back? 'Baby's a human being.'"

Marjorie laughed, trying to think up a better comeback than Rita's. But the car roared twice, startling Marjorie from her thoughts, and then quieted into a steady rumble. "Looky there," said Marjorie, touching Sam on the shoulder. Sam turned his head toward the car and saw a tomcat hunched like a porcupine next to the Oldsmobile.

"Oh, no!" Sam yelled, and a split moment before or after his yell the dog froze into a second of disciplined joy and sprang after the tomcat. The dog ran twenty feet and then the chain jerked her neck and lassoed her to the ground.

"It's not right to chain Pretty up, it's not right to chain her up!" Sam shrieked, running over to the dog and pulling her upright.

"Pretty's OK. You just leave her tied up," said Marjorie as the dog settled back on the porch beside Sam. Pretty was an ugly black and tan wolf-sized thing that Sam and Ruth had trained to jump the eight-foot fence around the back garden. Bertha had given the dog to them as a going-away present. Ruth had told Marjorie that Bertha stole the dog the night before Ruth and Sam left New Orleans, from under a house three blocks away from Bertha's on Prytania Street. According to Sam, the dog's owner had kept Pretty under his house: The house was raised on stilts, and like other people in the neighborhood with similar houses, he wrapped chicken wire around the stilts and kept his dog penned inside, so that if strangers came near, the dog would rush beneath the front steps, barking right under the visitors' feet and scaring them to death. Marjorie, who had grown up on Prytania Street, remembered that a lot of people had kept dogs like that in the old days. The dogs would become mean with imprisonment and isolation, and were often dangerous if they escaped. The dog Bertha had stolen for the children had grown too big for her hemmed-in space, according to Sam: she had had to stoop as she walked around under the house, and she would howl in a sad, houndy way as the children passed by. Bertha had gone down to the house at four o'clock in the morning with a pork chop and some wire cutters, and smuggled Pretty back to her Ford Falcon. Bertha had told the children that there were numerous circumstances in which stealing was acceptable, and this was only one of them.

Marjorie worried about the dog. Pretty had grown so big Marjorie no longer felt free to let her roam loose, despite the fact that there were no leash laws yet outside the Durham city limits. Sam was so attached to Pretty that he let the dog sleep under his bedcovers. Marjorie would come into Sam's room at night to pull the sheet up to his chin, and see the dog's huge shoulders and her monstrous profile lying against Sam's pillow. The children took Pretty everywhere with them, and she had grown insanely protective. The dog hated men, and growled and lunged at them if they came anywhere near the children.

Pretty looked at Sam, letting her mouth fall open in a ferocious yawn. Marjorie told her children, "That dog's getting mean. I don't want to see you two letting her roam around loose, you understand? I told you all once already, if I see that hound walking unchained I'm giving her away. I saw a notice up at the laundry mat saying there's a horse farm outside Durham that's looking for a watchdog."

Massive arms seemed to press against Sam's ribs, and a streak of heat ran up from the hollows behind his knees to the base of his neck. Some days passed without this fear coming to him or Ruth, but recently the terror that they would lose Pretty had begun to shadow the children continually. They would stop suddenly in the middle of a game of roll-the-bat and look at each other with a shared horror that drew them together. This fear circled in their stomachs as they ate breakfast, and it clung to their skin on hot days when the backs of their legs stuck to the car seat.

The face that Sam now trained on Marjorie made her feel terrible. She stooped down so that the hem of her uniform exposed her yellowish, stone-smooth knee. "I don't mean to make you feel bad, Honey." A stray hair curled around Marjorie's bobby pin and tickled Sam's neck. "I just want you to know I mean it. If you have to let the dog run, just take her down deep into the woods, that's all."

"Come on! Mama!" Ruth yelled, sticking her head out of the car door for a second time. Sam climbed off the porch and onto the hood of the Oldsmobile. Marjorie pried Ruth from behind the steering wheel and sat down, waiting to release the brake until Ruth seated herself securely next to Sam. Marjorie drove fifty feet down the road before Ruth and Sam motioned her to stop. They ran around to the side window and Ruth pushed her face into Marjorie's ear, making a loud, kissing sound that shattered like lightning inside Marjorie's head and made her tip sideways as if suddenly deprived of her balance.

"Oh, that hurt." Marjorie half smiled, pushing Ruth away from the window.

"Get me some pop at the store," Sam said, his hands pressed against the side window so that they lay flat and smooth on the bottoms like a lizard's.

"I'll come straight back after I see Rita."

"Rita drinks too much BEER!" Ruth laughed, her voice rising in volume so that the word "beer" carried to all the houses on the road. She and Sam jumped back from the car, and their mother drove away.

"You shouldena said that, Ruth. I bet you made her mad."

Ruth looked at her brother, half worried. "How come?"

" 'Cause Mama drinks too much BEER TOO!" he

screamed at the top of his lungs, and fell onto the road, clutching his stomach as if he would die laughing at his own wickedness.

"Shut up, Sam, just shut up." Ruth staggered down the road pretending to be drunk, and Sam followed her, trying to outdo her by falling every few steps.

"I am feeling no pain, feeling no pain," Sam chanted, and Ruth joined in. When they got back to the porch, Ruth unhitched the dog.

"Mom said not to let Pretty off the chain or she'd give her away."

"Then she can give me away too!" Ruth grabbed the dog by the collar. "We can run on the road so she chases us. Then she won't wander off till we get to the woods." Ruth sped down the street, and Pretty bounded in front of her like a kicked can. Ruth stopped when they came to an unnaturally tall and straight pine tree near the road's edge.

"This is where I saw him first." Ruth pointed to a mysterious bare space between a pair of saplings. "He was standing right there."

"What'd he look like?"

"Ugly. He had red hair and a dirty face. He just stood right there and stared at me. Didn't say anything. I cut home and got Pretty, and when I come back, he's leaning on a tree right next to the garden. He had on a green thing that said 'Texaco' over the pocket."

"Maybe he was an escaped convict."

"If we see anything this time, Pretty'll scare him off."

* * * *

They turned down a path that led toward the lake. Ruth and Sam were fugitives from the law. They walked so softly they had not broken one pine needle on the journey from Georgia. They ate acorns and possums and slept in caves. They had befriended a guard dog in the penitentiary and trained her to keep off the police when Ruth and Sam broke away. Then the dog had come with them, catching possums and leaving the food at their feet. Ruth and Sam always let the dog eat her share first, after they roasted the meat.

"We've gone crawstate lines," said Sam, a pine needle poking from his mouth. He had taken off his shirt, and now it hung like an animal skin from his back pocket.

"We've gone cross," Ruth echoed, running her hands over her chest like a man. She had wrapped her shirt in a bandanna around her head.

"Now we have to change our names. My name is Corn Pone."

"My name is Juice Henry," said Ruth, sniggering and leaning against a rock. "I will tell you how to stop a bloodhound. You find a hot pepper the size of your foot and tie it to the bottom of your shoe and walk like that. Then the dogs come by and sniff the hot pepper up their noses. They sniff so hard they fall over sneezing and can't keep on after the scent." Ruth shook her head and wrinkled her nose, then snorted and pretended to sneeze. The dog pushed its face into Ruth's ear. "We should try that with you and see what happens," Ruth said to the dog, with a sense of sacrilege. A chill ran down Ruth's back and for a moment she was afraid the dog would disappear because of what she had said.

"We can't do that to her," Sam intervened. "She's not a bloodhound. It's just bloodhounds are bad."

The dog's tongue swayed in her mouth, a long pink leaf. Her sides puffed in and out as if a wind had risen up inside her that was trying to escape.

"That's how dogs sweat," said Sam. "They don't sweat all over like us. They just sweat through the pads at the bottom of their feet and out their tongues." He and Ruth decided to go back to the house and leave Pretty with a bowl of water before going to the lake.

* * * *

Marjorie returned home by three. The dog was on the chain in the backyard, but Ruth and Sam were gone. Marjorie realized she should have gone ahead to Rita's and not worried about the children. She decided to call Rita once the car was unloaded and the fertilizer spread on the garden. As Marjorie opened a sack of bonemeal, she pictured Rita and herself talking, their voices coiling away from the telephones, running up through their roofs over the pin-shaped poles into the high wires, threading Rita and Marjorie together like two ends of a hemline.

Marjorie hoed a new plot where she wanted to plant impatiens, then pulled the suckers off the tomato plants and inspected the beans. Sweat trickled from her forehead and eddied in the lines at the corners of her mouth. She felt a strong longing to be with Rita, drinking a margarita in a plastic champagne cup with salt dusting its rim. Rita had found the recipe for margaritas in an international cookbook, and Marjorie had said she wouldn't be able to stand anything so different, but Rita had made Marjorie try one, and now she said she was addicted to them. Rita always made Marjorie feel much more daring and cosmopolitan than she really was. As Marjorie bent over the garden she could almost taste the salty drink in her mouth. She pressed the bean pods to feel the size of the green hearts inside them. Ruth's part of the garden was weed wild, but Sam's rows stretched out straight as picket fences. Already the peppers were egg-sized, and the okra looked just like the only thing in the world it would ever look like—little green horse penises. Marjorie bent down to weed Ruth's side of the garden.

The dog lunged away from her and the chain jumped like a snake at her collar. Marjorie looked over her shoulder down the road. Two men were pushing their two-tone shoes along the pavement. "Down, girl," she said to the dog, without taking her eyes off the men. The dog was almost on the street, having run the full length of the chain, and was making homicidal snarls and snorts and lowering her head at the men, who were walking faster but pretending to ignore the dog.

Marjorie bent back to the garden, and not ten feet from

her hand she saw a pair of men's brown leather shoes. She looked up at a malevolent face topped with red hair that stood straight up, making Marjorie think of pine needles. Tiny whiskers pushed under the man's skin like red splinters.

The dog, oblivious of the intruder, was still puffing at the end of the chain, eyeing the mirage left by the men rippling in the heat waves at the end of the road.

"I'm goin' to kill your dog," the man said. "I saw her from the woods yesterday and I dint like her. I'm going to come over here and kill her when your boy and girl are watching." Then he turned and vanished into the fringe of woods lining the back of the house. Marjorie had never seen the man before in her life.

* * * *

Marjorie called Rita on the phone and Rita told her what to do. She should go to the store and buy hatpins—weapons that would not turn on you, that could not be used against you, that unlike knives, batons, guns, or bombs were not easy to wrestle away and belonged to women in the first place. A hatpin was only as small and long as a woman's hand. Marjorie should insert one in her coat pocket and place one on the right side of her mattress, within easy reach. She should stick two in the linings of kitchen potholders. If a man attacked her, she could bayonet him and the long pin would reach into a vital organ. She should look under the sink through her dangerous cleaning chemicals to find a bottle of strong lye. Then tape paper to it and write in boldface: CAUTION: STRONG LYE, DO NOT USE WITHOUT GLOVES. MAY CAUSE BLINDNESS AND BURNS. The lettering would be convincing enough to threaten the man.

Marjorie should check the locks on every door, and even on the windows. And make sure she knew which doors in the house could lock from the inside: the bathroom, the bedroom—and make a mental note that the bedroom window was large enough to crawl out of. She should ask herself where she might run if someone jumped her in the front hall (she would try for the door), the bedroom (she would take the window), the bathroom (she would be trapped). She should never leave the house before seven o'clock in the morning or return home after seven o'clock at night.

"I can't live like that, Rita," Marjorie finally said.

"That's how women in the big city live every day of their lives," Rita countered in an omniscient tone, as if she were recalling Jersey City. "There's them and there's us. It's a war on and we got to see it. Anyhow, if you don't want to do that, what you going to do? You can't use the dog to protect you, 'cause it's the dog he's after," Rita added with relentless logic.

"Maybe the best thing would be to give the dog away," Marjorie answered.

"Maybe so. Maybe I guess you should," Rita told Marjorie. "It's a shame, a crying shame. Those kids are real attached to that dog."

"She's like a person to them," Marjorie agreed, and both women suddenly felt cornered and a little silly, as they had when Rita related her unsuccessful comeback to the man in her laundromat. Marjorie asked Rita to read her the telephone number off the watchdog-wanted notice left by the horse farm, and the two women promised they would get together on Sunday for a drink.

Before the children came home, Marjorie called the number, and the woman who answered said the farm was still interested in a watchdog. Marjorie lured Pretty into the car with a can of bacon grease, and was surprised to find that the stable was only fifteen miles beyond the hardware and seed store, on the same road as her favorite pizza parlor. She had not known anyone was raising horses so near to Durham. Marjorie considered Durham to be almost a city, and she did not particularly like horses and rich horsey people, and thought they belonged in the country, say Hillsborough or Roxboro.

When she drove around a John Deere dealer into the stable's driveway, Marjorie saw a girl standing against a green trailer, smoking a cigarette. She had piled her rusty brown hair under a baseball cap that said "Dodgers" over the visor, and was wearing men's dungarees and a faded cowboy shirt. She looked much younger than Marjorie expected her to be, maybe in her middle twenties. Marjorie steered the Oldsmobile near the trailer and rolled down the window. Pretty stuck her head past Marjorie and howled at the girl.

"I'm the lady with the dog," Marjorie said. "Are you Miss Yanulis?"

"You're at the right place. Name's Jeanie." A red bandanna trailed from her right pants pocket.

"You talk different," Marjorie answered. "You must be from somewhere."

"Brooklyn," Jeanie Yanulis said. "But I've worked here a long time. I dropped out of Duke years ago."

"Her name's Pretty," Marjorie said, as she opened the passenger seat's door to let out the dog.

"Hey there, Ugly Mug," Jeanie told Pretty, tickling the dog on the nose and taking her collar. She offered to pay ten dollars for Pretty, but Marjorie couldn't accept; it would be like selling a child. She thought of asking if the children could visit the dog, but realized this would only make the separation harder. As Marjorie pulled her Oldsmobile onto the highway, she saw she would miss Pretty. It was awesome the way she jumped eight feet.

* * * *

When Marjorie returned home, Sam and Ruth were standing like two angels of death at either side of the driveway. They watched her grimly as she got out of the car. Sam tried to speak, but instead whispered inaudibly, "Where's Pretty?"

Marjorie did not want to tell the children about the man for fear of scaring them. Sam felt as if his heart had been ripped from him, and Ruth sensed a distrust toward her mother rising up and separating her from Marjorie in a moment of terrifying aloneness.

"You had no right," Ruth said. "She wasn't your dog." Sam drew closer to Ruth. He suddenly envisioned his mother before him as he had seen her on so many weekends, working alone in the garden, or walking slightly off balance into his room at night to give him an alcohol-scented kiss. He stared at Marjorie, dazed by his understanding that from then on things could be taken from him. He opened his mouth, shouting, "It's mine, you can't take it!" but no sound came out.

The look in her children's faces immobilized Marjorie. For a moment she was aware only of the ferocity of the sun's heat and the taste of salt at the edges of her mouth. She breathed deeply, and the mud-and-pine smell of the woods pressed around her as if, in the silence, her other senses were trying to overpower her.

"I had to!" she yelled at the children, her voice the shriek of an angry fiend. Then her words returned partway to her, closer, quieter, yet still somewhere outside her. "A man was here! He said he'd kill the dog! He said he would do it while you all were here! I didn't want you to go through something like that!"

Ruth and Sam broke down simultaneously into tears, relieved that a reason had intruded into their shock to order and support it. They both clung to Marjorie's dress. She put her hands on their heads, stroking their hair, and felt her balance returning to her, the strangers beside her dissolving through their tears into her children.

Later, Ruth said that if the man had come back to kill Pretty, the dog would have had him by the throat before he said Boo! Yet when Ruth lay down to sleep, the image of the red-haired face lingered malignantly, manlike, in front of her, and blood pounded against her eardrums as loudly as a dog barking. Sam began waking up at night, afraid of the dark and alarmed by any sound he heard outside the window.

He would crawl into Marjorie's room and curl up next to her bed on the floor, then slink back out in the morning before she could wake to find him there.

GHOSTS OF MOTHERS

Marjorie and Bertha's mother, Geraldine, had been sixteen when she began working as a hospital aide in Baton Rouge, with the object of marrying a doctor. After two years she settled for Willie LeBlanc, an older man who worked as an x-ray technician. Willie LeBlanc had had difficulty marrying because of an attitude of gloominess that he was unable to shake after being wounded in World War I. Geraldine cooked her husband complicated dishes, using twelve spices in one meal, and never served fruit without laying a cushion of lettuce underneath, but he ate his food absentmindedly, sometimes chewing the lettuce in parsimonious bites and forgetting to taste the fruit, sometimes eating only the neck of a roast chicken stuffed with wild rice and liver and crabmeat. Geraldine wound her black hair into complicated silk scarves that billowed on her head when she opened the door to greet her husband, but Willie would only brush his whiskers against her cheek, his lips kissing the air, before he removed his hat and sat down on the porch, clicking on the radio.

On Sundays, Geraldine LeBlanc would dress Marjorie and Bertha in matching crinoline bordered with blue and violet ribbons. Although Geraldine's mother had been an unmarried washerwoman who spoke only French and came from St. Martin Parish, Louisiana, Bertha and Marjorie learned to say, "My grandparents were born in Paris, France, but the only French Mama knows is 'Parlee-voo francey,'" and to talk in high, mindless titters. Yet when Bertha and Marjorie, chattering in their studiously mindless manner, came into a room where Willie LeBlanc sat, he would eye them in his sullen way and go out to the front steps to smoke. During the fifteen years of Geraldine's marriage, a piece of shrapnel slowly worked its way through Willie LeBlanc's bent shoulders until it touched his heart and left him slumped in his chair one Saturday as he listened to news of World War II on the radio.

Geraldine found work as a nurse's aide in a home for the incurably ill. After his death, the photograph of Willie that hung over Geraldine's bed acquired a youthful vibrancy, while Geraldine's hair mildewed to gray and her sharp temper seemed to hone her down, so that she looked curveless and severe in her pink uniform. Throughout the ten years of her widowhood, Geraldine pined away for her dead husband, until she became so frail that a strong wind finally blew her off the front porch and killed her.

Geraldine had lived to see her older daughter, Bertha, accept a science scholarship to attend a northern college, where she was unlikely to meet any men from good families. After Bertha left, Geraldine kept a tight rein on Marjorie, who was four years younger and much more malleable. Geraldine's second daughter was the only triumph of her life: Marjorie was a poor student, conventionally pretty, and under her mother's guidance, entered nursing school at age nineteen to catch a doctor. During Marjorie's first year of courses, she lived at home. A week after Marjorie enrolled, Bertha wrote her sister a letter that said:

Dear Marjorie,
Run away.

Love, Bertha

Geraldine opened the envelope before Marjorie got home from her classes, and returned the letter to Bertha, enclosed in a second envelope.

In 1954, shortly after Geraldine's death and before Marjorie had finished one year of nursing school, she ran off to

North Carolina with a New Jersey army boy on leave from Fort Bragg. Byron Coffin was from a good family and had a college education. During his term of military service and the two following years when he remained in Fayetteville, Marjorie married him and bore four children, and then he returned to the North without her, to attend law school. Marjorie moved to Durham and found work as a hospital aide. Five years later, Byron Coffin came back to North Carolina for the purpose of legally dissolving his marriage. Every year since 1958, Bertha LeBlanc had sent Byron Coffin a Christmas card that said: "YOU SKUNK!" Bertha felt as if she spent her whole life defending her sister from evils Marjorie would never recognize.

*   *   *   *

During the summer of 1963, life with Aunt Bertha had proved pleasantly hair-raising for all of Marjorie LeBlanc's children. Before Sam and Ruth returned to live with their mother, Bertha had taken her nieces and nephew south of New Orleans, stopping at a cemetery in Franklin to show the children their origins, and Sam had fallen into an open grave and had to be pulled out by three teenagers with a rope. The children's aunt had driven them up the Natchez Trace, where her Ford Falcon stalled and they waited four hours by the Indian mounds until a gray-haired lady from Maine happened by in a pickup. Aunt Bertha could do a thing like ride with the LeBlanc children in the Falcon as it swayed behind the pickup, towed by a chain, while she cried, "This is dangerous!" in the same tone with which the children's mother said, "This is right nice!" Ruth and Sam had heard Aunt Bertha yell at a catcaller outside Stuckey's that "She might be fucking fat herself, but Lord, his stomach was so big, when he looked down he couldn't see his own pecker." The children's mother never cursed. After Sam and Ruth went back to North Carolina, Carla saw Aunt Bertha toss a plate of stewed okra in a man's lap at the Tulane cafeteria, just because he had pinched Karen and called her his "little angel."

* * * *

Karen and Carla LeBlanc arrived in Durham in September, springing out of the Ford Falcon with their hands looking bloodstained and their black hair flying wildly. The two girls ran toward Marjorie up the steep slope of the gravel drive, holding out their palms for her to see. Aunt Bertha trudged up the hill behind her nieces, wearing an orange India-print dress with horses along the hem.

"They've been messing with pokeberries," Bertha called to her sister. "We stopped by the road to pick them, and the whole back seat is spread with pink newspapers." Marjorie hugged Bertha and then stooped down to give Carla and Karen smacking kisses and said, "Oh, I missed you to death!" When the girls pulled away, they left purplish paw-prints on Marjorie's white stockings.

Ruth and Sam hung back, sizing up Karen and Carla, and deciding they looked more or less the same after two months of separation.

"Mama gave away Pretty," Sam told them. Carla and Karen had heard already about the dog, but they turned with Sam and Ruth to stare at their mother, who was talking to Aunt Bertha and did not notice.

"A man told Mama he'd murder Pretty if we kept her," Ruth added impressively.

Carla's lantern jaw dropped open, but then she remembered her own news and said, "Aunt Bertie kept letting us stop on the road to catch box turtles." Carla pointed to the car, and the children drew together, flocked toward the Ford Falcon, and watched Carla pull out a box turtle as large as a man's hat from the back seat.

"There's four, one for each of you," Bertha called across the yard, and then said to Marjorie, "I'm tired as a dog, and boy, would I love some ice tea. Leave the bags until later. All I have in them is dirty laundry anyway."

Marjorie took her sister by the waist, and the horses on Bertha's hemline herded together and jumped over her knees. When Marjorie reached the front door of her house she let go of her sister, and Bertha followed Marjorie into the kitchen, sitting down with a groan as Marjorie brought out a pitcher of tea and two glasses. Marjorie picked up a nurse's uniform lying on the table, folded the uniform over a chair, and sat down across from Bertha. Carla and Karen raced into the kitchen, lifting up their box turtles before Marjorie's face.

For a moment, Marjorie had a strange thought: She imagined her two daughters had come back in changeling form and were now turtles. "You aren't asking me to kiss those ugly things?" she teased.

Carla and Karen guffawed. Carla had a new, U-shaped scar over her eye, and Karen's bangs had been cut too short. Her fine hair stood up like black cat fur. Marjorie reached out and drew her daughters in, giving them a second welcome hug. "Oooooh, I missed you," she told them. "I felt like I had parts missing."

"Aunt Bertie said you were happy to have the extra time to yourself!" Karen blurted, and then looked around with raised eyebrows, as if surprised by what she had said.

"She was glad somebody who loved you was looking after you while she was straightening things out here," Bertha answered deftly.

Carla lifted her box turtle onto her mother's knees, and Marjorie felt its claws grab and push against her. She looked up at Bertha and said, "I've got a turtle in my lap!"

Carla laughed, picked up the turtle and sat down on Marjorie's lap. Marjorie tugged on a wild strand of Karen's hair, and Karen pulled away.

"Besides," Bertha told Karen and Carla, "I had a lot more fun with you all around."

Carla watched a ladybug crawl over her mother's shoulder and said in a menacing voice, "Your children will burn!"

"We've got a big night planned," said Marjorie. "We're

going to eat pizza and then visit the planetarium in Chapel Hill."

"The planetarium," Karen said to her turtle, as if mouthing the word for the first time, although Marjorie had been taking her children to the planetarium for years. The turtle tested the hinges on its shell, opening and closing.

"Hey, Carla and Karen!" Ruth called from outside. "Sam's painting the turtles with pokeberries!" Carla jumped off her mother's lap, and she and Karen ran out of the kitchen, carrying the turtles.

When Marjorie heard the screen door slam behind her daughters, she looked into her tea as if reading something there, and told her sister, "Karen's mad at me!"

Bertha looked at Marjorie, pondering the statement. Of all the children, Karen reminded Bertha most of Marjorie as a girl. Karen didn't roughhouse like her brother and sisters. She preferred staying inside all day, watching television or playing with her Tammy dolls. A homebody. She kept to herself and never let Carla near her things. Territorial was what she was. Marjorie had been just like that, and she had also had that same eagerness to please adults, who lived in that stable, solid world from which Bertha had always fled.

"Oh, I shouldn't have done it!" Marjorie cried out, her eyes wide, startling Bertha. "I shouldn't have let them leave me."

"They were only gone for three months, for Christ's sake!" Bertha answered. "Besides, now you're a nurse."

Marjorie's nursing program diploma had come in the mail two days before: a small cardboard rectangle with her misspelled name, "Marjory DeBlanc," embossed in gold over three lines of Latin.

"A real live nurse!" Bertha stood, sweeping up the nurse's uniform and holding it against her wider hips. She thought to herself that she and Marjorie were the exact same height and really looked alike: they had the same dark hair and yellow complexions and sloping shoulders. Bertha was just older and fatter, with darker circles under her eyes and spidery purple veins on the backs of her knees. Bertha laughed and shook out the uniform, laid it messily over its chair, and sat back down. "Anyhow, you know parents always miss their kids more than the kids miss them. You probably felt much more left behind than they did."

Marjorie noticed the magenta prints on her stockings and said, "Well, I hope they missed me just a little!" She glanced up at the nurse's uniform dangling from the chair. She thought the white dress looked more lively than it ever did when she was inside it, as if the uniform might jump up, ghostlike, of its own accord.

*   *   *   *

"We're off!" Aunt Bertha called, leaning out the window of the children's bedroom in nothing more than an apricot slip. The four LeBlanc children put their turtles into a cardboard box on the front steps.

Marjorie settled Karen and Carla into the seat beside her. Bertha rushed out of the house, still buttoning her dress, and sat in the back with Sam and Ruth. The Oldsmobile progressed slowly down the road, as Marjorie stopped and started, adjusting the children's seat belts. Karen watched out the window as her neighborhood passed by. She saw the three Budd boys hiding behind their family's truck while their father shouted for them angrily from the steps; Mr. Mintor, the undertaker, talking in his yard with Mr. Whitmore, the garbageman; Mr. Manson's daughters, Deenah and Dinah, spraying three naked Carmichael babies with a hose; Blue Henry carrying a twenty-two rifle and followed by his dog, also named Blue; Mrs. Katerwaller lifting a pot of red geraniums from the back seat of her enormous car; and a new man with a long black suitcase, who was walking unsteadily down the street, as if he might be drunk.

Carla stared at the odometer, because Aunt Bertha had explained earlier in the day the difference between the odometer and the speedometer. When a light rain began to collect on the windshield, Carla watched the wipers. Carla thought they looked like eyebrows rising and falling. She raised her own eyebrows and found this made her feel surprised; she drew them downward and felt cross.

Marjorie nosed the Oldsmobile into the laundromat's parking lot, and Rita ran toward the car, jumping over puddles. She stuck her head in Karen's window and said, "Look at all these LeBlancs!" Before Karen could say anything, Rita had unbuckled the seat belt, lifted Karen into her lap, and closed the door. Rita turned around in her seat and said to Bertha, "Hi there. I'm Rita Lopez, and Marjorie talks about you all the time." Ruth and Sam stared at Rita's glasses, which were sprinkled with drops of water.

"I hope so," said Bertha, "because I talk about her all the time."

What could she possibly have to say? Marjorie wondered.

After Rita tugged at the seat belt to widen and refasten it around her and Karen, Marjorie restarted the car, and Carla said, "I saw a movie last week on television, about this scientist whose wife gets killed in an accident, so he keeps her head alive in a tray."

Sam concentrated on the back of the car in front of them to see if he could guess the make from the taillights alone.

"I saw that one!" said Ruth. "The head gets mad and tries to kill him by winking at him from the frying pan on the table."

"Jesus!" said Rita.

Marjorie looked in the rearview mirror at Sam and then said, "No monster movie talk, you all. Sam'll get nightmares."

Sam, embarrassed, pressed his face against the glass and then said, "Buick."

"That's fine with me," said Rita. "I am sure certain I don't want to hear about a lady's head winking from a saucepan."

"The rain's stopped!" Carla told everyone.

Karen allowed her smaller hands to be cupped in Rita's big ones. Rita pushed her nose against Karen's neck and kissed her nape, and then opened Karen's hands absentmindedly, spreading them flat.

"Marjorie!" Rita cried. "This girl has scarlet palms!"

"That's blood!" Ruth volunteered.

"It's pokeberry juice if I'm a day," Marjorie countered.

* * * *

There were no parking spaces at the pizza parlor, so Marjorie drove a short distance down the two-lane highway and left her Oldsmobile in front of the hardware and seed store. The children jumped out of the car, calling, "Horses! Horses!" Marjorie looked past them and saw two horse rumps inside a green trailer parked on the far side of the lot. A girl with rusty brown hair stuffed into a hat leaned against the trailer. Marjorie had the feeling this moment had happened before: the children tearing away from her to look at the back ends of two horses, Bertha and Rita joking under their breaths about something, the seven o'clock sky reddening at the end of the road. Then Marjorie realized that it was not the moment that was familiar; it was the girl herself, whom Marjorie finally recognized as the one who had taken the dog only a few weeks before. Marjorie called her children away from the trailer, wondering why it was parked in the same lot she had chosen, when the horse farm was only a little way down the road.

"Come on, you hooligans," Marjorie told her children, hurrying for fear the girl would recognize her. "If you don't move fast, me and Bertha and Rita are going to eat all the pizza." The children turned in unison, walking backward and drawing themselves slowly away from the horses. "You all have to be careful around big animals like that. You never know what they might do."

"Yes ma'am, yes ma'am, yes ma'am, yes ma'am," Ruth

chanted in time to her swaying steps, walking slowly so that she was the last person to enter the pizza parlor.

* * * *

Ruth, Sam, Karen, and Carla sat down at one end of the table, concentrating on the pizza. When they finished eating they grew restless, and Marjorie told them they could go outside, making them promise to stay together and not to wander.

"The planetarium doesn't start for another two hours," Bertha told her nieces and nephew, "so I have a feeling us girls are just going to sit here and talk our heads off for a while."

"Stay away from the road. There's plenty of space behind the restaurant," Marjorie said to Carla, catching her by the back of her shirt and giving her a kiss before she squirmed away.

When the last of Marjorie's children disappeared out the door, the waitress leaned over Marjorie's shoulder and said, "I heard on the news about how they caught a man with two dead little girls in the trunk of his car."

Before Marjorie could think to answer, Bertha said, "Lucky for him he didn't run into my nieces and nephew, or he would have ended up in the glove compartment."

"My children wouldn't get into a strange car," Marjorie said, having had a moment to assemble herself. The waitress was a mousy woman with narrow-set eyes.

"They know not to wander," Rita joined in, looking pointedly at the waitress.

"Well now, don't you all gang up on me. I didn't mean anything. Things just aren't how they used to be, that's all, and anyway I needed to know if you all want more Co'-Cola."

When the waitress brought three Coca-Colas, Bertha took a metal flask out of her purse and poured Wild Turkey in the paper cups.

Two nurses sitting at the far end of the restaurant waved to Marjorie, and she waved back.

"My sister the nurse!" said Bertha. "Marjorie Kildare."

"I'd rather be married to a doctor," Marjorie answered.

"Not me," Rita told her. "Imagine being touched by someone who's had his hands in somebody's guts all day."

"Mama's greatest hope was to marry a doctor, but she got stuck with an x-ray technician," said Bertha.

Marjorie looked at her reflection in her cup of Coca-Cola and whiskey: an oval face scattered and gathered on the surface. "Well, she *loved* him anyway."

"From the time we could talk, Mama was always pressing us to marry," said Bertha. "The last thing she said to me before she died was: 'Old maid!' She was standing on the front steps and yelled it out so the whole neighborhood heard, and then she dropped dead."

"Bertha!" Marjorie cried, enjoying the blasphemy in spite of herself. "Don't believe her, Rita; she's making that up."

Rita had made two piles of sugar packages on the table, and was dividing the ones with state birds on them from the ones depicting Civil War heroes. She stacked the Civil War heroes in a wet spot on the corner of the table. "The last thing my mother ever said to me was: 'Rita, you're so dark!' " Rita held up her arm and pointed to it. "After we moved here, Mom warned me not to tell anyone I was Puerto Rican. Well, I wanted to be dark. I never walked in the shade even on boiling hot days, just to spite her."

A young man sitting to the left of Rita leaned forward and asked if he could borrow the women's garlic salt. When Rita handed it to him, she saw that he was wearing a fraternity shirt that seemed to say "KKK" on it. He smelled like stale beer. After the young man returned the garlic salt, he said, "Would you girls mind a whole helluva lot if I joined you?"

"We'd mind a whole helluva lot," Rita told him.

The women sat in silence for five minutes. Marjorie was embarrassed by Rita's abruptness and stared at her pile of sugar packets. Bertha and Rita felt too self-conscious to talk when they might be overheard.

After the young man finished wolfing down his pizza and

left, Marjorie sipped her Coca-Cola thoughtfully and said, suddenly mournful, "Mama would turn over in her grave if she saw me now, unmarried with four kids." Marjorie pictured her mother, her hands on her hips and scolding Bertha about something: a memory intact with the details of the kitchen and the pattern on Bertha's messy apron, but Marjorie could not recall the words her mother had been saying.

"Right before Marjorie moved to North Carolina, Mama tried to set me up with a spot of grease named Thomas Ray," Bertha told Rita. "An army recruit who was an insurance salesman in real life. He had come to Orleans with Byron Coffin when they were on leave from Fort Bragg—"

"Lord, let's not talk about Buy My Coffin," said Marjorie.

"So I told her I didn't want to marry, I was going to keep on with my studies, and she called me an old maid. And she was still mad the next day at lunch, when she said, 'You want to be a shriveled-up spinster, Bertha! You don't have the ghost of me in you!' Then she rummaged around in the kitchen drawer where she kept her knives, and I thought she was going to kill me, but she pulled out a deck of Old Maid playing cards and waved the Old Maid in my face and then threw the cards all over the table. One landed in my soup. And she stamped out onto the porch and said something about the wind messing up her hair and fell off the front steps."

"*My* mother once—" Rita began, but Marjorie interrupted her.

"When you all talk this way, it makes me worry what my kids are going to say about me!"

Bertha and Rita looked at each other in the kinship of childless women, understanding that Marjorie obliquely had put them down while also succeeding in killing the conversation.

"I never wanted to marry," Rita said, "but I would of liked to have kids. Well, who knows—I might of been an awful mother."

Something made Marjorie think of the woman in the hardware and seed store parking lot. "You know, I think that girl by the horse trailer is the same one I gave the dog to."

Bertha told Rita, "I was really sad when Marjorie wrote and told me about that dog. I liked her. I stole her in the dead of night from a man who kept her under a house."

Marjorie waved to the waitress to get the check. When it came, Bertha snatched the check from Marjorie and handed the waitress a five-dollar bill and a tip.

"I wouldn't have given away the dog," Bertha told Rita. "I would have waited until the man came back and then done something to him."

"What? What would you have done?" asked Marjorie.

"Something," said Bertha.

"You know I work!" Marjorie told her sister accusingly. "He could have killed the dog anytime after school, before I got home, right in front of the children."

"Hey, Margie," Bertha said, "I was just talking. I'm sure you did the best you could."

"We never did find out who it was," said Rita, leaning forward and feeling the whiskey sway inside her. "But then, he never came back."

As soon as the words escaped from her, Rita found herself thinking: I wish he had come back. I wish he had come back and the dog had pinned him to the ground, and then I could have tied him up with old shirts and heaved him in the car and taken him to the laundry and thrown him in the dryer and watched him twirl around inside. I wish I knew his name, and then he wouldn't be every red-haired man with whiskers I meet in Durham since Marjorie gave the dog away. I wish I had his address and telephone number and social security number and the number on his dog tags. I'd like to stick him on an ironing board and press him flat and wrap him in pink laundry paper and send him to Mississippi.

Rita finished the last of her cola, narrowed her eyes, and pushed her glasses to the top of her nose to get an accurate look at Marjorie LeBlanc. For a terrible moment, she reminded Rita of her own mother, who had sat in that same embedded-in-her-seat kind of way, as if she could stay put even if the world rolled out from under her. Maybe it was the tiredness, the run-roughshod-over look Marjorie got from having married and had so many children. Maybe that's what made Marjorie seem sort of a faded version of her sister Bertha. Bertha had that high crime look and fiery fatness of spirit that Rita had noted all her life in ugly women. The problem with Marjorie LeBlanc, Rita thought, was that she had probably been pretty long enough for her prettiness to soak in and stain her with all sorts of things like: eagerness to please, eagerness to make peace, eagerness to stay put.

Marjorie, Rita thought and almost said, we should have waited in ambush for that red-haired man. This Wild Turkey makes me feel a need to fight and scramble and hit back, and that's maybe what I'll do, and when are you going to do it? After your children are grown and gone? What got into me that I let you make me tell you to give that dog away? It was that stay puttedness. Marjorie LeBlanc, I love you, but don't you get tired of just staying put?

CALL THE POLICE

Carla had found a rhinoceros beetle on the overhang behind the restaurant. The beetle was olive green, with black spots and a black horn, and almost three inches long. He was clinging to a mesh guard around a light bulb, and all four children could see that they had never yet encountered a beetle so perfect in size and so enormous. Ruth had once found a female rhinoceros beetle, who was small and hornless, with faint black spots, and Sam had once brought home a damaged male, already dead and with part of its shell broken.

"He's bigger than a house," Ruth said.

Carla decided she would stay under the light while Sam

and Ruth and Karen scattered to find a sapling or a pole to knock the beetle down with and a tin can in which to keep it.

On the road between the car and the restaurant, Karen had seen an orange-and-blue Maxwell House coffee can, the lid still next to it. The can had been on the far shoulder of the road, and so she crossed the state highway, leaving Sam and Ruth behind in the parking lot. A loud, honking cement trunk, with its high beams on, blinded her for a moment before she reached the other side. Twilight was deepening into a darkness that took the colors from things, and so she walked fast, looking back and forth across the road shoulder for the glimmer of orange and blue that would be the coffee can.

She passed a black-and-white police car hidden in a clump of bushes by the road, and hurried on. She stepped over a board with four nails sticking out of it. At one point twenty feet ahead of her, Karen saw orange and blue rings flicker beneath a telephone pole with a streetlight on top, but as she approached the pole she was disappointed to see that the rings belonged to the top of a boy's sock, an old boy, almost a man. He was standing with his hands in his pockets, leaning against the pole, and he reached out and seized her ponytail.

"Hey, Little Lady, where you running off so fast to?" Karen smiled up at him, a little lady, and he let her go.

On up the road under the next streetlight, a snake, dead but not yet flattened against the asphalt, lay stretched out on the highway, its head just over the edge of the road shoulder. Karen thought about something Ruth had told her: A snake can bite when it's dead, so after you kill it, cut off its head, dig a hole, and throw the head in. Karen walked out on the road around the snake's tail, and two long horse vans, a station wagon, and a car pulling a boat raced by.

When Karen returned to the road shoulder outside the rim of light, the ground had darkened almost to invisibility, and she went more slowly, passing the hardware and seed store without noticing it, and walking along a cyclone fence, dragging her fingers along the metal mesh. The fence gave way to a posted iron gate with lamps on either side, and a black dog with gold eyebrows snarled at her. She stopped to watch its teeth flicker and to listen to its snarl, remembered Mr. Mintor's coon hound, who had once bitten Blue Henry on the ankle, and hurried on toward a streetlight farther down the road, still searching for the orange-and-blue flicker. Just as the ghostly tent of light thrown from above began to mingle with the air around her feet, she heard a truck stop behind her and a hoarse voice call her. She turned, and a man in a visored cap stood in front of her and grabbed Karen by the shoulder.

* * * *

Sam and Ruth came back to Carla only five minutes after leaving her, and they brought with them a piece of string, four rocks in a rusted tomato can, a metal pole, a length of hose, and a branch broken from a tree planted in the restaurant parking lot.

"It's still here," Carla whispered to her brother and sister. The three children studied the beetle, and Sam and Ruth set down everything but the branch. Ruth lifted it to the ceiling behind the beetle, and then cocked the branch backward to bat the insect off the light. The beetle opened its shell, and Ruth saw two black wings fragile as burnt paper.

"Wait! It'll fly off," Sam told her. Ruth stopped moving the branch, and the beetle pulled its shell back into place, leaving a piece of black wing showing, so that Sam thought of a shirt tail a man had forgotten to tuck in. Carla decided they should knock the rhinoceros beetle down with a rock and slam the can over him as soon as he hit the ground. She lifted up one of the rocks, and Sam told her, "No, don't, you'll smash him!" Sam picked up the metal pole, leaned it against the light, and moved the pole toward the beetle. The beetle showed his wings again, and Sam held the pole still. He and Carla and Ruth waited silently for so long that they became self-conscious and vain about how patient they were being.

Carla imagined she was a burglar, standing quietly in a living room until she could be certain that all the house's inhabitants were asleep.

The beetle crawled toward the pole, grabbed it with his foreleg, and in one motion pulled the bottom half of his body onto the pole, just as it slipped from Sam's grasp and clattered to the ground. The beetle fell backward after it, landing with a sound like an egg shattering. Carla slapped the can down before Ruth or Sam could estimate the damage done to the insect. In a moment, the children heard the beetle buzzing and knocking against the sides of the can. Carla lifted the can slightly and one of the beetle's black legs poked out. Sam inched the square of cardboard beneath the rim, and Ruth slipped her hand under it, pushed the cardboard against the can and inverted it, and then pulled back the cardboard partway to peer inside. The beetle, alive and unharmed, butted his head through the opening. Sam grabbed him by the horn, pulled the beetle slightly upward, and grasped him by his shell. Carla tied the string around the beetle's shapely, muscular-looking leg, and for half an hour the three children watched spellbound as the beetle flew ahead of them, back and forth over the parking lot.

* * * *

"It's time to go!" Aunt Bertha's voice startled them from the front of the restaurant. "Come on, you all!"

Carla towed in the rhinoceros beetle and the children took a long, admiring look at him before walking around to the front of the restaurant. Carla held the beetle inside her cupped hands. He poked at her fingers with his pointy feet. Ruth carried the tomato can and cardboard, and called, "Looky this, everybody, a man rhinoceros beetle!"

Carla held up the beetle for her aunt to admire.

The beetle's leg reminded Bertha of a black silk stocking. "He's handsome," Bertha told her niece.

"He's the handsomest man I've ever seen," Rita said.

"Mom!" Sam shouted. "It's a rhinoceros beetle."

But Sam's mother was looking across the darkness of the parking lot and demanding, "Where's Karen?"

Sam, Ruth, and Carla looked around them, disoriented by having to return to the world outside the rhinoceros beetle.

"She *was* here," said Ruth.

Rita and Bertha circled the parking lot, calling out Karen's name, and then Bertha went back into the restaurant to look in the bathroom, while Rita walked down the road to the car. Marjorie stood motionless with her son and two daughters, as if she thought she might lose her remaining children if she went anywhere. She felt weighted to where she stood, lifeless as stone or salt.

Bertha came back out of the restaurant with the waitress who had served them. Marjorie looked away; she did not want to hear the woman relishing the news. But the waitress put her arm around Marjorie's shoulder and said, "Don't you worry, Hun. She's bound to turn up in the last place you'd expect. Don't you even think about what I said earlier about those dead girls. That was in New York, not way down here. I didn't tell you my name—it's Lizzie. The day we wake up in a world where a little girl can't play outside in the boondogs after dark, I just don't want to live in this country anymore."

Rita came back from the hardware and seed store parking lot, shaking her head.

"Maybe she's hiding somewhere," said Lizzie. "My little boy Rusty once hid himself in a tree for a whole afternoon, just because some friend of his spat on him at church. Boys are that way."

"I'll wring her neck when she comes back if she's dared to run off on purpose!" Marjorie felt embarrassed by her words.

"I don't know," said Bertha. "Karen's not the kind to just run off. Now, Carla maybe—" Bertha looked down at Carla, and Carla nodded.

"You could stay here with the kids by the restaurant," said Rita, "and I could go wait out by the car in case she decides to head that way."

Lizzie said her shift was more or less over, and she offered to drive Bertha up and down the highway to see if they could spot Karen on the road shoulders. Rita walked back to the Oldsmobile and Marjorie and the children sat down on a planter in front of the restaurant doors. Lizzie went inside and came out a minute later with her apron balled under her arm and keys jingling in her hand, and Marjorie watched Bertha get into Lizzie's car. The children stood up and set the beetle whizzing around their heads.

"Don't do that! Get over here and sit down!" Marjorie snapped, and her children came and sat slightly away from her with sober expressions. They kept quiet out of a superstitiousness, thinking their silence might bring Karen back more quickly, before it was too late to go to the planetarium. Carla closed her eyes and felt the beetle's legs prickling her hands. Sam and Ruth looked straight down the road until their eyes grew tired.

Marjorie broke the silence by saying, "If any of you ever try anything like this, I'll tan your hides." She thought she sounded like an old witch, but her voice somehow got the better of her. "This is the worst time of night for a driver to try to see someone on a road."

Carla opened her eyes and watched Lizzie's car pull back into the parking lot. Lizzie yelled out, "No luck!" and she and Bertha came and sat down on the planter. Bertha pulled Carla on her lap and Carla looked down and saw a row of horses jumping over her aunt's left knee.

Lizzie said, "I gotta get back to my little boy. The sitter's mother won't let her stay out late. I could drive Bertha back to you all's house just in case someone finds your little girl and decides to take her back there. I could leave a message here at the restaurant to look out for her. Maybe you should go down to the police station. It's sort of a long way, but you can follow this road to the 7 Eleven and turn down the street there."

"The police station!" Marjorie answered.

"If she got lost, someone might take her there, Marjorie," Bertha said.

Marjorie pictured herself sitting at an oak desk with a state trooper standing behind it, looking down the front of her dress, which she had known was too low-cut when she bought it. The state trooper offered to take her out on a ride in his police car. Then Marjorie saw herself sitting in front of a respectable-looking man in a blue cap, something like a police captain on television. He chuckled at her and asked her what might have made her daughter want to run away.

"I'll go if I can take Rita with me," Marjorie answered. She closed her eyes for a minute, feeling as if she were going to cry, and then opened them to keep away the startling image in her mind's eye: She had seen the red-haired man who had threatened to kill the children's dog. He was standing on top of her house, balancing by holding her television antenna, and gazing down on her with a mocking smile.

* * * *

A half hour after Lizzie drove off, Marjorie called home and Bertha answered the phone and told her that Karen was not there. Marjorie said she would drive to the police station. She led the children down the road to the car and Rita, and they all got into the Oldsmobile.

Rita remembered the last time she had been to the police building, to argue in vain against the dumb stupid idiot state trooper who had pulled his car out from beyond a clump of bushes and almost collided with her in order to give her a speeding ticket, when she had been doing barely forty-five on the highway. All around her in the police building, men had been milling: There were men in khaki state trooper uniforms, and prosecutors and public defenders sweating a reeking man-to-man smell in their suits and ties, frowning men in handcuffs, and men bailiffs smoking cigarettes in the corner and telling each other bawdy jokes. There was a man judge who floated by, looking as if he were wearing a black bustle, and there was a court clerk who winked at her while he was pretending to shuffle though a stack of pink papers. Rita had been struck by how the whole mixture of law and crime was a man's affair. She had realized that she had no more business committing a crime or ferreting out justice than a man had walking into her laundromat. This was why Rita did not protest when Marjorie stopped the Oldsmobile halfway down the road at the 7 Eleven and said, "Let's just call home again and make sure Karen didn't get there ahead of us." But when Rita called Marjorie's from the telephone booth, Bertha said there was still no sign of Karen.

Marjorie continued driving the car in the direction of the police station, the children huddled against each other by the right back window and watching Durham whipping by. Houses rushed toward them and ran away more quickly than they had come. Ruth, Sam, and Carla saw a drunk banging his head against a brick wall in a vacant lot, and a girl and boy rubbing against each other under a tree, and a dead possum lying in a gutter. Suddenly a row of police cars and the police station were in front of them, and then, as suddenly, the station was gone and their mother was saying, "Oh, Rita, I can't walk in there just yet. Let's us try going home and waiting a little longer."

"Marjorie," said Rita, as the Oldsmobile turned back toward the highway.

"What?"

"I keep thinking about that man."

"What man?"

Rita leaned over and whispered, so the children could not hear. "The *Dog Man.*"

"This is a fine time to bring that up!" Marjorie cried.

Rita sat in silence for a minute and then said, "You don't think he's been around since then, enough to know Carla and Karen came back today?"

"The very idea!" Marjorie answered.

Rita felt the Oldsmobile speed up, and watched the head-lights burrow into the darkness over the road.

* * * *

As Marjorie LeBlanc rounded the corner to her house, she saw two horses grazing under the streetlight that shone in the corner of the LeBlancs' yard. The horses seemed no more unreal to Marjorie than anything else that had happened in the past two hours. They looked more substantial than Mar-jorie's yard—the horses stood rust-colored on a pool of bluish grass under the light, while the yard and street and house were intermingling shades of gray. As the car came closer to the yard, Marjorie noticed a horse trailer parked at the edge of her driveway, and before she could think clearly, she won-dered from within her state of exhaustion whether the girl with the horses was some sort of judgment on her, connecting her giving the dog away to Karen's disappearance, and to Marjorie's marriage and everything else.

"There's horses right by our house!" Ruth called out.

Rita looked out the window, ducking down to see up the slope of the yard, and said, "There's a crowd on the steps. It's Bertha and Karen, sitting beside that woman we saw with the horses."

Marjorie stopped the car when it was only halfway into the driveway, its back end still in the road. She jumped out, for-getting to turn off the headlights.

"Here she is, safe and sound!" Bertha called as Marjorie ran up the gravel drive. "They showed up right after you phoned the second time. Jeanie here picked Karen up because she looked lost. She was way out past the hardware and seed store, where the road just turns into woods. Karen thought Jeanie was a man and screamed bloody murder. Jeanie said she sounded just like a lady in a horror movie."

Karen sat in her aunt's lap, leaning against her pillowy breasts and stomach and pretending to be asleep. Marjorie lifted up her daughter and folded Karen against her. "Why didn't you ask to be taken back to the restaurant!" Marjorie said, sounding harsher than she wanted.

"You didn't tell me the name!" Karen answered, her words muffled by her mother's shoulder.

Jeanie stood up and said in an easygoing voice, the voice Marjorie wanted to have spoken in, "Oh, man, we drove all over, looking for that pizza place. I went inside two pizza parlors and a barbecue restaurant and a corn dog place and Hardee's, but we couldn't find it."

"But the restaurant was right there!"

"Marjorie," said Rita, coming up behind her and touching her arm.

"You know, your daughter's smart," said Jeanie, squatting down and lighting a cigarette and drawing on it so that it blossomed in the gray air. Her hair was hidden under her cap, and her square jaw made Marjorie think of a man's face, an outlaw's or a cowboy's, lit by a fire in a cigarette commercial. "Once we got to the neighborhood, Karen knew all the curves and turns in the road and the names of all the streets around here."

"I should hope so," said Bertha. "Sam can tell the make of a car just by looking at the taillights, so I'd expect that at least one of the kids could find their own house."

Sam and Ruth and Carla clustered around their mother, staring at Karen.

"You gave me such a fright!" Marjorie told her.

She let Karen go, and Karen followed her brother and sisters down the slope of the yard toward the horses, which Marjorie saw had been tied to the two spindly pines in the yard. Before Marjorie could warn the children away from the horses, Jeanie said, "It's OK. Those two old brood mares aren't anything to worry about. Hey, isn't it funny I know you already? Rita told me you're the lady with the dog. I'm Jeanie Yanulis, remember?"

"Don't walk behind the horses' feet!" Marjorie called down to her children.

"Jeanie told me she had to give that dog away too," Bertha said. "It jumped a man at the stable."

"Mama, their noses are soft and scary!" Carla called from the bottom of the yard.

"The owner's son," said Jeanie. "It wouldn't have been a loss to anyone if she'd eaten him for dinner. I found a lady way out by Mooksville who wanted her. I liked that dog too. The guy I work for went out and bought this Doberman and some Doberkinder—" Jeanie paused, but Marjorie didn't seem about to appreciate her joke. "He keeps them down the road behind a ten-foot cyclone fence with barbwire stretched across the top. Now those dogs give me the creeps. You know what they say: The same way a lawyer isn't a human being, a Doberman isn't a dog? Your dog was nice," Jeanie continued. "She just didn't trust men. A man probably mistreated her once. Dogs get that way."

"Mama, you left the headlights on!" Ruth cried from the bottom of the yard.

"You better turn them off!" Bertha called back. "We're taking Marjorie inside and sitting her down. You all have worn your poor mother ragged."

Marjorie heard the children's shrieks of laughter as they raced each other to the car. She walked through the dark living room into the kitchen, where Rita was already brewing a pot of coffee.

"That's just what I need," said Jeanie.

"You have to take those horses somewhere for tonight?" Rita asked.

"I ought to leave them here and teach the lady that owns them a lesson. Give them a night off and give myself a night off too."

"They look kinda nice out there on the lawn," Bertha said. "Grazing by the light of the street."

"Grazing by the light of the street," Marjorie repeated in a dreamy way. She listened without really following as Jeanie's quick voice rose and fell and darted in and out of Bertha's and Rita's slower ones.

"So the owner calls me up," Jeanie was saying, "and tells me that due to an 'inexplicable failure of courtesy,' she fired the driver after he drove all the way up from Louisiana with the mares. What he said was, she could come get her own fucking horses because he fucking quit, since they'd told him at the stable she intended to pay him fucking late fucking again. So after he drove to the nearest pay phone, he left the horses right there, a mile down the road, and then I go hitch all the way there and wait for her to show up with the extra set of trailer keys. I wait hours, and she finally sends down her 'hired man' after I call her up and curse her out. I was ready to drive along to the next dirt road and let those horses loose in a clump of woods. Tulane Highway and Bayou Hullabaloo—those are their names, the horses' names. Can you believe it?"

Bertha laughed and Marjorie took a sip of her coffee and found that Rita had slipped whiskey into it. Marjorie felt the coffee burn her tongue and throat and curl like an animal inside her stomach. She closed her eyes and continued savoring the coffee until she heard Carla's shout climb up the yard toward the house. Marjorie stood and said, "You all go ahead and stay here. I'm going to round up the kids and air out my head and move the car up the drive."

When Marjorie got outside, Karen was asleep in the weeds by the steps, Carla was squatting under the front light playing with her enormous beetle, and Ruth and Sam were at the bottom of the yard, trying to coax the horses to eat pine cones.

Marjorie walked down to the bottom of the driveway, and as she reached the car, she was startled by a man standing only a few feet away in the road. It was too dark to make out his features, although she could see by the streetlight that he was tall and heavy, and wearing a hat and a tie and a ghostly yellowish shirt.

"Baby, I saw your car sticking out onto the road," he said, "and I was just wondering if you forgot to put on the parking brake and the car rolled down the hill maybe." The man took a step forward as he spoke. Marjorie recognized Mr. Mintor, the undertaker who lived down the street.

"Oh, I just left it there." Marjorie laughed. She felt muddleheaded and a little drunk, and thought she probably sounded strange. "I'm going to drive it up now."

Mr. Mintor took another step toward her and placed his hand on the small of her back, whispering, "Hey, why don't you put the kids to bed, and you and me go have a drink?"

Marjorie got in the car and closed the door before she realized she had forgotten to answer. She steered the Oldsmobile up the driveway, and thought that the wheels on the gravel made a homey sound. As Marjorie stepped from the car, Bertha came outside and rounded up Ruth and Sam and then Carla, who looked bleary-eyed for a moment at her beetle and dropped it in a can on the steps, then covered the can with a brick. Marjorie saw that the turtles had overturned their box but had hardly strayed more than a few inches from each other. Ruth collected the turtles and put them back in the box, and the three children followed Bertha into the house.

Marjorie lifted Karen from the grass, saying, "You're nothing but a sack of potatoes." Karen murmured something about the planetarium, and as Marjorie opened the front door, she wondered if Mr. Mintor was still at the bottom of the driveway. She hadn't wanted to be rude or hurt his feelings; she was just tired. Marjorie imagined him standing there every night, lurking in the road, waiting for her to come to him. She looked back but could not see into the darkness that edged the yard. She shut off the porch light and stepped into her home, closing the door.

2. What Are Men Good For?

ELECTRIC TRAINS

The clouds moved in magnificent curls on the horizon, like vapor puffing from a steam engine. The sun glowed dully behind them, the same pale yellow as Marjorie LeBlanc's Oldsmobile station wagon as it slipped on a thin layer of ice covering a rise and lost momentum. Marjorie honked at Jeanie Yanulis, who had parked her pickup truck in front of the house.

"Don't you dare turn around or I'll wallop you!" Marjorie told the four children in the back seat. They laughed and stared conscientiously in front of them, at their boots, at the scrap of newspaper on the car floor advertising Butterball turkeys for the Thanksgiving of 1965, at the icy road that tugged at their eyes as it raced behind them. The station wagon zigzagged up the hill and hairpinned into the LeBlancs' gravel drive. The children heard Christmas wrapping tearing in the back of the station wagon. In the rearview mirror, Marjorie saw the twenty-five-dollar Flexible Flyer sled poking through the wrapping.

"All four of you climb out of the car without looking back," Marjorie commanded. "Then get in the kitchen and close the door!" The children scattered like a dropped bag of marbles. They ran into the house and ostentatiously slammed the kitchen door, then watched through the cracks between the hinges as their mother huffed and hauled the six-foot sled out of the Oldsmobile, tearing the paper and banging her head on the car ceiling. Jeanie picked up the back end of the sled and helped Marjorie maneuver it in the front door and up the stairs.

"Well, get a load of this!" Jeanie's voice sailed down the stairs. "Who's going to be spoiled rotten!"

The children's mother answered, "You're telling me, driving all the way to Raleigh and Christmas shopping on Thanksgiving just to be sure I could get the right size. Nothing but macaroni and cheese for a week! I don't know what got into me, there's never more than a handful of snow days anyhow. Well, this is what they wanted."

The children heard the sled banging over the threshold of their mother's room, the closet creaking open, a scattering of hangers and crackling of paper, and then the closet door slamming.

"Whoosh!" Marjorie told Jeanie. "That just about broke my back. Lemme rest my feet a minute." Marjorie sat down next to Jeanie and watched her take off her hiking boots. Jeanie had found a new job in November at a different race-horse farm which paid her better, and she had bought herself the boots and a fringed suede jacket as presents. She was wearing the jacket now, over a work shirt. Her hair was pulled back in a crooked ponytail and she had on green imitation jade Maori earrings. She tugged at her boots, which had been tied haphazardly, the laces skipping holes and doubling back and entering some holes twice. In the two years that Jeanie and Marjorie had been friends, Marjorie had never seen Jeanie tie her shoes properly. Jeanie had a generally reckless quality, which gave Marjorie's life a vicarious sense of danger. As she watched Jeanie now, Marjorie suddenly saw herself in her mind's eye: a spare woman in a blue cotton dress, her wishbone legs descending into white nurses' shoes. How long have I looked like this? she wondered to herself before refocusing on Jeanie.

"I swear I should get work boots just like those, Jeanie. Maybe that'll keep my feet from aching. I bought these things"—Jeanie watched Marjorie raise two thin ankles with shoes sticking up from them like knobby goose heads—"because they were supposed to be the going thing in nurses' shoes, with extra supports in the arches. Ha! They don't work worth a D! I should have stuck to my old kind."

Jeanie laughed because Marjorie still couldn't bring herself to curse, even after eleven years of raising children, holding bad jobs, fighting with landlords and bill collectors and neighbors and, more recently, listening to Jeanie's own foul mouth when she got mad.

"I'd sure like to see you wearing hiking boots in that hospital," Jeanie said. "And those doctors wearing those dumb little white hats—"

"Look at that mud, Jeanie! Put your boot on that newspaper there."

Jeanie laid her boot on top of a picture of Richard Nixon. "Rita's already gone out and bought a pair. She wore them last night when we went to see a movie. You should have come with us."

"I fall asleep in that kind of thing."

Jeanie and Rita had started going to a political-documentary film series in Chapel Hill because good entertainment was hard to come by in North Carolina. The first two films had been on domestic violence and the underfunding of sickle cell research. As Jeanie unknotted the laces in her second boot, she imagined herself as a member of an underground women's organization. The organization had been founded twenty years earlier by a black nurse's aide who had been denied admission to Harvard Medical School. At night, she worked as a janitress in the Harvard Medical School laboratories. She gave the floors a perfunctory scrub, and then sat down to work in front of a row of microscopes, searching for a cure for sickle cell anemia. She worked for thirty years and died just short of reaching her goal. If there had been twenty people conducting the research for two years instead of one person for thirty years, the cure would have been found. Instead, the remedy that the nurse's aide discovered had a peculiar effect. Fed to wife-beaters, it would make them bruise easily and feel unsteady and weak, too weak to hit their wives anymore. The men's wives were sometimes told about the secret medicine, but more often than not, the organization acted independently. They raised money through bake sales, and would administer the medicine by mixing it into cakes and pies and brownies, which the organization would take to the houses of the men targeted. The remedy would take effect only if the men ate more than their fair share of the pie or cake. In the entire history of the organization, every man had eaten more than his fair share.

"What are you thinking about?" Marjorie asked. "You should see the expression on your face."

Before Jeanie could answer, Marjorie leaned out the bedroom door and called, "Hang up your coats and put your muddy boots in the back! Don't run off anywhere. Jeanie's staying for dinner!" Downstairs the children, in an unusual display of obedience, looped their jackets on pegs near kitchen door and threw their boots in a heap on the back steps.

Ruth rearranged the boots from largest to smallest. Then the nagging idea came to her that as the oldest, she was expected to do things like lining up her brother's and sisters' boots in an orderly fashion. She kicked them all down the steps, one by one. When she was done, she looked beyond the row of garbage cans and across the vacant lot and saw Winston Budd leaning over the hood of the Budd boys' rusted Chrysler.

"You sure do love that ugly hunk of junk!" Ruth shrieked in an eleven-year-old's high-pitched shout, and her sisters and brother ran up behind her to peer out the door. They settled their heads alongside hers, so that coming up behind them, Marjorie thought her children looked like a row of dirty cabbages. She turned to Jeanie, who was pulling off her socks at the top of the stairs, and said, "I'm too beat to make anything fancy. Let's just throw together some vegetables and a meat loaf."

Ruth leaned farther out the kitchen door and yelled, "Why don't you marry it!" Marjorie looked past the children's faces and saw Winston Budd stick up his middle finger at Ruth.

Marjorie pushed the children inside and shut the door. "I told you not to bother with the Budd boys. I mean it! Every last one of them is nasty and bent for trouble." Marjorie prodded her four children out of the kitchen and added in emphasis: "Don't let me catch you messing with them, not even to ask them the time of day."

* * * *

The children flocked out of the kitchen to their bedroom window and watched Winston Budd across the vacant lot, which a construction company had cleared recently of its pinewoods. Yesterday had been a memorable day. Ruth, Sam, Karen, and Carla had torn down and pushed into the vacant lot the prefabricated tree house their father had sent them in the mail a year before. The tree house was a perfect six-feet cube made of varnished plywood, with a door on one side and a barred window on the other. Sam discovered that if he got inside and leaned against one of the walls, the tree house would flip over and roll to the next wall, along the same principle of motion that set a wheel spinning in a hamster cage.

"You can drive it from the inside! Look, get in here," he had directed his sisters, and together the four LeBlancs set the tree house rolling floppily along the vacant lot, picking up speed as they came to a slight downhill.

"Watch out for the human tank!" Ruth had yelled, and the box house abruptly stopped, the rectangular hole that served as the doorway flat on the ground. The LeBlancs heard someone climb onto the wall that had come to rest in a ceiling position over them.

They looked up and saw through the barred tree house window Winston and Joshua Budd, massive boy-men in their midteens, with sunburned skin and ghost-colored hair.

"Hey there in there." The children heard through one tree house wall the disembodied voice of Lou, a third, slightly younger Budd. "We ain't never going to let you out!"

The four prisoners hurled themselves together against the wall that faced away from the voice, but Joshua jumped from above and threw his weight against the outside of the wall, and held the tree house in place.

Winston squatted like a toad above them and leered through the window. "We'll only let you out if you say the worst word you can think of, Lady Bug," he told Carla.

Carla looked in collaboration at Karen, who whispered something frantically to her younger sister.

"OK," Carla told him.

"OK," said Winston. "OK, let's hear it."

"Ain't," she said.

Laughter exploded around the tree house. "Ain't! Oh, haw haw!" the LeBlancs heard Joshua say.

Suddenly Joshua was standing up above them again, Winston and Lou on either side of him. All three Budds unzipped their flies and peed down into the house.

*　*　*　*

Over the sound of the television, the children could hear the laughter of their mother and Jeanie rise high over their murmurs of approval or disapproval, which traveled from the kitchen, mixed with the smell of fried okra and baking meat.

"*They* have a father," Marjorie was saying to Jeanie in the kitchen, "but they act like they don't have anyone to bring them up at all. I walked right over to the Budds' garage, where Mr. Budd was working, and told him what happened and said, 'Your boys don't have any home bringing! I've never seen such a sight in my life, those four little children crying, come home with pee all over them!' He just kind of snickered back at me and wiped his nose on his dirty oily car rag. I was so mad I was fit to be tied. Then his wife comes out the house, her eyes all black as bruises around the edges like she hasn't slept in a month, and a bottle of gin in her hand. 'Hun,' she says, 'maybe you should talk to those boys.' 'Maybe you should shut up,' he says back. Then she just kind of slinks into the house in her slippers. It was twelve o'clock midday, and she wasn't even dressed. She just had on this flimsy light orange bathrobe. It's times like this I wish I had a man around who could stand up for us. Not that Mr. Big would have been much help."

Marjorie occasionally spoke of Byron Coffin, now that they had been apart longer, but she never called him by his name. She called him Buy My Coffin or Tightwad or Mr. Big or Mr. Do What I Say.

Jeanie poked at the wheels of okra flecked with cornmeal simmering in the pan. "He sent a package for Sam. It came while I was waiting in the pickup for you guys."

"What am I supposed to do? Leave the neighborhood?" Marjorie continued without listening. "I can't be here all the time fending off big boys like that. I don't get home from work until two hours after the kids get home from school— Who sent a package?"

"The children's father. He sent it UPS. He must have thought you wouldn't pick it up if he sent it through the post office."

Marjorie laughed. "Well, he's right."

"I put it in the back of the truck."

Marjorie laid out six forks on the table. She walked to the stove and stirred the vegetables, opened the oven door to check the meat loaf, and then shut the door with a bang.

"Do you know what he sent Ruth for her last birthday? A radio! A radio to an eleven-year-old child! And it's everything I can do to make the rent and keep them in half-decent clothes. He wants to buy them from me. It's so easy for him, he's never here so he doesn't have to scold them or buy Karen orthopedic shoes instead of taking them all to the movies, and then he comes riding in once every year or two like a knight in shining armor or he goes acting like Santa Claus. I can't wait to see what he does when he comes next month! Last Christmas the kids hardly paid attention to the clothes I bought them."

Jeanie thought of how Rita had told her yesterday, "Nobody knows how to spit fire like Marjorie. I only wish she'd get rattled up about important things."

"They just sat around the whatchamacallit, the remote-control dune buggy he sent them. 'Why don't you send money?' I wrote him. 'Why don't you visit them more or invite them to spend a summer with you?' I don't think one of the children could still recognize him but Ruth. But now he's got to ruin this Christmas too—."

"It's a birthday present," said Jeanie. "It was supposed to be for Sam's birthday last week. Look, Marjorie, why don't you just give it to him? You know the kids are going to love that sled; it doesn't matter." Jeanie opened the oven and played with the temperature dial, enjoying the little explosion the oven made when she turned down the gas too far and had to relight it.

"He never writes a word to me," Marjorie said abruptly. "He never puts an envelope or a card on the package or anything, not even a hello."

"It has a card on it saying that electric trains are useful toys because they teach boys about electricity, about transformers and wiring and that kind of stuff."

A car horn rigged to play the first line of "Dixie" blared across the lot into the kitchen. Both women looked out the window and saw the three Budd boys waving to them. Marjorie drew the blind.

* * * *

The trains did not come in a cardboard box arranged and sealed by the manufacturer. The train cars were packed side

by side, evenly as cigars, in a solid-pine crate. They had been
selected and laid in wood chips with painstaking care, like the
pears wrapped in shredded cellophane the children had once
seen their mother take to the hospital. The hand that packed
the cars had selected without frugality, for both kind and
color: a bright-orange engine embossed with "Union Pacific"
in blue; a black coal carrier; four brown and red boxcars; a
cattle car with four iron bulls in it; a green oil tanker; and a
deep vermilion caboose. The train cars weighed down your
hands with the perfect heaviness of small things that are
truly lead heavy. Sam picked out the cars one by one, savored
each for a moment in his palm, and then passed them to his
sisters, who held the cars up to the light to prove their den-
sity and opaqueness and then let them sink down in the
swoop of an arm to test their weight.

Under the cars were wood and gossamer wire tracks, which
seemed weightless in comparison, more delicate than the
tracks left by sleds on snow. Sam unstacked the foot-long
pieces and placed them beside the box in piles of straight and
curved lengths. Then he lifted the gloriously heavy black box
encasing the transformer and placed it in his lap. After this
came red and yellow and blue rubber-coated wire strands, a
roll of pure copper wire as fine as his mother's hair, a matching set of pliers, screwdrivers in four sizes, and a wire cutter,
all with bright-orange handles, and assorted bags of differ-
ent-size screws. Under these were wood chips with a friendly,
hamsterish cedar smell.

When Sam finished unpacking the crate, his mother and
Jeanie came to the doorway of the children's bedroom to see
the present. The smell of horses followed Jeanie into the
room. Karen saw that Jeanie's sock had a hole over her big
toe. Karen gave her own socks a self-assured look. They
matched and were bleached to stainlessness.

"Jesus," Jeanie said, surveying the pieces, arranged in a
miniature trainyard around Sam. "That's really an OK present."

Sam stared at his knee, and at his sisters, whose tight, expressionless faces turned in unison toward Marjorie. Sam felt a part of him led across the faces like so many stepping stones. He looked up at his mother, whose lips were pressed together so that her mouth disappeared entirely. Her eyes were glistening with tears held back and her forehead seemed to sink down into them. Her face reminded him of a stream bank on the verge of collapsing.

"Yeah, they're OK, but you can't really do much with them. You have to stay inside to use them," Sam explained. Jeanie nodded. But Karen saw Sam's hand curl around the engine and tighten, and after Jeanie and Marjorie left, the girls watched spellbound as Sam turned the engine upside down and uprighted it several times. Rolled onto its back, the engine would let off a low, steady moan, *Hoooooo,* as if an insect whose security depended on being upright on its belly. When Sam flicked his wrist back downward, the engine would fall into a magnificent hush.

* * * *

Although Marjorie's children were as close as possible in age, running from eight to eleven, they were so lacking in personality traits endearing to adults that teachers in school did not even make generalizations about them. When she went to school to pick up Carla's report card from the same teacher who had instructed Ruth and Karen and Sam, Marjorie was always dumbfounded that the teacher did not realize she had taught four LeBlancs. Mrs. Lookingbell or Mrs. Snodgrass or Mr. Small never said, "I'm sure Sam will catch on like his sisters" or "Carla is just a late bloomer; Karen had the same trouble reading *wh* words in first grade." Marjorie's children would cluster around her, unnaturally sullen in a room full of shouting, laughing, crying, or sharply sober classmates. Ruth, Karen, Carla, and Sam looked drab and indistinguishable and stood stoop-shouldered under an invisible weight.

Marjorie had to assume that her children were hiding their personalities for personal use, for times when they were alone with one another. She was not surprised when three weeks before Christmas the children seemed to gather and ungather in the house with an obvious crackling energy, like a wool fabric shooting off threads of static electricity. Sam in particular would patter down the stairs early in the morning, his brown eyes glinting over his oatmeal, his mind on something distant.

* * * *

The children were tactful about the electric trains. They kept them in a shed that bordered the vacant lot, burying an extension cord under dirt and leaves and connecting it through their bedroom window. They were careful to play with the trains when their mother was at the hospital, or in the kitchen gossiping with Jeanie or Rita, or visiting one of the neighbors' houses. Ruth, Karen, and Carla hovered around Sam as he worked on the trains, and not merely because the girls were enthralled by the minuteness of the wiring and the threatening beehive sound of the transformer. They had become charged with the sheer rapture that radiated from their ordinarily quiet and self-effacing brother as he labored over the only gift from their father any of the children had ever liked.

The first time the LeBlanc children had received a present from their father had been Christmas two years before. The package had come by UPS when their mother was at work, and contained a box of frilly yellow dresses for the girls and a dark suit for Sam, all wrapped and mailed by the store. Ruth and Karen and Carla, dressed in cutoff shorts and T-shirts and high-top sneakers, glared in astonishment as they tore back the pale-blue tissue paper. The dresses had wire and papier-mâché corsages attached to slender white belts and were made for much smaller children. Carla's dress had plastic underwear attached to the waist. Sam's suit, on the other hand, was large and hulking, and undertaker gray. The pants, when he put them on as the girls shrieked with delight, bent at his soles as if from an extra joint, and extended eight inches along the floor. At a loss about what to do with the clothes before their mother arrived home, the children stuffed the dresses and suit into the spare-tire compartment of a rusted car behind the scrap-iron dealer's.

Once Carla's father had sent her a cardboard-bound children's Bible, its edges weakly dusted with gold and containing only four brown and white illustrations. Another time Ruth opened a tiny box and found a silver-plated kitten fashioned to attach to a charm bracelet. Ruth had never owned a charm bracelet, and the kitten had fallen in the back of a box under her bed, full of copper staples and nails and twenty-nine barbs cut from a barbwire fence. Karen had received a pink plastic dune buggy that whirled within a wire diameter so stingy only a slow-footed toddler could have liked the toy. The presents were never accompanied by a note of explanation; aside from an AM radio Sam and Ruth dissected to fiddle with the wiring and memorize the contours of the transistors, the children had never found any use for the gifts. They were as awkward and impersonal as a misaddressed letter mistakenly opened.

This time, after Jeanie deposited the late birthday present in the children's bedroom, Sam had read in amazement the note stuffed into the red envelope inside the box. "Sam—" the black scrawl began. "The best thing about these trains is the electricity. Hope you can figure out how to hook up the wiring and transformer."

Sam deftly strung the wires and laid out complicated track formations, huddling over the trains as if they were a small miracle. The girls would snigger at Sam, and assemble the track pieces upside down in long lines as he screwed together complicated networks of curves and straightaways. Giggling so hard that their hands wobbled uncontrollably, Sam's sisters would touch the wrong wire to the screw on the transformer to watch the blue sparks jump up in fits of anger. Amid howls of laughter, they set the iron bulls on top of the boxcars or on the tracks in front of the engine. Sam worked amid his sisters' haphazard actions with steady concentration, because he was powerless against them, and because they also concocted plans that revealed their admiration for the trains.

Every now and then, Jeanie liked to pile Marjorie's children into the back of her truck and take them to Billy Arthur's hobby store at the only mall in Chapel Hill, and buy them stink bombs and Estes rockets. In early December, Jeanie had driven them to Billy Arthur's, and the children had noticed for the first time that the store sold switches, iron switchmen, cork roadbed inclines, and a flatcar with a detachable semitruck trailer that said "Food City" on it. All of these things demonstrated to Sam's sisters the absurd lushness of the gift—alone, Sam could not have mustered the change to buy a single piece of track. But Carla and Karen and Ruth, entertained by his earnestness, helped him comb the vacant lot, the scrap-iron dump, and the used-car dealer's for empty returnable soda bottles, worth three cents each. For a week, the girls spanked the bottles on their bottoms to empty out the dirt, rinsed the cobwebs from inside, and stacked the bottles like dead soldiers into crates, which Sam lugged to the Winn Dixie supermarket. Then, when they grew tired of washing, Karen and Ruth and Carla collected deposits on crates of bottles filthy with mud and spewing insects swaddled in spiderwebs. Carla, in an unprecedented moment of brilliance, discovered that the Winn Dixie piled repurchased empty bottles in shopping carts behind the store. Every day for a week she took the same cart heaped with empty Coke and Fanta bottles from the back to the front of the Winn Dixie and received payment amounting to six dollars and seventy-two cents each time. When the store manager finally caught on and scolded her, he herded all three LeBlanc girls out of the electric doors.

The store manager was startled by how similar the three slack-jawed, black-headed girls were. He watched them huddle together in a clannish way in front of the supermarket. The quirky thought occurred to him that if the girls ever had to stand together in a lineup as adults, no crime victim would be able to tell them apart. As he watched them a little longer, however, he decided that their expressions might distinguish them: The middle one, with the brushed hair, looked slightly bewildered, while the other two had outlandish grins and rebellious hair. The oldest girl turned to look though the plate-glass window at him when she noticed him staring. She put her hands on her hips and said something he could not hear, which made the smallest girl laugh.

The store manager walked back through the plate-glass doors and said, "Y'all break up and move off now. You go somewhere else."

The three girls walked as slowly as they could around the corner of the supermarket and into the parking lot. They ran right into the parking space that had a sign saying "Store Manager" in front of it. The tone the man had used in talking to them had given Ruth an uncomfortable feeling, like a knot just over her heart, which did not go away until she wrote an anonymous note on a paper advertising fatback and pinned the note under the windshield wiper of the store manager's car. The note said: "You better stay away from my Woman, or I'll kill you one night right soon."

The LeBlancs had enough money for the time being to buy everything Sam needed for the train anyway, and they kept busy buying and assembling new parts for Sam's railroad. On the six snow days, the girls pushed Sam outside and stretched him flat on the Flexible Flyer. The children barreled down the steepest hill near the house, overturning on curves and smashing into pine trees. Ruth sat in the front and steered with her feet, while Karen closed her eyes and Carla whooped with joy.

TALKING RAGES

Two weeks after Christmas, when the three girls were back to searching for bottles in the vacant lot, Ruth walked up a

small rise and saw, partly obscured behind a row of pines, the
Budd boys taking the muffler off their Chevrolet.

The Chevrolet had once been a bright-blue two-door family
sedan. The Budds had painted various parts of the car a rust
color. They had soldered the doors closed so that in order to
enter the Chevrolet, you had to grab the top of the front window and swing yourself in, feet first. Winston had bought a
special license plate that read HO-BABE, and underneath this
Joshua had screwed in a second plate, with a Confederate flag
on it. There was a decal on the back window saying "Guns
Don't Kill, People Do" and a bumper sticker reading "Bomb
Hanoi Now."

Ruth squatted behind a pine tree and watched Lou crawl
out from under the car. "It's about time we did that," he told
his brothers. Winston got inside the car and revved the motor,
which made a noise like an unending row of slamming doors.

Carla and Karen ran across the lot when they heard the
noise, and crept behind Ruth to see what she was looking at.
Just as they stumbled over the rise, the motor cut off in a
moment of terrifying silence. Karen screamed, "Oh no, get
back! It's them!" and dropped the two bottles she was holding. The bottles clanked against each other, and one broke at
the bottom of the rise next to Lou's foot.

"Well, if it ain't Miss Ain't," Lou said to his brothers.

Karen and Ruth whirled around and ran halfway across
the lot before they realized Carla was not with them.

"Carla!" Karen gasped. "Where's Carla?" The girls
turned and saw their sister still standing on the rise, her
hands on her hips and the bottom of her ponytail resting
crookedly on her shoulder.

"You dumb fucks!" she shouted down at the Budds. "Get
the hell out of my vacant lot!" The rest of what she said was
drowned out by the sound of the engine restarting. Ruth and
Karen watched Carla disappear down the rise and then scam-
per back toward them, wild-eyed at her own daring and jubi-
lantly holding the unbroken bottle.

For the next week, the three girls scrounged the territory behind the scrap-iron dealer's, while the Budd boys remained in the vacant lot, taking out their car engine and putting it back in.

* * * *

One afternoon in early March when Marjorie was working, Karen and Carla came home without their shirts on. Ruth was behind the house helping Sam fasten corkbed and track onto a nine-by-nine-foot piece of plywood Ruth had dragged home from a construction site. It was a bright, relatively warm day, but Karen walked into the kitchen shivering. Carla stamped her hiking boots, a Christmas present from Jeanie, and took her time coming in. Carla was breathless, either from running hard or from excitement.

Ruth looked up and saw that Carla had no shirt on. "Mama said you can't take your shirt off outside anymore," Ruth said, "because pretty soon people will be able to tell you're not a boy." Ruth said this in an even tone, intended to indicate pleasure in disobedience rather than to relay her mother's command.

"Ha!" Carla answered. She ran her hand through her hair the way Chuck Connors did on *The Rifleman.*

Ruth looked up a second time to answer Carla, and saw Karen standing in the kitchen door, sniffling. "They took my shirt!" Karen said, putting a nylon jacket on her bare back.

"You're gonna sweat," said Carla. Carla had only just noticed that she could sweat if she exerted herself especially hard. She could rarely work up more than a little-girl sweat, but on a very sunny day, if she ran with her jacket on, she could make a mustache of perspiration appear over her lip. As far as she knew, she had not been able to sweat at all the year before.

Ruth walked over to the kitchen door and leaned in. "Who took your new shirt, Karen?"

Now Sam laid down his screwdriver, looked at Carla, and said matter-of-factly, "Mama's going to kill you both."

"She gave it to them!" Karen sobbed, standing in the doorway and pointing at the back of Carla's head.

"Carla gave away your shirts?" Ruth asked.

Karen shook her head and looked at Ruth with a mournful expression, unable to go on.

Carla explained patiently, "I didn't give them Karen's shirt, I only gave them my shirt, that baby-blue one that used to be Sam's."

"Mama's going to beat your butt." Sam affirmed his earlier pronouncement.

"Where's Karen's shirt?" Ruth pressed.

"OK," said Carla. "We were down at the new house they're building, looking for plywood."

"Just like you were yesterday!" Karen accused Ruth.

"So Lou Budd saw us and he grabbed Karen's arm and said he would take us to the police because we were stealing, and I said go ahead! but Karen started crying and then Joshua said why do you dress like boys in overalls and boys' pants and boys' shoes? I said noner your business. And he said maybe you aren't girls at all, you better prove it, so he held Karen and Winston pulled her shirt over her head and took it off to prove it and Karen tried to stop them but he held her arm up behind her like this—" Carla demonstrated a half nelson on herself. "So then they held her for a while longer and let her go and told her to put her shirt back on and I said, *She* surely doesn't want it. You look pretty raggedy to me, so why don't you keep it, and just take mine too why don't you."

"So she took off her shirt and threw it on the ground!" gasped Karen.

"Ha!" said Ruth.

"We better go back and find them," Sam decided. "Come on, Ruth, I'm not going alone."

Ruth picked up a rock and followed Sam, pretending to be his bodyguard. They took the route through the woods to the house where the new lot lay, being careful to look out for the Budds.

When they reached the lot, Sam said, "There they are, up in that pine tree." Carla's shirt was halfway down the tree, but Karen's was a tiny red speck at the top.

Ruth tried to shimmy up the tree to get the shirts, but the pine was the kind whose branches do not begin until the high middle of the trunk, about twenty feet up. Ruth shimmied back down. She and Sam threw rocks at the shirts until they finally knocked down Carla's, which had a large rip in the right shoulder. They were unable to dislodge Karen's shirt. In the end, they came home, and the four children decided that it would be best not to tell their mother about the incident, in the hope that she would never notice Karen's shirt was gone. The plan succeeded, since Marjorie only missed the shirt the Sunday after laundry day, when she went into one of her talking rages as she sorted the clean clothes, finally concluding that the shirt had been lost in the wash.

*   *   *   *

Marjorie LeBlanc's talking rages had started shortly after she began working full time as a nurse and generally came on days when she worked overtime, although they were otherwise without forewarning. The children could rarely detect the source of the trouble, but when the talking rages began, they fed on whatever difficulties might be present as a forest fire snaps twigs in two and roars over dried logs. So that Marjorie might hum around the house for weeks, picking T-shirts off the floors, wrapping an old piece of sheet around a leaky sink pipe, or hovering over a skillet and deftly flipping pancakes the children caught in their hands and raced off to eat on the steps or the curb or even while running across the street. Then the simplest object, like a dirty plate or torn shirt collar, might make Marjorie freeze where she stood, her lips drawing tight and her face paling.

"Do you think I'm just your workhorse!" she shouted on Sunday as the children huddled at the door to her bedroom. She picked up shreds of socks and balled-up T-shirts from a mountain of laundry she had set down on her bed. "Am I supposed to wash the same T-shirt twenty-seven times a week?" Marjorie went to Rita's laundromat every Saturday, and until then the children had thought their mother enjoyed sitting with Rita, sipping gin and tonic or margaritas and howling at jokes the children seldom understood. "This whole house is a pigsty!" Marjorie continued. "I can't even walk into the bathroom without tripping on some gray, raggedy pair of underwear that Karen has left in the middle of the floor. I'd be ashamed to leave my underwear on the floor! I can't even invite my neighbors over here because I'm embarrassed to let them see the mess. Hope George from over the way stopped by and could barely walk across the floor for the coats and bottles in the hall. 'You must really have your hands full with working and watching after those four children, Mrs. LeBlanc,' she says in her big ugly rough belting voice, and I have to sit there listening to her talk about her Girl Scout bake sale and all the cooking awards she's ever won while the filthy dishes are sitting piled on the stove behind her instead of washed and stacked like someone named Karen told me she'd do. 'Can't even keep her own house straight and her children run around like wild things in the middle of the street just waiting to get knocked over by cars!' she'll be saying next to all her snooty PTA friends."

Marjorie paused while she seemed to wonder over something. "How do you think I feel when I come home after working myself silly all day and leaning over some rotting old man's smelly bedpan and then that mincing nosy Mrs. Katerwaller across the street with her one-hundred-dollar dress tells me, 'I believe I saw your little daughter Karen and her brother standing in the middle of the street for a whole hour after dark yesterday, and they didn't move an inch when a car barely missed hitting them. It was just around when we were all eating supper together.' Have you decided to live in the street, is that it? Why don't you sleep out there—" Marjorie grabbed her mattress by the corner and began tugging it off the bedframe. "Why not take this with you and sleep out there, since I'm not even around to feed you supper?" Clothes began sliding from the mattress onto the floor. "Then people can see how I really care for you, why don't you just sleep outside—"

"Mama, stop it, stop it!" Ruth called out, picking up the clothes as they fell to the floor and balling them into her arms.

"What were you doing at the end of the street?" Marjorie said to the mattress, tugging it toward Karen and Sam so that it finally slid to the floor in frenzied jerks, then balanced on its end. Ruth frantically continued to pile up clothes in her arms.

"Looking for luna moths! They like the streetlights!" said Carla, as Sam and Karen crumpled into tears.

The mattress stood upright for a moment and then tipped over toward Karen. "Mama! Mama!" she shrieked as the mattress tumbled down on her.

Suddenly Marjorie drew her hands to her mouth and then pushed them back out again and ran over to lift the mattress. She watched Karen struggle out from under and then cried, "What am I doing!" Marjorie stared at the teary faces of her children as if they were strangers lined up to pass judgment on her. "I'm a monster, a monster. I didn't used to be like this! What's happening to me? I'm not myself, I work too hard, I haven't been myself since the day I was born, so many demands!" She ran out of the room. The children stayed behind, speechless, lugging the mattress back onto the bed and loading the laundry into the basket.

A quarter hour later Marjorie, her eyes red, returned to the bedroom and took the ironing board down from the wall. She sniveled as she ironed the clothes, pressing even the socks and the sheets. Finally, she said, "Don't mind me, I'm so tired. Mrs. George is just an old battle-ax. She hasn't kept her nose to herself one day of her life." Marjorie set down the iron. "What's a luna moth?"

"They're big and green," Karen said soberly, wiping her face on the pair of socks she had worked into a ball. "They have pink and yellow eyes on the wings and long tails, and they lie down on the street right outside where the light hits under the lampposts. You don't ever find them this time of year, but Sam found one!"

"Well, I'll be," said Marjorie. "I don't think I've ever seen one of those."

"I'll show you!" Sam said, eager to please, running out of the room and coming back with a cigar box. He opened it, and inside, Marjorie saw a mint-green moth lift up its wings and then resettle them neatly into a symmetrical stillness.

"It's too beautiful for words," Marjorie pronounced.

After that the children sat on the bed, wrestling and joyously calling each other Battle-Ax and joining in when Marjorie sang:

> Rich girl uses cold cream,
> Poor girl uses lard,
> My girl uses axle grease
> and rubs just twice as hard.
>
> Oh, ride that humpback goat,
> ride that humpback goat,
> The only song that I can sing
> is ride that humpback goat.

"Whoosh!" Marjorie called out at the end of the chorus. When she finished sorting the laundry into piles, she said, "I swear those washing machines eat clothes. I know I put something red into the wash, but Karen's new shirt isn't here anywhere! I'll bet that skinny lady who was in such a hurry to use my dryer didn't even stop to check if she got everything before she crammed her clothes in! Well, I'll ask Rita to look for it."

* * * *

"I got a telegram from Mr. Big, saying he's coming in April," Marjorie told Jeanie. "A telegram! My heart almost stopped—I thought someone had died. Well, I don't want to be here to see him."

Outside in the street, the women heard a car go *Rum! Rum!*

Rum! Jeanie lifted the curtain on the kitchen window and remarked, "Christ, those guys are still out there laying a patch."

Marjorie stared over Jeanie's shoulder. "They've been doing that all February. They're going to kill somebody if they're not careful. I don't even think that boy's old enough to drive a car." Joshua was racing the Chevrolet up and down the street. When he reached the LeBlancs' house he stopped the car, restarted it, and then took his foot off the clutch, spinning his wheels before he raced off again. A stripe of burnt rubber remained behind him opposite Marjorie's house.

"All the children play on this street! I really should talk to that boy's mother, but I sure don't have the strength to right now. Right now my feet are aching the living daylights out of me." Marjorie propped up her feet on a kitchen chair. "I don't see how you can stand me, Jeanie. All I ever do is moan and groan!"

Jeanie sat down and started cutting her fingernails with a toenail clipper. "You need a night off, Marjorie. Why don't you let me take the kids out to the movie theater or something? Ruth wants to see that vampire picture."

"Oh, no!" said Marjorie. "I'll have Sam and Karen sleeping in my room for a week. They always beg me to take them to those things, and then they sit stuck to their seats the whole time and look like they're going to faint when they walk out. After the movie, Carla and Ruth start jumping around and pretending they're wolfmen or vampires, while Sam and Karen get scareder and scareder to death by the minute. Then Karen drags herself into my room around midnight and snuggles into my bed. As soon as I begin to fall asleep, Sam comes in, all quiet and secret like he doesn't want me to know, and curls up in his bedclothes on the floor or in the armchair."

Jeanie laughed. "I could take them out to the farm tomorrow."

"That'd be kind of nice." Marjorie looked at her feet. "I swear I'm so beat sometimes I think I'm losing my marbles."

"You just stay here and soak your feet and watch a monster movie on *Science Fiction Theater.*"

"Oh, Jeanie, you're so nice to me," said Marjorie. "Sometimes I wish you were a man!"

Jeanie pushed her ponytail off her shoulder and laughed. "I think that too—why do we both have to be women? You could be a handsome young man with four children, just dying for a lady to come and bail you out."

The two women couldn't think of anything to say next.

Jeanie leaned over and tied her shoelaces in double knots. "I'm going to show Carla how to put pine tar and bacon grease on the hooves of that horse I'm keeping for that rich lady. Carla's not afraid of anything, I swear. It's funny—she isn't scared of walking across a bull pen, but Karen can't sleep for the werewolves."

"That's because not one of those ragamuffins has a lick of sense. Oh, Karen's an odd one. She's all shy, but she's listening and watching all the time. Do you know what she told me the other day? She said, 'Don't be lonely, Mama. You'll find somebody.' Just like that, right out of the blue!"

Jeanie frowned. "Some kids just pay more attention to what adults are thinking."

Ruth's high shriek pierced the kitchen window: "You take your hands off!"

Marjorie stood up and opened the curtain, and she and Jeanie saw one of the Budd boys holding Sam in the middle of the road while another Budd revved the motor of his car twenty feet away, as if he intended to run Sam over. Sam wrenched himself free and ran from the older boy, who bent double laughing. After Sam reached where Ruth stood on the road shoulder, the Budds' Chevrolet backed up, shifted gears, and went racing down the street. Ruth turned toward the Budd boy standing in the road, picked up a rock, and drew back her arm in a threatening gesture.

"That's it!" Marjorie cried, jumping up and opening the kitchen door. "I'm not going to let this go on one moment longer. Those boys are asking for trouble. Why, little children play on this street all the time. You stay here, Jeanie. I'll be back in a minute. I'm going to go talk to those boys' mother." Marjorie walked quickly out the kitchen door and Jeanie sat down, watching her friend's figure recede across the vacant lot.

THE WOMEN PUT THEIR HEADS TOGETHER

From her battered house at the top of the road, Faith Budd could see most of what happened in the neighborhood. She had watched the fatherless LeBlanc children walking back and forth from the orange U-haul like little pack animals, five years before. The Leblancs' box of a house, with the big ugly fence around it, had been vacant and considered unsalable for years, and Faith's boys had used it as a hideout, where she suspected they sat together smoking cigarettes when they were young and dragged girls when they were older.

Mrs. LeBlanc had never repainted the house or fixed the pothole in the middle of the driveway, but immediately after moving in, she had invited over a whole motley assortment of friends, including the woman who worked in the laundromat down the road; a fat lady who came during the summers, wore outrageous clothes, and appeared to be a relative of some kind; occasional packs of nurses, all in uniform; and also a hulking, boyish lady friend who dressed like Daniel Boone in tall boots and a fringed suede jacket and hauled manure to the LeBlancs' backyard garden in a pickup truck. She looked like the kind of person who might do anything. Sometimes this friend sat in her pickup in front of the LeBlancs', waiting for them to come home, or she would wander around in the yard, whistling through a piece of grass. Didn't Mrs. LeBlanc ever worry about bad influences on her children?

Ordinarily, Mrs. Budd minded her own business, but in the last year Mrs. LeBlanc had not been minding hers. Right before Thanksgiving, she had walked up to Mr. Budd while he was screwing new commercial plates onto his truck and screeched at him in a high-pitched quavery voice about something Winston and Joshua and Lou had done to the LeBlanc children. The Budd boys were barely teenagers, and Mrs. Budd believed it was wrong to meddle too much in disputes among children. She had little choice, since her own boys were so gloomy and secretive. Right now she had no idea where Lou and Winston were. Joshua was driving up and down the street, testing out his rebuilt motor. He coasted to a stop by the driveway, and Faith saw him look up and sneer as Mrs. LeBlanc came out of her house. She was wearing her nurse's suit and heading across the vacant lot that dipped down toward that high-and-mighty Mrs. Katerwaller's house. Mrs. LeBlanc's face was flushed with exertion, and she walked in a straight line in ridiculously small steps, like a little red ant. Faith Budd narrowed her eyes when she saw Mrs. LeBlanc pause and look up at Faith's window before continuing.

Faith's eyes were so deeply set that when she was a girl, people had accused her of wearing brown eye shadow: her coppery irises glimmered from inside two dark circles. Once when she peered into the washing machine at the laundromat and saw a penny glinting from the bottom of the dank, muddy water, she thought she had caught her own reflection. This was years after her husband, a rough-shaved boy covered with car grease, had first loitered on Faith's doorstep, thinking her eyes made her look cityish and interested—years after she bore three bad-mannered boys who collectively ignored her in a sullen conspiracy with their father. It was only last week, in fact, when she had been emptying the boys' oil-stained clothes from a gunnysack into a washing machine while her husband waited in in his truck, parked outside the laundromat's front window. She had noticed him staring slightly to the side of her left hip. Faith turned around and saw Marjorie LeBlanc's behind, fleshless and shaped like an onion, sticking out as she bent over in her nurse's uniform to pick up a green sock. Her children were sitting on the orange plastic chairs nearby, small and wrinkled like so many sacks of groceries. When Marjorie straightened up, she hollered something at her children, exposing her pinched yellowish face. Faith had looked back at her husband's truck and seen him turn away, shuttering his eyes.

Faith stuck her feet in her slippers and walked to the hall-way mirror to look at herself: she pushed back some stray hairs into the bun that had slid over her left ear and said, "Aren't you a fright!" After entering the kitchen and pour-ing herself a jigger of gin in a milk glass, Faith carried the bottle and glass to the front room. She set the bottle on a low table, but kept the glass in her hand when Mrs. LeBlanc knocked on the screen door. Faith opened it, saying, "Well, come in here and mingle with us floozies," and she let sail a high, hollow laugh, tossing her head. She let Marjorie in and plunked down on a ratty armchair.

Marjorie sat on a couch upholstered in cloth that depicted cowboys galloping over a desert landscape. In front of the couch was a low table stained a deep brown, with a gin bottle on it. Beside the couch, Mrs. Budd's television rested on a chest stained the same color, with handles shaped like eagles. The other furniture in the room was also dark brown, and it made Marjorie feel that she was out of place, like a woman entering a men's bar to ask for directions.

"Would you like something?" Mrs. Budd asked, raising her glass.

Marjorie looked down at her lap and saw that her hands looked as small and fine as girls' Sunday gloves. Something tempted her to want to say, "I think I'll have a glass of milk," but she caught herself in time. Marjorie had the peculiar thought that people were always sizing her up and deciding she was one kind of person or another. Mrs. Budd was cocking her head in an expectant, mocking way that made Marjorie feel prim and prudish. But when she looked into Mrs. Budd's deep-set lonely eyes, which seemed to sink into the brownness of the room, Marjorie shifted in her chair and tugged at her belt and then retied it so that it hung more loosely about her waist.

"I'd love a gin and tonic," she said.

Mrs. Budd pattered to the kitchen and came back out with an economy-brand bottle of tonic and a glass of ice with a lemon wedge perched on the rim. Marjorie looked down Mrs. Budd's hallway, and was startled by a Halloween mask—Frankenstein—hanging on a doorknob. Mrs. Budd set down the glass and the tonic bottle and said, "The tonic cools you off and the gin makes you hot!" Marjorie poured in equal amounts of each.

"Mr. Budd's out?" Marjorie asked, leaning back to sip her drink.

"He's taken his vacation time to go up to his parents' in the mountains for two weeks to do some hunting. I tried to get him to spend the time with me. I said, 'Hun, can't you just stay here to keep me a little company?' But he just had to go. What are men good for anyway!" Mrs. Budd gave off a little bark of a laugh. "He was planning to take the children, but they don't like hunting so much."

Children? Marjorie thought.

"They say only grits hunt."

Marjorie raised her eyebrows quizzically, thinking: Why, but they *are* grits!

Mrs. Budd misunderstood. "Oh, that's what they call hicks, they say grits. They got to act real cityish now all the time with that car of theirs, and Winston says they'll wait till they go into the army to shoot real guns, they wouldn't be caught dead hunting painters and possums. Franklin Delano just stumps around the house when he hears that, but I've never seen him to lose his temper. He says it's good the boys are learning all about cars anyway. But I wouldn't really call it learning, cars are just like second nature to them what with a father like Franklin Delano."

"Franklin Delano's your husband?" Marjorie asked, this time taking two long gulps so that the tonic burned the middle of her throat and tingled in her nose the way she liked it to.

"He's not my first," Mrs. Budd continued, refilling her own glass from the gin bottle.

"Oh?" said Marjorie.

"I married my first when I was fifteen. He died young."

"I'm sorry to hear it," Marjorie said.

"You know how he died? He was standing in a bar in Raleigh, and a man walked in and shot up the bar with a pistol. You know how some men do when they get drunk? Then he ran out the bar. So Skeet got up and followed him out the bar with his hand in his pocket, pretending he had a gun. Then Skeet said, 'You stop right there!' and the man stopped. So next Skeet said, 'Draw!' and pulled his hand out of his pocket. Well, what could the man do but shoot him dead in self-defense! No one even blamed the man afterwards."

"That's awful," Marjorie said. She poured herself some more gin and tonic and squeezed the lemon into the glass.

"I was lucky I didn't have the boys yet. Then I met Mr. Budd when I was walking out the cemetery after the funeral. He was working on the road, laying a pipeline. He just said hi and wiped his forehead with his hat. Then later he asked around about me and came to my house to invite me out, then we got married and he got a job at the garage and then I had the children right in a row, three boys in diapers at the same time, and later he started managing the garage when the man that owns it moved to Florida."

Mrs. Budd paused, and Marjorie waited for her to fill in the rest of the story, from managing the garage to the pre-

sent. Marjorie thought she could then find a way to bring up
the Budd boys and their car again. Outside, she heard the
Budds' Chevrolet going *Rum! Rum! Rum!* up the hill in the
direction of her house.

"I saw your little girls with a group of children down by
the crick a while back, and I do think they were killing a
snake," Mrs. Budd said abruptly.

"Snake?" Marjorie sat forward slightly on the couch and
set down her glass in the circle of water on the table.

"I do think it was a water moccasin. That older boy, I
can't recall his name, he owns that brindle dog named Blue,
tried to shoot the snake with his BB gun and then they all
threw bricks at it and finally cut off its head, then they took
it down the street and hung it on the sign at the corner. I am
so afraid of snakes I could hardly watch. I know some people
don't feel one way or the other about a snake, but if I just
see one, I can't sleep for the next three nights. Franklin
Delano comes back from hunting and tells me about all the
different kinds just out of personal interest, the ones that
curl into hoops and roll down the road and the kind you drop
and they break like glass and the copperheads and cotton-
mouths that will chase you. And I just tell him, please
Franklin Delano don't, I don't care to know there's ever been
more than one kind of snake on this earth.

"When I was a girl my mother was keeping some geese,
and the best layer once laid seventeen eggs and my mother
decided to let her hatch them all; she had a love for geese.
But every morning we'd come out and there was another egg
gone, so one night I sat up with the lantern, waiting to find
out was it a rat or raccoon or what eating the eggs, so we
knew what kind of trap to set. Didn't anything come the
whole night. But in the morning, when the roosters started
crowing, I open my eyes and see a five-foot snake snaking
toward the goose. Well, I was frozen stiff. I thought that
goose would jump off her nest at it, pecking and hissing and
all. But she just got up real slow like a hypnotized person

and walked sideways to the edge of the barn and drew her neck straight up in the air and let that snake slink up and dip its head into the nest and stretch out its lip over the crown of an egg. Then its lip stretched even farther and its head fell back and he closed his eyes like he was dreaming, opening his mouth wide. I screamed! My mother came running and my brothers came out and chased the snake out the barn and down a hill and along a fence until it leapt into a tree and got away. I never could get out of my mind the picture of that goose stepping aside like that, just out of scared stiffedness, while that snake came and took the eggs she was spending so long sitting on. Her eyes just seemed to open wide and turn all glassy, and I remember that her beak just kind of snapped up and down on air. In the end we never did catch the snake. My mother drove over it with a neighbor's tractor one day, but it just slid away like it was a shadow and hadn't felt a thing. My mother even waited for the snake with a gun, but he came only in the very minutes when we were off doing something else, sometimes even in the middle of the day, and he ate all the eggs until there was six left and then the goose just took up and left those."

Mrs. Budd set her glass down in a delicate motion, balancing it on the arm of her chair, and asked Marjorie if she would like a little something to eat. Then Mrs. Budd said, "You know, Mrs. LeBlanc, I thought you were kind of standoffish before, but I can see I was wrong. I think you're right nice."

"You call me Marjorie," said Marjorie.

"And you call me Faith."

"Well, I'm going to have to ask the girls about that snake," Marjorie said. "You know how kids are, they don't have any fear of danger. Sometimes I come home and see them standing in the middle of the road there when your boys' car is racing up and down, just like they don't have a stick of sense. You don't think you could warn your boys to be a little careful, maybe drive farther down the hill? Since God Himself couldn't keep my kids off the roadway."

"I'll be sure to talk with them," said Faith. "Mr. Mintor next door already set his dog on them once because they parked the Chevrolet on the edge of his property."

"You mean Mr. Mintor who runs the funeral home? The one who wears the yellow shirt with the dirty gray tie?"

Faith sniggered. "That's him. The fellow who kind of snorts when he talks!" Faith snorted in demonstration.

"Do you know—" Marjorie put her face in her hands, holding back little gasps of laughter. "He—he—came courting a couple years back!"

Faith let out another snort.

"He came over to my yard one night and almost scared me out of my skin, and do you know what he said? You'll never guess what he said. He said"—Marjorie paused to snort— " 'Baby, why don't you put the kids to bed' "—snort—" 'and we go out and have us a drink?' "

"He said that?" Faith cried out.

* * * *

When Ruth braved her way over the Budds' front yard to get her mother, great howls of laughter were coming through the screen door. All their lives the LeBlanc children would cringe when their mother accompanied them to movies or sat in kitchens with their friends' mothers, letting out her great uncontrollable funny laughs. Ruth stood on the Budds' front steps for a minute, surveying their yard. She savored the sensation of invading Budd territory. Then she kicked a brick in the walk out of place, knocked on the screen door, and called through. "Mama! Hey, Mama, Jeanie's here, and we want to know can we go out and get some barbecue?"

"My goodness! Look at the time!" Ruth heard her mother say. "I'm starving my family to death!" Marjorie appeared in the doorway, and Mrs. Budd came up behind her, pushing the screen door open.

"I'll talk to the boys about the car," said Mrs. Budd. Then Faith watched Marjorie grow smaller as she and her daughter walked down the hill. Faith muttered to herself, "But whatever makes her think they'll listen!"

* * * *

"I'm not going to be here when your father comes," said Marjorie. "I'm going over to Rita's with Jeanie and Mrs. Budd. I left the phone number right here." Marjorie pointed to a blue slip of paper on top of the phone book. "You tell him he's to bring you home by nine o'clock tonight and give you supper first."

"I bet we won't recognize him," said Ruth. "Remember last time when he came with a mustache?"

"He said he was going to shave it off," said Sam. "It must be gone by now."

Marjorie tied a yellow scarf around her head. Karen watched, fascinated by the triangle that hung like a drooping hen's tail on her mother's neck.

Carla sat quietly, pounding a pile of pepper out of the shaker onto her grits. Marjorie kissed her on top of her head. "You be good now," she said. She opened the kitchen door, stepped out, and then turned around. "Don't whine and complain and give him a hard time, or he'll think I'm raising you wrong."

"We promise," said Ruth, although she felt strange promising. They would no more have acted badly around him than around a minister in a friend's church, or the school vice-principal, or similar allegedly important adults with peripheral relevance to the children's lives.

When the children heard the Oldsmobile starting, Karen and Ruth cleared the table and stacked the dishes in the sink. Sam and Carla went outside, walked down the vacant lot to the street, and peered inside the gutter.

All of the LeBlanc children were still small enough to slip through the iron slits where the gutters emptied into the storm sewers. The sewers dropped five feet into a cement well, and were connected to one another by wide pipes, which the children could walk through if they stooped over. Sam had discovered the pipe network one day when he tossed a roll of firecrackers into the sewer and heard them explode halfway down the street, where the next gutter well opened.

It was a hot April day, so Sam and Carla decided to climb down into the coolness of the storm sewer. They lay on their stomachs and slipped feet first through the slit, hung from their hands, and dropped to the bottom. Then they bent double and walked along the inside of the sewer pipe until they came to the next gutter well. Carla leaned against the chilly cement, and Sam pulled himself onto an iron rod two feet up the wall and peered outside. The gutter well was directly across the street from the Budd house, and Sam noted that the long, slender sewer opening was just like the window of a tank.

"We should roll right over there and knock down their house," said Sam.

"We should mash them like pancakes," Carla agreed. She pulled herself up next to her brother and saw their mother's Oldsmobile parked outside the Budds'. The heat glaring off the pavement hurt the children's eyes. They felt bored and impatient. Mrs. Budd came out of the house with a load of laundry, waved to their mother, and then walked past the Chevrolet to the station wagon and got inside. The LeBlancs' car slowly pulled around the corner. Carla jumped down, peered into the mud to the left of her foot, then stooped and picked up a penny. "Oh, no—tails!" she said.

"Toss it up the pipe," Sam advised.

Carla flicked her wrist and the penny leapt ten feet, ricocheted against the wall, wobbled at the bottom of the pipe, and then lay still.

"I'm going back to the house," Sam said suddenly.

"I think I'll stay here awhile," Carla told him.

"Come back and mess around with the trains."

"I'll come in awhile," Carla said, climbing back on the metal rung after Sam jumped down. Carla laid her face against the warm cement outside the gutter's mouth and listened to Sam scuttling along the pipe. Then she saw Winston Budd coming toward her. She drew back her head rapidly, and in half a minute Winston's boots walked across the street in front of her and then over to the Chevrolet at the bottom of the Budds' drive. Winston squatted down, his side to Carla, leaning against a back tire. He took out a long green object, pressed the top of it, and a rusted switchblade knife shot out. He held the knife by the tip of the blade and turned the handle around to admire it, with a slightly bored expression.

Carla squinted and saw that the handle was a naked lady carved in green stone. And abruptly, she experienced a feeling in her stomach more intense than thirst, deeper than the pit that had been there that morning when she woke up and thought of her father coming. She held still for a moment, pondering the feeling, and realized that it was pure longing. She wanted the knife with the naked green woman on it more than she had ever wanted anything in the world.

She watched Winston throw the knife into the grass, so that the naked lady did a flip and landed with her head in the air. Carla never took her eyes off the knife as Winston polished it on his pants, closed it, and laid it down on the hood of the car as he checked his pockets for a pack of cigarettes. He took out a Lucky Strike, lit it, and then picked the knife back up and stuck it halfway into his back pocket. He reached into the front window of the Chevrolet, pulled out a wrench and a pile of rags, and opened the hood of the car, his back to Carla. He threw the rags on the ground behind him, pulled out a metal rod and propped up the hood, then leaned over and stuck his head so far down it was as if, Carla thought, he were going to kiss the motor.

The knife fell out of his pocket and onto the pile of rags, as quietly as the swishing of a nylon slip. Carla pulled herself upward through the gutter opening. She walked soundlessly in her sneakers across the street to the Budds' driveway, and then stooped over and picked up the knife.

She backed up slowly, but just as she reached the middle of the street, Lou and Joshua sprang through the door of the Budds' house, and Lou yelled, "Hey, Winston! She took something from you!"

Carla whirled around and raced across the street, ducked down and tried to get into the storm sewer, changed her mind and threw the knife through the opening, then ran across the vacant lot and behind her house. All three Budds, not realizing that Carla had let go of the knife, raced after her, and Winston caught her just as she reached the shed.

"Give it here!" said Winston, whirling Carla around and shaking her by the shoulder.

"I don't have it!" Carla answered, breathing hard.

Karen came to the doorway of the shed, then stepped back as Sam and Ruth rushed past her from inside. Ruth was carrying the train engine and Sam had a piece of track in his hand.

"Tell your little thief of a sister to give me back my knife!" said Winston.

"What knife?" Ruth asked, but before she could understand, Joshua pushed by her into the shed, and Lou grabbed the train engine from her hand.

"Man, oh, man!" Joshua's voice echoed inside the shed. "Look at these trains." Lou followed Joshua, and before Sam could turn back around, the train engine came flying out of the shed and slammed into the wall of the house. The back end scattered on the ground, and the front turned over and moaned, *Hoooooo.*

"Don't, oh, don't!" Sam cried out, running into the shed, where the Budds were already tearing up the track and lifting the train cars in armfuls. Winston let go of Carla and joined his brothers in the shed. He grabbed two of the train cars and threw them out over the vacant lot, where they crashed against some bricks.

Carla ran after him, yelling, "It's in the sewer, it's in the sewer, I threw it in the sewer!" But the Budds ignored her now, either because they could not hear her through their shouting and laughing, or because they were completely diverted by Sam, who was whirling in circles around them, trying to grab the train cars and pieces of track. Ruth threw a mop, leaning by the back door, high into the air, so that it arced and came almost straight down on Joshua Budd. He hardly seemed to notice.

Ruth darted to the right and ran in front of the house, yelling, "Help! Somebody come over here and help us!"

Karen stood rooted by the shed door, watching the Budds pry up and break the last pieces of track. When they all turned their backs to her, she leaned over and slipped the transformer and the caboose inside her shirt, and then slowly backed through the kitchen door, down the hallway, and into the bedroom. She watched from the bedroom window as the three Budds emerged from the shed, scattering the remaining train cars in front of them around the back garden plot, while Carla raced in crazy zigzags after the Budds. When the last car hit the ground, Karen heard Winston turn to Carla and say, "I don't even like that knife! I got two just like it that are even better. But you better learn to stop stealing." Then the three Budds walked back across the vacant lot, slapping each other on the backs and making whooping sounds. Carla trailed after them, stopped, turned, and ran around the house after Ruth. Then Karen took the caboose and transformer out of her shirt and laid them under Sam's pillow.

Sam sank down with his back against the lintel of the shed door. When he looked up, a tall shadow blocked the light in the doorway, making him start. Then it stepped backward, a slack-jawed man in a brown hat. Sam could see a strange gray car behind the man, on the street near the yard. Sam realized with detachment that the man must have come around the left side of the house and seen nothing of what happened.

Carla and Ruth walked back toward the shed and stopped when they saw the man.

He removed his hat, and as Karen came outside through the kitchen, she saw that his hair was yellowish-brown and rumpled, making her think of a wilted lettuce leaf.

"Dad! OhmygodDad!" Ruth whispered.

The man blew his cheeks in and out, making little puffing sounds as he surveyed the wreckage. A bent boxcar lay in Sam's hand, and the other cars radiated out from him in the vacant lot.

The children's father spoke in strange muffled gasps, like a small boy holding back tears. "You—didn't—appreciate?" he said. He pivoted on the edge of one shoe and walked in a wobbling stride toward the street corner. He took off his hat, got in the gray car, and turned on the ignition.

Ruth broke loose from where she stood in amazement next to her sisters. She ran down the grass and grabbed the car door handle and pounded on the glass. "He didn't do it! It was them! It was them!" She gestured wildly to three teenagers loitering around a souped-up Chevrolet across the vacant lot. To Sam, the boys looked small and far away, as if they were figures in an advertisement stuck to a distant fence. His sister's voice had an unbelievable tone—it sounded thin and tinny as the worst lie Sam had ever told. The gray car pulled slowly away from the curb, and when it was a safe distance from Ruth, picked up speed. It was almost racing as it reached the horizon, one hundred feet down the road at the top of a hill. The car seemed to flatten, until it was thinner than corkbed and then a mere coppery wire and then nothing.

On the edge of the lot, the train engine emitted a hoarse *Hoooooo!*

Sam laid down the boxcar, looking at it like a man who suddenly wakes from a fit of violence and wonders at the weapon in his hand.

He turned to Carla and spoke, but instead of the sentence he had intended, he heard himself say, "Oh oh oh oh oh!"

Karen looked at her feet, and Carla watched Ruth walking back toward them from the corner. Then Carla's eyes focused just above her sister, who turned around when Sam and Karen began staring in the same direction.

A coppery wire flickered at the end of the road, widened into a silver car, and swooped down toward them, gathering momentum and then slowing as it approached the Budds' house, finally coming to a halt before the LeBlancs' drive. The children's father emerged from the car, walked around to the passenger's side, and pulled something out of the glove compartment. Then he ambled up to the Budds' house and spoke something the children could not quite hear as they crept down their yard and onto the road. Their father took his hat from his hair with his left hand, and Winston Budd answered something back as his brothers sat down nonchalantly on the stoop, shaking their heads and smirking at each other. Slowly their expressions changed, and to the LeBlanc children it looked as if the change were being created by invisible wires drawn from their father's right side.

He put his hat back on his hair and with his right hand raised a black pistol shaped like a horse's head. He appeared first to be aiming at Joshua Budd, but then stepped back several feet and turned the gun slightly. He shot at the Chevrolet's windshield, shattering it in a symmetrical spiderweb that seemed to tug at the hearts of the open-mouthed children standing in the road. Then, pausing as the Budds stumbled backward in astonishment, he lowered the gun and shot several times at the hood, leaving four holes in a straight line over the motor.

3. Eavesdropping

HARDLY A FAIR PORTRAIT
OF BYRON COFFIN

Byron Coffin was a stoop-shouldered tall man who worked in
New Jersey as a prosecutor. He had met Marjorie LeBlanc in
1954, while doing army duty at Fort Bragg, and had suc-
cumbed to marriage two weeks later, not out of irresistible
desire but from an inability to withstand the weathering effect of her passion, which rubbed down his few sharp edges
until he was no longer sure of what he felt. He had been introduced to Marjorie by his army buddy Thomas Ray, while
the two young men were on leave in New Orleans. Thomas
Ray had taken Byron Coffin to a shadowy bar with sawdust
and peanut shells on its cement floor, where Marjorie's sister,
Bertha, was working as a waitress after finishing college in
the North. Bertha served the two men several glasses of Wild
Turkey, which Byron paid for, and she later sat down at
their table and introduced her younger sister, Marjorie, when
Thomas Ray offered to buy them drinks, which Byron would
also pay for. Marjorie, who was a nursing student at the
time, wore a candy-striped hospital aide's uniform, which
showed off her figure. It seemed to Byron's memory, which
was worn and battered like a piece of glass tossed in the sea,
that she had fit his image of southern beauty. She was a bottle blonde, voluptuous and with a lazy way of talking, like
Marilyn Monroe. When Byron took Marjorie dancing, she
would lay her face on his shoulder and whisper to him in

warm, sugary breaths. He remembered that he had barely learned her name when, eyes burning with love, she waved a bus ticket to Raleigh at him, having resolved to follow him to the ends of the earth.

Marjorie found a dishwashing job at a bar in Fayetteville, and while Byron lived separately at the barracks, she set up house in the bar's back rooms. When Byron saw Marjorie, it was usually through a haze of Jax beer, and the red-faced children whom she presented to him as regularly as tomatoes picked from a garden were no more real to him than anything else from that period in his life.

To Byron Coffin, reality was gray and somber, with a musty smell. It could be mapped through time in the leather-bound books he kept in his law library, or framed in an old family photograph with his father on the right, his mother slightly below in a chair, and Byron in the center, gazing unflinchingly into the camera. It was peopled by men and women who spoke an English uncluttered by hyperbole, rages, tears, and manners of speech that indicated the speaker probably could not read and write.

Incapable of appreciating his good fortune in being a member of one of the rare generations that come to maturity between wars, Byron had never fully recovered from the shock he felt the day he received his draft notice. Every male in his family for the past two generations had been able to pull the strings necessary to avoid military service. The draft notice had arrived two months before Byron Coffin graduated from a prestigious men's college (whose purpose, a stringy-haired girl arrested on drug charges had recently told him, "was not to foster upward mobility but to preserve the sons of the privileged from downward mobility no matter how inept they might be"). Before military service, Byron had never doubted his competence. He had made gentlemen's B's in school, although he spent most of his time drinking in fraternities and engaging in outdoor sports with his peers (whom the same drug user had denominated "cavemen in brownshirts"), and he had never wavered from his plans to go into banking or stockbroking or law.

However, Byron Coffin spent his first two years out of college as the victim of a terrible accident, mingling with big-eared country boys at Fort Bragg. After he finished his term of military service, there followed a dream-like period in which Byron cruised the countryside in a yellow Dodge convertible with Thomas Ray, drinking and carousing and selling life insurance. When Byron Coffin later recalled the three and one-half years he spent near Marjorie LeBlanc, he remembered most clearly the tickling, medicinal smell of pine needles outside the army barracks, and the salesman's voice of Thomas Ray, coaxing Byron to buy liquor or lend money or play a game of poker which Byron inevitably lost.

One day, as the yellow Dodge sped into Raleigh, Thomas Ray swerved to avoid a possum in the road. The car leapt into a ditch, throwing him and Byron into the air, and leaving them brusied and battered, but not seriously harmed. Shaken, Byron gathered a pile of life insurance brochures from the road. As he did so, he felt himself gradually coming to his senses—he was overwhelmed by an awareness of life's instability, of his need for an orderly existence. The dry tobacco field that stretched out before him looked unruly, its uneven rows tangling crazily around stumps and rocks. Byron climbed back into the convertible, thinking of New Jersey and longing for his old life.

For the next several months, he avoided Thomas Ray and stayed in Fayetteville, spending long hours writing letters to his family in New Jersey, poring over legal textbooks he ordered in the mail, and staring distantly at his wife and children when they interrupted him. One morning he came to the breakfast table dressed in clothes his uncle had sent him: a spectral white shirt, scarlet tie and gray three-piece suit. His oldest child backed away from him, as if sensing his complete strangeness to her world. Byron told Marjorie he was going to New Jersey, and promised to call her as soon as he reached

the house of his parents, whom Marjorie still had not met.
Byron then explained to Marjorie with some excitement that
he had been admitted to a well-respected law school in New
York City. It was his intention that she continue to work as a
waitress to help defray educational expenses and support the
children, and that she stay in North Carolina, which had a
lower cost of living, until Byron got his legal career under
way.

"Why do you want to do that for?" Marjorie LeBlanc had
asked.

"I'm doing it for you, Marjorie. I know it'll be hard to be
apart, but with some teamwork, we'll all pull together and
everything will turn out," he had reassured her.

"But I mean, why do you have to be a lawyer? You were
brought up nice and have a good education; you don't have to
be something like a policy man or an undertaker or a lawyer."

Byron Coffin had looked at his wife in astonishment, fath-
oming for the first time the depth of the difference between
himself and Marjorie LeBlanc. "What in heaven's name is
wrong with becoming a lawyer?" Byron had managed to ask.

"What's wrong with it?" Marjorie had answered. "Why,
everyone knows—don't feel bad, Honey, but everyone knows
lawyers are the scum of the earth."

During the three years when Byron Coffin was away at law
school and his two years of clerking for a New York Southern District court, these words had returned to him like the
first line of a childhood riddle: when he tightened the noose of
his tie before entering classes; as he bent over a particularly
intriguing case in the latest legal supplement; or when he visited his uncles or grandfather in their law office, with its
stuffed leather chairs. As time passed, Byron Coffin was unable to remember any other words spoken between him and his
wife. For three years, he continued to visit the children on
Christmas, Easter, and the three weeks following Memorial
Day. He wrote Marjorie monthly and read her daily letters,

but he always failed to reconstruct even moments later her
stormy professions of love or his words of advice. In the first
year of his absence when he fell asleep and dreamed of her,
she would climb onto his bed and lean over him whispering
intimate, unrepeatable phrases in his ear. But more and more
frequently, she surfaced in nightmares in which she would
drag her body, heavy as a brick house, over his bedcovers and
repeat, "A lawyer? A lawyer?" in a twangy, banjo voice that
gave the words an irrationally horrifying meaning he could
not explain when he awoke. Byron began writing Marjorie
less and less. He saw the children only at Christmas during
his first year out of law school, when he was studying for the
bar and beginning his clerkship. The following year, he gave
up visiting and writing, and he left Marjorie's letters uno-
pened on the bureau in his parents' front hall.

Two years after being admitted to the bar, when Byron
Coffin had entered the public-spirited occupation of prosecutor for the State of New Jersey, he returned to Fayetteville
to collect his wife and children. He had reached that stage in
his career where it was right to buy his own house and have
his own family. When Byron Coffin arrived at the bar where
Marjorie had washed dishes, a waitress gave him Marjorie's
forwarding address, explaining that she had decided to move
to a city where she could return to doing hospital work.
Byron found Marjorie living on the periphery of Durham, in
a run-down neighborhood occupied by dirty-necked children
who gathered in packs and followed him hungrily at an uncomfortable, lurking distance. He passed vacant lots filled
with ancient garbage piles and rusted farm machinery. Here
and there, new lots cleared of woods and topped by nice
houses still under construction caught his attention; the
neighborhood was changing for the better, at least. There was
one old pillared mansion in the grand southern style, its
walkway lined with geraniums, which Byron speculated pre-
dated the neighborhood. When Byron Coffin arrived at the
ramshackle house indicated by the address, he saw that

Marjorie had painted her maiden name on the mailbox. He
cleared his throat, scraped his shoes on the welcome mat, and
knocked. He thought of Ulysses returning to Penelope when
Marjorie appeared at the screen door, the children peering
shyly at him from around her hips.

Byron recognized his wife by the rings-of-pearls wrinkles
circling her neck, and by the fact that she was wearing the
same green sundress she had worn the day he had left Fort
Bragg. Otherwise he would not have known her; she bore no
resemblance to the tow-headed, round-figured beauty he saw
in his mind's eye when he sometimes thought of her with embarrassment and regret. He felt deceived and confused.
Marjorie's hair had turned black from lack of care, and her
features had sharpened amazingly. Under the sundress, her
stark collarbones sloped like a coat hanger. Her legs were
swollen and almost ankleless, straight as broomsticks, and
her high, round cheekbones stood up under her skin like two
soup spoons.

"Who's that?" the tallest girl, dressed in faded overalls,
asked Marjorie.

Marjorie LeBlanc had stared at Byron for a full minute
without moving. Byron thought she looked stunned, as if she
were seeing someone who had risen from the dead. Finally,
she said in a choked voice, "It's no one, Sugar." She backed
away from the screen and closed the door.

Byron, who felt guilty about his long absence but somehow
proud of the strong sense of duty that had returned him to
his family, stepped backward, his lantern jaw dropping so
that his mouth hung open. He felt an emotion swell inside
him that he had never experienced before, and he stood still
trying to imagine what it was. He looked around him at the
twilight sky, which was the startling color of purple velvet.
The sky seemed to be ripped in half by a clothesline with four
pink hospital orderly uniforms dangling from it. He wondered why Marjorie could not muster the ambition to finish
nursing school. Now the emotion inside Byron Coffin rubbed

him across the middle like a rope burn. After a moment, he realized the feeling must be outrage.

He stepped forward and pounded on the door.

"Who is it?" Marjorie had asked from the other side. "If it's you, Mr. Big, go away."

"Marjorie. Marjorie, I want to talk to you. If the problem's another man—" Byron Coffin heard a dry, voiceless laugh on the other side of the door. "Perhaps we should arrange for a separation of some kind."

"Arrange for a separation!" he heard, followed by another moan of a laugh. "For a year he hasn't so much as touched me with his fingernail, and now he wants to separate!"

"I demand to see the children!" Byron heard himself say, at the same time wondering why. It occurred to him that all along, his real reason for visiting might have been to disengage himself permanently from Marjorie and her family.

A moment later, the door opened and four black-haired, lantern-jawed children burst through one at a time, as if pushed from behind. They clung to each other and stared up at Byron Coffin with curiosity as he put his hands in his pockets, withdrew them, and then turned on his heels and walked quickly away from the house.

Byron Coffin arranged to have his marriage legally dissolved in Louisiana, where just and impartial methods existed for protecting men in his position from paying alimony and child support. Because he was a fair man, Byron more than equitably divided his property with Marjorie, allowing her to keep the children's clothes, all the family furniture, including expensive bunk beds purchased for the older girls, and the used but well-maintained Oldsmobile station wagon. Out of a sense of honor alone, he continued visiting the children almost once a year, usually bringing a prudent allotment of money in an envelope for Marjorie. But with time, Byron Coffin's duty to his family became less insistent, as if his marriage were a murder case in which the victims' relatives and witnesses gradually died or moved away.

Christmases, he asked his mother to shop for presents, although he cautioned her against calling or writing. Her gifts were becoming more outlandish each year, and against his better judgment she also had started sending the children birthday presents. In November she had bought her grandson an overpriced set of electric trains. Byron had objected to the extravagance of the gift, but the store (within its legal rights) had refused to take back the trains because Byron's mother had removed the cars and tracks from their original boxes to pack them in a wooden crate. Afterward, Byron forgot that he had originally disliked the present. He began to pretend to himself that he had picked it out, and he even wrote a message on the card his mother showed him lying inside the box. Byron liked to imagine Sam LeBlanc opening the gift. In Byron Coffin's daydreams, Sam actually was not Byron's own son but a boy in one of those unfortunate families where the father had been killed in a sawmill accident. The boy opened the box, and his round, dirty face beamed with gratitude and wonder.

* * * *

Except at his work, Byron Coffin was a taciturn man who did not ask questions. He was made uncomfortable by his children's incessant talking, full of exaggerations and bald-faced lies and uttered with an unspellable accent, all of which made him feel that he was losing hold of himself, being quartered into four parts and left in the same uncollected state he had experienced during his years in Fayetteville.

On what would be the last visit Byron Coffin ever made to North Carolina to see his children, he had barely arrived in Durham when he acted in a manner that, if made known, could cost him his job at home. He intended to be a district attorney in the near future. After placing the gun back in his glove compartment, Byron sat in the driver's seat, feeling as stunned as if he had shot himself.

Before the children could yank open the doors of Byron's

car and clamor around him asking him to explain his behavior, he decided to use up his visit doing things that would make it impossible for them to converse. He would take them to the theater and let them sit through the movie three times in a row, or to the Chapel Hill planetarium. Or to the traveling amusement park he had passed on the road out of Roxboro, where he could wait down below with his hands in his pockets while the children's legs dangled from the top of the Ferris wheel or they lost themselves in sordid sideshows; or to whatever entertainment he could find near Durham, which he considered the edge of the world, so far from the metropolitan Northeast as to be barely more than a waking dream.

Sam sat in the back seat and stared out the window, after proclaiming, "Christ in a bucket!" under his breath.

Byron's three daughters insisted on cramming themselves into the front seat of the car. Karen, a gaunt nine-year old with nervous, sweaty palms, sat pressed against him, her legs knocking the stick shift when Byron changed gears. His oldest daughter, Ruth, asked to see his "police special," and when Byron refused, explaining that he carried the handgun only because it was a necessity in his line of work, she began talking with the youngest girl, Carla, about killing a snake. Byron wondered to himself if Ruth was a bad influence on Carla, who had the same discourteous way of jerking up one corner of her mouth in a smirk and then rolling her eyes. Carla answered Ruth's questions animatedly, turning to Byron to tell him about a dog or a boy named Blue, and that they all knew how to shoot a twenty-two, but that snakes could move faster than a bullet, and how they had resolved to kill a water moccasin by stoning it to death.

* * * *

Carla and Ruth were trying to get their father to talk. During the interval that had passed since he turned and walked across the street from the Budds and sat in his car waiting for his children to get in, and in the minutes after he flipped the safety catch on his gun, locked it in the glove compartment, and put on his seat belt, Byron Coffin had uttered only a fragment of a thought: "I'm very sorry it had to come to that." Then he had started the car, pushing Karen's knee from the stick shift, and looked directly in front of him with the absorption of a careful driver.

"We thought," Ruth was saying, "it was a lie about how a cottonmouth will chase you, but he did chase Carla."

Carla interrupted. "After I saw that snake, I took out over the baseball field and then jumped over the crick and ran through the parking lot and knocked on the door to Pepper's house and then ran and got Blue and Blue the dog. And when Blue and me and Blue and Pepper came back out, that snake was sitting right in the smack middle of the road, ten feet past Pepper's into Blue's yard. Did you know that? Did you know they would chase you?" Carla and Ruth looked intently at their father, who shook his head and put on his blinker.

Carla paused a moment longer to wait for an answer. When she did not get one, she continued. "We had to throw a ton of bricks and rocks on it before it got discombobulated and bent up and stopped racing along. It was Ruth threw the brick that landed right on the back of his neck." Carla reached around Karen's shoulders and touched Byron on his nape. He pressed his foot lightly on the brake before Carla removed her hand. "Then he couldn't move. Then Blue stood on the brick and pushed it down with his shoe and took out his knife and sawed through the snake right behind the brick. So we dug a hole for the head. Is it true you have to bury the head because they can bite after they die?"

Byron Coffin scratched his leg and frowned.

"Because it's true," Ruth interjected, "that when its head was just lying there cut off I stuck a stick in its mouth and it clamped down on it and wouldn't let go. Of course, maybe it's just a reflex, like a man kicking on death row after they kill him. So we buried it in a hole."

"Like a man kicking on death row?" Byron Coffin asked. The girls looked at him, waiting for him to explain himself.

"You think?" Ruth prompted. "You think that a snake head can bite when it's dead?"

"I thought we might go to that amusement park between Durham and Roxboro," Byron Coffin answered.

* * * *

The rides did not look safe. He watched what appeared to be the most terrifying one in the lot, a rickety metal structure supporting a forty-foot girder with a rusted capsule built to hold two people at one end and an iron weight at the other. Set in motion, the Bullet would twirl, lifting the capsule in an arc until its occupants were suspended upside down in their seat belts, forty feet off the ground. Then the Bullet would gather speed and twirl without stopping, while the riders miraculously stuck to their seats and did not fly out into the air.

Byron Coffin turned to his children and said, "That works by centrifugal force. The spinning pushes you outward so that your feet stay on the floor and you don't fall out and get hurt." The children took the words uttered by their father, and turned them over until they were smooth as stones. Ruth held up two fingers to Carla to signify that he had spoken two complete sentences in succession.

Sam repeated "centrifical force" out loud, savoring the magical certainty of it, but inside he felt too hollow from the morning's encounter with the Budds to summon up a state of fearlessness. He decided to save his tickets for the sideshow tent. Karen looked doubtfully at her father as the Bullet whirled by and a child's scream circled past them and leapt upward. She pulled him toward the Ferris wheel, which to Byron Coffin looked as if it were made of chicken wire and papier-mâché. Corroded metal bars held up seats patched with a white material.

"Let's just watch for a while," he told her.

* * * *

Ruth and Carla stayed behind to ride the Bullet. They wanted to ride the Bullet for the same reason that they relished late-night television films in which slim, yellow-haired women carried lanterns to basements to investigate noises. The same instinct that prompted the two girls to beg their mother to take them to movies in which handsome men pretended to kiss women, only to suck their blood, drove Ruth and Carla to overturn rocks looking for nests of copperheads; to follow a pistol-wielding drunk down a back alley in Raleigh while their mother was shopping; to seek out and bully rather than avoid boys in school who had bad reputations; to hide behind gravestones in the town cemetery and watch funerals with open caskets; to cross pastures that penned in bulls, climb fences that warned of high voltage wires, and ignore adults who waved the girls away from ferocious domestic disputes carried out on public sidewalks. Both girls instinctively felt that the secret to life lay simply in knowing the smell and shape of danger. When Carla and Ruth sat down in the Bullet, Ruth said, my hair is *standing on end,* and Carla imagined she could feel her own hair pricking up on the back of her neck.

* * * *

Sam was not taken in. Not by the Bearded Woman, who was simply an old lady with a fringe of mustache, like Sam's fifth grade teacher; not by the Largest Dog in the World, which he recognized to be an undersized Great Dane; not by the two-headed woman in the dark box, who he saw was an overrouged old lady surrounded by a complication of mirrors that reflected the image of a hidden younger woman's head. Sam felt sorry for the live Guernsey cows with fifth legs sewn onto their hips or noses through crude operations that still revealed scars left by stitches. He studied with some enjoyment an electric eel that lit up a row of light bulbs above its fishtank, and he also looked carefully at the tapeworms and two-headed pig fetuses preserved in formaldehyde. But even these things did not hold his interest for very long; his thoughts kept returning to the more startling fact of his father's stinginess.

Sam's father had bought himself and the children only two tickets apiece. Two tickets would buy each of them one ride. Whenever Sam's mother took him and his sisters to traveling amusement parks or circuses, she filled them with saltwater taffy and cotton candy and let them take every ride at least once. The better ones she would allow them to ride over and over, even offering to sit next to them on rattling roller coasters which made her sick to her stomach.

When the woman in the ticket booth had told Sam's father the price of the rides—twenty-five cents each—he had pressed his lips together and handed her two dollars and fifty cents.

She had looked up at him and said, "Well, don't burn a hole in your pocket!"

"I'm not a rich man," Sam's father answered.

"And I'm not ugly," the ticket seller told him, staring at his clothes. Sam read her plastic employee's name tag, and saw that it said Angelita Galuba. Angelita Galuba was an ancient woman, with brown-splotched hands jutting from an orange nylon shirt. Her hair stood up like rooster feathers and her sharp beak of a nose pointed straight at Sam's father.

"I'll take twenty tickets," a tall black woman with a salt-and-pepper Afro called over Byron Coffin's shoulder. Her two granddaughters, willowy girls in yellow dresses, glared at his back, willing him to move. Sam studied the woman's dress: a nurse's uniform, with yellow and black daisies embroidered on the collar. He recognized her to be Nurse Arrington, who worked at his mother's hospital. Her granddaughters, Sherry and Tamika, went to his school.

Mrs. Arrington noticed Sam and said, "Hello to you!" and then gave Byron Coffin a brief, clinical look. Tamika made a face at Sam: a long, underbitten face hanging forward over stooped shoulders. Sherry doubled over with laughter.

"You can just cut that out," said Mrs. Arrington, dropping the tickets into her pocketbook. "I don't know why I let you talk me into this to begin with. I always thought these amusement parks were as strange as strange can be. Well, we're here!" Mrs. Arrington looked at Sam and then at Byron, and back at Sam again. "Say hello to your mama for me," she told Sam, tugging her granddaughters behind her.

Byron Coffin parceled out the tickets. When Sam's sisters plunged into a discussion of which ride they would choose, Sam stood still, his long jaw slightly open, trying to reconcile the slenderness of the cardboard he held in his hand with the gaudy image of the train engine still burning in his mind.

All morning Sam had felt himself reeled in and out like a fish cruelly played on a line. First there had been his jubilance in watching the engine charge over the incline of newly laid rockbed, to him a symbol of the indestructible generosity of the distant father to whom he felt tenuously connected. Then came the horror of watching the trains smashed into a rubble of plastic and metal by the Budds. The subsequent fulfillment Sam had felt at his father's shooting the car had been quenched instantly by the miserly gesture with which Byron Coffin had locked the gun in the glove compartment. Sam's hand had ached to feel the warm metal in his hand, to fill his emptiness with the pistol's leadenness. But Sam's father had not made the obvious gesture of flipping the safety catch and spinning the cartridge to ensure that no bullets remained inside. He had not even hooted with joy at the destruction of the Budds' car as he turned on the ignition of his own new Ford Galaxy 500. Instead, he had pressed the lever on the dashboard that shot cleaning fluid onto the window, and then turned on the windshield wipers. When Byron Coffin leaned back in his seat, Sam noticed that his father had a nickel-sized bald spot in the empty brown pocket of his rumpled hair.

Sam ducked under the back of the sideshow tent and saw Ruth and Carla standing close enough to a row of cages to become queasy from the rank odors of the animals inside. He

walked slowly across a field behind the tent toward a cluster
of pinewoods, and heard his mother talking to Rita and
Jeanie: "Do you know Buy My Coffin once went to Raleigh
on leave from Fort Bragg, and I asked him to bring me back
a present? I had to ask, because, just like a man, he wouldn't
have thought of it otherwise. And do you know what he gave
me? A clothesline he bought at a dime store. Imagine even
thinking of such a thing!" Sam's mother's voice rose to a
higher pitch in his mind, and he recalled her saying, "And
when Ruth got too big for a crib, he went out and bought a
rickety pile of sticks for a bunk bed that shook and wobbled
and scared me to death when the kids climbed in it. 'This is
pure pine!' he said. 'Cheapest coffin's made of pine,' I told
him." Sam's mother's voice dropped to a low pitch and she
said, "There's only thirty-five dollars in this envelope!" and
then: "I wouldn't shed a tear if the whole penny-pinching
state of New Jersey fell into the ocean!" Rita argued, "Not
everybody up there is like Byron Coffin, Marjorie." "Ha!"
Sam's mother answered.

When Sam reached the pinewoods, the turpentine smell of
the air made his head feel light, and he was glad to come to a
cool creek behind a tangle of blackberry bushes. Behind him
he heard the screams of girls on amusement park rides,
voices enticing people to enter tents and spend money, a siren
in the direction of the road and, back in the woods, a man's
voice calling, "This way, this way!" and men's heavy foot-
falls snapping dead branches. Sam let the noises drift away
from him, and he concentrated on the coolness of the creek as
he waded in up to his knees without taking off his sneakers.
The gold flecks on the water's surface made his eyes burn.
The creek quickly reached his crotch, its sudden cold startling him, and he turned back.

He lay down near the bank, his head dangling over an out-
cropping above the water and his legs running uphill. Above
him, the long branches of oaks looked like roots clutching the
sky. He stared long enough to make himself feel that he was

at a great height, looking down onto a blue landscape. He tried to make a clump of bushes on the far side of the river appear to be the vegetation on the tops of the trees growing in his inverted world.

A woman was watching him. She lay on a far bank with her head turned sideways on a rock, as if it were a pillow. Half of her face lay under water, and the top half joined with its reflection to form a wide, perfectly symmetrical head. Sam closed his eyes and held himself dead still. He stood, turned slowly around, and looked: There really was a woman on the bank. Her brown hair was tangled in a nest of reeds and sloshing against a stone. A pale slip clung tightly to the surfaced part of her body and rippled in the water next to her sunken half, leaping and twisting like a live animal. Her bare left arm and foot knocked against the roots sticking out from the streambank. Her glassy eye stared at Sam from a face frozen in anger or astonishment.

"Hey, boy! Boy! Don't look at that. There's a boy down here!" Three men approached Sam through the woods, two of them in the tan uniforms of state troopers and carrying a stretcher and a blanket, and the third wearing a shirt of such a brilliant royal blue it made Sam think of the costumes the magi had worn in his school's Christmas play. "Boy, git away from there!" the blue-shirted man called; his face was flushed and purposeful. The two policemen drew closer behind him. Sam whirled and ran up the slope, looking for his sisters.

* * * *

Byron Coffin had sat with his daughter Karen for nearly an hour, watching the Ferris wheel. She was a quiet girl, who did not needle him with questions in the manner of her two sisters. She seemed happy just to sit with him. She alone among the girls was wearing a skirt and blouse and strapped black shoes instead of overalls and sneakers. Her skirt was made of a green nylon that Byron Coffin associated with salesgirls in the cheap stores lining the courthouse's avenue in Newark. He saw pretty girls on the Ferris wheel wearing stylish flannel plaids and freshly ironed ginghams. His own daughter was very homely. She had a sallow complexion and a long, cavernous face, which made her hair seem too short. Her ponytail looked like a dirty whisk broom. But she was well-behaved. Byron had been afraid Karen would ask for something sticky, like cotton candy or a snow cone, yet she sat quietly beside him on the wooden bench, watching the Ferris wheel, and whispered that she did not want to ride it after he expressed his belief that the Ferris wheel looked a little rickety.

Byron was carrying a leather briefcase, which contained papers too valuable to leave in a hotel or in the car. At one point, he opened the case and pored over a document, and seemed to forget where he was. He continued reading the document for almost twenty minutes. Karen looked into her father's briefcase and saw an address, and underneath it the beginnings of a letter, poking from a pocket in the lid:

April 25, 1965

Byron Samuel Coffin, Esq.
25 Maple Grove Way
Upper Montclair, N.J.

Darling Byron,
  I will hurry home tomorrow, you know I have never been able to fall asleep at night when I sleep alone. I will always

Karen did not know there were still people living who called each other "Darling." She memorized the address at the top of the paper and the two lines underneath.

When Byron Coffin closed his briefcase, he summoned the energy necessary to ask his daughter a question. "I have something important to tell you children. I had hoped to talk with all of you at once, but perhaps I could just tell you, Karen, and you could pass the word around?"

Karen squeezed his hand in a reassuring gesture, as if she were a nurse and he a hospital patient.

"I'm getting remarried."

Karen withdrew her hand. She barely listened to the stream of words that followed: "As you know, your mother and I . . ." Karen pulled her green nylon skirt over her knobby knees and looked straight ahead of her. Tomorrow her father would be gone for good. Since he would be gone, she wanted to choose the words he would say. She wanted to string his words together like a row of knitting, so that she would have something to look at and consider the next day. And all the days after that. Beside her, his words followed one another with a monotonous, reasoning rhythm; he looked straight at her profile, and talked without stopping to her ostensibly attentive ear, but all she heard was *knit two, purl one, knit two, purl one.* She closed her eyes.

Byron Coffin sat in the front seat of his new Ford Galaxy 500 beside a beautiful thin woman with a yellow ponytail. "Darling," she said. "Darling, just kiss me and kiss me. I haven't slept in four days." Byron Coffin kissed her a long time, and then turned toward the back seat and said, "Karen! I didn't see you sitting there. I'd like you to meet my darling daughter, Karen Coffin. Karen, this is—"

"What's her name?" Karen opened her eyes and turned on the bench toward her father.

Byron Coffin stopped talking and let out a gasp of air, as if he was thankful that he had been given such a simple question to answer.

"Miss Meeks."

"Miss *what* Meeks?" Karen continued in a businesslike manner, as if filling out a form at a hospital desk.

"Cindy."

Karen clasped her hands together in a crisscross pattern and turned the name over in her mind. "Cindy Meeks." She tested the words. "How old is she?"

"Nineteen, a very nice age," Byron Coffin answered.

Karen turned to him and raised her eyebrows in a way that reminded her father of Marjorie. "Nineteen?" she asked. The age of Claire Murkington's sister Dee Dee, who worked as a waitress at the corn dog stand? Dee Dee wore a short-skirted cowboy suit for her job. She cried when Paul McCartney got married, and she would scream at Claire and Karen if they took the romance novels Dee Dee had bought at Winn Dixie. Nineteen was also the age of the college girl Minnie, who sometimes baby-sat for the LeBlancs and whose bed at Duke was littered with a wealth of stuffed animals Karen never thought of without being pricked by a needle of envy. Dee Dee and Minnie were old enough to drive a car, but they could not drink whiskey. Karen could see Minnie lying on her bed reading *Seventeen* magazine and complaining, "I'm tarred and embarrassed by all the Shirley Temples I gotta drink!"

Karen smoothed out her skirt and asked, "How old are you?"

Byron Coffin placed his hand on Karen's leg, right above her knee. He tapped on her leg to emphasize certain words as he spoke.

"I'm thirty-five. Now, Karen, it's normal for a man to have a young wife. I'm sure, if you try, you can think of more than a few of your mother's friends who have older husbands. But I'll bet you can't think of one man who's married to a woman much older than he is."

Karen rolled these words up and put them aside to unknot and save for possible later use.

"How did you meet Cindy?" Karen pressed.

Her father removed his hand from her knee. "I had the good fortune to receive an appointment instructing an undergraduate Legal Ethics seminar at a prestigious university."

Karen waited patiently for an understandable word.

"Miss Meeks was one of my students. She'll be leaving school now, to start a home with me."

"Oh," said Karen. She could not think of any further information she needed at the time. She tucked her hands under her thighs and began swinging her legs and staring in front of her. The bench bounced and wobbled under Byron Coffin with an annoying vivacity.

"What do you say we forgo the rides and go look at that sideshow tent your brother was so excited to see?" Byron asked his daughter.

"Fine," Karen answered. "But you won't like it."

"Oh, now, I'm sure we will." Byron was relieved that his daughter seemed satisfied by the answers he had given. He had dealt very professionally with her, responding honestly to each question. He squeezed her hand and told her that of all his children, she was the one who understood him best. Karen was glad to hear it.

* * * *

Byron Coffin immediately regretted his decision; he was horrified by the crudity of the freak show inside the tent. He told his daughter, "The Shetland pony and Great Dane are not as depraved as the other exhibits, but it's tragic to think people here could be so ignorant as to pay good money to marvel at such things." Byron pulled Karen quickly past the five-legged cows and would not let her stop to examine the specimens inside the jars of formaldehyde.

When they stood outside the tent, Karen voiced her first words of protest all day. "I would have liked to see the electric eel light up the lights," she whispered.

"I think it's time to go," Byron Coffin answered. "Let's find your sisters and brother."

Byron spotted Ruth and Carla on the other side of the Ferris wheel. The girls were staring longingly at the ride and pretended not to hear him when Byron said he was ready to leave.

* * * *

Byron Coffin was resisting Ruth's pleas for more tickets. He looked over his children's heads at the Ferris wheel, frowning. An irregularity in the shape of the thing caught his eye. Then the irregularity detached itself from the top of the Ferris wheel and spread outward like a swooping bird. There was a moment when Byron Coffin saw that it was actually a flattened metal bar descending toward him, and he thought: See? See? Just as I said. It's unsafe! Then the bar struck him on the collarbone, bowling him over so that he fell backward, his head hitting a rock.

* * * *

A crowd larger than the one in the sideshow tent collected around Byron Coffin.

The ticket seller, Angelita Galuba, called, "Now everybody step back," as Ruth and Carla tried to push their way through the gathering people to where Karen was already standing. "I know what I'm doing. I worked as a helper in the home for terminally ill patients. Someone call an ambulance," Angelita Galuba yelled. "*You* move back," she said, pointing authoritatively at a spectator. "Everybody else clear out of here. This man has a concussion and what he needs is air, not a pack of jackasses hanging over his face trying to see blood!"

Ruth and Carla heard Karen shrieking from within the crowd, "That's my daddy! That's my daddy!" Sam came up behind Ruth and startled her by taking her hand.

An older woman's voice answered, "Now don't you worry; I'm sure it's not that serious." It was Mrs. Arrington, a head higher than anyone else in the crowd. "Let me help there. I'm a nurse—"

"Let the nurse lady in!" Angelita Galuba yelled.

Sam followed Ruth and Carla as they squeezed through a space between two women.

"He do look like death's door," one woman said to the other, clutching her pocketbook as if afraid that the very momentousness of the occasion might take it from her.

"I don't know, I think he must always look kind of broken-jawed like that," the other woman answered.

Mrs. Arrington had cushioned Byron Coffin's head with a green sweater. Byron's eyes were closed, and his long jaw was relaxed so that the LeBlanc children could see into his mouth. His tie hung crookedly, like a broken exclamation point.

Angelita Galuba stepped deftly over Byron's long legs in her high-heeled shoes and pushed back the inner circle of on-lookers. She was enjoying herself. "There's nothing to see," she shouted, "so just move and go on about your business. Little girl dropped a stick of lead she was carrying, that's all. Hit him in the head, and now he's going to be fine, so let's all get lost."

The crowd gradually grew bored, and dispersed.

* * * *

Ruth and Carla were embarrassed by the scene Karen made as the two attendants lifted Byron Coffin onto a stretcher and carried him to the ambulance. "I want to go with him!" she cried, grabbing on to her father's leg so that his sock slipped down, exposing a milky ankle.

"There's a dead lady down in the crick," Sam told one of the attendants. The man frowned at the weight of the stretcher, and did not seem to hear.

Mrs. Arrington pulled Karen away and led her by the hand to an old green Buick sedan. "Come on, you all. I'm taking you home," Mrs. Arrington told Sam and his sisters. "Tamika and Sherry, you two get in the front with me."

On the ride home, Mrs. Arrington's granddaughters kept turning around and staring, as if they found the LeBlancs a curious spectacle. Sam looked out the window toward the woods, and Ruth and Carla stared back at Sherry and Tamika. Karen held her face in her hands and sniveled.

Mrs. Arrington watched Marjorie LeBlanc's son in the rearview mirror: He had that same unraveled look his mother always wore. Marjorie LeBlanc was the kind of woman you had to pull out of herself to find her, like tugging a bit of yarn on the edge of a sweater and watching it unravel into a heap of wool. Marjorie LeBlanc and Penny Arrington had been saying hello to each other for years, but try as she might, when Penny thought about Marjorie and tried to summon up that piquant sense of who she was that lies at everyone's center, nothing came to mind. It was because of this, among other things, that Penny felt protective toward her but also knew that Marjorie would never be a truly close friend. And, Penny speculated, Marjorie's son looked like he'd probably be the kind of man who would attach himself to women in order to have a sense of who he was, to feel that he was more than the ghost of someone. Right now he was gazing down the road with that same blank look Marjorie got after a long day of doling out sedatives and lowering temperatures.

"I wonder what that girl was doing with a piece of lead up in the Ferris wheel," Penny Arrington commented, to startle Sam from his thoughts.

"I know her," said Carla. "She goes to my school, and her name is Jeanette Winsted."

Tamika added, "She's bad, everybody knows it."

Sherry nodded. "I bet she didn't let it slip from her hand like she said. Bet she been carrying that piece of lead around for a week just looking for a head to throw it at."

Penny Arrington put a damper on her granddaughters' discussion: "I'm sure it was just an accident."

"Daddy'll sue her," said Karen in a choking, poisonous voice, lifting her head. Her face was streaked with red dirt and tears. "He's a lawyer."

"Well now," said Penny Arrington.

"Her family's poor as peanuts," said Ruth. "He wouldn't get a nickel out of her."

CARR ISLAND

Four years later, Karen LeBlanc sat on the back steps eavesdropping as her aunt and mother and their friends chattered and howled with laughter in the kitchen. Karen tugged at her skirt with the gesture that had now become characteristic of her, and pushed her hair forward over her sloped shoulders. She had started curling her hair and arranging it at the sides of her face to hide her profile, which was her least flattering angle because it accentuated her lantern jaw. She never went out without first putting on pale eye shadow to lighten her eye sockets. Marjorie would not let her girls wear rouge or pancake makeup, mascara or red lipstick, so that Karen had to keep most of her cosmetics in her locker at school, and put on her face in the girls' bathroom before first period.

"Oh, boy," Karen heard her mother say inside the kitchen. "I was prepared to commit mayhem when he looked me in the eye and said, 'I won't be coming back down here. I see you have sufficient resources to make it on your own.' " And then he took out his wallet and showed me a picture of this teenager who looked like a movie star and he told me *that* was his wife-to-be. Golden hair, and violet-colored eyes just like Elizabeth Taylor's."

Marjorie LeBlanc looked out the window and saw that the day had turned to evening. Her nurse's suit bobbed on the clothesline next to a family of blue jeans and T-shirts and a white dress of Karen's.

" 'Member that girl Whoyoucallher, who lived on Jefferson Avenue?" Bertha asked her sister. "She's the only other person I ever saw with violet eyes. You know, the one who got tapeworm?"

"Tapeworm!" Mrs. Budd hooted.

"Tapeworms are hard to get rid of"—Jeanie altered the subject slightly—"because any part of them can turn into a new worm, in all his glory. If you chop them up into pieces, all the pieces become more worms. They don't even need a lady worm to breed with."

"Oh, Miss Tapeworm!" Marjorie suddenly cried out. "I remember her now. Ooooh, she was an awful little prissy thing with new dresses."

"I'll never forget the day her mother let out she'd got a tapeworm." Bertha turned to the other women. "She told Mama in secret, and Mama tromboned it all over the neighborhood. 'That poor pretty little Nattie Sue, I wondered why she hadn't gotten her shape yet!' That's it, Nattie Sue! After that, Nattie Sue wouldn't come out of her house for a week."

Marjorie and Bertha exploded with laughter, and the other women had to follow.

"They say those diet pills you send away for in the back of magazines are just capsules with tapeworms in them," said Rita.

Bertha seconded her. "I've heard models take tapeworms on purpose to stay photogenic."

"I've got you a tapeworm story," Mrs. Budd began, waiting for her friends to quiet down a little. "Now, in the town I was born at, outside Kannapolis, there was this girl named Pamela, who was out one day with her group of girlfriends. She didn't hang around with the likes of me, so I wasn't there, but I was the first person to hear about it. They were sitting on chairs on Pamela's porch, and all of a sudden my best friend at the time, Bonnie, who didn't put on airs and loved me to death, but who came from a hooty-tooty family just like Pamela, says, 'Hey, what's that hanging out the bottom of your dress?' So everybody looked over and saw this long flat ribbony thing dangling down. First they thought it was bias tape come loose from Pamela's hem. But somebody says, 'It looks like a piece of macaroni!' Then everybody saw the macaroni flipping around by its own self. But somebody else called out, 'A TAPEWORM!' The horrible, gospel truth was that that tapeworm was still half inside Pamela and letting its other half dangle out through an unmentionable hole. Pamela was so embarrassed that her family got up and moved to Kannapolis, since Pamela could never face any of the well-to-do boys in town again after that. Everybody knew."

"Christ!" said Bertha.

Rita crossed her ankles and said, "It's hard to be rich," and Jeanie and Rita laughed together.

"Poor Pamela!" Marjorie thought to add.

"Marjorie's full of disease and hospital stories," Bertha said. "She told me there's a Dr. Mooks and a Dr. Leaks at the hospital who sewed up a live cigarette inside a heart patient."

Everyone looked at Marjorie expectantly.

"I'll tell you, the worst horror story I know," Marjorie said, bringing the conversation full circle, "is Tight Wad walking out on me in the hospital that day. And I never told any of you the full tale. This is what happened. The children's father was laid out on his hospital bed with a broken collarbone and a concussion, his mouth open just like it was always closed when he was up and walking around. Lord, he's a northerner who never did learn the meaning of conversation—"

"Don't you go on about the North," said Jeanie. "Where I grew up, lots of people talk all the time." She nodded at Rita.

"That's right," said Rita, getting the distant look she did when she was thinking of Jersey City. "She can't go blaming Byron Coffin on the whole North."

"All you two do nowadays is gang up on me," said Marjorie, almost pouting. "Well, all right. He failed to talk in a way I've never seen a man down here not talk." She paused and looked at Rita and Jeanie to see if they'd interrupt her again. "Anyway, he wasn't assigned to my ward; he was being looked at by a Nurse Arrington—"

"I know her!" said Rita. "She has two little granddaughters she's raising since her own daughter was killed ten years ago in Raleigh by a man driving drunk on the highway—"

"I didn't know that," Marjorie gasped.

"She's the first black nurse to be hired at the hospital. I met her back a couple years, at a meeting for integrating the movie theater in Chapel Hill. I know her real well."

"That theater used to be segregated?" asked Marjorie.

"Lord, Marjorie," Rita answered. "What planet do you live on?"

"I went there last month with Marjorie and her children to see *The Boston Strangler*," said Faith Budd.

"Hey ho, my story!" Marjorie continued. "It was Penny Arrington drove the children home after Tight Wad got brained in the head by that Winsted girl. Penny went out of her way to be nice, she'd tell me when the coast was clear so that I could come and stare at Tight Wad in all his glory. He was out cold for a whole week from hitting his head on a rock. The doctors didn't know he was my thrown-off husband, because of our names being different. I didn't take on Le-Blanc to burn my bra or anything, I just never could stand that Coffin. Especially as a name for a nurse—think of it! So I came in each day and turned him on his bed a little, and checked his chart, and smoothed back his hair. Just to make sure he wasn't dead, that's all. I'd sit next to him for about fifteen minutes. He never made a noise. The man in the bed next to his was always moaning and carrying on, and I had to be careful because some doctor was always coming to check in on him. He was a study. I remember he had blue circles around his eyes and little yellow bruises all over him like someone had beat him up, but they never could find out what was wrong. They've had cases since on that ward and still don't know what they are."

Jeanie cleared her throat and shifted uncomfortably in her chair, as if she might be the person responsible for the man's illness.

Marjorie continued: "The man's wife used to stay next to his bed for hours a day. She was a scared little thing, she looked like someone had slapped her in the face every day of her life. Sometimes I'd talk with her a little and then I'd get up to go back to work when Penny warned me some doctor was coming. Then on Monday of the week Penny was working a night shift, I walk in, and there Tight Wad is, sitting up, his lips pressed together like this."

Marjorie made a face, curling in her lips so that her mouth became a pencil line. Jeanie and Rita imitated her, holding up their faces to each other like two mouthless masks and then laughing.

"He's crazy as a loon," Faith Budd added, turning to Bertha. "He shot my little boys' Chevrolet right in the motor. They wouldn't even cross the street to talk to Marjorie's children after that, they were so afraid he might come back any minute and do it again. It took my little boys months to get their car running again. They had to put in a whole new engine."

" 'Marjorie,' he says, 'I see you have sufficient resources to make it on your own.' Here he is brought back from the dead over the weekend, and that's the first thing he says to me. Now there's a horror story for you!"

"Marjorie doesn't have to worry anymore anyhow," said Bertha. "I'm going to convince her to come up north and stay with me." Bertha had won a fellowship to study at UNC for a year, but right after arriving in Durham, she had flown to Wisconsin to interview for a job at a college there. After learning that she got the position, she had spent every living minute of every day trying to convince Marjorie to move there with her. "But you know Marjorie," Bertha added. "She doesn't want to leave the South."

"All my friends are here!" Marjorie cried, looking around at the circle of women. Faith Budd nodded.

"Oh, it's cooold in Wisconsin," said Faith. "You step outside and it freezes your nipples right off."

* * * *

Karen got up from the back steps and walked away from the women's voices and into the girls' bedroom. She lay down on her bed after closing the door. Karen was old enough now to have the sense to be embarrassed by her mother's friends. By herself, Karen's mother was ordinary enough, but she made up for this by surrounding herself with the lunatic fringe. Mrs. Budd reminded Karen of a picture of the Old Woman Who Lived in a Shoe from a childhood book: that hair pulled too tightly back into a bun with stray threads flying loose, and her exhausted-looking eyes. Rita always wore the same dress, and Jeanie never dressed up at all, and what was more, Karen knew something her mother did not: Two months before, Karen had seen Rita and Jeanie kiss for a full minute on the couch while Karen's mother had been in the kitchen squeezing some lemonade. And even Nurse Arrington, who came by every so often, was bizarre despite the air of respectability her age and uniform gave her. She had worn that big Afro back when all the black girls in the high school were still straightening their hair, and there was something off kilter about her that Karen couldn't put her finger on. Not just the fact that the very day Karen's father had been rushed to the hospital, Mrs. Arrington had driven by the new neighborhood pool and said something like: "You know they killed Bill Kearny's dog when he insisted on bringing his family there to swim. They said he had too many children, but of course they refused him because he brought back that little son of his from Vietnam."

Bill Kearny was a hospital orderly, who lived at the end of the dead-end road and had at least ten children. Karen was irked by the way Nurse Arrington had stated her opinion right out. It was how she had said it, as if she were commenting on the scenery in Karen's neighborhood. After that, whenever a member of the neighborhood pool took Karen there, she could hear Nurse Arrington's singsong voice gnawing at her ear. The older black people Karen had encountered were quiet and, well, dignified, and would not have thought to talk to white children they barely knew about such a thing. Especially at such a time, when Karen believed she had been *traumatized* by seeing her father hurt. Mrs. Arrington was a nurse, and Karen thought she might have been more sensitive, especially later, when she went into a long list of all the people whose dogs she remembered being killed out of vengeance: There was a man who had stolen another man's girl, and a lawyer who was defending a black man against a white man in a robbery case, and an auto mechanic whose customer felt he had overcharged. "Why, dogs are like a symbol here," Nurse Arrington had told the LeBlancs and her granddaughters in a pleasant, small-talk voice, as she turned her green Buick up the hill. "Some white folks think the worst insult you can give someone is to kill their dog." Karen had not liked feeling she was being called a "white folk."

More than once, Mrs. Arrington had come calling on Karen's mother, wearing a far-out African dashiki of a type only college students in Chapel Hill might be caught dead in, and asking Karen's mother to make a pie or a cake for a bake sale, to raise money for some political cause. Mrs. Arrington was eccentric. Karen's mother would agree to make lemon meringue pies to help fund an antiwar poster drive or pay the bail of someone in a civil rights trial, but Karen knew for a fact that her mother did not even vote in presidential elections, much less know the difference between North Vietnam and North Carolina. She just went along and baked the pies to be agreeable. She had never learned to be judgmental.

Karen longed to surround herself with normal, popular people, and what was more, she had learned how to do it. If Hubertine Fox or Clara Sandra Phillips broke down right in the middle of class, it was Karen who guided her to the bathroom and comforted her because Leroy Jackson Ackridge III had been two-timing Hubertine or because Clara Sandra had heard on the radio that Paul McCartney was rumored to be dead. Then Karen would return to class with a benevolent expression that made the other girls burn with envy. Karen saw that the girls in the most important cliques got A's in school and ran for student government and tried out for cheerleading, so Karen studied dutifully, cheating when necessary. She spent all summer practicing straddle splits and stag kicks while Ruth and Carla fell on the ground behind her, pretending to die of laughter.

It was because of her sisters and brother that Karen felt her small victories—being a runner-up for junior homecoming queen or the elected class treasurer—were especially admirable. Ruth always wore a green army jacket with red and white numbers sewn onto the shoulders and what Ruth claimed was a real bullet hole through the breast pocket. More likely, Karen thought, it was a burn hole left by a hand-rolled cigarette. Ruth's stringy black hair had been untrimmed for years, and her ragged blue jeans were covered with embroidered sew-on patches she bought in Chapel Hill: an ecology symbol, a peace sign, a marijuana leaf, a black fist clenched before a green, yellow, and red background, and a yellow smily face. For her fourteenth birthday, Ruth had asked for a real American flag to make a curtain out of, but their mother had refused. At least she had refused to purchase the flag herself, although she did not meddle when Sam bought one for Ruth at an army surplus store. Carla gave Ruth a Coca-Cola can with a strobe light that flickered in the direction of Ruth's fluorescent Jimi Hendrix poster, lending the girls' bedroom a nightmarish quality. Karen suspected that Carla had stolen the can from a store in Chapel Hill that sold such things. Ruth's side of the room was covered with posters of Janis Joplin, Martin Luther King, Bob Dylan, a naked girl in a straw hat running across a field of wildflowers, Malcolm X, and Country Joe and the Fish. Ruth hung around with other fifteen-year-olds at school whose rooms Karen suspected looked the same—like Sherry Arrington, who had once grabbed Karen's sliced celery and carrots from her lunch at school, crying "Black Power!" and Truman Sharpless, who had a two-foot ponytail and probably dealt heroin. Ruth never dated Truman—she just let it be known that they had most likely done the bold thing together.

Then there was Sam, with that permanent look of melancholy sunk into his face since the day their father had suffered the accident at the amusement park. Rita and Jeanie and Aunt Bertha loved to talk about how boys grew up just fine without fathers, but Karen had checked out a psychology book from the school library, which showed how little Aunt Bertha and Rita and Jeanie knew. The book explained that a boy who grew up without a father would probably never turn out right. He would have women trouble—either he'd resent them or he'd ruin himself running after loose older women. Children who grew up with only mothers also had difficulties finding and keeping work and were likely to end up criminals. Only in some cases was there any hope: if, for instance, a boy's father *died* and then the mother kept the father's presence alive by talking good about him all the time. But Karen saw that in Sam's case, there was probably no hope.

Anyone could see that Sam had been scarred permanently by seeing Byron Coffin's accident, after which Sam had had screaming nightmares about houses filled with dead ladies. He did not have any girlfriends, and if anybody at school got beat up and had his head pounded senseless against the blacktop, when Karen penetrated the crowd of onlookers she was certain to find Sam on the ground at the center, his eyes closed and his long jaw hanging open. All of his friends at school were boys who had beat him unconscious at one time or another. Whenever Sam got knocked out, he and the boy who started the fight would become instant heroes solely because of the dramatic nature of being able to lose or cause someone else to lose consciousness. They would walk around like best friends for weeks. Karen knew that if Sam had a father to teach him to fight, her brother would be a completely different person.

And Carla was getting more and more like Jeanie every day. Carla was in her last year of middle school, but she still dressed like Huck Finn and even carried chewing tobacco so that it poked halfway out of her pocket for everyone to see. She spent all day in the woods by herself, carrying sticks she had sharpened with her own switchblade, and studying animal droppings and pretending to be a caveman. Once Karen had spotted Carla squatting before a line of boys outside the school. As Karen approached the circle, she saw that Carla was showing the boys twelve dung beetles she had yoked together by their horns to a toy wagon loaded with stones. She was saying, "Lay yer bets! Lookathem pull that thang!" There wasn't another girl in the whole crowd. Karen wondered if Carla had even discovered yet that she was a girl.

Karen was the only regular person in the LeBlanc household. Sometimes she pictured the LeBlancs as a family consisting of one mother and three children wholly unrelated to Karen herself. When Karen had studied Carr Island at school, she allowed herself to imagine the LeBlancs confined there at the leper colony. Karen would come visit them on a little boat, bearing a picnic basket full of their favorite foods—usually wine, cheese, crackers, and fruit—and chatting with a nurse dressed in a Florence Nightingale outfit sitting across from her. Karen would be living with her father and his elegant wife, Cynthia Meeks, who would have just bought a summer house near Myrtle Beach.

Karen's clique of friends at school pitied her for her family, and she turned their pity to use, going into tearful episodes in which she was too choked with crying to explain the problem. She would later hint with a martyrish expression what the source of pain was—her brother showing everyone the forty-four stitches in the back of his head, Ruth getting suspended for smelling like marijuana, Carla wearing a T-shirt with a large hole over her right nipple. And Karen's girlfriends would cast meaningful glances at each other, feeling grown up as they put their arms around Karen and helped her keep her mascara from running. Then Karen would rise, smiling cheerfully, so that she developed the power to make her girlfriends tell each other, "She's such a good person, so sweet and likable, and never complains, despite all the hardships she has to deal with!" Karen would walk to the ladies' room and reapply her rouge, mascara, and special white lipstick, all the while making silly jokes to let everyone know how bright and happy and normal she was, notwithstanding everything.

Karen would spend hours with Hubertine and Clara Sandra, doing harmless, girlish things, like going through the telephone book to find what Clara Sandra said she had "a knack for telling what were colored names right off," and then calling up and saying, "I still haven't received the last payment on the refrigerator," pretending to be a bill collector's secretary, and hanging up on a threatening note when the person on the other end of the line began to sound genuinely anxious. Or Hubertine would show Karen how to pluck her eyebrows and then draw them back on with a black pencil in a more flattering shape. Or Clara Sandra, Karen, and Hubertine would tell each other all the latest gossip about the sluttier girls in the school, tactfully omitting Karen's own sister Ruth, and speculating on abortions and which girls had boyfriends who beat them and whether it was really true that Mary Rockenbach slept in the same bed with her father.

Hubertine and Clara Sandra and Karen had discussed more than once the strange scene between Jeanie and Rita that Karen had witnessed in her living room. Clara Sandra knew the word to use if two women French-kissed: "lesbianism," and she declared that lesbianism was a defect you were born with and could not help, like a clubfoot. Hubertine said that everyone had control over his own destiny and could keep himself from doing something he knew was wrong. Karen told her friends what Marjorie LeBlanc had once said to Ruth when Karen was eavesdropping outside her mother's door: Ruth had asked what lesbians did when they had sex, and Marjorie had answered in an objective, nurselike manner that she believed they kind of rubbed up against each other.

Karen, Hubertine, and Clara Sandra had been working together all May on their idea for raising money for the ninth grade fall dance. The ninth grade would hold a picnic the third week after school started, and everyone was to come dressed like an ancient Greek. Karen and Hubertine would sell tickets for the slave auction, in which people from the other grades as well as teachers would bid money just like at a real Greek slave market. The ninth grade would plant people in the audience who would bid high to raise prices. Some of the money would go to pay for the picnic lunches, served by the auctioned students to the students who had bought them. The remainder would go to the class treasury. Hubertine and Clara Sandra had agreed to renominate Karen as class treasurer, and in return she would nominate them as president and vice-president.

Karen already looked forward to controlling the auction and subsequent dance, but had not yet decided who would be her escort. Karen could date any nice boy in the school she wanted, although the boys who were not considered nice she suspected of snickering at her when she walked down the hallway between classrooms. When Clinton Paley, who came from a good family and was already a senior, asked Karen out, she tactfully let it be known through her chain of acquaintances that although she did not have a bigoted bone in her body and had nothing against Clinton personally, she could not date him. If she dated black boys, the white boys would not want to take her out, she explained to Hubertine, who relayed the words elsewhere. And, Karen added, it was too early for her to close all possible avenues and prejudice her future. Her caution had paid off, since a short time later Clinton Paley had begun to hang around with Sherry Arrington and let his neat hair with the part shaved into it grow long enough to braid into cornrows. He even tied a black armband around his neck, which he said he would not take off until the war ended. The armband gave him a reckless look, like the man in a dark scarf standing in a snowstorm Karen had once seen in a book on the Klondike.

Karen's biggest problem was keeping those boys she selected to be her dates from coming into her house, where no doubt her mother would be cackling with a pack of her bizarre friends, or Jeanie would be showing Carla how to soften a saddle with castor oil, or Sam would be sitting by himself in the loud, flowered armchair, staring out the front window with the heartbroken expression that had become his trademark.

* * * *

Karen tiptoed into the living room to look under the sofa cushions for her favorite lipstick. In the kitchen, the women were back to the subject of Wisconsin. When she found the lipstick—flat on the end as if Carla had rubbed it on a piece of cement—Karen lay down on the sofa and stared at the ceiling. The couch was more advantageous than the front steps for eavesdropping, since Karen had only to lean forward to see into the kitchen. Karen disapproved of most of what she heard, but she found the urge to listen in on her mother and the other women irresistible.

Karen discovered she had come at just the right time, because a minute later Jeanie said in a strange voice that made Karen lean forward, "Me and Rita are planning to go to New York City for a while."

"Stay in the Ritz!" said Faith Budd.

"For how long?" Marjorie asked.

"A few years anyway," said Rita. "I'm selling the laundry mat."

"What!" Marjorie cried out, as if stricken. "Since when?" Marjorie raised her hand to her throat as if defending herself from attack.

"Oh, since a while," Rita answered. "It'll be a nice change."

* * * *

"Change?" said Marjorie. Marjorie was feeling for the right word, and that was not it. She wanted to speak a word so perfect that it arrested Rita and Jeanie where they sat, and kept them from saying anything more. Marjorie wondered why she had not thought before of the possibility of Rita and Jeanie's leaving. For a year, they had been reminiscing about New York City as if it were the promised land. And they were different, somehow. They had become even more, well, *political,* always running off to some student thing in Chapel Hill or painting banners and sheets behind the laundromat.

"I would never of left Brooklyn if they'd had cows and horses there," said Jeanie.

"Country girl," Faith Budd told her.

"Sometimes I think I was crazy ever to have come back from Jersey City at all," said Rita. "There's not one other Puerto Rican around here that I know."

"*I'm* here," said Marjorie.

"Bertha, you've got a grasshopper on your sleeve," Jeanie broke in. "No, it's a katydid!"

"Brush it off!" said Faith.

"What about your work with the horses?" Marjorie asked Jeanie. The katydid jumped over Marjorie and landed on the windowsill.

"It's just that I'm beginning to get sick of that job, Marjorie," Jeanie answered. "I liked it at first, when it was just the racehorses, but now they've got all their weird show saddle horse crowd moving in. Do you know what they do to those horses? Those Saddlebreds and Tennessee walkers? They break their tails to make them stand up, and after that the horses can't swat flies anymore. Then they slit the bases of their tails with razors and stick ginger in their assholes so they hold up their tails even higher to ease the pain." (Karen made a face and lay back down on the sofa.) "And to teach the horses to lift up their feet, men put acid on the horses' legs and wrap balls and chains around the burnt places so that whenever the horse puts her foot down, it hurts so much she jerks it back up. Haven't you ever seen how those horses walk in that spiky way like they had high heels on, lifting up their knees until they bash themselves in the heads? That's because they remember how much it used to hurt to walk like a normal horse. And if they didn't put acid on some horse's leg, it's because they drove nails into the bottom of her hoof, so long that they pierce into the quick whenever the horse puts down her foot. They teach them to rack and pace, to move in all sorts of ways they weren't meant to, and whip them if they try to run like a normal horse. Shit, they try to breed the running out of them; I don't even know if a Tennessee walker could gallop if it wanted to. And the bits they put in their mouths—these double-twisted wire snaffles that can tear their tongues in two! And do you know where all that came from? Because some slave owner wanted to ride around on his plantation all day without his butt getting sore. He wanted a horse like a Cadillac, with big-springed shock absorbers."

Marjorie never knew what to say when Jeanie talked about politics. "You sound like that book *Black Beauty.* I think it's really nice you care about the rights of animals, Jeanie."

Jeanie laughed and said, "Oh, Marjorie, you're something else. I didn't mean that—"

"Or what's that other book where the animal tells the story?" asked Faith Budd. "The one my little boys had to read in school and brought home? *Beautiful Joe,* about a dog. I cried at the end."

"I didn't mean that!" said Jeanie. "I meant this place is crazy, you know?"

"What place?" asked Marjorie.

"The South, she means," said Bertha.

"You sound like Buy My Coffin," said Marjorie. "He used to do that too, go on and on about how ignorant and backwoods everybody down here was."

"But he only did that because he thought he was better than everyone else," said Rita. "We just want to spend some time in a big city. See some culture!"

"There's culture down here!" Marjorie exclaimed. "Why, James Taylor is a Chapel Hill boy."

"Oh, Marjorie," said Bertha. "They just want to get away from all the rednecks."

"And you sound like Ruth," Marjorie told her sister, and then thought: Why doesn't anyone sound like me anymore? When Ruth first began coming home wearing a braided headband in her stringy hair, she once sat at the head of the kitchen table, her ham steak half eaten, and entertained her sisters and brother by doing an imitation of Ruth's idea of a redneck: "So that grit jes set there in his sleeveless T-shirt with his sack-of-meal stomach hanging over his belt, thinking about eating harmony grits and hawg jows, and said to me, 'You communist fascist pig!' And I had to laugh at him and say, 'You can't be both communist and fascist. They're diametrically opposed!' " Karen had sat still, testing the phrase "diametrically opposed" in her small, carefully shaped mouth, while Carla and Sam slapped the table and almost fell out of their chairs, repeating, "Cain't I have sommore hawg jows?" And Marjorie had cleared the table, wondering: But aren't we rednecks? Don't you eat grits and pigs' feet? Don't your relations have those big bellies and talk just like that?

Bertha leaned toward Marjorie and said, "Don't be such an old dried dead fish, Marjorie. I think you should get out of here yourself and see the country some."

Marjorie did not respond at first. She felt as if she were standing still while the world was spinning around her, turning upside down and righting itself like a clothes dryer. Finally, she said, "I'm not going to let you drag me off north on one of your crazy ideas, Bertha. Like as not, you'll be itching to leave there after a year or so."

"Well, probably," Bertha answered.

Marjorie ignored her. "Anyhow, I think Ripon, Wisconsin, sounds like a hellhole."

"Marjorie said 'hell'!" Jeanie cried.

Marjorie told Jeanie, "It's your bad influence. You've just been chipping me away, piece by piece, all these years. And it does sound like a hellhole!"

"It's bound to be cold as a witch's tit," Faith Budd agreed.

THE CARMICHAELS

Karen stuck her head inside the kitchen and said, "Mama, I'm going over to Sally Ann Ruby's."

"You don't think you're spending a little too much time there?" Marjorie asked. "This is the third night this week, and maybe her family would like her to themselves more."

"Don't worry, Mama," Karen said in a consoling, adultish voice. "She's baby-sitting her little sister by herself tonight, and I'm just going to keep Sally Ann company. I'll get dinner over there."

"Well, OK, Honey."

"Karen's such a little grownup!" Faith Budd hissed.

As Karen walked back down the hall to the bedroom, she wondered what new excuse she would have to think up for going out the next week.

Outside the window, Karen heard Blue Henry. She looked through the curtain and saw Blue and the LeBlancs sitting under the light on the back steps. Ruth and Carla were wrestling on the porch, pretending to choke each other and exclaiming, "I'm the Boston Strangler! I'm the Boston Strangler!" Blue Henry stood on the steps singing "Feel-like-I'm-Fixin'-to-Die Rag" by Country Joe and the Fish, and his dog joined in howling. Blue was a notoriously bad student but, Karen noted to herself, intelligence was not so important in a man. He was tall with curly hair, and older than any of the LeBlancs, old enough to have his own draft card.

When Carla and Ruth and Sam looked toward her window, Karen stepped back and pulled the curtain closed. The sky outside had turned from a royal purple to an impenetrable blackness. Karen changed into navy-blue corduroy slacks and a dark brown shirt. She pulled her hair back into a barrette and added a layer of Morning Glory Blue eye shadow to her eyelids. She thought for a moment about the tail end of the conversation she had overheard in the kitchen. She looked at herself in her round mirror circled with light bulbs (which Carla called her "Miss Priss glass") and said, "Mama would never move in with Aunt Bertha. Aunt Bertha is clean out of her mind." The face that looked back at Karen from the mirror was cool and steady, and nodded in agreement. She pictured Blue Henry standing behind her, also nodding, as if thinking about Aunt Bertha. Aunt Bertha was even stranger than Marjorie LeBlanc's friends, always talking about bones and apes and strange customs, and dressing in what Karen thought to be a shifting back and forth between bohemian and white trash. Some days, Bertha came out of her room wearing a red hairband, black stretch pants, and a loud pink shirt, and other days she dressed in cutoff jeans and a T-shirt with an antiwar slogan on it. At least Marjorie LeBlanc appeared to be normal on the outside.

Karen turned off the lights on her mirror and slipped out of the bedroom through the hallway and the living room. As she closed the front door behind her, she heard her aunt say, "I'll bet she has a secret boyfriend out there."

"That wouldn't be like Karen," her mother answered with such self-assurance that it irritated Karen.

Karen had taken up a habit that she knew was destined to cause trouble if she was not careful. She had started wandering the neighborhood during the evening, staring into people's windows. It had not occurred to her that people might see something wrong in this until she had watched an afternoon drama on television about a Peeping Tom. But then she distinguished the television character from herself: He peered into women's bedrooms because he was a sick man whose mother had henpecked him and who had had an accident in the war that interfered with his ability to marry. Karen's interest, on the other hand, did not have anything to do with the unnatural things that came to pass between grown men and women. She did not look into people's bedrooms; she looked into their living rooms. And her motives for doing so were reasonable. She wanted to see how normal families lived, families with a mother who did housework and a father who came home at seven o'clock and a son who emptied the garbage and a girl who helped her mother in the kitchen. How else would Karen know, when the time came, how to raise a family? She certainly was not going to learn from the LeBlancs.

Karen would stand at the windows of certain houses almost every evening. She had perfected the art of threading through windowside bushes without making a sound, and she knew which windows were generally left open in the summer, so that she could hear conversations carried on inside the houses. She would stand close to the glass and listen until she had learned at least one essential fact—say, that Mr. Speck had talked to his boss about a promotion or that Mrs. Booth would have to have her wisdom teeth pulled. Night by night, Karen gathered as detailed a knowledge about certain families as a faithful soap opera watcher might acquire concerning the lives of regular characters. Sometimes Karen suspected that she knew more about the families than they knew about themselves.

There were certain people in the neighborhood whom Karen particularly liked to look in on. The Carmichaels were probably her favorites, although the Mansons ran a close second. Lydia Carmichael's living room was spotless, all the furniture placed just so. Mr. Carmichael liked to lie on the living room sofa reading Zane Grey paperbacks while his wife sat opposite him on an armchair upholstered in a tasteful beige fabric. Their children watched television on a screened-in back porch connected to the living room. Every now and then Mr. Carmichael would rise from the couch and read some passage out loud. Lydia would put down her knitting and listen attentively, with a quizzical, affectionate look. Sometimes one of the children—who were all early grade school age, with yellow hair and gray eyes—would wander into the living room, and Mrs. Carmichael would get up to make popcorn or bandage a finger or jokingly show the oldest boy how to knit a one-inch square.

The Mansons lived between the Rubys and the Carmichaels and were less predictable. Their dining table was in their living room, and sometimes Mrs. Manson, a heavy, square-shouldered woman with a piled hairdo, would snap at her children if they drank directly from the soup bowl or reached over the table or set the ketchup bottle down on the tablecloth instead of emptying the bottle first into a small bowl. It had never even occurred to Karen that there was a right way to serve ketchup. Mrs. Manson had her own white Eldorado, and she had once run over the family's Pekingese, Dixie, squashing him flat in the driveway. Mrs. Manson had walked around the living room dabbing her eyes with a lavender handkerchief all evening, while her two daughters, Deenah and Dinah, sobbed on the couch. The next night, Mr. Manson had brought home a German short-haired pointer puppy, which Deenah and Dinah sulkily refused to look at, while Mrs. Manson said flatly that Dixie could never be replaced. But when Karen returned three nights later, the new puppy, now named Stonewall, lay curled in Mrs. Manson's enormous lap. After Mrs. Manson ran over Dixie, Karen always thought of her as someone big and hulking, capable of squashing things, but at the same time well-meaning.

Mrs. Manson's daughters and her son, Colonel, took after their father, and were slender and red-haired. Both Deenah and Dinah curled their eyelashes with eyelash curlers and put up their hair every night with Dippity-Do, wrapping it around orange juice cans. Dinah was older, and sometimes her father would have to speak to her authoritatively in a deeper-than-usual, rumbling voice about a boy she was dating or the eleven o'clock curfew he had set. Occasionally Mr. Manson would have to shout, and Dinah would run out of the living room, but later she would return in a pink bathrobe, a scarf wrapped around her hair and looking apologetic.

Both the Mansons and the Carmichaels were proof to Karen that a world existed outside of the dingy, sleazy one concocted by her mother and her mother's misfit friends like Rita and Jeanie and Mrs. Budd. Mrs. Budd would bring over stories about her neighbor Mr. George, who was "a raving maniac who just last night opened the door to his wife's closet and peed on all her clothes because his dinner wasn't ready, ruining a lot of the hand-washables." There was Mr. Booth, who "stalked around the house stark naked and slept in his children's bedroom," and Oscar Renaud, always drunk as a skunk with three sheets to the wind, who had fallen out of his car one night and slept until morning in his front yard.

Mrs. Budd liked to gossip about the neighborhood, but Rita would reach high and wide into any part of her life to talk about a psychiatrist who had kicked his wife in the belly to make her miscarry; or a stepuncle who had slept across the street with his mistress but brought her over each morning to eat breakfast with his wife and children. When Karen's mother would protest and say, "Little pitchers have big ears," Mrs. Budd would let fly her high, witchy laugh, and Jeanie would answer, "Let them hear. The sooner they know, the better!" And then Aunt Bertha would be sitting at the kitchen table the next day, telling Jeanie about priests who tried to feel up Marjorie and herself at parochial school, turning them forever against the Church, or unlikely stories about women who got so mad they had poisoned their husbands and cut off their offensive parts. Karen's mother would invariably bring up the time Byron Coffin had been robbed of his dog tags and all his money after his army buddy Thomas Ray got him drunk and led him to a whorehouse, only one night after Sam was born.

None of these stories had any basis in real life, as far as Karen could tell. Mr. Mintor, whom Jeanie claimed to have elbowed in the stomach after he pinched her in Woolworth's, could be seen any Sunday prying the dandelions out of his lawn or pruning his roses with a friendly, peaceful expression. Karen had never seen a schoolteacher "wolf-eyeing and feeling up the homecoming queen as big as you please and my boy Winston caught him and that's why the man threatened to fail him." Presbyterian ministers, whose refined manners were "skin-deep, and don't let a soul tell you otherwise," when Karen met them on Sunday mornings after spending the night at girlfriends' houses, were shy, fervent men whose well-dressed congregations adored them.

Karen feared there was a side of things she was not getting, being raised in a house full of women and one hopeless brother, who couldn't even make the third-string football team if he tried, which he did not. She had often been told she was precocious by teachers and friends' mothers, who meant to say Karen was adultlike in her understanding of complex emotional subjects. Such people probably did not grasp the truth: Karen had a profound understanding of the very adults who complimented her, of their needs and preferences, of which they themselves might not be aware. Karen could make teachers favor her in such a subtle way that no one could accuse her of being the class pet. All of her girlfriends' mothers had exclaimed to her at one time or another that she was just like one of their own daughters, and none of the women ever suspected that they were far less special to Karen than she was to them, since she collected the admiration and approval of adults in general.

* * * *

Karen arrived at the Carmichaels' house a little earlier than usual; Mr. James Earl Carmichael was not yet home, and Lydia Carmichael was standing by herself in the living room. Karen could see the children through the glass of the shut door leading to the television room. Lydia stood over a bucket full of cleaning supplies. She was wearing black slacks and a faded blue shirt, and had an orange bandanna tied around her head and a trash can dangling from her left hand. Her right hand held a vacuum cleaner with a detachable suction component. Karen thought it would be better to go on to the Mansons' house and return later to the Carmichaels', but something held her watching awhile longer. She pictured Byron Coffin and Cynthia Meeks Coffin, and then

Blue Henry and herself, sitting on the couch and armchair in the Carmichaels' living room. Blue Henry read a passage from a book, and Karen paused in crocheting an afghan to listen.

Mrs. Carmichael began cleaning by sponging the coffee table. She cleared off the magazines and laid them on the couch, and wiped a pile of crumbs lying on the table into a pile. She whisked the pile a foot through the air onto the wooden floor that showed along the edges of the carpet, and then kicked the crumbs into a central heating vent with the toe of her shoe. Instead of going back to the coffee table and restacking the magazines on the table, Lydia halfheartedly dusted the top of the Carmichaels' stereo console. She picked up five records and stuffed two into one record jacket, and when the remaining three would not fit together into a second jacket, she dropped them onto a spread-out pile of records, pushed the pile together, and slid the records into a cubicle next to the turntable, slamming them into the back of the console. When she stood up, she knocked an ashtray sitting on top of the console onto the carpet. She placed her hands on her hips and looked down at the ashtray before she stooped to collect the cigarette butts and scrub the gray spot they had left in the carpet.

As Lydia scrubbed, the spot grew wider and darker against the powder-blue background. She stood and pulled the armchair across the rug until the chair lay directly on top of the stain. She plugged in the vacuum cleaner and batted some pieces of paper, shoes, an empty Maxwell House coffee can, and other clutter from under the sofa with the detachable nozzle. She picked a gold pen out of the litter. Karen recognized the pen as Mr. Carmichael's favorite, the one he used to underline especially good passages in his Zane Grey books. Lydia held the pen up to the light, examined it, and then tossed it back under the couch. The rest of the clutter she threw into the cleaning bucket.

Lydia started stacking the magazines, but stopped abruptly and drew out one, then sat down on the couch and began turning the pages. On the front of the magazine was a naked woman with the word GIRLS! in hot pink letters above her. Lydia turned the pages slowly, stopping for almost a minute to look at one of them. When she came to the end of the magazine, she bent over and pushed it under the sofa. Then she stood, turned on the vacuum cleaner, and vacuumed the rug around the sofa and in between other pieces of furniture. She moved the armchair over slightly, sat down in it, took the bandanna off her head, looked out the window, and then picked up her cleaning rag and carried the bucket and vacuum cleaner out of the room.

Karen heard Mr. Carmichael coming up the walk, and she ducked down between the house and the bushes. She watched Mr. Carmichael close the front door behind him. He dropped his hat on the armchair, lay down on the couch, and kicked off his shoes. He rested his head on a pillow and looked around the room, stopping to survey the coffee table. When Lydia Carmichael stepped into the living room, she was wearing a red-checked dress, and her yellow hair shone with brushing. She carried a basket of gray yarn, heaped with a half-finished man's sweater.

"Lydia," Mr. Carmichael said, as his wife bent to kiss him. "Have you seen my gold pen? I thought I had it this morning when I left for work, but maybe I forgot it on the coffee table last night."

"Oh, it's around. I'm sure it will turn up." Lydia sat down in the armchair and began knitting.

Karen almost called out to Mr. Carmichael, "Why, she knows it's under the couch!" Karen pushed her face closer to the glass.

*   *   *   *

Blue Henry and Ruth, Sam, and Carla LeBlanc stood in the middle of the street looking at a luna moth flattened against the pavement. The moth looked to Sam like two green ears directed upward toward their voices.

Blue told the LeBlancs: "Who knows what the hell that

girl is looking at when she stands there looking? I crouched
down behind her for a whole half hour at one place last night
and there wasn't a thing to see. Just a lazy slob lying on a
couch and his two Martian daughters with their hair all
strangled around beer cans pinned to their heads."

"That'll be the Mansons," said Ruth.

"They're the ones used to have that little monster Pekingese dog," said Carla. She added, by way of explanation to
Blue, "One day me and Ruth were out by their house with
that German shepherd, Lady, that lives up the road. Lady
sees the Mansons' Pekingese and runs across the street and
clamps her jaws around his head. In a friendly way, just to
play. And when Lady stepped back, that dog's eye had fallen
out of his head and was hanging by a thread outside the
socket. So Mrs. Manson runs out and says, 'Put his eye back
in, put his eye back in!' clutching up her hands in front of
her mouth and standing there like her feet are nailed to her
yard. So Ruth took the eye and pushed it back into the
socket. Then Mrs. Manson tells us that the breed has this
problem, that their eyeballs can fall out when they get
alarmed, they're so bug-eyed. Boy, did that give us the wil-
lies. We lit out of there, and I always avoid that house now.
Cross to the other side of the street when I see their mailbox
coming."

"Jesus!" said Blue Henry.

Ruth told him, "They're creepy folks, no question about
it."

Blue thought over Ruth's statement, and then said,
"Karen stays about twenty minutes at each house. I followed
her to four or five until I got bored stiff."

"We should sneak up behind her tonight and crack her on
the head with something so that they find her there in the
morning, crumpled up in the flower beds," said Carla.
"Won't she have some explaining to do!"

"We should fan out and find where she's at and then meet
back here," said Ruth.

"I dunno," said Sam, and that was all Ruth expected him

to say. He had been tongue-tied and soft in the heart even since the day he had seen a dead woman in a creek outside Durham four years before. Ruth had wanted to ask Sam about what the dead woman looked like, when he had first mentioned her. Ruth's mother had been spooning the ham bone out of a pot of collards to give to Sam because he was sitting at the table with such a gloomy expression on his face. Carla and Karen had left the table already, and Sam still had not eaten half the food on his plate. Their mother had said, "Sam, you'll grow up stunted if you don't eat more," but he had just picked at the ham bone as if it were the source of his sorrow. "Sweetheart," she continued, "you look like you've seen a ghost." Then Sam had told them, never taking his eyes from the ham bone, that he had seen "a dead lady in a slip floating around in the crick." Their mother had dropped the soup ladle and taken Sam by the arm to her bedroom, where Ruth could not hear, and then called the police. Afterward, Ruth's mother told her, "Don't you mention this to Carla and Karen, and don't you ever bring it up with Sam." Marjorie LeBlanc was the kind of person who believed that you could make something disappear by just not talking about it. "You promise me to keep silent," she ordered Ruth. "Sam's real upset, and he needs to put it out of his mind." Ruth had felt as if a twenty-ton boulder had been dropped in her lap, all because she was the oldest daughter, there to be confided in and to have ugly secrets deposited on her. But Ruth never did question Sam about what happened, and he never mentioned it. "Sam," Ruth said to him now, "aren't you dying of curiosity to follow Karen and sneak up on her?"

"I dunno," Sam repeated. He thought of that day four years before when he had lifted his pillow and found, like black and red jewels, the caboose and transformer Karen had hidden there.

A yellow Impala dotted with rust spots pulled up beside the LeBlancs and Blue Henry. Rita stared out at them through her thick glasses.

"Hi there. Me and Jeanie are on our way to my house, and

your mother asked if I'd drive down the block to tell Karen to get home. I thought I'd swing back and drop her off. You all know where that Ruby girl's house is at?"

The children drew together, and Rita suspected they were conspiring about something. Her hair lifted slightly on the top of her head with a passing wind, and then settled back down. She opened her car door to throw some light on the children's faces.

Blue Henry spoke up. "Sally Ann Ruby's is one place you're not going to find Karen LeBlanc."

Ruth could not hold herself back. "Either she's at the Mansons'," she said, "or else at the Booths' or the Carmichaels'. Or at the Specks', looking in *their* windows."

Rita raised her eyebrows behind her glasses. The children peered inside the car, as if they wanted some kind of information in exchange for their secret. They saw Jeanie sitting beside Rita, and between the two women, a stack of magazines bound with twine. In the back seat were a spare tire and a jack, a carton of Salems, a picket sign, road maps of the Northeast, a toolbox, and a lacy black slip draped over one window from a coat hanger.

"I know where the Carmichaels live," said Jeanie. "And the Mansons and the Booths. I just don't know where the Rubys' house is."

"It's just at the corner right there," said Carla, letting out a little gasp of laughter. "But you have to go farther than that far to find her. You should try the Carmichaels' and the Mansons' at least."

"Well, you all are just cloaked in mystery," said Rita. "I guess we'll find her all right."

* * * *

Marjorie LeBlanc stepped out of the shower, wrapped a towel around herself, and walked quietly past the kitchen, where Faith and Bertha were still talking. They would stay there all night cackling and gabbing away, while Marjorie forced herself to sleep because she had to get up at five o'-

clock for work. Marjorie would have liked to be a housewife, or a graduate student who had every summer off. She would sit around knitting and watching television and throw a frozen dinner into the oven five minutes before six o'clock. Faith and Bertha had it easy, while she, Marjorie LeBlanc, was a workhorse. And Rita and Jeanie could run off to the North Pole together, since neither of them had children or any responsibilities in the world.

Marjorie stood in front of the full-length mirror she had bought on sale. The mirror had a warp at the top, so that she had to stand back to see her true face. She stepped forward and her face angled off toward the right edge of the mirror. Not ten minutes before, Jeanie Yanulis and Rita Lopez had stood in Marjorie's bedroom and told her they were *in love* with each other. Marjorie had not been surprised—maybe she had known all along, known up to the extent that she could not imagine how two women made love with each other. Marjorie dropped her towel and stared at her body in the mirror. It looked like someone else's body—her breasts stared back at her, tired eyes with dark circles around them. Who would guess it possible, Marjorie thought to herself, that a body could go so many years with so little touching and loving? She turned from the mirror, pulling on a nightgown, and then twisted the towel around her wet hair like a turban before she shut off the light and lay down on the bed.

I should try to have a dream about kissing a woman, Marjorie LeBlanc thought. She laughed out loud and then held herself perfectly motionless for fear that the women in the kitchen would hear her. Marjorie wrapped the bedspread around her; it was softer than the sheets, and she was too tired to get up again and crawl under the sheets anyway. She fell asleep almost immediately and dreamed she was standing on a boat dock, watching her two oldest friends, Jeanie and Rita, wave to her from a ship. The ship stayed where it was, but the land Marjorie was on moved backward from the boat, and drifted and drifted until Marjorie was a tiny white spot on a ribbon of land, and then invisible.

* * * *

Blue Henry, Carla, Ruth, and Sam watched Rita's Impala move slowly down the road. It stopped first in front of the Rubys'. Jeanie ran up the Rubys' lawn and knocked on their door. The Rubys' porch light was on, but their house windows were all dark. No one opened the door, and after five minutes, Jeanie ran back down to Rita's car. The car drove on to the Mansons'. Jeanie rang the Mansons' doorbell, and Mrs. Manson came out in her nightgown, looking wraithlike under her porch light. The children could hear snatches of her high-pitched, excited voice as she waved her arms while talking to Jeanie, but Blue Henry and the LeBlancs could not make out what Mrs. Manson was saying. Jeanie stayed on the steps for a while, chatting with Mrs. Manson, and finally returned to the car.

Now the Impala drove toward the streetlight that stood on the corner near the Carmichaels' yard. There, the car stopped dead, its back lights shutting off. The children saw Rita get out of the Impala and walk over the yard, across the circle of yellow thrown down from the streetlight. When Rita reached the circle's outer rim, she became invisible for a moment, before the children saw her reappear about ten feet from the Carmichaels' window.

* * * *

Rita stood behind Karen in the darkness, wondering what to do. She could see Karen's head poking up from a bush and backlit against the living room window. Rita at first thought of calling out, but she saw that the living room window was ajar, and she did not want to attract the Carmichaels' attention. She wondered what Karen could possibly be staring at.

Sitting on an armchair was the peculiar woman who often came into Rita's laundromat and insisted on washing her clothes without soap. The first time the young woman had done this, Rita had directed her toward the soap-vending machines on the back wall, but the woman had shaken her head and kept piling the clothes into the washer—blacks and purples and whites together. Rita thought of offering to lend her a little soap, thinking that the problem might be money, but then she remembered the blue Cutlass Supreme she had seen the woman step out of earlier. Rita had kept her eye fastened in a sneaky way on the young housewife. When Mrs. Carmichael heaped the cleaned clothes, shrunken and still spotted with stains, into her basket, Rita had seen the young woman's smile—midway between a frown and a smirk. After that, Rita left Mrs. Carmichael alone. Other days, Rita had noticed her pairing mismatches of socks, reds with greens and children's with men's, and twice Mrs. Carmichael had stuffed an entire T-shirt into a wool sock. Once she had thrown an expensive-looking man's crewneck sweater into the dryer, and then proceeded to cook it, turning up the dryer to "linens" and smiling gravely into the black hole of the machine. When the sweater came out, it was hardly bigger than a doll's dress. Rita thought that Mrs. Carmichael was probably a different kind of person, maybe an interesting lady, once you got to know her.

However, Rita could not see what Karen found so spellbinding about the Carmichaels at the moment, other than the mere fact of being able to watch them displayed from such a revealing angle in such detail. Mr. Carmichael was orating from a book with a cowboy on horseback depicted on the front cover. On the back cover was a fleeing cow, the noose of the cowboy's lasso suspended over its head. Every now and then Mrs. Carmichael looked at her husband with the same frown-smirk she used on the dirty clothes at the laundromat. Suddenly Mr. Carmichael's mouth paused in an open position in the middle of a word and he stared straight ahead of him, taking a step toward the window.

It was not until Karen's head ducked down that Rita realized Mr. Carmichael was looking right at her. For a moment, she had the strange sensation that she had been watching a television movie, and suddenly the movie had turned around and begun watching her. Then Rita realized that the light thrown off from the living room must be making her easily visible to the Carmichaels.

"What in hell's name!" Mr. Carmichael thundered, bursting through his front door. Rita heard Jeanie get out of the car and walk down the Carmichaels' driveway.

Karen backed out of the bushes, crying "Oh!" when Rita caught her by the shoulders to keep from being run into. In a moment, all of the Carmichaels were at the door, looking down with grave expressions at Karen and Rita, and then over at Jeanie. Three blond children of grade school age lined up in front of the parents, and came to rest open-mouthed before them. For a moment, Rita thought that the Carmichaels looked like a Norman Rockwell painting, or a Christmas card. In the foreground would be something humorous, like Santa Clause with his reindeer.

"It's not here anywhere," said Karen.

Rita tried to make sense of the words.

"I've looked and looked, but it's just no point in all this darkness."

"Young lady," said Mr. Carmichael, trying to ignore Rita and Jeanie. He seemed to fish around for something to say next. He added sternly, "Can we be of some assistance to you in some way?" He spread his arms, indicating that "we" meant the entire bulwark of the Carmichael family.

"My little brother threw my charm bracelet into your bushes from his bicycle," Karen said, in such a levelheaded tone that Rita was mildly impressed. "I guess I should have waited until morning to search for it, but I just love that bracelet to death." She threw up her hands in a hopeless gesture and smiled.

"Well," said Mr. Carmichael. "Well, I don't think you'll be finding it tonight. My wife will take a look in the bushes tomorrow morning for you." Mrs. Carmichael did not make any sound or gesture that committed her one way or the other.

"That'd be right nice of you," said Karen. Rita held Karen more firmly by the shoulders and tugged her toward the Impala. The Carmichaels backed through their door into the house.

When Rita got into the car, Jeanie shifted the front seat so that Karen could sit in the back.

"I sure hope she finds that charm bracelet!" Karen said, sitting down on the bottom of Rita's slip, so that it slid from its hanger.

Rita answered, "You don't have a little brother, Karen."

"Oh," Karen answered, with what Rita thought was a strained sort of laugh. "I always think of Sam as younger. You know, he's so silly sometimes."

"Sam wouldn't throw your charm bracelet into somebody's bushes," said Jeanie.

This time, Karen took longer to answer. "It's not what it looks like!" She fell silent again for a moment. "Don't tell Ruth! Don't tell Blue Henry and Carla and all!"

"Karen—" Jeanie began.

"Promise!" Karen said in a half desperate, half threatening tone.

"Everyone already—"

"I saw you and Rita!" Karen leaned forward, pushing her head over the front seat between the two women and putting her hand on Jeanie's shoulder. "I saw you French-kissing on Mama's couch."

Karen felt Jeanie's body stiffen, but then Jeanie laughed and lit a cigarette on the lighter in the car's dashboard. She lifted the orange burner, coiled like a bulls'-eye, and Karen saw Jeanie's mouth curl downward but could not tell if she was frowning or suppressing a grin.

Rita stopped the car on the edge of the road, half a block from the LeBlancs' house.

"I know what you are," said Karen, adopting an ominous tone. She could hear the voices of Blue and the LeBlancs approaching from up the street.

"If I were you," said Rita, "I'd stay out of people's

bushes in general for a while, before people start to talk mean about you."

"I know why you're running away from here to go to New York together. You're queer," Karen answered.

"And that's about all you know," said Rita.

"I'll tell what I saw," Karen pressed.

"I'm shivering in my boots," said Jeanie.

"Karen, what the hell were you staring at?" Rita turned around in her seat and looked where she thought Karen's face must be.

Now Blue Henry's voice rang out clearly in the darkness near the car.

"Don't tell Blue Henry and them all. Don't or I'll tell my mother."

"Oh, Jesus," said Jeanie."

"Blue Henry already knows," Rita told Karen. "He and your sisters sent us down to the Mansons', and Mrs. Manson told me that Lou Budd told her you're always staring in her window, and Carla pointed out the houses we could find you at."

Jeanie opened the car door and pulled her seat forward to let Karen out, feeling a small surge of compassion for her. Jeanie almost turned toward Blue and the LeBlanc children to call, "You all lay off Karen. It's no big deal." But instead she said, "You talk to your mama about this before she hears it from a neighbor."

The Impala drove past the Booths' and Mansons' and Carmichaels' houses, and disappeared around the corner. Behind her, Karen heard Blue Henry cry out, "THE LADY BOSTON STRANGLER HAS RETURNED!"

His shout jumped through Marjorie LeBlanc's window, hitting the far wall of her bedroom and coming to rest at the head of her bed. The shout woke her: Marjorie found herself uncovered, her bedspread having slid to the floor. She wriggled under the sheets before falling back asleep.

4. *Wyoming*

KILLER HEARTS

From behind the black Pontiac, Carla LeBlanc and Ivy Lee
Moody watched the man park his car in the yard. It was a
battered car, muddy yellow, with a single headlight and
treads worn smooth as asphalt. Carla and Iva Lee made no
attempt to hide; they stared at the man shamelessly. The
man's name was Mr. Renaud, and he was pulling a laundry
bag and a musical instrument case from his car to carry inside the right half of the duplex. It was late August, but Mr.
Renaud was wearing a long-sleeved green shirt, with a white
T-shirt glimmering ghostlike underneath. His brown nylon
pants, which his belt pulled tightly as a drawstring around
his waist, fit badly over his jutting hipbones. He had the kind
of hips only occasionally seen on men, which taper downward
into legs and upward into waist, almost like a woman's.

Iva Lee's mother, Ellen Moody, was sitting on the duplex's
porch, playing cards with her neighbor Faith Budd, and
Carla's mother and Aunt Bertha. Ellen Moody had moved
into the left side of the duplex at the end of May, right after
the man who lived on the other side, Mr. Renaud, had de-
parted on an unusually long summer vacation. Ellen and Iva
Lee Moody had brought all their belongings in the back seat
of their black Pontiac. They had moved five times in twelve
years, from Amarillo, Texas, to just outside Leslie, Arkansas, and from there to Bolivar, Tennessee; Cameron, Louisiana; Bude, Mississippi; and finally Durham, North Carolina,

the first real city they had been in since Amarillo. Ellen Moody said that the day she discovered she could get a bad job anywhere, she didn't see any point in tying herself down to one place.

Mrs. Moody thought that the next time she changed location, she would like to head upward and to the left on the map, maybe to Minnesota or one of the states you never met anyone from—say, Oregon. But all morning Carla's mother had been trying to convince Mrs. Moody to make Durham her permanent residence. Marjorie LeBlanc said she had lost her oldest friends, Rita and Jeanie, to New York City that year.

As Mr. Renaud struggled up the walk with his load, Carla could hear her mother saying, "Jeanie moved down here from New York City in the first place, but Rita was born and raised in Durham. Then a year ago Rita fixed up the garden in front of her laundry mat, and the next week she had sold the business and was gone, and Jeanie with her." Marjorie LeBlanc scooped up a trick of diamonds and moved it to the edge of the table, as if to illustrate her words, and then added, "Well, I know I can't hold a candle to New York City!" The tone in her voice indicated she felt hurt that Rita and Jeanie had not thought otherwise. "But it was like the rug had been pulled out from under me. As if the world had been dumped upside down. Here I thought I could always count on old friends because I wouldn't be one of those people always whipping around the country, like Bertha here."—Marjorie pointed with her cards at her sister. Bertha's summer semester anthropology courses at UNC were almost over, and she was leaving to start her first teaching job, in Wisconsin, at the beginning of September. Marjorie gave her a narrow stare. "But now I see if you stand still, everyone just gets up and leaves you!"

Ellen Moody looked over Marjorie's head at Mr. Renaud, and then Marjorie and the other women turned around to look as well. Carla saw Mr. Renaud's eyes gather in the four women seated around the card table. Ellen Moody and Faith Budd were dressed in hot pink bathrobes and furry slippers, all of which Faith had bought at a sale for herself and her new neighbor. The two women's deep-socketed eyes buried the middle of their faces in shadow, and Faith's bun had slid slowly down the back of her head and now lay like an uprooted tulip bulb on her shoulder. Ellen Moody, who was swaying caterpillar-like in her green hammock, had pulled her hair back into a lopsided and overly tight ponytail secured by a length of packing twine.

Marjorie and her sister had the same look of being intruded upon. Two days before, Bertha had convinced Marjorie to accompany her to the beauty parlor to get a pixie cut. Now the sisters' hair, instead of lying flat on their heads in stylish caps, stood up in a multitude of black cowlicks. Marjorie and Bertha gazed out of dark eyes set in olive-toned faces, two short women with identical nosy expressions. However, while Marjorie was wearing her nurse's uniform (she had fallen behind in the wash since Rita had left), Bertha had dressed in a sari given to her by a fellow anthropology student who was from Calcutta. Earlier that morning, Bertha had run across the street in her nephew Sam's raincoat, calling out, "Look at this! I had to dare to wear it outside just once!" She had flashed open the raincoat and revealed a green midriff T-shirt and a translucent cloth wrapped in a complicated pattern that exposed her stomach. Faith and Ellen had convinced Bertha to leave the raincoat off, and she had been playing cards so long by now, pushing the sari up on her shoulder in an unselfconscious manner, that she failed to remember how she must appear to Mr. Renaud.

Mr. Renaud looked quickly away from the women and turned back toward Iva Lee and Carla. It appeared as if he might be about to say something to the girls, but suddenly his face reddened with embarrassment, perhaps because of the brown pants belling out over his suitcase to accommodate his wide hips. He did not wait for the girls to greet him but walked with heavy, sad steps, swaying over small black leather shoes which seemed to hurt his feet. Carla and Iva Lee watched him, checking for signs of drunkenness. He rushed inside his half of the duplex before he had to say hello to the women on the porch. He did not seem to realize that Marjorie was sitting in his rocking chair. She was holding still, to make herself less noticeable.

The Moodys' side of the duplex had a kitchenette, a bathroom with a shower, a bedroom which barely accommodated Iva Lee's bed, and a front room with a foldout couch, where Mrs. Moody slept. The Sunday Ellen Moody moved in, she had planted wildflowers behind the house, not bothering to distinguish between what might be her half as opposed to Mr. Renaud's half of the backyard. Mrs. Moody also had dragged Mr. Renaud's rocking chair from his side of the porch to her side, and had strung a green hammock in the middle. Carla's mother and Faith Budd had dropped in on Mrs. Moody and brought her a secondhand mailbox acquired at a garage sale. It was a fancy mailbox: fiberglass, with a picture of a vixen and a fox cub on it, and the name PURDY in block letters at the top. Mrs. Moody had whited over the PUR and painted MOO in unsteady, ascending fluorescent orange letters. When erected, the Moodys' mailbox towered over Mr. Renaud's, making his invisible from the road.

Mrs. Moody worked the day shift as a cashier at Eckerd's drugs and the night shift as an usher at a movie theater. Sometimes when she was working the night shift, she would take Carla LeBlanc and Iva Lee with her, and the girls would sit through *Cool Hand Luke* or *Butch Cassidy and the Sundance Kid* or old movies like *Birdman of Alcatraz* four times in a row, until they knew every line. On Ellen Moody's time off—Sundays and an occasional Saturday—she would lie in the green hammock and give the rocker to whoever came to visit first. Usually Marjorie and Bertha would arrive after breakfast and pretend to fight over the chair. Faith Budd would straggle along later, out of breath and her hair flying loose as if she'd been chased the whole way. She would be carrying a bottle of Wild Turkey in one hand and an electric fan in the other.

On Ellen Moody's second Sunday off, Iva Lee and Carla found out about Mr. Renaud, who occupied the right half of the duplex. "You stay clear of him, Ellen," Faith Budd said, gesturing toward the other side of the duplex so that the whiskey sloshed in the bottle she was holding. The women were just beginning to lay out a game of hearts, and Faith Budd stopped in the middle of what she was saying to pick up her cards. When Marjorie, Bertha, and Faith Budd played what Carla called Killer Hearts, the women would cackle wickedly whenever they dealt someone a heart or the queen of spades, and hoot if they got a coveted card. If Faith won, Marjorie and Bertha would good-naturedly accuse her of cheating, and Faith would reply with a happy nod of her head. Ellen Moody appeared to have learned to play cards in a similar tradition, for she also hollered if she got a heart and grinned menacingly before she prepared to drop the queen on someone. She would hold the queen to her breast, and pull it out rapidly, as if it were a dagger, and toss it over the table. The hearts games were always punctuated with informative gossip and reminiscences about the injustices of childhood, which trailed away whenever an important card was about to be ferreted out of someone's hands.

Toward the end of the morning, Marjorie LeBlanc cried out, "Oh, how can you be so wicked, Ellen! I was holding on to that card. I need it more than you!"

Ellen scooped up the jack of diamonds with an evil expression and dropped it in her pile.

Then Faith Budd pointed toward Mr. Renaud's side of the house for the second time that morning and said, "Any sane person likes a little liquor, but that one drinks like a fish, comes home every night three sheets to the wind. You can hear him stumbling up against his porch, trying to find where the stairs have gone to. Men don't hold their liquor like women. A man who drinks starts stamping around on the floorboards and heaving his couch through the window."

Mrs. Moody's voice faltered. "Where's—where's he now?"

"They say he left in June to dry out somewheres. More likely he went off fishing all summer with his buddies. Probably drunk as a skunk right now and floating belly down in the river. Oh, you wicked woman! You're trying to shoot the moon! Marjorie and Bertha, don't give her any more hearts! She's trying to shoot the moon!"

The falter in Ellen Moody's voice caught in Carla like a hook. Before this, Carla had assumed Mrs. Moody was not afraid of anything. She was a tall, bony woman with a pockmarked face and no-nonsense hollows in her cheeks. She had slender legs and long feet that reminded Carla of catfish. Ellen Moody spoke in a hoarse, rasping tone, and her deepset eyes narrowed and disappeared when she heard something she did not like. Her voice had a subtle north Texas twang and she said "harse" when others would merely have said "horse."

Ellen Moody's daughter, Iva Lee, spoke somewhat differently. Iva Lee could not remember Texas, and had perfected a nasal, mountainish accent, culling the more extreme manners of pronunciation from each place she had lived in since Texas, and from movies she had seen on hillbillies and cowboys. However, Iva Lee had adopted the sandpaper roughness of her mother's voice, and had the same eyes capable of vanishing, and Carla had sought out Iva Lee after she used these attributes on Faith Budd's youngest son, Lou.

Mrs. Budd still called her sons "my little boys," but Lou, the only Budd boy young enough to be living at home, was now a huge seventeen-year-old, with a chest as hairy as a pig's back. Two days after Iva Lee arrived, Carla had been standing in the road midway between the LeBlancs' and the Budds' houses, looking at a dead dragonfly. Iva Lee had come strutting up the street in the direction of the shortcut leading to the supermarket. She was wearing a tie-dyed shirt and jeans cut off at the knee, high-tops, and a green cap that said "John Deere" over the visor. Carla herself was wearing cutoff shorts, her brother's T-shirt, and a Red Rose Feed cap, into which she had piled her unbrushed black hair. The cap accentuated her jawline, which swung sharply downward into her underbitten smile. Carla calculated Iva Lee to be around thirteen, Carla's own age.

At the top of the Budds' driveway, Lou Budd appeared and began to make the queer, ratlike noise reserved for passing women that many men believe sounds like kissing. Then he said, "Oh oh oh oh. Oh, sweetheart, gimme somma that sugar, um, um, um."

Iva Lee had turned toward him, narrowing her eyes, and said, "It's a crying shame you like how I look, 'cause I think you're the ugliest thang I've ever laid eyes on that wasn't awready dead." Her voice had such a pure, deep twang that it bled all the color out of Lou Budd's face.

When Iva Lee began walking again, her high-tops slapped the asphalt.

"You bitch!" Lou Budd called after her. "You filthy two-dollar whore!"

Once again, Iva Lee stopped and faced Lou Budd, this time not even bothering to narrow her eyes. Short, fire-colored hair poked under the visor of her John Deere cap. "I guess I never gave it much thought befawr," she said. "But I am a bitch. I like being that way. Why, it's what gets me up in the mowerning and puts me to sleep at night."

Carla decided to shadow Iva Lee the whole way to the supermarket.

When Iva Lee got there, she walked through the electric doors and immediately walked out again. Then she entered and exited again and circled back around for a third and a fourth time, all the while watching the door hinges. It occurred to Carla that Iva Lee had never seen electric doors up close before. But what made an even greater impression on Carla was how, after the fourth time in and out of the super-

market, Iva Lee walked on toward the hardware store, as if
she would never give that entrance another thought. She had
thoroughly digested, in less than a minute, her movement
from a world with plain swinging doors to one in which doors
opened of their own accord.

Carla slunk into the hardware store behind Iva Lee. She
followed Iva Lee into the tool section and saw her study a
row of wood compartments filled with screws and pick up a
hammer to test its weight. Iva Lee ambled to the back wall
and stopped before a glass case with Bowie knives and jackknives in it. She stared particularly long at a yellow jackknife with three blades. She crossed back through the tool
section and picked up four forty-watt light bulbs, a bag of
nails, and a package of clothespins, and walked to the cashier's counter.

How Carla LeBlanc got the yellow jackknife out of the
glass case without being detected is worth some speculation.
The case was soldered shut at the corners, and the back sliding panels were fastened together with a combination lock.
Nevertheless, when Carla shadowed Iva Lee out of the store,
the yellow jackknife was in Carla's front right pocket.

Carla followed Iva Lee from barely ten yards away, along
the asphalt leading to the shortcut, and then over the red clay
and pine needle path trailing to Carla's neighborhood. After
a while, it was impossible that Iva Lee did not know she was
being followed, and it was unlikely that Carla did not know
Iva Lee knew. Finally, Iva Lee turned around, setting down
her bag from the hardware store. She looked at the yellow
knife handle poking out of the top of Carla's pocket.

"You're Miz LeBlanc's dawter," Iva Lee told Carla. "I
seen you playing up the road with your brother and sisters.
I'll tell you a joke," she continued, "I heard a lady with New
Jersey plates tell over a picnic table in the Natchez Trace."
Iva Lee looked down into her sack as if the joke might be
there, and then said: "A man goes to a doctor's awfice, and
when it comes his turn, he goes into the back room and says,

'Doctor, I have a strange problem.' And the doctor says, 'Well, what?' and the man just looks kind of shamefaced. So the doctor says, 'You kin tell me, don't be shy. I'm a doctor.' The man says, 'Awright. You see, Doctor, I have five penises.' 'FIVE PENISES?' the doctor hollers out. 'How do your pants fit?' So the man tells him, 'Like a glove!' "

After Carla and Iva Lee walked home side by side, and began to spend every waking moment of the summer with each other, this punch line became a sort of code phrase to them, which bound them together and cut them off from everyone else. They used the phrase indiscriminately, whenever they passed a particularly ugly or unfriendly or stupid man: a catcaller, a state trooper, or a wealthy-looking businessman stepping out for lunch in his striped tie, or Lou Budd. Whenever the girls said the words, Carla imagined a little udder flopping around at the man's waist level and dissolved into a wicked, criminal sniggering.

When, at the end of the summer, Mr. Renaud reemerged from his side of the duplex only a half hour after his arrival, Carla leaned over to Iva Lee and said, "Like a glove!" and Iva Lee doubled over laughing.

Mr. Renaud hurried past them, studying the ground immediately in front of his shoes. He was carrying the instrument case, and he propped it up in his front seat, so that the case poked above the seat back like a person's head. When he drove away, Carla and Iva Lee watched with disappointment as the receding car made a perfect left hand turn on its treadless tires; if Mr. Renaud was intoxicated, he was failing to act accordingly.

Carla and Iva Lee were not afraid of drunks. One had camped on the corner outside the bank for a whole week, cursing at bank customers and showing a big stain on the seat of his pants to passing traffic.

After Mr. Renaud's car disappeared, Iva Lee said, "He don't look bombed yet."

"I once saw that wino outside the bank piss right on a

man," Carla lied. "I saw his thang hanging out one day when I was walking home," she added, this time speaking the truth. She reflected a moment on this fact, suddenly imbued with a sense of worth, with the knowledge that she had seen plenty and not been shaken.

"I saw the police pushing him down the street, day before yesterday," said Iva Lee. "I awmost fainted when they passed by, he smelled so bad. Smelled like a zoo."

* * * *

In early June, long before Mr. Renaud returned and shortly after Mrs. Moody had taken over the backyard and appropriated Mr. Renaud's rocking chair, Iva Lee and Carla had extended the Moodys' territory further. One night, Iva Lee pulled on the rope suspended from her bedroom ceiling, and a set of folding stairs held up by a spring stretched down to the floor from the attic. She had never seen anything like the stairs but accepted their appearance calmly, ready for the unexpected. When she crawled up, she saw a second hinged rectangle in the attic floor, to which she guessed stairs to Mr. Renaud's quarters connected.

Later, when Carla came to sleep over on a Saturday night, she and Iva Lee ascended the Moodys' attic stairway and pushed on Mr. Renaud's attic door. It creaked open about three inches. Inside, Iva Lee and Carla could see the gloomy moonlight settled on the room below. A thin, empty bed stretched out beside the back wall. There was no other furniture, except for a desk and a chair. Iva Lee unfolded the steps by pushing down on them. The two girls descended. They were small for thirteen, and so they climbed down together, each holding one side of the ladder. Carla's feet shone silver in the moonlight. Iva Lee looked bluish and spectral.

"Ooooh," she began to croon softly, like a ghost.

"Shut up! Your mama will hear us through the wall," Carla warned her, but Iva Lee wouldn't stop. She pretended to float around the house, moving slowly and rising up and down on her toes as she walked. Carla could not keep from laughing as she followed Iva Lee around the apartment and back to the bedroom.

Mr. Renaud's side of the house was just like the Moodys'— a kitchenette, a small front room, and a bathroom, but mysteriously reversed.

Iva Lee turned on a lamp and then lay down on Mr. Renaud's bed.

"You're messing up the sheets!" said Carla, but she felt happy, intoxicated by Iva Lee's daring.

Iva Lee picked up a pillow and threw it on the floor. "What do you mean? This is my house! Looky this, he really forgot to take the sheets off! And he sleeps with two pillows." She picked up another pillow and began kissing it. "Darlin', my darlin'," she said, burying her face in the dusty pillow cover.

After this preliminary visit, Iva Lee and Carla returned regularly to Mr. Renaud's rooms when Mrs. Moody was away at work. The two girls sat on Mr. Renaud's couch and tinkered with his straight-backed piano. They played Carla's James Taylor records on Mr. Renaud's stereo and drank glasses of water from his own kitchen sink.

* * * *

Now at the end of the summer, faced with Mr. Renaud's return, the two girls stared at his front door, wondering what to do next. Iva Lee frowned. Although the uninhabited half of the duplex had no doubt served all summer as an attraction for rats and raccoons, squirrels and black widow spiders, Iva Lee found the idea of a man living there unsettling.

Carla's feeling of foreboding matched Iva Lee's. Iva Lee was the first person Carla had met in the neighborhood who was also being raised by her mother alone. There was something irritating to Carla's territorial sensibilities about a man coming to rest inside the walls of the Moody house. It was as if the Moodys were suddenly a run-of-the-mill family with a father, mother, and child.

Both girls felt that something should be done before the problem of Mr. Renaud got out of control.

"Let's make one last rondy-voo inside his quarters," said Iva Lee.

"We don't know when he's coming back."

"Not tonight then. Let's study his habits first, like we're hunting him, and find out when he likes to go out."

"Hey, you girls, you!" Mrs. Moody called. "There's some pop in the Frigidaire. Help yourself before you fry out your brains thinking."

The girls circled around to the back of the house, pretending not to have heard Iva Lee's mother. They studied the windows and noted which shades had and had not been drawn. Mr. Renaud's side of the duplex looked much more forbidding than it had before he returned, and this raised the girls' spirits. Iva Lee pulled out her new yellow jackknife and threw it. It whirled, wheel-like, toward the house and landed at a perfect angle, its point embedded in the dead center of the wood slat over Mr. Renaud's back door.

*　*　*　*

Whether there was in fact a dearth of good men, or whether Marjorie LeBlanc's experiences were singular, was a question that Marjorie turned over many times in her life, and that the women on the porch debated the following Sunday evening, between hollers and exclamations pertaining to their card game. Marjorie, Bertha, Faith, and Ellen had been playing and smoking cigarettes and drinking a special punch concocted by Bertha, and now that dusk was falling, the card game had taken on a momentum of its own. Marjorie was joking about men who had asked her out, and the women were encouraging her between ruthless maneuverings of the cards. Carla looked up from the mayonnaise and pickle jars she and Iva Lee had been cleaning out with the garden hose. Carla generally admired and enjoyed her mother when she got into such a state.

During those rare moments when Marjorie LeBlanc was in a carefree mood after work, she would entertain her four children by imitating her various past callers, whom the children were relieved to see so reduced to jokes and caricatures; ordinarily, their mother's loneliness was a constant, grave preoccupation for them. It was the worry that drew Carla and her sister Ruth from the street on nights when Marjorie was alone in the house. It was what made Carla's sister Karen rise at six o'clock each morning to curl her hair and paint a second face of lipstick, eyeliner, and eye shadow over her own face with a superstitious perfectionism. And it was the worry that led Carla's brother to keep too much to himself. It made Sam LeBlanc lean against the corner street sign, his hands in his pockets and his lantern jaw drooping, staring at the ground as if he were building up his resistance against inevitable attacks of loneliness in his adult future.

When Carla's mother ridiculed her own solitary condition, she liked to begin with Mr. Mintor, the undertaker, who was rich but cleared his throat and snorted all the time, blowing into his handkerchief; or Old Goat Eddie, who drooled when he kissed; or Cold Joe, who had an eye patch and spoke in a monotone. Marjorie would lean over, snuffling into one of the children's ears, or grab one of them, threatening, "It's time to give you an Old Goat!" and plant terrifying wet kisses on their foreheads. Once when a neighbor's dog, six feet standing on her hind legs, jumped up on Joe and knocked him over, the children and Marjorie heard him say, lying on his back and without inflection, "She has a cold nose." So that when Marjorie imitated Old Goat Eddie's kisses, Ruth or Sam would circle their mother in stiff, Frankenstein steps, pronouncing, "She has a cold nose, She has a cold nose," or try to give each other snorting Mr. Mintor kisses. Carla would lie down on the ground and fold her arms over her chest and invite her mother to "Come into my coffin, where it is nice and cool, and we will go at it, Baby!"

"Don't, Carla, don't!" Marjorie LeBlanc would say when her youngest daughter got out of hand.

Now Marjorie ran through descriptions of Mr. Mintor and Old Eddie and Cold Joe for her friends, who gathered closer on the porch as the evening deepened into night. The forty-watt bulb above them gave off a yellow light shaped like a bird's cage. At the end of her repertoire, Marjorie pronounced, "You have to kiss a lot of frogs before you meet a prince." After studying her hand of cards, she added, looking around to make sure that Iva Lee and Carla were out of earshot, "Well, I've met a few men who could really tear up the town. I might of remarried if it wasn't for the children."

But Carla and Iva Lee heard every word. They had moved just a few yards outside the porch's birdcage of light, and were wandering after fireflies, which were plentiful that August and sometimes could be brought down two or three at a time. It was Iva Lee's belief that if you filled a quart jar with forty lightning bugs, you could tie a wire around the top and use the jar as a lantern that could be seen from two miles away. Carla stepped away from the large mayonnaise jar she and Iva Lee had set aside for this purpose, and peered through the darkness toward her mother.

"Well," whispered Carla, "I certainly didn't come to this earth of my own accord!"

Iva Lee answered in a melodramatic voice, "If it wasn't for you, I could have married the President! I could have seen the Empire State Building! If you weren't here, I could have been a model for la-di-da *Vogue* magazine, I could have been a lady astronaut, I could have swum across the sea!" She lifted the jar lid and then tightened it after Carla dropped in a handful of fireflies.

"There was an awful fellow"—Marjorie's voice continued to seep beyond the porch into the darkness—"who told me to put toothpaste on his whangdoodle. He said it felt good. Imagine! I wouldn't even of wanted to see him in a pitch-black room with his birthday suit. Can't remember his name;

he was an ugly little man with a mustache and a rash. I met him at one of Hope George's parties. Oh, that snooty Mrs. George always has a jack-in-the-box at her parties. Once some relative of hers insisted on walking me home, and when I got out the kitchen door, he pulled down his pants and asked me to give him a massage. 'A massage,' is how he put it. 'No, sir,' I said. 'Thank you very much, but I'd rather not!' Then when I walked on around him, he pulled up his pants, like as not forgetting to zip them, and followed me down the street, begging me on bended knee not to be mad and to let him walk me home. I could smell the liquor on his breath from ten feet in front of him. I never would of shook him if Ruth and Sam hadn't been out in the front yard, having a wrestling match. It seems Carla had made some kind of bet, and even Karen, who's so big for her britches now, was out there raising Cain and egging Sam and Ruth on. You could hear them clear down the block, and Mr. Massage was not in a mood for children and stopped dead on the street, where I left him. In the end, I think the children decided it was a tie."

"Ha!" said Carla, moving close to the jar and squatting down. At the girls' feet, the fireflies flickered and streamed across the jar.

"The worst one *I* ever had to deal with was Iva Lee's father," Ellen Moody followed Marjorie. "Didn't he promise to marry me, and then a nosy lady in Amarillo tells me she heard him bragging he had more women on the side than he could count. Said he had left a wife behind in the Arkansas half of Texarkana and another in Brownsville, Texas, and hadn't divorced either one of them. I told the nosy lady I didn't believe it, but then she got specific, and could even tell me the name of the Brownsville wife: Marguerite Fate, never will forget that name. The nosy lady says, 'That's bigamy, is what it is, and if you marry him too it'll be something even worse, double bigamy.' So when T-Bird comes by the house that night, I say, 'T-Bird, is it true you're harsing around?

Is it true you've got women on the side?' And he says to me—
now listen to this one—'Sure I got women on the side. I got
women on both sides. But you're in the middle.' Next day I
packed up my clothes and Iva Lee, who was hardly more than
four months and smaller than a loaf of Wonder Bread, and
we took a Greyhound to as far as I could pay to go. I didn't
want to be where T-Bird was hanging around, forcing me to
make up my mind every living minute about whether to see
him or give him the cold shoulder. I'll never forget how on
that bus ride Iva Lee didn't cry once the whole way. You
know what it can be like to have to go a long way with a baby
on a bus, everybody shushing you and staring at you as if
you were the one squalling. But Iva Lee just lay against my
shoulder, looking out the window all contented." Ellen
Moody shifted in her seat to get comfortable and stretched
out her legs, bumping Faith Budd under the table.

"Let me put my two cents in," said Faith. "I heard a lady
at the laundry mat say that once when she got restless for
some loving, she tried applying to one of those dating services. She got a call from a hundred-year-old man who was
spending all summer in Florida but had flown back home to
bury his dog. It was a weimaraner, who had run into a cement mixer, and the man told her everything about the funeral; it was a full burial with all the trappings, including a
Methodist minister. She said that that cured her for good
from worrying about getting a man."

"Every man I even thought about when I was young
enough to care," Bertha followed, "I either ran off from or
he should have stayed away in the first place."

"Oh, Bertha," Marjorie told her sister. "You don't always
have to say that like you're proud of it."

"Well, I'm not ashamed of it."

"I, for one, wouldn't mind remarrying!" Marjorie cried,
stamping her foot on the porch so that the card table rattled.
As if embarrassed by the quaver of seriousness in her voice,
she added in a lighter tone: "I wouldn't mind a Daddy War-
bucks who could support me in my old age."

"Amen!" said Ellen Moody.

Carla felt a ghostly emotion rise within her: Marjorie Le-Blanc's loneliness, so unappeasable and desperate, entered Carla and became a sense of longing inside her. Carla looked at the dome of light around the women, and it seemed to whiten and ripple at the edges like a specter. "Whoo!" Carla cried, shaking off the feeling and wading a few steps through the cool darkness to where Iva Lee stood, holding up the mayonnaise jar against the night.

"I guess there's no truth to it," said Iva Lee, in her level-headed way. "I count thirty-seven lightning bugs, and the jar hardly throws any light at all. It must be another super-stition."

"Let's unscrew the lid and watch them fly out."

Iva Lee took off the top, and the insects soared upward in uneven flashes of light, like sparks from a fire.

"Holy bejesus," said Carla. "Looky them go."

"They're like firecrackers without the sound," Iva Lee decided. Both girls instantly longed for real firecrackers.

A block down the road a loud noise issued, the noise that always first registers in the listener's ear as a slamming screen door or a gunshot: an engine backfiring. Mr. Renaud's car, which in daylight looked as if it had not had a paint job in a decade, was rounding the corner. Its one yellow eye moved steadily toward the girls, blinking off when it reached the yard.

OSCAR RENAUD

Mr. Renaud backed out of his car door, dragging his instrument case after him in his right hand. Carla thought the case contained a violin, and Iva Lee said it had to be either a trombone or a shotgun. In Mr. Renaud's left hand were notebooks, sheets of music, and smaller papers, which Carla and Iva Lee could not identify in the feeble light thrown from inside his Plymouth. Mr. Renaud pushed the door closed with his foot and scuttled by the girls without seeing them, dropping some papers behind him. After he passed, both girls stepped under the streetlight in front of the Moodys' to investigate the papers.

They were literature from Alcoholics Anonymous. The girls read the pamphlets out loud to each other for entertainment, adding in phrases like "Onward Christian soldier," and "Turn to Christ and you shall be saved." Then they sang "Swing Low, Sweet Chariot" with grave, pious faces, and concluded with "Carry Me Back to Old Virginny."

Over the next two weeks, the girls discovered that Mr. Renaud went to AA meetings on Mondays and Fridays between eight and twelve o'clock. At first, Iva Lee and Carla thought he might be carousing, but his headlight always appeared at midnight and proceeded down the road in a straight line, unfaltering as a lantern held steady. When he stepped out of the car, his arms were always full of pamphlets, as if he had lost the old ones during the course of the work week.

Iva Lee invited Carla to spend the night on Friday, August 29. Iva Lee had promised not to talk in bed with Carla after ten o'clock, since Mrs. Moody had to get up at six-thirty to work the following morning. The girls held themselves still as corpses in their beds, not so much to respect Ellen Moody's beauty sleep as to assure that she would be dead to the world by eleven.

At eleven, Carla and Iva Lee rose. Iva Lee took from under her pillow the flashlight Carla had borrowed three days before from the glove compartment of the Budd boys' Chevrolet while Iva Lee had distracted Lou by walking slowly along the edge of his yard. Carla had tied orange cheesecloth over the front end of the flashlight to soften its beam. She and Carla lowered the attic stairs, crept up, pulled the stairs closed, and repeated the same movements in reverse on Mr. Renaud's side of the duplex. The girls' bare feet whispered along the rug in his bedroom, and they lay down on his bed.

Iva Lee switched on the flashlight. Two pairs of Mr. Renaud's pants lay balled up in separate corners of the room. His desk was littered with papers, and his shoe, with a tie half coiled in its mouth, lay on the desk chair. A long-sleeved shirt stirred on a hanger hooked over the curtain rod. The shirt looked to Iva Lee and Carla like a man staring wistfully out the window into the darkness. The view from the window was similar to one Iva Lee saw every night when she went to bed: the black square of a neighbor's backyard, and beyond this, the street surfacing in a pool of green under a street-light; a lone light bulb on the Budds' porch; and yellow squares of windows in distant houses. Iva Lee liked to pre-tend that the windows were stones, and the darkness around them rivers of pure blackness full of unexplored mystery. The rivers could not be discovered in the daytime. Iva Lee had explained the view to Carla before, so that now, when both girls looked out the window, they saw the same thing. Carla liked to imagine being in a world that only she and Iva Lee inhabited.

Carla rose and took down the shirt, then buttoned it on over her T-shirt and cutoff shorts. She picked up the tie and let it dangle around her neck, as she had no idea how to knot a necktie. She lifted her foot into the shoe and clomped around the bed in slow, melancholy steps, hunching her shoulders.

Iva Lee gasped, "Oh, stop! Stop it! Don't make me laugh." Carla clomped across the room into the kitchenette.

Iva Lee followed her, trying to think of something to match Carla. Iva Lee shone the flashlight around the kitchen-ette and then stood on the counter and began rummaging in the cupboards.

"What're you looking for?" Carla asked, climbing beside her.

"Booze!" Iva Lee whispered. In the orange circle thrown from the flashlight into the cupboard, the girls could make out more sheets of music paper, empty orange juice jars, and a few cracked plates. They opened all the cabinets over the sink, and then jumped off the counter and opened all the cabinets below the sink, but they could not find any liquor bottles. Carla looked in the drawer under the stove, but discovered only a pot lid.

"He's coming!" Carla exclaimed, and darted out of the kitchenette into the bedroom, grabbing the flashlight from Iva Lee.

"Liar!" Iva Lee whispered after her. She heard Carla open and close drawers in the bedroom.

In a minute, Carla reemerged and said, "He don't have a thing in this world worth a dime."

Iva Lee took the flashlight and began removing the dishes and jars from the cupboards and laying them on the counter. Then she switched them around, putting jars and cleaning fluid above the counter, and the plates in the cabinet under the stove. Carla slid one plate inside the stove. Iva Lee had to stop every two or three dishes to keep from snickering too loud.

After this, they went into the bathroom and turned on the light. Carla and Iva Lee each shaved one side of one ankle with Mr. Renaud's razor, not wanting to remove all the hair that had just started to appear. They put down the toilet seat, and they stood together on Mr. Renaud's scale, weighing themselves in unison. Then they turned off the bathroom light and went back into the bedroom. Carla hung up Mr. Renaud's shirt on the curtain rod and put his tie back in his shoe, and stuck the shoe on the chair.

The girls wandered into the front room, which looked nothing like the Moody's side of the house. The room was lit from the porch light, because Mr. Renaud had forgotten to pull down his shades. There was a low, murky brown couch in the corner, a coffee table with a chessboard and the instrument case resting on it, the straight-backed piano that the girls had tinkered with in the weeks before Mr. Renaud returned, and a bookcase, which had not been there before.

Iva Lee walked over to the piano, lightly touched the key

on the farthest left and said, "A giant!" Then she pressed down the highest key and said, "A lady screaming!" She swayed back and forth, hitting the same two keys and chanting, "A giant, a lady screaming! A giant, a lady screaming! A giant—"

"Shhhhh!" said Carla, hitting the low key once herself before pulling Iva Lee away from the piano. Carla focused the flashlight's beam on the bookcase.

"Looky that!" Iva Lee exclaimed, and they examined the odd assortment of specimens laid out on the shelves: piles of rare, especially colorful, and root beer bottle caps; an old chewing tobacco tin; cadmium-blue milk of magnesia bottles; a rattlesnake skin oiled with glycerin; two whelks and two sand dollars; a wasp nest in the shape of a heart; a city of quartz crystals, which rose in uneven heights, reminding Carla and Iva Lee of New York skyscrapers; a shellacked three-inch stag beetle; four bicycle chain wheels of varying designs, suspended from tacks at the front of the third shelf, and throwing lacy circular shadows on the back of the bookcase; a scallop shell; a patchwork quilt, twelve by eighteen inches, cut from pieces of material no larger than the stars at the cores of apples; a twisted root that looked exactly like a man carrying a knapsack; a box turtle shell; four woodcut portraits signed "Annie Zalokar," bearing the legend "For Oscar," and stating the name of the person portrayed at the bottom: Annie Oakley, Ulysses S. Grant, Thelonious Monk, and Arthine Renaud; four broken watches, two compasses, a violin bow made of black wood and chestnut horsehair; and a row of eight-sided bolts, laid out in descending order of size.

Both girls made involuntary internal adjustments concerning their opinion of Mr. Renaud.

"Where did he get all this stuff?" said Carla. She picked up the stag beetle and put it back down.

Iva Lee traced her finger along the patterns on the quilt and snakeskin, and knocked lightly on the wasp nest. "You gotta be around a long time to get a collection like this going."

A lone lantern swung into the front yard, outside the window. The two girls heard the sound of a car motor.

"Uh oh," Carla commented, but there was no fear in her voice; Iva Lee heard an agreeably scary tone that indicated interest in rising to the occasion.

The two girls pressed themselves flat against the wall and inched along it until they reached the wall belonging to the front door. The car light outside blinked off. Carla and Iva Lee ducked down and crawled along the floor to the piano. They glided like shadows into the space between the bench and the pedals.

* * * *

Oscar Renaud had been back at his job for only two weeks now, and already the dead batteries and unaligned tires, broken fan belts, loose clutches, and worn-out brake linings, were beginning to depress him. Mr. Coleman, who owned the auto repair store, had been so glad to take Oscar back that the old man's voice had risen to a high, boyish peak as he talked excitedly about the garage, his cottony brown eyes brightening with tears. Long-time customers had complained and drifted away in Oscar's absence. No one could diagnose the source of a car's trouble with such uncanny accuracy as Oscar Renaud. For him, an old motor that had been stalling for years would suddenly become young and nimble, its pistons rising in a choreographed smoothness; the spark plugs would explode in their cylinders with a timing more precise than that of a timpani drum in the New York Philharmonic; air and gasoline would meet in the carburetor like two harmonizing voices. For Oscar Renaud, dead batteries would take on new life and outlive their warranties, and realigned fifteen-year-old station wagons would turn on a dime.

But Oscar Renaud resisted his profession like a prophet denying his calling. If he could have chosen his occupation,

Oscar would have been a musician and composer, and he secretly hated cars and rebelled against his work. Most of his
rebellion was directed against his own Plymouth, which he
allowed to rust and collect dents. He seldom checked its oil,
and he never changed the tires until one acquired a bubble or
ran over a nail. His license plates dangled from single screws
and his left headlight had been out for three years.

Oscar Renaud had grown up in Kinston, North Carolina,
five blocks from the locally renowned Parker brothers, some
of whom later recorded with world-famous musicians. Oscar
believed that with hours of practice and dedication to the
study of music, he could one day meet similar luck. As a
young man, he had spent all his evenings, when he could have
been dating, composing songs on his bassoon in the back room
of his father's optician's office. This had been during the fif-
ties, when a handful of musicians were experimenting with
the bassoon as a jazz instrument. In his lifetime, Oscar
Renaud had written four hundred and seventy-one songs for
the bassoon and oboe, all of which he had copyrighted, but
only one of which had ever been sold: a gentle blues piece
called "Annie Zalokar Has Two Big Hearts," after Oscar's
first and last girlfriend, who had lived with him for seven
years in New York City before going back to her husband.
The song had been bought by a country singer in Nashville,
adapted to the guitar, and renamed "Two-timing Girl."

After Annie had left him, Oscar Renaud quit his job as a
music instructor in a New York grade school and returned to
North Carolina. Unable to face the optician's office, he had
moved to Durham and started working at Coleman's. He
knew almost nothing about cars when he took the job, and
had lied to get it, but within a week Oscar Renaud discovered
his own mocking genius for handling automobiles, which so
far excelled his musical talents that for a whole year he was
unable to tinker on his straight-backed piano or even play old
songs on his bassoon. Oscar Renaud began frequenting bars
and buying liquor in the state-run ABC stores on Fridays to

ensure that he would not pass a dry Sunday. After three years, he stopped going to bars and drank all his liquor at work or at home. On weekdays, he would drive from work directly to his side of the paint-peeling duplex, with its dirt and crabgrass lawn, and sit in his rocking chair, trying to hear a single chord of new music in his head. Instead, he heard only the thump and beat of the chair against the porch. Sometimes, after a long Saturday of drinking, he would lean back in the rocker and a strain of someone else's music—say "Locomotive" or "Anthropology"—would well up inside him, making him long to be anywhere other than where he was. He would refill his glass and gaze at the house windows glimmering like the nickel silver of woodwind keys, the columns of darkness rising around them, black as the brasiletto from which oboes are made.

After seven years of living alone in the duplex, during which time Oscar's salary quadrupled, he came home one morning in early June to find in his yard a black Pontiac with a sagging muffler and broken antenna. On his porch were a beautiful woman and her little girl, swaying together in a green hammock. They were lying head to toe, and the woman's feet were hidden in a fold of hammock, which seemed to curl up from her waist like a mermaid's tail. Oscar put his car in neutral, but his shame kept him from pulling into the front yard. He had spent the night asleep in his Plymouth on a back road. Three empty Cutty Sark bottles clinked on the seat beside him, and when he looked in the rearview mirror, he thought that his eyes looked red as brake lights. He circled back to the highway and did not stop driving until he reached Myrtle Beach. He had nothing in his car but a pile of dirty laundry, his bassoon, and his last paycheck. At a hotel in Myrtle Beach, he wrote Mr. Coleman a letter of regret. Then Oscar Renaud drove to Cape Fear, where he rented a beach cottage and spent the summer staring at the ocean, playing his bassoon, and applying for jobs as a music instructor in high schools all over the United

States. When the urge to drink became intolerable, he would drive along the coast, often to Myrtle Beach, but sometimes as far as Ocracoke and Cape Hatteras, and once all the way north to Chincoteague, to watch the Chincoteague ponies swim across the water to the island. The wild ponies' manes and the grass that struggled from the sand on the harsh Atlantic shores reminded him of the hair of the beautiful woman who had appeared in her hammock on his porch.

Simple things like a bird's nest hidden in beach grass or a blue bottle found in a scrap heap near his cottage could fill Oscar Renaud with feelings of gratitude and rapture so intense that he could barely contain himself—he was sentimental and romantic. But this was because he had to be. Oscar Renaud was an ugly man, and life dealt him happiness in parsimonious allotments. Other than Annie Zalokar, no woman had ever looked once at him. On the rare occasions when Oscar Renaud rode buses, he would sit in the window seat, trying to look forbidding and hoping that no one would squeeze into the seat next to him. He would stare fearfully at stuffy-looking women and necktied men, sticky children and mothers with howling babies, but when they all chose other seats, he would end up thinking: Why, what's the matter with me, I'd like to know? Why did everyone pass me by?

Annie Zalokar was the only person who had not passed Oscar Renaud by. She was a short, fat woman with ink-stained hands, who worked as a printer in Greenwich Village. No one else had thought her pretty, but Oscar became spellbound by her beauty if he simply studied the angle of the bobby pins in her hair or the half-moons in her thumbnails.

It had been seven years since Oscar had been touched by a woman. When he came home at the end of the summer, he feared that the lady he had seen in the hammock would have disappeared, as if she had been merely an apparition. But when Oscar's Plymouth reached the duplex, he saw four women playing cards, sprawling onto his half of the porch as if they accepted and included him. When he walked through the duplex into his dusty bedroom and lifted the shade, an ocean of wildflowers rose to meet him. He sat down, overwhelmed by the generosity of the woman who had planted his side of the yard as well as her own.

* * * *

On the night of August 29, when Oscar Renaud unlocked his door, the blue coolness that had settled inside the front room welcomed him. He propped open the screen door with his bassoon case and then made two trips back outside to carry in the two seven-foot Japanese maples that he had bought that day at Fred's Nursery. He unlashed the trees from the top of his car and almost lost his balance when he lowered the heavy burlap bags filled with dirt in which the maples were wrapped. He was not a strong man, and so he had to rest every ten feet as he carried the trees.

When the Japanese maples were both safely inside his front room, Oscar Renaud walked to the piano and, without sitting down, absently tapped out the melody of "Straight, No Chaser." The toe of his small shoe brushed against Iva Lee's knee, but he did not appear to notice. He played the first six bars of "Don't Get Around Much Anymore" with a light heart, and then wandered over to his bookcase. He pulled a perfectly spherical stone from his pocket and laid it on the second shelf, and then walked to the corner of the room and collapsed on the couch, not bothering to kick off his shoes. He began whistling "Round Midnight," and when his whistle failed on the high notes, he switched to an O-mouthed hum in imitation of an oboe, and closed his eyes.

Oscar Renaud's AA pamphlets flapped on the floor next to his bassoon case as a summer wind filled the room with the smell of wildflowers. He tried to pick out the other smells: maple leaves and wet earth, a nicotine odor as if tobacco were being cured nearby, the alcohol scent that lingered in his memory and accompanied him everywhere, and something that reminded him of a little girl smell, a tomboyish odor of wet shoe leather and burning rubber and gunpowder. He opened his eyes and admired the maples. They gave him the sensation of sleeping outside, or on a porch. Tomorrow he would surprise his neighbor, Mrs. Moody, by planting the trees in both halves of the front yard. His eyes closed again, and he meant to get up and change into his pajamas and move into the bedroom, but sleep put dark, cool arms around Oscar Renaud and dragged him downward into blackness.

Iva Lee and Carla waited an impressive amount of time under the piano. Even though their feet began to tingle and their calves felt cramped, they continued to sit motionless long after Mr. Renaud sang the final note of his song. They stared at the shadowy mound of Mr. Renaud on the couch, the tree branches above them, and the darkness in which the distant windows crowded together. Finally, Carla touched Iva Lee's leg, and the two girls walked more silently than the swish of a nylon dress past the couch and into Mr. Renaud's bedroom. They ascended the hanging stairway and pulled it up behind them in a patient, cautious motion that kept the springs from moaning. They descended Iva Lee's attic stairs and pushed them back into the ceiling, and then crawled into bed. They pressed their sides against each other and Iva Lee twined her feet around Carla's ankle.

"He sleeps with his shoes on," Iva Lee whispered.

"He brought trees into his living room," said Carla.

"What do you make of him singing like that?" Iva Lee asked. "Gave me the heebie-jeebies." She closed her eyes and saw images of tree branches stretching toward the ceiling.

"He sounded like the way ghosts would sing, if they sung," said Carla.

YOU KNOW THAT WYOMING WILL BE YOUR NEW HOME

Mrs. Moody's car battery went dead on Saturday morning, so Marjorie took Ellen to the movie theater at six o'clock, and drove back to pick her up at twelve that night.

"I'm so glad my car broke down," Ellen Moody said as she slid into Marjorie's Oldsmobile after work. "I hate it when they play those scary movies all day. I would of been afraid to walk across the parking lot by myself tonight. After six hours, I can't get the noise of wolfmen growling and ladies screaming out of my head. It's so nice of you to come pick me up, Marjorie."

"You know I'd do anything for you, Ellen."

Ellen touched Marjorie on the arm and told her, "You're sweet."

Marjorie turned the car onto the road and said, "I was just thinking on the way over that I can hardly remember back to a Sunday before our card games. I feel like I've known you all my life."

"I like you too, Marjorie!" Mrs. Moody felt a wild rush of emotion, which seemed all out of proportion to the occasion. She almost put her arm around her friend, but did not since Marjorie was driving. "I'm real happy here. I think me and Iva Lee like Durham better than any place we've been yet."

The Oldsmobile nosed through the darkness of Durham, and the dimly lit houses rushed forward to greet the two women.

As Marjorie turned into her neighborhood, Ellen Moody said, "Iva Lee sure is head over heels for your Carla."

"I think Iva Lee's the first real close friend Carla's had besides her sister Ruth," said Marjorie.

"She's growing upward and out into the world."

"Carla and Iva Lee look like two wild women roaming around together. They were sitting on the front steps carving spears two days ago."

Ellen chuckled. "Iva Lee loves that yellow knife Carla gave her as a welcome present."

"Carla's always saving up to buy jackknives. I don't think she ever spends her money on anything else. I once had to take away one of those switchblades from her. It was real fancy, with a green handle, and was she mad! But she was just a little girl, and those things are dangerous. I think they might even be against the law."

When Marjorie pulled up in front of the Moodys' mailbox, the two women sat quietly in the dark for a minute.

"Well," said Marjorie, "if we were on a date, this would be the time to kiss!"

Ellen laughed as she got out of the car and watched the Oldsmobile drive away. She did not notice the Japanese maples when she turned up the duplex's walkway. She was looking squarely in front of her, haunted by scenes from the wolfman picture that had been playing all week at the theater. The light on the porch was not working, and she could barely find the stairs. She glanced to neither the right nor left as she opened her door.

"Oh!" she said, for she had opened the wrong door, and was looking into Mr. Renaud's front room: Before her, a small lamp illuminated a piano. Ellen closed the door quietly and felt along the wall for her own doorknob. When she stepped into her front room, Ellen turned on the lights in the hall. As she got ready for bed, she checked inside the hall closet and behind the bathroom door to dispel the visions of leaping and springing wolfmen that kept appearing in her mind. She checked inside the shower and thought to herself: I wonder if there's a woman in America after that movie *Psycho* who left by herself isn't scared to open the shower curtain. Alfred Hitchcock should be shot! Ellen Moody scrubbed her face and slipped into a nightgown. She left the hall light on when she got into bed.

In the morning when Iva Lee awoke, her mother was glaring out of the window with her hands on her hips, examining the trees whose red leaves reminded Ellen Moody of bloody paws or strange jagged gloves.

"Well!" said Ellen Moody. "If he didn't approve of the wildflowers he might have said something, or just pulled them up, instead of going about making his point in such a backhanded way."

Later on in the morning, when the women were settled into a card game and Iva Lee and Carla sat on the porch steps, whittling saplings into spears, Ellen Moody said, "I know a lot of people think wildflowers are weeds. But I never went in for those artificial-looking flowers like carnations and gardenias and roses. I like a flower you stick in the ground and it holds on by itself. Come rain, come hail, come hot weather, it grows on and on. And that's all there is to it. I never thought a plant had to be some fancy-pancy tree to be nice."

"If I were you, I would just pretend not to notice," said Faith Budd.

"Well, *I* like those trees," said Marjorie, leading with a three of hearts. "No one in this neighborhood has ever planted trees like that."

"You can't play a heart until hearts have been taken!" Faith Budd cried. Marjorie withdrew her card and replaced it with a club.

"Hearts doesn't work as well with so few people," said Ellen. "I wish Bertha had of come with you." The three women looked at the empty rocker. Marjorie had chosen to sit in a low wicker chair, perhaps to dramatize her sister's absence by leaving the rocker unoccupied.

Marjorie scooped up the trick of clubs. "Bertha's working like a maniac because her classes at the university are almost over. 'Not on Sunday!' I told her. 'Nobody's work is so serious they can't take off a little time on a Sunday.' 'Women have to work twice as hard as men to get half the gravy,' was her answer. Well, I don't know. I don't think a woman should give up everything to work. She doesn't even spend a minute a week looking at a man."

When Marjorie stopped to consider which card to play, the other women felt uncomfortable. Ellen Moody looked at the rocker, which appeared to be leaning forward in an attitude of objection, as if the spirit of the absent Bertha were listening indignantly to this gossiping that occurred the moment her back was turned.

Carla and Iva Lee held up their spears and compared them. The girls had decided that the spears' points had to be perfectly symmetrical for the sticks to travel straight. It had taken them several experimental throws the day before to break the light bulb on the porch.

"Bertha's leaving me in just eight more days!" Marjorie said abruptly in a reedy, hollow voice as she dropped a diamond.

"I've already bought canned chocolate icing for a going-away cake," Faith Budd told Ellen Moody in a carefree tone. "Next Sunday, we'll have to throw a little party for her."

An eerie, moaning sound that appeared to be a melody of some kind issued out of Mr. Renaud's side of the duplex.

"There he goes again," Ellen whispered.

"Oh, he used to do that all the time a few years back," said Faith Budd. She stopped and her mouth formed an O as she listened to the music. "I used to kind of like it. That was before his drinking became so noticeable, before he took to moaning on his porch at night."

All three women drew fans of cards to their bosoms and craned their necks toward the right half of the duplex.

Ellen Moody was the first one to break her pose. She rearranged her cards and said, "I have to admit he hasn't engaged in any drunkness since he got back. He must be on the wagon. But he's never even introduced himself, and I think that's a sign of bad manners. Of course, it could just be that his manners are too good. He could be standoffish."

A short while later, the music trailed to a finish, and Mr. Renaud was seen leaving in a diagonal path across the right half of the yard.

"Look at that!" said Ellen Moody. "He went out the back door so that he didn't have to pass us on the way out!"

Faith Budd studied Mr. Renaud's receding figure. "He must be going to the 7 Eleven. Nothing else close by is open on Sundays."

Two games later, Faith Budd congratulated herself. "I was right! Here he comes now."

Carla, Iva Lee, and the three women watched him approach, hunched over a 7 Eleven bag.

* * * *

When Oscar Renaud saw all the women's heads turn toward him, he had visions of himself dropping his grocery bag and running into the pinewoods bordering the road, never to return.

All morning he had been trying to summon the courage to amble out nonchalantly onto the porch, hands in his pockets, and begin some small talk with the women out there. They were playing a card game that he did not recognize. The only card game Mr. Renaud had ever learned was solitaire, but even that he had been unable to recall the few times in the recent past when he had thought of playing. He would begin to lay out cards in the proper formations, but then he could not remember how you were supposed to make the first move. He would stare at the cards, thinking: Why, I'll never know again how the game goes! People were only interested in teaching card games that they could then immediately play and beat you at. Who in the world would ever teach someone else solitaire? How had he learned the rules in the first place?

The thought that he would never even relearn solitaire had filled Oscar Renaud with desperation, and increased his longing to step out onto his porch. But the desperation was quenched by a paralyzing timidness which held Mr. Renaud to the couch, where he sat clutching his bassoon. When he realized he had to buy some frozen dinners and some toilet paper, he almost resolved to go without dinner that night and to wait to use the bathroom until work the next day. He put down the bassoon and walked aimlessly around his kitchenette. Finally, he decided to sneak out the back door.

Once at the 7 Eleven, he found himself buying things he had not intended to. He looked at the popcorn and pictured a taller, more debonair Mr. Renaud walking out his front door with a large yellow bowl and a salt shaker and saying, "Buttered popcorn, anyone?" When Oscar saw a roll of silver tape, he imagined himself repairing the outside of his screen door and explaining, "Just thought I'd cover up this hole here." In all, he bought two frozen beef pot pies, toilet paper, popcorn, silver tape, a bucket for cleaning his car with (he could offer to clean the Pontiac and then to fix it), a box of pudding mix that served eight, a jar of mixed nuts—which he had always associated with parties—and a one-hundred-watt light bulb to replace the broken bulb above the front steps. As Oscar Renaud turned to go home, he felt a growing resolve to walk onto the porch.

This resolve left him as soon as he saw the women's faces all fixed on him.

But he continued forward in small steps on his pitifully small feet, past the Budds' house, across the road, through the yard between the maples, and onto the porch. He sat down in the rocking chair. Ellen Moody narrowed her eyes and looked at Marjorie meaningfully. When Mr. Renaud stood, put down his grocery bag, and adjusted the rocker over a warped board, moving it farther onto his side of the porch, Ellen raised an eyebrow and pursed her lips in a restrained smile.

Iva Lee stuck her spear into the ground beside the steps, and Carla grinned with a sinister expression.

"Mr. Renaud," Marjorie LeBlanc began. "We were just remarking on how pretty those red trees are." Later, Marjorie would grow to regret her simple words, which opened the first path between Ellen Moody and Mr. Renaud.

"I only thought," Mr. Renaud said in an airy voice like a broken reed. He cleared his throat. "I only thought I should do something in return for those beautiful flowers my new neighbor planted in the backyard." Oscar Renaud's heart pounded inside his chest, like the footsteps of a man fleeing across a wooden floor. He felt his face turning red.

Carla suddenly wondered what Mr. Renaud had thought when he found the plate inside his stove.

Faith Budd leaned over to sneak a look at Ellen Moody's cards, but Ellen put them face down on the table with an absentminded gesture. "I always did like wildflowers," she said in a conversational tone. "Some people think they're just weeds, but I like them because they're so hardy. I like flowers that have those kinds of seeds that grab onto your socks when you walk and the ones that travel hundreds of miles in the air. Everyplace Iva Lee and me have lived, I've planted wildflowers." Both girls noted with interest how an hour before, Iva Lee's mother had pronounced almost identical words but with an opposite feeling behind them.

"Have you lived a lot of places?" Mr. Renaud asked.

"TexasArkansasTennesseeLouisianaMississippi, then here. We've moved all over the states," said Mrs. Moody. "We like moving. Sometimes I just get this itch to go see a new place, and off we go."

"This time she's here to stay, though," said Carla's mother.

"That's nice to hear," said Mr. Renaud. He worried that his words sounded too forward. "Well, don't let me interrupt your game."

Faith Budd, who had a good hand, was itching to get back to the cards, but she said, "Would you like to join us? Do you know how to play hearts? We could always show you, if you don't know how." She hoped Mr. Renaud would refuse, as she really did not want to stop the game.

"Oh, no, no, well, that's—well, no," said Oscar Renaud. "I was really just going to—wash my car. And I noticed Mrs. Moody's Pontiac was—" He was going to say "dirty," but realized that didn't sound right. "I noticed your exhaust pipe was a little loose, and I thought I might be able to take a look at it."

"Oh, do you know about cars?" Mrs. Moody looked doubtfully at Mr. Renaud's disintegrating Plymouth, but said, "My battery's been dead since yesterday. I was going to get someone to jump it tomorrow."

"Oh, that's no trouble. I've got some cables in my trunk, and I can charge it for you right now."

"Well, that would be pretty nice."

Iva Lee and Carla followed Mr. Renaud over to the Plymouth, still carrying their spears. He pulled a cardboard box of metal parts from the back seat, and then took from the trunk a toolbox, a board on casters he called a dolly, a jumper cable, and four car antennas.

"Where'd you get all those?" asked Carla.

"At work," Mr. Renaud told her. "I work fixing cars." He had been pirating old antennas from the scrap heap behind Coleman's all week.

"You can make our radio work?" asked Iva Lee. "This boy Leroy Legree in Mississippi bent off our antenna and threw it into a soybean field."

"If you fix cars, how come this one is such a wreck?" said Carla, pointing to the Plymouth.

"I hate cars," said Mr. Renaud, matter-of-factly.

Carla and Iva Lee thought this was funny, and followed behind him, repeating to each other, "He hates cars! He hates cars!"

Mr. Renaud allowed Iva Lee to start his Plymouth. She handed her spear to Carla, turned on the ignition, and then slid over so that Mr. Renaud could pull the Plymouth alongside the Pontiac. They got out of the car, and he showed Carla how to fasten on the jumper cables. The girls laid down the spears on the grass, a few feet from the Pontiac.

Mr. Renaud worked the broken antenna out of its socket and fitted in a new one. Carla and Iva Lee told each other, "Like a glove!" and then pulled the dolly to the side of the Pontiac and slid under the car.

"Hey, Mr. Ree-node, what's your real name?" Iva Lee called.

"What?" Mr. Renaud's voice worked through the metal over them.

The girls pushed against the ground with their feet until

they poked out headfirst on the dolly under the passenger's side of the car.

"You know, your first name—what's your real name?"

"Oscar."

"Hi, Oscar!" said Carla, and the girls disappeared back under the car.

* * * *

The next Sunday, for Bertha's going-away party, Oscar Renaud made popcorn, laid out a dish of mixed nuts, and brought his stereo speakers onto the front porch. Marjorie, who liked musicals, put on *Man of La Mancha* and *Camelot* and *Brigadoon* and told him that the records sounded ten times better on his stereo than on her old record player. Faith Budd brought over Tennessee Ernie Ford and Glen Campbell, and Ellen Moody's eyes misted with tears as she listened to "Galveston." She told Oscar Renaud she thought it was the best song ever written.

Iva Lee and Carla sang "Galveston" over and over in a mournful, theatrical style, and then tried to sing James Taylor's "Fire and Rain" in serious voices.

Aunt Bertha stopped in the middle of raising a forkful of devil's food cake to her mouth, and said, "You sound like dying bloodhounds."

Carla barked at her, and Iva Lee sang, "but I always thought that I'd see you owooo!" and went back to cutting her piece of birthday cake with a jackknife.

Ruth and Sam LeBlanc howled from where they lay piled together in the hammock.

Karen helped Mrs. Moody carry out the butter pecan balls she'd baked especially for Bertha.

Oscar Renaud told Ellen Moody they were the best butter pecan balls he'd ever eaten in his life.

After that, things escalated. The following week, Bertha ran around the house in a flurry, packing up her books and files and index cards. Faith Budd and Marjorie loaded card-

board boxes and suitcases and coolers into Bertha's Ford
Falcon, and by the time they were done, Marjorie had become
all quiet and red-eyed. Oscar Renaud brought out some
Roman candles and giant sparklers from Myrtle Beach,
which Iva Lee and the LeBlancs set off in front of the Le-
Blancs' house as Bertha inched the Falcon down the driveway and Marjorie trotted beside her, crying and saying,
"You call me the minute you get there!" Faith Budd and
Oscar Renaud and Ellen Moody waved from the top of the
driveway, and Bertha honked the horn as her Ford Falcon
disappeared into the skyline at the top of the hill. Oscar
Renaud asked Ellen Moody if she would like to go to the
planetarium in Chapel Hill that Sunday night.

* * * *

Hearts was not a game that could be played by two people
alone, and so Faith Budd and Marjorie LeBlanc sat on the
duplex's porch, listlessly laying out a gin rummy game, while
Ellen Moody dressed up in the front room. Faith sat sideways in the hammock, her stomach bunched up between her
knees and chin, and Marjorie tilted forward in the wicker
chair. Even with Faith cheating, gin rummy was a dull game.
It lacked the potential for scheming and friendly animosity
inherent to hearts.

"I think you should be careful with those, Carla,"
Marjorie said to her daughter. Carla and Iva Lee had taken
out a cardboard box filled with used shotgun shells the girls
had been collecting all summer. They were scraping leftover
gunpowder from the shells with their knives, and emptying it
into a tobacco tin.

"Oh, we're just fooling around," said Iva Lee. "We already tried this before, and we couldn't even get the gunpowder to light on fire."

The whole truth was that two days earlier, Carla and Iva
Lee had taken a full tin of gunpowder to a cleared lot in an
area where new houses were being constructed. The lot was

covered with dry, yellow grass and bordered by two drainage ditches, a dirt road, and a weedy yard partly occupied by a new house in the finishing stages of construction. In the middle of the lot were some rusted cans, an old tarp, and a pile of broken bricks. Carla had taken a piece of cord soaked in kerosene from a plastic bag in her pocket and uncoiled the cord in a ten-foot line along the ground. The cord was to serve as a fuse. Iva Lee emptied gunpowder out of the tin onto one end of the cord, and covered the gunpowder with little stones, broken bricks, and bottle caps. The two girls lay down in a depression in the ground at the other end of the cord and set it on fire. They wanted to watch a little flame dance down the line and then explode the pile of gunpowder, as they had seen outlaws do on *Gunsmoke*.

A feeble orange light which occasionally burst into flame crept down the cord to the gunpowder, but no explosion followed. After five minutes, the girls smelled smoke, and saw that a patch of grass had caught fire. They stamped on it, but the fire only ran away between their feet, crackling in other clumps of grass. Finally, Iva Lee thought to pick up the tarp and throw it over the burning area. She and Carla stomped on the tarp, and the fire died down just as a young, blond-haired couple, holding hands but walking fast and looking worried, approached the girls from across the lot.

"We saw some boy over here lighting a fire!" Iva Lee yelled out to them. "He ran off when he saw us, and we just put it out in the nick of time!"

Carla thought it was funny the way the couple continued to hold hands as they stumbled over the bricks and cans in the lot.

"Where did he go?" the man asked. "Do you know who he was?"

"Don't know his name, but I've seen him before," Iva Lee said. "He's a big kid, about seventeen. He never wears a shirt and he's got a hairy chest and lives somewhere over thataway." She pointed in the general direction of the Budds' house, and the man and woman turned to look where she pointed. Carla picked up the tobacco tin. The gunpowder was gone, kicked into the air while the girls were putting out the fire.

"You see," said the young woman, "We were just over there looking at our new house, and I got so frightened when I saw a fire!"

Carla looked at the woman, poker-faced.

"Well, I guess it's out now," Iva Lee said. She and Carla walked away across the lot, and turned once to see the man and woman picking up the tarp and looking underneath it to assure themselves that the fire really had been extinguished.

When Carla and Iva Lee got back to the house, they noticed that their eyebrows and eyelashes were singed. The individual hairs had tiny balls of melted brow and lash at the ends. Neither of the girls' mothers had noticed. Carla and Iva Lee felt drawn together by the fact that they might be the only two people in the world with eyebrows and eyelashes that looked like theirs.

Now Carla and Iva Lee sat scraping the residue gunpowder out of the remaining shotgun shells, because the girls did not want to just heave the shells; they were obviously good for something. As Iva Lee bent her face over the tin, Carla leaned forward and said, "Partners in crime!"

"Partners in crime!" Iva Lee echoed, wiggling her burnt eyebrows. Iva Lee was in good spirits. Ellen Moody had been bustling back and forth through the front door all afternoon, trying on dresses, skirts, slacks, even her work uniforms, and asking Faith and Marjorie for their opinions. For Iva Lee, Ellen Moody's happiness and excitement were catching.

"You better hurry," Faith Budd called through the left front door of the duplex. "It's ten o' six!"

"How do I look?" Ellen's voice sailed through the doorway, slightly ahead of her. She was wearing a nylon dress Faith had lent her, with minute pink and yellow flowers running in a polka dot pattern over a green background. Ellen had put on a touch of pink lipstick. She held out a black patent leather purse and looked down at her navy-blue pumps. "Does this purse look really bad with these shoes?"

Iva Lee put down the tin and studied her mother, who rarely dressed up. "You look like a beautiful lady, Mama. Just so long as you never make me dress like that."

"Oh, you'll go to your own wedding in army boots," Ellen told her daughter.

"You'll be the belle of the ball!" said Marjorie. She imagined Oscar Renaud and Ellen dancing with other couples in the darkness of the planetarium.

"I'm not going to my wedding," Iva Lee answered her mother.

"It hurts my eyes to look at you," Faith pronounced.

Oscar Renaud knocked on the inside of his own door. He had stayed in his side of the house all day, not wanting to bother Ellen Moody as she tried on her clothes for her friends. He had busied himself perfecting oboe and bassoon reeds, mopping and waxing his linoleum floor, changing the sheets on his bed, and searching frantically through his closet for the necktie he always wore to the AA meetings but had been unable to find that morning. He finally discovered the necktie in his sock drawer. He dressed in his only shirt that had holes for cuff links, remembered he had lost his pair of cuff links ages ago, and then put on his green shirt, which was his favorite anyway.

When Oscar Renaud knocked, Marjorie cried, "Come out, come out, wherever you are!" He opened his door and looked at Ellen, as Marjorie and Faith stared at him.

"You look prettier than Elizabeth Taylor," Oscar Renaud thought to say, and then he turned a brighter shade of red than Carla and Iva Lee had imagined possible.

"You look like the cat's pajamas," Faith told him.

When Oscar and Ellen drove away toward the end of the street, Marjorie first imagined herself as Oscar Renaud, her heart racing faster than the Pontiac as it rounded the corner.

Then Marjorie imagined herself as Ellen Moody, her head held at a cocky angle and a smile playing on her lips as she contemplated how she felt about dating a homely man who had misbuttoned his shirt, so that his right collar edge seemed to be grabbing his left pocket in a fist. When the Pontiac's taillights flashed into darkness at the top of the hill, Marjorie felt as if she were nobody at all.

"I've never seen Ellen look so happy," said Faith Budd.

* * * *

Faith could have predicted what would happen next. Ellen Moody, who Faith had always known was something of a fly-by-night, gave Oscar Renaud free tickets to the ten o'clock shows and let Oscar drive her home from work at the movie theater. After only a few weeks, she allowed Oscar Renaud to sleep in the left half of the duplex. Ellen gained weight, and the hollows in her cheeks began to look like dimples. On the last warm Sunday in November, she leaned forward as she sat playing hearts on the porch with Marjorie and Faith, and said:

"Oscar's the sweetest man I've ever known. He's the *only* sweet man I've ever known." She looked across the front yard to where Oscar stood next to his Pontiac, teaching Carla and Iva Lee names for parts of the motor.

"I think it's so nice about you and Oscar," Marjorie answered her. And the sad thing, Faith thought, was that Marjorie meant what she said. Faith watched Marjorie's unmarriageable face, examining her crow's feet and the fading line that marked the curve of her top lip, and the white strands that had first appeared in her hair the week after her daughter Karen was born. And either because of or in spite of the fact that Faith had been married for twenty-five years to a man who rarely touched or looked at her, she felt a pain for her friend so sudden and piercing it made Faith think of a sewing machine needle.

"Marjorie!" Faith Budd cried out, and then had no idea

how to answer the surprised faces that Ellen and Marjorie
held up to her. Faith tucked a stray wisp of hair into her
topknot to buy time, and then she said, "Marjorie, watch
your cards! If you tilt them down like that you can hardly
expect a cheater like me to resist the temptation to look at
them."

"Oh, Faith, you were just born bad," Marjorie told her,
drawing her cards closer to her stomach in mock horror. The
two women waited for Ellen to play, and Marjorie cried,
"Cheater, cheater," when she played her own card and Faith
took the trick. Then Marjorie turned back to Ellen and said,
"You know, Carla thinks Oscar's the salt of the earth. He
just tickles those girls to death. He showed them how to hot-
wire a car just to make them giggle. Carla and Iva Lee came
over and started the Oldsmobile without a key! Ruth has
been calling them Bonnie and Clyde ever since, and Carla's so
full of herself she can hardly sit down. Oscar really has a
way with those girls. I like a man who isn't afraid of children."

"He used to teach music to grade schoolers in New York
City," said Ellen Moody. "He said the kids there pronounced
his name 'Ahskuh.' ' "

"New York City?" Marjorie said.

"He was a teacher?" asked Faith. She looked over at Oscar
Renaud's feet sticking out from the bottom of Ellen's Pontiac. Iva Lee's and Carla's feet poked out on either side of
his.

"For seven years," Ellen Moody answered. "Now that his
rough period is over and he's himself again—"

"Thanks to you," said Marjorie.

"—he's planning to go back to teaching. He's applied for
jobs all over the country, and he should be hearing back from
the schools sometime in November or December."

"Well, well," said Faith. She dealt a new game, and the
women played in silence for a few rounds. Every now and
then the voices of the girls vibrated in the air and pricked
Faith in the back.

"Mama, come getaloadathis," Iva Lee cried. "Come on, put down your cards and come looky this."

Ellen did as her daughter directed, and Faith and Marjorie followed single file down the stairs and across the yard. Iva Lee and Carla were bending together over the closed car hood, and Oscar Renaud was sliding out from under the Pontiac. Iva Lee stood back from the car, her chin pointing toward a hood ornament Carla was holding up on the front end of the Pontiac. Carla stood back, and all the women looked down at the hood ornament: a naked lady with outspread wings, her feet barely touching the car, as if she were about to jump upward into flight.

"Goodness!" Ellen Moody cried. "Wherever did you get that thing?"

Faith Budd thought the ornament looked a lot like one her son Lou used to have on the front of his Chevrolet, which she repeatedly had asked him to remove. It occurred to her that the girls had stolen the ornament from Lou, and then Faith was surprised by the next thought that came to her: Well, the joke's on him! She felt one of those moments of pleasurable spite toward her son that she had experienced occasionally with all her boys. After all, she thought to herself, no one could be expected to love them every minute of every day.

"Don't you like it?" Iva Lee asked her mother. "I want to drill some holes in the hood and fix the hood ornament on."

"It's supposed to be like a figurehead," Carla explained, while Oscar Renaud came up behind the women and turned red, as the women by now assumed he would.

"Not on my car," said Ellen Moody. "Not in public on the front of my car."

"OK, Mama," said Iva Lee. "Just thought I'd try." Carla handed Iva Lee the ornament, which Iva Lee had stolen from Lou Budd's car two nights before, while Carla had been siphoning gasoline from his tank. Iva Lee held up the ornament like a trophy.

"My Pontiac sure looks like new," said Ellen. "Oscar's

done every little thing imaginable to it. It's such an art to know how to fix cars."

"I'll be glad to get out of this line of work," Oscar said modestly.

Marjorie stood back to admire the car. It still looked rusty in places and hadn't been cleaned in weeks, but Marjorie accepted on faith that the inner workings of the Pontiac had been improved through skills beyond her comprehension.

"It sure is nice you're teaching Carla about mechanical things," said Marjorie. "Heaven knows we could use a fix-it man around the house." She added, "It's hard being a woman alone, you know. People like plumbers and mechanics love to take advantage of you." Carla rolled her eyes, because she believed she had heard this line at least one thousand times in her life. Marjorie, who was not looking at Carla, continued: "Once when I had a man tune up the Oldsmobile, he charged me a hundred dollars, and I swear after that it worked worse than before. I wondered if he'd stolen a part."

"Well, maybe I could take a look at it for you?" Mr. Renaud asked.

"Oh, no! I wasn't hinting," Marjorie said, embarrassed. "I was just thinking out loud. The car's not giving me any kind of trouble right now."

"They won't get away with cheating Mama again," said Carla. "Next time I'll hang over their shoulder like a vulture. I'll make sure they do just what we did on the Pontiac."

Iva Lee patted the Pontiac. "This car's ready to go places," she said.

"I think it's in decent shape for a long journey," Oscar Renaud agreed.

Marjorie did not assign any special meaning to his words.

* * * *

However, two Sundays later, Faith Budd was not surprised when Ellen Moody leaned over the Thanksgiving turkey she was cleaning and said, "I'm afraid I've got some good news. Iva Lee's already told Carla."

Iva Lee and Carla were laying out items from a box containing things Iva Lee had collected: a bird's nest, a geode, a silver dollar, the tobacco tin filled with gunpowder (which also belonged partly to Carla), bottle caps Oscar Renaud had given Iva Lee, and above all, the winged naked lady hood ornament, the prize of the collection. Iva Lee had promised to let Carla keep the hood ornament as a Christmas present.

Marjorie, who was concentrating on scraping a can of cranberries into a double boiler, was only half listening to Ellen. Faith Budd busied herself mincing chicken livers and gizzards to make stuffing. Marjorie, Faith, and Ellen had been playing hearts that morning in the front room, because the weather had turned too cold for the porch, and as Marjorie emptied out the last cranberry, she noticed that the jack of diamonds had slipped to the floor near the couch. She put down the double boiler and picked up the card so that it wouldn't be lost, preparing to slide it into the box with the others.

"Oscar got a job in Wyoming!" Ellen Moody pronounced. "I'm so excited. Wyoming!" She gave the turkey an enthusiastic pat. "I've never been to a place so far up on the map." Marjorie stopped dead, holding the card before the lip of the box.

Iva Lee and Carla sang in a cowboy accent:

> It's yer misforchun
> And noner my own.
> Yippy Hi-yai-yay
> Git along little doagie
> You know that Wyomin'
> Will be yer new home.

"You're not thinking of leaving us?" Marjorie asked Ellen. Marjorie dropped onto the couch, letting the jack of diamonds slip to the floor. Faith Budd watched Ellen and noted that she did not have the courage to face Marjorie.

"Oh, I know I'll just cry myself silly the day we leave," said Ellen. "But we've got to be there right after Christmas. Wyoming!"

Marjorie wanted to say: "But you're not even engaged. But you haven't known him half as long as you've known me." She wanted to get up and throw the double boiler at the far wall and run out the front door, up the hill to her house. She wished she could grab Ellen Moody from behind and shake her. But something held Marjorie still: It was as if a strong man had grabbed her by the shoulders and was pinning her to the couch. She could not arrange the thoughts she needed to string together to say what she wanted to say. "You can't leave me for a man!" were the only words she could think of, and even to her they did not sound right.

Carla picked up the winged hood ornament, lay down on the carpet, closed her eyes, and pictured a snowy landscape with cows and horses wading across it. Behind them came Iva Lee, riding a buckskin mule. Carla felt exhilarated, as if by virtue of being Iva Lee's closest friend, Carla herself could be there in the landscape too. Iva Lee would carry away to Wyoming that part of Carla which Iva Lee knew. Carla saw herself wading across an ocean of snow. The wind bit her cheeks, and when she breathed in, the cold air had an exciting, minty taste and the cattle seemed to be walking upward into an endless blue sky, as if even the earth did not set limits on where they could go.

5. Rebellion

SAM LEBLANC, DON'T LEAVE ME

Faith Budd, Marjorie LeBlanc's last and only friend in the world, had been in Florida since April. Bertha was spending the summer of 1972 in Iceland, excavating bones and pot shards and ancient houses and Marjorie did not know what else. It was June, and Marjorie felt desolate. She clattered aimlessly around her home like a kicked can. Weekends were the worst. She would pull herself out of bed, make a pot of coffee as dark as nightshade, and spend the day cleaning the kitchen or shampooing the rugs. Marjorie felt as if her life had been strung together with long periods of uselessness and lonesomeness. Here and there on the long river she had to follow was an island of friendship: Rita or Faith, Bertha or even Ellen Moody, or the children in the moments when they weren't flying off somewhere. But mostly it was Marjorie LeBlanc alone against the world.

It was because she had never remarried. Faith could always say, "I've got to run home and fix Franklin Delano some supper." Ellen Moody had sent out Christmas cards with a picture of Oscar Renaud and herself watching Iva Lee race down a hill in a tobogan. Marjorie LeBlanc wasn't tied to anyone; she just had to grab on here and there when people would let her. When the children ran off and forgot her, she'd hardly be more than a leaf in the wind. Marjorie would never understand Bertha, the way she actually seemed to like being on her own, as if work were enough to live for. Marjorie couldn't imagine living for her nursing job; after working all day, she felt half dead.

When Marjorie stepped into the hospital, she put herself on hold. She joked with the other nurses and the hospital aides, and sometimes they met after work or on weekends, but it seemed mutually understood that no one really wanted to see anyone associated with the hospital after hours. They shucked each other off like so many uniforms and went back to their lives. Even after all these years, Marjorie had never actually come to think of herself as a nurse—she felt more as if she were dressing up in nurse's clothes to humor life's demand that she make money to raise her children. Not that she didn't take her work seriously while she was doing it. It was just that the real Marjorie LeBlanc was someone else, the person she inhabited in her real life. But then, who was that, exactly? Marjorie couldn't say. There had been times—after friends moved away, or whenever Bertha's visits ended—when Marjorie had sensed herself dwindling away, when she had felt as if she were hardly more than a breath and a thought.

Once, at the hospital, Marjorie had seen a case of what the doctors called "stocking and glove hysteria" and what Marjorie diagnosed to herself as an incurable case of lonesomeness. The woman patient had come down from a hospital in the mountains. She had been unable to move her hands and feet, although the doctors could not find any physical cause for the loss of control. Marjorie knew what it was: You only had to look into the lady's eyes to see they had that kind of bottomless, farsighted glassiness eyes got if they stared too long at all the things that made you feel left behind, at horizons and at semitrucks pulling over far-off hilltops. Some mornings, it was everything Marjorie could do to move her feet up and down all the times it took to walk to the kitchen. This morning, when she thought of the name "stocking and glove" she imagined her arms and legs were unoccupied pieces of cloth, Raggedy Ann limbs. But really, they were funny words to use for sickness—they made Marjorie think of some rich European lady with elbow-length gloves and silk hose.

Marjorie pulled on her bathrobe and opened her bedroom door. She heard her son Sam, and Lorna Winsted and her little boy, talking in the kitchen. Marjorie shut the door and sat back down on the bed. She did not need to eavesdrop. She did not meddle in her son's affairs, even though Hope George had told Marjorie that the Winsteds were trash. Marjorie liked it when Lorna came over, and not just because Marjorie had felt an affinity with the Winsteds ever since Lorna's sister Jeannette dropped a lead pipe from a Ferris wheel onto the children's father, seven years before. Lorna said it had been an accident, but Marjorie couldn't be sure. Marjorie liked the way Lorna sat in the kitchen, laughing and talking her head off, scaring away the silence in the house. Besides, she was over twenty, with a five-year-old child, and she and Sam seemed to be friends only, and not romantically inclined. Sam had met Lorna through his summer job busboying at the Whiteside Manor Country Club. Faith Budd would like her.

Faith's absence was such a sharp pain that sometimes Marjorie could not even remember what it had been like having her friend around. Faith was visiting her mother, who had just had an operation and was recuperating at her sister's house. Faith had called Marjorie from Florida City and said in a low voice, "This place is crawling with relatives." After that, the whole conversation had taken place in a whisper. Faith told Marjorie, "Sometimes I wonder if it's even Mama. She's all skin and bones, there isn't the ghost of how she looked in her. I have to clean her and change her and everything, and meanwhile Uncle Barry expects me to muck out the toilet and mop the floors. I think Mama enjoys it. She's getting stronger every day, but she won't let on. I hope I don't drop dead before I leave. I can't stand it here much longer—makes me feel like a girl again."

If you hated it all that much, you'd come back home, Marjorie had wanted to say.

"I do like the beaches, though. I even took a little trip in the car and went on a hydrofoil through the Everglades. I saw some alligators. Of course, mostly I'm not having any fun at all, just looking after Mama."

Marjorie had been surprised to find out that Faith's mother was still living. When Faith and Marjorie sat on the porch discussing the injustices of childhood, Faith always talked about her mother as if she were a thing of the past, and not just living in another state. Faith would tell Marjorie, "I can't remember one scene from my girlhood but my mother wasn't standing there with her face red as a cardinal and her mouth open, screeching something at me. It's a miracle I'm not deaf. That's why I never raised my voice to my little boys." Or she'd say, "I've always been a late riser, because my mother got up at the crack of dawn, and the only time we got along was when one of us was sleeping."

Marjorie on the other hand talked about her mother, who had been dead for seventeen years, as if she were still alive. Marjorie was almost thirty-eight years old, but a week didn't pass when Geraldine LeBlanc's voice didn't well up inside her and say, "That's very nice, Honey" or "You little monster! I can't believe you're my own daughter." When Dr. Mooks at the hospital would loiter around a patient while Marjorie was trying to turn her over or give her an injection, it was all Marjorie could do to keep from saying, "Get out from underfoot!" or, to Dr. Leaks, "I should beat you until you can't stand up." The way he'd push you into a corner and put his big ugly face up next to yours when all you wanted to do was go about your business.

Marjorie had never talked back on the job, however. This was also because she was her mother's daughter. Marjorie wanted to look dignified at work and not be joking around like a crowd of women on somebody's front steps. The year Dr. Leaks kept taking out people's parts without good reason, Nurse Arrington would say to his back whenever he walked by, "What *he* needs is to have his pancreas taken out." Marjorie would laugh, but she never dared to talk that way herself.

Marjorie pulled on her nurse's shoes. They wouldn't keep her feet from hurting, but at least her legs wouldn't swell up and ache as much as they did with other shoes.

Marjorie thought of the year her father had been transferred to the Veterans Hospital in Temple, Texas. While Willie LeBlanc worked twelve-hour days bent over his x-ray technician's machines in the hospital, Geraldine LeBlanc convinced all the society women in Temple that she came from a wealthy family with oil interests in the Gulf. She dropped her Louisiana accent and developed a Texas drawl, which she knew to be more refined. She held teas and gossiped with the doctors' wives and helped them decide who was trashy and who was not. If someone told Geraldine, "Morna Hincock is the lowest kind of trash you can find in east Texas," Geraldine would nod solemnly and say, "I *pity* her, that's what. I don't think two of those children have the same father." And the society women would cluck, and sip their iced tea, never dreaming that Geraldine's own mother had been a washerwoman who had eight daughters and no husband.

Lorna laughed loudly in the kitchen, and Marjorie heard her say, "So Jeannette told him, 'You can lie there and cry your eyes out, Sugar. I'm too old to mercy-fuck anymore.' "

Marjorie's stomach grumbled. She tightened her bathrobe belt and made her way toward the kitchen. Sam was sitting opposite Lorna, and her son, Dace, was perched on Sam's shoulders and holding on to his forehead. Marjorie thought of a postcard of a totem pole Bertha had sent once, with a little face grinning on top of a large one. Dace still had all his baby teeth, and rust-red hair that matched his tie-dyed undershirt.

Sam leaned forward and Dace widened his eyes and mouth in astonishment and said, "Whooooah." Seated, Sam was the same height as Marjorie when she stood, so that she had to look up at Dace. At seventeen, Sam had grown far enough beyond six feet that some people calculated his height at seven feet. His long face sloped down into a row of perfectly straight underbitten teeth, which he flashed at Marjorie as she came into the kitchen. Lorna had her back to Marjorie and kept talking.

"Jeanette says, Think of it like this. You're walking down the street at night and someone comes up behind you and holds a knife to your throat. Don't no one have to tell you it's a man. You know it's a man. No way can it be a lady. Jeannette says that's how and why she don't like men anymore. It's not men in particular once you get to know them; it's all the men out there that you haven't met yet. She says you have to hate the ones you don't know, just to stay alive. See, once Jeannette was standing out on the dock at Myrtle Beach, dropping down bacon on a string to catch some crabs. She had a bottle of Boone's Farm strawberry wine with her, and she was looking out over the ocean. All of a sudden, this arm comes out of thin air and wraps her around the waist."

Marjorie dumped two heaping spoonfuls of coffee into her mug and felt a shiver go up her spine as she put the water on to boil. She dropped two English muffins in the toaster so that she would have an excuse to stay in the kitchen and listen longer. Since Sam knew she was there, it wouldn't be eavesdropping.

"Jeanette said that at first she felt her whole body freeze. She couldn't make herself turn to look. She said she felt like maybe if she stood real still, that arm would just disappear, like it wasn't any more real than the moon bobbing on the water.

"She says all sorts of funny things went through her head. Like: 'It's funny how I know it's a man and couldn't be a lady, even though I can't see him.' 'This bottle is shaped just like a woman with a long dress.' 'If he disappears, I am going to stay here looking at the water, and then I'll come back here every night the rest of my life and stand on the edge of the sea braiding my hair and looking at that row of lights right there.' She thought things like that. Then she said she felt her hand jerk her shoulder around so that the bottle broke on the man's ear and he hit his head hard on the post sticking up on the dock and fell off it. Jeannette saw his shadow falling, and the shadow of the knife in his hand, and his necktie sticking out like an arm wanting to break his fall, and then he made a splash and was gone. To this day, Jeannette don't know if her mind was tricking her, cooking it all up, or if it really happened."

When it seemed as if Lorna had stopped talking, Sam said, "So who found the body?"

"Hi, Mizz LeBlanc," Lorna told Marjorie.

"Hi there. What a story to hear before morning coffee! You want an English muffin, Pumpkin?" Marjorie asked Dace.

"Yeah."

"Yeah what?" Lorna asked.

"Yeah, please."

Sam remembered when he had fished off a dock once, near Cape Hatteras. Someone had lent him a fishing pole with a fancy reel and a ten-foot rod. He was going to catch snapper blues. But it turned out you didn't need a fancy reel. All you had to have was about ten feet of line tied to the top of a pole, and you hardly even needed to use bait. The baby blues were so crazy they would throw themselves on the hooks. He had even caught one by the tail. Sam was filled with a sudden longing to go fishing. He could see the ocean in front of him, churning with baby blues. Then he saw a man swimming toward the fishing pole, doing an Australian crawl, a knife still in his hand. He came to the dock and held out his arm, and Sam pulled him up.

"It was a misunderstanding!" the man cried. "It was dark and I thought she was my wife. She told me she was going down to the dock to fish, and I was just bringing her the scaling knife."

"Jeanette's been going to these secret women's meetings in Chapel Hill," Lorna told Marjorie.

"Sounds like fun." Secret from whom? Marjorie wondered.

"There isn't a thing they don't talk about. Sometimes they mostly complain about their boyfriends, but then sometimes they talk about sex murders, and Jeannette tells me all about it. Last night it was on mercy-fucking. Excuse my French."

"Hun, you want some strawberry jam?" Marjorie said, looking in the refrigerator.

"Yeah, thanks," said Lorna. Sam watched Lorna frown as she tried to unscrew the lid to the jam jar. "Won't budge," she said, shaking her wrist from the effort. Then she banged the jar on the edge of the table, the jar made a sighing sound, and Lorna opened it with a delicate twist of her hand. Lorna was tall, with dirty hair she pulled back into an oily ponytail. Her ears were small and stuck out. Almost every day for a month, Lorna had worn the same pair of cutoff shorts and a yellow bandanna she had sewed into a middy blouse, which she tied just above her navel. She had long, knobby legs, and her stomach was perfectly flat and decorated with stretch marks. Sometimes she smelled like the incense sticks she burned in her room, and sometimes like marijuana, and other times she had a strong odor that filled Sam with an overpowering feeling of longing, a cross between the smell of bacon cooking and burning leaves. Sam knew that Lorna was too much older than he was to take him seriously, and he respected her as a friend and did not press her to be anything else. But what he wanted to know was why the one woman who liked him wouldn't sleep with him, when he knew dozens of boys who were total assholes and had all the girlfriends they wanted.

Sam imagined himself lying on a stretcher on the side of the road, the last of the nice men left in the world. A Ford pickup had hit him and left him there. Lorna bent over him, wringing her hands and saying, "Sam! Sam LeBlanc, don't leave me."

"What's mercy you-know-whating mean?" Marjorie finally made herself ask. She pulled the English muffins out of the toaster and handed one to Lorna and a half muffin up to Dace. She handed the other half to Sam, but he did not notice. He was off daydreaming somewhere. He was always drifting away to another world.

"You know, where you sleep with a guy just because you feel sorry for him. Well, *I* sure know better than that by now." She looked up meaningfully at Dace's head and added, "You Know Who was this poor tired army man from Georgia, and Dace's hair's exactly the color of Georgia red clay. But who could care less?"

Lorna stood up and peered through the kitchen door. "There's that Mrs. Katerwaller," said Lorna. Marjorie watched Mrs. Katerwaller drive slowly down the road in her gigantic blue Lincoln. "My mother once cleaned house for a whole month for those Katerwallers. Their maid, Gracie McPherson, quit on them because Mr. Katerwaller was always rubbing up against her. Gracie said the Katerwallers never even picked their underwear up off the floor. She says Mr. Katerwaller's a redneck slimeball from Winston-Salem, always off rooting around like a pig with its nose in the ground for a piece of some woman and hardly comes home. Mrs. Katerwaller just sits by herself all day, reading books on the patio. Mama says when she went to work there, the bathroom smelled like the inside of a garbage truck and looked like the men's room in a service station. Sam and me have seen Mr. Katerwaller at the Whiteside Manor dining room with women-not-his-wife, but when Mrs. Katerwaller comes in with him, they both act so prim and proper you'd think they'd never seen themselves naked."

* * * *

Before he started working as a busboy at Whiteside Manor Country Club, Sam LeBlanc had longed for years to meet the Winsteds. Near the high school was a section of street where everyone looked like a Winsted—there were Lorna's mother and Jeannette, Lorna and her baby, and four or five other girls, who all loitered on the front steps of a brick apartment building, smoking or eating honeydew melons or listening to the radio and dancing to "My Baby Does the Hanky-Panky," or anything else they felt like doing. Sam had once seen a Winsted give a baby a sip of hard liquor, and two of the Winsted women sat together on the windowsill one day, wearing orange sundresses and no underwear. When Sam was in ninth grade, a Winsted had once leaned out her window in a yellow slip and called, "Hey, Sugar," and then waved to Sam and pulled down the window shade. Sam could not believe his luck when he applied for a job busboying at Whiteside Manor and discovered that Lorna Winsted had been working there for a year.

Whiteside Manor Country Club had that subtle elegance acquired only through a firm sense of history and tradition. It had a place to check coats, for instance, and if a young man happened to forget to dress appropriately, there was another cloakroom in the back, with suit jackets and ties that could be borrowed without a fee. Beside the register at the dining room exit was a scalloped crystal dish filled with green and white anisette mints. Diners were guided into the dusky rooms by the club's manager, a brittle, well-dressed widow with an opal brooch, named Mrs. John T. Rollins. She could tell you that an unescorted woman had never set foot in the Whiteside Manor dining room. Mrs. Rollins was the widow of an ex-president of the club, and Lorna said it was the spirit of John T. lurking around the barstools that kept Mrs. Rollins from being thought of as an unescorted woman. Mrs. Rollins received no salary; she managed the club restaurant out of a sense of civic duty.

The Whiteside Manor Country Club restaurant did not employ waitresses, whom Mrs. Rollins associated with pancake houses and truck stops; there were waiters dressed in black jackets and ties, and the country club was so refined that even the waiters were white. The dishwasher, Allison Paley, was black, and so were class two busboys, who cleared the dishes and plates. But then class one busboys, who served water, butter, rolls, and the pickle plates, were white. The butter they served came in precut squares stamped with a crown, and they poured ice water into goblets too fine to be run through a regular dishwasher. At the Whiteside Manor dining room, when judges sat down with doctors and senators and architects, the radishes in their pickle dishes were decorated with little flutes, and the cucumbers had been cut with a zigzag pattern.

Lorna Winsted, the assistant cook, was paid minimum wage for her work with the pickle dishes. She sliced and peeled vegetables slowly, with a sneer on her face, and sat next to Allison Paley, whose responsibilities included cleaning the water goblets too fine to be put through the dishwasher. There were three sinks, one each for washing, rinsing, and disinfecting the goblets, in the spare room off the kitchen where Lorna and Allison worked. On Sam's first day at Whiteside Manor, Mrs. John T. Rollins stood nodding behind the headwaiter as he explained to Sam that class one busboys had to first water the clients, and then butter and roll them, always from the proper side. As Sam stood listening, he saw Lorna put a whole green olive into her mouth and then spit it back out into a newly prepared pickle dish.

After Mrs. John T. Rollins left the kitchen, Allison pulled two goblets from the disinfecting sink and cheered, "Water 'em, roll 'em, butter 'em, screw 'em."

Lorna parceled the carrots onto the pickle plates and said, "Mrs. John T. Rollins is a gold-plated bitch who could piss through flint rock." Lorna looked up at Sam and dazzled him with her smile. Then she handed a bundle of peeled and quartered carrots to Allison, who passed them through the soapsuds in the first sink, rinsed them and then dunked them in the dish-disinfecting solution, and handed the carrots back to Lorna, who parceled them out onto the pickle plates.

Sam had to buy a pair of thirty-dollar black wing-tip shoes, and a ridiculous black cummerbund and jacket, custom-made in downtown Durham. He spent his first week of work earning back the money he had spent on his uniform. The only employees who did not wear uniforms were the cooks and the dishwashers. Lorna was into women's liberation and would not even wear a hairnet, and Allison had radical-looking short hair, and usually came to work in a man's jumpsuit that said "Fred's Diner" on the breast pocket.

Business was slow, because most of the club members sat at the bar, where they became too drunk to navigate their way to the tables. When Sam was not busy, he would sit in the kitchen alcove, rolling his own cigarettes and listening to Lorna and Allison talk. Lorna's sister Jeannette was moving to Alaska because people said that there was work aplenty there and you could earn two hundred and fifty dollars a week just waiting tables. Lorna and Allison talked about going with Jeannette. Allison wanted to see her brother Clinton, who was living in Canada, near Alaska, evading the draft, and she said she'd be glad to live anywhere north of North Dakota. Lorna then turned to Sam and asked him if he had thought about how he was going to evade the draft.

Sam sensed that Lorna and Allison were not going to pay him a moment's notice unless he convinced them he was politically cool. The next day, Sam brought to work the letters that Blue Henry, who was three years older than Sam, had sent him from Vietnam. The letters said:

Dear Sam,
Stay the fuck away from Uncle Sam.

> *Sinsirly,*
> *Blue*

Dear Sam,
I mint to write, I cant remember if I did. I just want to tell you, stay the fuck out of here.

> *Blue*

Dear Sam,
Do what you can to stay the fuck out of here.

Blue

Sam told Lorna and Allison that he and Blue had bought some Boone's Farm apple wine one morning and driven in Blue's pickup to the city limits for the purpose of getting drunk enough to shoot each other in the foot with Blue's shotgun, in order to cripple themselves and render each other unfit for military service. But in the end they lost courage and spent the afternoon shooting at highway road signs.

Sometimes the club members drinking at the bar demanded Sam's audience and would not let him escape back to the dish room to be with Lorna and Allison. The hardest people Sam had to deal with on the job were the state senator and Bobby Sanford, the Duke medical student. They would come in around ten o'clock at night, and by eleven they were drunk and by twelve blind drunk and by one stinking drunk. The state senator would grab Sam by the back of his cummerbund and say Sam was just like his own son, and tell him, "Listen to this, listen to this," trying to include him in conversations with Bobby Sanford. Bobby turned out to have gone to the same northern men's college as Byron Coffin, and so Sam listened to Bobby with some curiosity. Bobby liked to talk about his college days. He said there weren't many places left in the world where men could get together to be men, and that the day his college let in females he personally would never give it another dime, no matter how many games the football team won. He talked at length about those nights he had spent in college when buses came from neighboring girls' schools. He laughed uproariously when he told Sam that the buses were called fuck trucks. Bobby Sanford shared with Sam the secrets of fraternity initiation rituals, in which seniors tested freshmen's capacity for trust and love by shaving their heads, or drunkenly swinging chain saws near their faces, or sodomizing them. Bobby said that he would die before the day came when they let faggots into his fraternity, a national organization that had been around for fifty years and would be around another fifty thousand more.

After listening to Bobby Sanford, Sam decided he did not want to go to college. What he really wanted to do was go to Alaska with Lorna Winsted and Allison Paley. Sam did whatever he could, in addition to trying to keep up with their politics, to get on their good sides. When Allison wanted to step outside to smoke a cigarette, Sam would stay in the dish room and watch out for Mrs. Rollins. When Lorna brought her son to work, Sam would sometimes take Dace outside and let him light Sam's cigarettes, or Sam would make smoke rings or blow smoke out of his nose to entertain Dace.

In mid-June, Sam was sitting in the back parking lot of Whiteside Manor, showing Dace how to roll an unlit cigarette from one side of his mouth to the other, when Allison came running across the street by the parking lot, late for work. She was wearing her jumpsuit. She was tall for a girl, and her short hair and jumpsuit made her look almost like a man.

Just as Allison reached halfway across the second lane, Mr. Katerwaller's car shot out of the parking lot in an attempt to make a yellow light and almost hit her. The light turned red, and Mr. Katerwaller put on the brake at the last possible moment. Sam recognized the car before he did the driver. Mr. Katerwaller's car was a 1965 yellow Chrysler New Yorker, too big to fit in one lane. There was a tenth grade girl from Sam's high school named Carol Buttons sitting in the seat next to Mr. Katerwaller. She hid her face behind her brown suede purse when she saw Sam.

Mr. Katerwaller leaned out of his window and yelled at Allison, "You big ugly black ape! What the hell you doing in the middle of the road!"

Allison stopped where she was, her right knee grazing the front bumper of the Chrysler. She walked around to the passenger-seat window and leaned her head in, over the suede purse.

She told Mr. Katerwaller: "You're a dumb hick asshole who can't keep his own fly zipped."

Mr. Katerwaller threw open his car door dramatically and stood up. Allison straightened and stepped back from the car. Sam could not see Allison's face, but he could see Mr. Katerwaller's and thought he appeared stunned, like a person who has encountered his own ghost. The cars behind him, which could not fit around the Chrysler, began honking, and the driver directly in back of the Chrysler leaned on his horn. Carol Buttons reached across the car seat and tugged Mr. Katerwaller's jacket, whispering something in a high, frantic voice. Mr. Katerwaller glanced down at her, and then got back in his car and slammed the door. The Chrysler jumped forward under the light.

The next day, Mrs. Rollins fired Allison when she arrived for work. Sam pointed out Mr. Katerwaller's family car, a large blue Lincoln on the far side of the parking lot. On her way out the back door into the parking lot, Allison picked up a piece of pipe from the garbage can, and while Sam kept a lookout on the steps, she battered the back fender of the Lincoln until there was a square depression the size of a kitchen sink over the left tire.

ADVENTURES
WITH HELEN KATERWALLER

On a dreary Saturday morning in mid-June, Marjorie spent three hours making an angel food cake with drip-down orange-coconut icing. She was going to bring the cake to Mrs. Katerwaller as a present. Now Marjorie walked across the vacant lot between the LeBlancs' house and the road leading to the Katerwallers', holding the cake tightly against her side. Ordinarily, she would not have dreamed of visiting Mrs. Katerwaller, but that morning when Marjorie woke up, she had felt desperate, and hadn't Lorna said Mrs. Katerwaller spent too much time alone?

In the past ten years, Marjorie had talked to Mrs. Katerwaller rarely. Marjorie went to the Georges' Christmas party almost every year, and the Katerwallers were always there. No one else from the neighborhood was invited. Mr. George was an important real estate broker, and Marjorie suspected Hope George invited her because Hope thought Marjorie had a better education than she really did, or came from a wealthier background than in fact was true. Marjorie vaguely remembered having once led Hope to believe that Willie Le-Blanc had been a high-ranking member of the A.M.A. And then Marjorie had mentioned to Mrs. Katerwaller in Hope's presence that Marjorie's own sister, Bertha, had an advanced degree.

Still, Marjorie had never seriously considered Mrs. Katerwaller as a possible friend. Mrs. Katerwaller came from money. Marjorie believed it was Louisiana hot pepper money. Mr. Katerwaller owned something having to do with cigarettes, and he came from money too. Tobacco money. He drove a car the size of a house and dressed to the nines.

The Katerwallers' brick house had been built in the neighborhood before the neighborhood had crept that far down the road. Marjorie thought of the Katerwallers' as a sort of reverse eyesore. The house had a lawn and front garden as manicured as a fancy cemetery, and a patio in the back. As Marjorie crested the rise in the vacant lot, she could see the patio across the road, behind a curtain of oak and pine trees. Marjorie headed toward the trees, avoiding the middle of the lot, which was overgrown with blackberries and poison ivy, and walked along the edge near a gully. She stepped over broken bottles and used condoms, rusted contortions of wire and an ancient piece of electric-train track, and as she reached the row of pines, she saw Mrs. Katerwaller sitting on the patio.

Both Mrs. Katerwaller and the patio were like nothing else on the block. The patio was covered with wrought-iron chairs painted white, and in the center was a table made of a sheet of glass balanced on white metal legs. There was a green and yellow umbrella over the table, and all around the patio were

ceramic pots full of geraniums. The patio was swept so clean
it hurt Marjorie's eyes to look at. And Mrs. Katerwaller
looked like a movie star. Like Grace Kelly. Her yellow hair
was pulled back in a chiffon scarf, and she had on a yellow
gauzy thing tied at the waist with a gold chain belt, and gold
sandals that laced halfway up her legs. She even had on lipstick, although she did not seem in a hurry to go anywhere.
She was reading a hardback book, and there was a tray with
a pitcher of iced tea and two turned-over glasses next to it, as
if Mrs. Katerwaller might be expecting someone. Marjorie,
who was wearing a flowered shift that looked as if it was
made from upholstery material, decided to turn back, but her
feet kept going forward, so she followed them through a
clump of trees, past a stone birdbath, and onto the patio. An
overpowering tobacco smell rose from the flowerpots of
geraniums.

"Hey there, Helen!" Marjorie cried through the trees. "I
just thought I'd bring you a little angel food cake!"

Mrs. Katerwaller looked up, startled. She peered at
Marjorie as if trying to place her, and then said, "Well,
Margie LeBlanc, come over here and take a seat. You're just
in time for some ice tea. Mr. Katerwaller was going to join
me, but he had to fly out of the house on a moment's notice."

Helen put down the book, turned over the glasses, and
poured some tea. Marjorie put the cake next to the book,
which was called *The King Must Die*. Helen set down the
glasses but did not say anything about the cake. Marjorie
saw a plate of Pepperidge Farm cookies behind the iced tea
pitcher. They were fancy cookies, delicate flutes with choco-
laty edges.

Marjorie sat down, glancing at the cake as if it were a child
she feared might misbehave. It was heaped with coconut
gratings and was a brighter orange than Marjorie had
thought. Maybe she had used too much food coloring. She
couldn't think of a thing to say. She squeezed some lemon
into her iced tea. Helen Katerwaller watched her the whole

time, without speaking. When Marjorie finished with the lemon, Helen told her, "Mr. Katerwaller's gone to a special meeting at the Masonic Temple."

Marjorie thought of repeating something Faith Budd had once said she'd heard somewhere. The Masons cut you on the hand with a knife, suck your blood, spit it into a dish, and then write your name on a wall with the blood. They could tell the exact date of your death by looking at your name, and nothing you did could change your fate after that. Marjorie giggled.

"Pardon?" Helen Katerwaller looked questioningly at Marjorie.

Marjorie decided not to risk telling the story to Helen. Then Marjorie thought of something else: how her daughter Ruth had once yelled out when Mr. George drove by in his Shriners' hat, "There goes the Grand Imperial Wizard!" Marjorie decided not to say that, either.

"You have the most beautiful geraniums," she told Mrs. Katerwaller. "Try as I might, I never can get them to bloom like that."

"I use a tobacco leaf mulch. And then I fertilize them once a month with dried beef blood and bonemeal," Helen Katerwaller answered.

"The tobacco doesn't crinkle up the roots?" Marjorie asked.

"Not to my knowledge."

Marjorie nodded. The angel food cake seem to have slumped toward Mrs. Katerwaller. *Menacing,* Marjorie thought. It looks menacing, as if it's trying to protect me. She had to drink her iced tea all the way to the bottom to keep from giggling again.

Mrs. Katerwaller saw Marjorie staring at the cake and said, "Would you like me to get a knife and cut you a piece? I'm afraid I'm going to have to do without. I'm saving room for a big dinner tonight. Mr. Katerwaller's taking me to a special buffet at the Whiteside Manor Country Club. Do you

know it? Mr. Rollins' widow, Ladybird, helps keep it together, and everything there is done so tastefully—do you remember Mr. Rollins from Hope's Christmas party a few
years ago? He was a fine figure of a man, let me tell you. If
he'd lived, I believe he would have been a North Carolina con-
gressman."

"My son has a summer job at the Whiteside Manor!"
Marjorie answered, beginning to get a toehold in the conversation.

"Oh?" said Mrs. Katerwaller. "I think that's important,
for young men to work in the summer. It gives them character."

"Sam's working there as a busboy," Marjorie said, leaning
closer to Helen.

"Oh, I see," said Helen, leaning back.

Marjorie thought Helen looked worried about something.
It occurred to Marjorie that Mrs. Katerwaller might be such
a snob that she didn't approve. No, thought Marjorie. No
one's that much of a snob.

But Mrs. Katerwaller was smiling politely, her mouth
drawn up in the same expression she might have worn if she
had just bitten into a lemon. Mrs. Katerwaller seemed to
want to end the conversation.

Although Sam was working in order to help pay for his
school supplies and clothes in the fall, Marjorie said, " 'Of
course,' I told Sam, 'you don't have to work, Honey. You
should take off a little time and enjoy yourself. After all,
you're only young once!' But he has a mind of his own. He's
always been grown up for his age." Marjorie remembered
how Geraldine LeBlanc had referred to any jobs Bertha and
Marjorie held as "volunteer work." Even waitressing.

"Well, I guess he has to be," said Mrs. Katerwaller, "since
he's always been the man of the family. That's quite a burden
for a boy to grow up with."

Just what did she mean by that? Marjorie wanted to know.
Mrs. Katerwaller gave her another sour smile.

"Well, thanks for the refresher!" Marjorie said, standing up.

"You aren't going already?" Helen asked her. "Please stay and have some more tea." But Marjorie saw Mrs. Katerwaller's hand already reaching for her book, as if she couldn't wait to get back to it.

"Oh, I'd love to!" said Marjorie. "But I've got a million things to do at home. I've got to finish up the potato salad for lunch. You know how a growing boy is, my son Sam eats more in one meal than I eat in a week, so I try to keep the house full of potato chips and potato salad and popcorn and corn bread, so he doesn't stuff on meat. If I didn't, he'd just run me out of house and home. He once ate a whole chicken for lunch. I'll be seeing you!"

Marjorie walked quickly toward the curtain of oak trees, and Mrs. Katerwaller did not say another word. When Marjorie reached the road, she rested against the mossy side of an oak tree, her heart fluttering in her chest like a blue jay in a birdbath. After a minute, she looked back around the tree toward the patio. Mrs. Katerwaller had picked up her book again, but she was not reading it. She was staring at the cake and holding the book to her throat like a fan.

* * * *

The next morning, Bertha called all the way from Iceland to talk three minutes on the telephone for a special Sunday rate. Marjorie clutched the phone much longer than that, conscious that she was talking a blue streak and hardly letting Bertha get a word in edgewise.

"So then the old battle-ax says, 'That must be an awful hard burden for your son to bear,' " Marjorie told Bertha. "I didn't give that nosy Helen Katerwaller the time of day. I just got up and left." Marjorie fell silent for a moment and then laughed at something Bertha said. From the hallway, Marjorie could see Sam heaping potato salad on his plate. Lorna Winsted scraped an uneaten half of hamburger from

Dace's dish onto Sam's and chattered in a low voice with her son.

"You take care too, Bertha," Marjorie told her sister. Marjorie hung up the phone and realized she'd been talking for over an hour.

When Marjorie entered the kitchen, Lorna was trying to scare Dace with a story.

"So the little boy's father dies, and his mother sends him to the store to get some liver. Only he don't feel like walking all the way to the store, so he goes to the cemetery and digs up his father's grave, and takes his liver, and brings it back, and his mother cooks it in a pan. That night, he's asleep in bed and he hears this scary voice—" Lorna deepened her voice and made it sound hollow and ominous.

" 'Johnny,' the voice says, 'I want my liver back.' Then the boy hears a footstep." Lorna tapped her shoe on the kitchen floor. "And the voice is closer this time and says the same thing: 'Johnny, I want my liver back!' " She tapped on the floor again. " 'Johnny, I want my liver back.' " Tap. " 'Johnny, I want my liver back.' " Tap. Lorna seized Dace by the shoulders and yelled in his face, " 'HERE, YOU CAN HAVE IT!' "

"Oh, haw haw haw," Dace said, squirming in his chair. "Haw haw."

"We used to tell one like that," said Marjorie. "It was called 'Bloody Boots.' I don't remember how it goes; I just remember the end: 'Bloody Boots is on the first step. Bloody Boots is on the second step. Bloody Boots is on the third step. BLOODY BOOTS HAS GOT YOU!' " She grabbed Lorna, and Lorna and Dace shrieked agreeably.

There was a knock on the screen door.

Everyone turned around. A tall woman stood backlit behind the doorframe.

"Margie? It's me. Helen."

Marjorie rushed to the door and opened it. "Helen! Come in and make yourself at home."

Mrs. Katerwaller walked into the kitchen, carrying a china plate with a red glass cover. "I just made a tomato aspic and I thought I'd bring it down here to eat with you all." She lifted the cover, and Sam and Lorna looked at each other in mock horror, behind Mrs. Katerwaller's back. Dace pulled himself up in his chair and stared at the aspic: a pink ring speckled with green. Dace was not even sure it was something you could eat.

"You know what this is?" said Marjorie, shooting Sam a meaningful look. "That's elegant." She pulled a tray from under the sink and put the aspic and two plates on it, and then added a dish of lemon wedges, two glasses, and gin and tonic bottles. "Us ladies are going to sit in the living room and leave you hooligans in the kitchen."

Sam, Lorna, and Dace watched with relief as Marjorie carried the aspic tray to the living room. Mrs. Katerwaller followed, and Lorna heard her say, "That girl in there seems familiar, but I can't recall where we met."

"Why, it must have been at my comin'-out party," Lorna said under her breath to Sam. "It must have been my comin'-out party at the country club. Is your mother a friend of hers?"

"I don't think so," Sam told Lorna. But he was glad that anyone at all had come over to distract his mother a little. Even if it was Mrs. Katerwaller. You couldn't blame Mr. Katerwaller on his wife. And recently, whenever Sam came home, his mother seemed to be sitting in the kitchen, scrubbing listlessly at the stove burners with a piece of steel wool. She acted overjoyed when he walked in the door, and she would linger around whoever was in the kitchen, making herself unobtrusive and offering people things to eat. Sam could remember when his mother had been someone else—sharp-tempered and shrill, ordering them to bed or out from underfoot. He recalled a whole year in which the first thing she said when she came home from work was: "I hardly get my foot in the door, and all I hear is demands." And then: "This house looks like a tornado hit it!" "Set the table!" "Didn't anyone put dinner in the oven?" Now he'd come home to find his bedroom floor swept and his bed made, and one of his baby pictures stuck into the frame of his closet mirror.

Recently, the house was almost eerily clean—sometimes when he walked through the front door he had trouble recognizing where he was, as if he had entered the wrong home. The LeBlancs' house had always been messy. When he was a little boy, Sam used to be startled by neighbors' kitchens, with their refrigerators devoid of handprints and their shiny floors. He used to long for the sofa in the living room, with its coffee stain shaped like a map of Louisiana on one of the arms and clouds of lint under the cushions. Sitting in a school friend's home that reeked of floor wax in the kitchen or deodorizers in the bathroom, he would get homesick for his own house's smell of boiling ham hock and wet dirt.

In the living room, Sam's mother let out one of her high-pitched, witchy laughs in response to something Mrs. Kater-waller said. Sam sat back in his chair, relaxed. Maybe Marjorie LeBlanc would get back to herself now.

Dace climbed down from his chair and crept along the short hallway leading to the living room, in order to get another look at Mrs. Katerwaller. He stuck his head around the corner, and the women kept talking without seeing him.

"Thump, drag—thump, drag—thump, drag, they heard on the stairs," said Mrs. Katerwaller. "It was the baby-sitter, with all her arms and legs cut off, pulling herself up the steps by her chin."

"That's awful!" Marjorie laughed. "I think my sister Bertha, the professor, used to tell me the same one, except that the man had a hand made out of a golden hook and—"

Mrs. Katerwaller started. "Hi there, Buster Brown," she told Dace.

"You scared the living daylights out of us!" said Marjorie. "You look like a little jack-o'-lantern, with that grin of yours. This is Lorna's boy, Dace."

Dace kept grinning and leaned against the couch.

"Just remembering that story gives me goose pimples!" said Mrs. Katerwaller. Dace ducked his head around the couch, watched Mrs. Katerwaller rub her leg, and saw the little places on her skin where it pricked up. Dace reached out and ran his hand down her shin.

"Oh!" Mrs. Katerwaller called out, and Dace ran back into the kitchen.

* * * *

Helen Katerwaller called Marjorie and invited her on a shopping spree. "There's nothing like buying clothes when you're down in the dumps," she told Marjorie. "And I happen to feel like cheering myself up. I usually go over to Atlanta or Dallas to buy clothes, but Belk's is good for a hat or a purse."

Marjorie remembered Geraldine LeBlanc leaning forward over a bridge game and saying to a Mrs. Tuttle, a dentist's wife, "Whenever I'm feeling under the weather, I go out and buy myself a small present. There's nothing wrong with spoiling yourself a little!" Marjorie thought her memory might be playing tricks on her, because Willie LeBlanc had been tightfisted with his paychecks and never given his wife more than a monthly allowance for groceries. Geraldine Le-Blanc had bought the sewing machine on which she made all her own clothes, with Blue Chip stamps.

"That sounds wonderful," said Marjorie. "I'm in need of a dark-red pocketbook. What I really need more than anything right now is a nice big dark-red pocketbook."

But once they got to Belk's, Marjorie remembered that she did not own anything red. In addition, all the purses at Belk's looked like something someone else would use. She spent a few minutes examining a red patent-leather pocketbook with a gold chain, and a large magenta purse shaped like a paper bag, which cost twenty dollars.

"Yoo-hoo, Margie What do you think of this?" Helen

Katerwaller called from the hat section. Marjorie walked through the purse racks and saw Helen facing her, wearing a smart scarlet hat with a black veil. She looked exotic, like Ingrid Bergman. A thick curl disappeared seductively under the veil.

Before Marjorie could answer, Helen turned toward a mirror and said, "It's awful. It looks like one of those ridiculous things Shriners wear. What do you call them? Fezzes. It looks like a fez with chicken wire hanging off the top." She dropped the hat on the counter and picked up a man's felt hat and put it on. "How do you like this, Baby?" She looked like the young Gregory Peck.

A sales clerk rushed through a green curtain, carrying three hatboxes, and put them down on the glass counter. "Do any of these interest you?" he asked Helen, with such a look of concern that Marjorie thought he must be paid partly by commission. There was a kelly-green silk thing shaped like an army private's cap, and a wide-brimmed black cowboyish hat, and something that looked like a pink suede frying pan lid.

Helen put on the cowboy hat and studied herself in the mirror. "Hmmm," she said. "Do you have this in some other color?"

"Let me see," the clerk answered, ducking behind the curtain. While he sorted through boxes, Helen wandered back and forth between the hat counter and the purses. She winked at Marjorie and then leaned forward and took the wig off a male mannequin and hid the wig inside a navy-blue purse on the purse rack.

"Imagine how the person will feel who opens that pocketbook!" Helen whispered to Marjorie, who watched, astonished, as Helen closed the bag.

When the clerk came back, Helen Katerwaller settled for the cowboy hat in a gray-blue.

As Marjorie and Helen walked out of the store, Helen whispered to Marjorie, "He looked a lot better without hair, don't you think?" and the two women dissolved into giggles.

Marjorie had always believed that well-to-do ladies had a prankish, wild-woman streak to them. She remembered once seeing a lady who lived in a mansion on Audubon Place in New Orleans dancing naked in the rain on her veranda. And that was in 1951.

*   *   *   *

Helen Katerwaller was more fun than Marjorie could have imagined. Helen made Marjorie feel like a schoolgirl. She hadn't felt so wicked in years.

The next weekend, Helen called Marjorie on the phone and said, "Let's take the Lincoln out for a spin and visit the historic section of Winston-Salem. We're lucky we live in the South—it's just crawling with history." Helen belted out a drunken sort of laugh.

Marjorie wore her nurse's shoes, because she thought she might be doing a lot of walking in order to go sightseeing, but she put on a shimmery nylon dress usually kept for parties, which was too hot for the weather. She went to her daughter Karen's room and snooped around in her makeup drawer. Marjorie smeared on a little rouge and thickened her eyelashes with mascara. Marjorie thought she almost resembled Dr. Zhivago's wife. She wished she had a yellow hat with a black veil to set off her coloring. She looked exotic. Maybe she would walk around Winston-Salem talking in a Russian accent, just to make people turn and look.

However, Helen and Marjorie got only as far as ten miles outside Durham, when Helen turned her Lincoln onto a dirt road running alongside a tobacco field.

"Where're you going?" Marjorie asked, bouncing in her seat and straining forward against her seat belt to see the deep potholes in the road.

"Oh, I don't know," said Helen. "I always wanted to see what these fields looked like up close." She drove past a wood building, and a man in a short-sleeved tan shirt and a brown tie came onto the front steps and frowned at her. Helen honked and waved, then turned around, drove behind the building, and came racing by the steps again. This time the man was standing on the road, slightly in front of the steps, and Helen whizzed by so close to him that Marjorie could see that his shirt was missing a button. Helen maneuvered the car back up the road and raced onto the highway. Marjorie was laughing so hard she couldn't even moan when her head hit the side window as the car bounced through an especially deep pothole.

"You're out your mind, girl!" Marjorie told Helen.

Helen sped down the highway, just ahead of the speed limit. The highway was divided by a deep, grassy gully. When the Lincoln passed a break that crossed the divide and led into a second dirt road, she said, "Let's try that one." She moved into the left lane and traveled almost a mile down the highway, but there was no sign of a second crossroad over the divide, where she could make a U-turn. She slowed down the Lincoln and nosed it over into the divide; the embankments leading into the gully were steep and about twenty feet tall on either side.

"You'll never make it," said Marjorie. The Lincoln bumped down into the bottom of the depression and started climbing, but stopped midway up the other side, at a thirty-degree angle.

"Let's try something else," said Helen. She let the car roll back down the embankment and drove down the middle of the gully, between the two sides of the highway, in the direction of the dirt road.

"You're going to get caught!" said Marjorie.

Helen just raised her eyebrows.

She drove a half mile before the women heard a siren. Above them on the right, Marjorie could see a state policeman's car running parallel to the Lincoln on the road.

Helen honked at him and drove another fifty yards before she said, "Let's see what he wants," and halted the Lincoln.

The state trooper stopped his car and walked sideways

down the embankment. Marjorie had noticed recently that
every time she turned on the television, there seemed to be a
movie on about a black lawyer or detective coming down
south to fight against a bigoted state trooper. The state
trooper was always fortyish, and usually wore dark sunglasses and had a cigarette in his mouth. It occurred to her
that North Carolina state troopers really did look like that.
This one had on dark sunglasses and was fortyish and was
even chewing tobacco.

He walked around to Helen's side of the car, and she rolled
down the window. He rested his arms on the car door and
peered at Helen with a sarcastic expression.

Helen looked stunning. She was wearing black pants and a
blue silk shirt and her cowboy hat. She had on just a brush
of face powder, delicately applied. Her hands on the steering
wheel were long and elegant, and her nails were painted with
magenta polish.

She looked toward Marjorie, and the right side of Helen's
mouth twitched up in a smirk. Then she turned to the officer,
and spoke to him in a plaintive, debutantish drawl. "Oh, Officer, I'm so glad you're here! I was just driving my husband's car along the road, and it's such a big old car, and it
just seemed to steer itself down underneath the highway! Oh,
please don't give me a ticket; Roland would never understand. I'm so scatterbrained today! First I lost the bridge
game, and then I missed my appointment for my hair, and
now I'm late for the club." Helen's voice thinned as if she
were going to cry. "I knew I shouldn't even have tried to
drive this big old car, it's too much for me, but I was just
hurrying and hurrying, trying to find something to put on,
and I DON'T EVEN HAVE A MAID!"

"Hey. Hey, ma'am," the officer told Helen. "Don't you
worry now; we'll get this big old car back on the road." He
opened the door and signaled for Helen and Marjorie to get
out. He climbed in the car and drove it down the center of the
divider. The Lincoln bounced and teetered dangerously as he

tried to drive up a more gradual slope of the embankment. Then the car drove almost half a mile forward, finally climbing up a shallow bank near the dirt road and circling back onto the highway.

Helen was laughing so hard she had to grab Marjorie by the arm to keep from falling over.

"Helen, stand up straight!" Marjorie said. "He's almost here."

The state trooper stopped the Lincoln above Marjorie and Helen, got out of the car, and looked down on them. Helen took off her high heels and walked up the embankment in her stockings, and the officer leaned down and helped her over the edge. Marjorie scrambled up behind.

"Oh, thank you, thank you!" Helen told the officer breathlessly. "I thought I was simply going to break down! I thought we'd be stuck there all day! We would have died if you hadn't come along."

She got into the driver's seat, and Marjorie walked around to the passenger's side and buckled her seat belt. The officer drove in front of the Lincoln, and Helen followed him for a hundred feet or so. He flashed his police light at her and finally waved her ahead. Helen drove off the first exit on the highway and stopped the Lincoln on the road shoulder. The two friends looked at each other and then sat for five minutes, howling with laughter. The phrase "above the law" flashed through Marjorie's head. She's *above the law,* Marjorie thought, and felt thrilled by the idea.

* * * *

The next Saturday, Marjorie called at Helen's house, and Mr. Katerwaller answered the door. Marjorie had not seen him since Christmas. He was tall and important-looking, with all his hair, and had broad, football-player shoulders.

"Yes?" he said, without letting Marjorie in.

"Is that you, Margie?" Helen called from inside the house. "Come on in and make yourself at home." Mr. Katerwaller stayed exactly where he was, as if he were going to refuse to allow Marjorie to enter. Then he smiled down at her and moved out of her way.

Marjorie sat in a stiff-backed oak chair in the living room, and Mr. Katerwaller walked out the front door, slamming it behind him. As Helen came in from the hallway, Marjorie saw the Chrysler pulling away from the house. It was only ten-thirty in the morning, but Helen was carrying a tray of drinks. She told Marjorie they were highballs. Marjorie had never had a highball before.

"He's all mad because the Lincoln has a dent. He says I shouldn't get expensive presents if I don't know how to take care of them."

Marjorie sipped her highball. Helen had not put on makeup, and she looked exhausted in a dramatic way—like Vivien Leigh after Tara had fallen to the Yankees.

"He took the Lincoln down to the gas station, and the Budd man who runs it told him it would cost two hundred dollars to fix a dent in the back. I think that state trooper might have winged the Lincoln on that embankment. Or maybe it's *been* that way."

Helen seemed sad about something. Marjorie did not believe it was the Lincoln.

"I told Roland not to worry about it. Frankie Budd always overcharges, and any other place would do it for fifty."

"You mean Mr. Budd, Faith Budd's husband, who lives right near me?" Marjorie asked.

"That's the one," said Helen. "Hooo, that Faith Budd is a bag of tricks. You know, before you moved to the neighborhood, I used to spend a lot of time with Faith Budd. She's not real educated or anything, but we got along. Her husband was such a monster. Just once Faith went out and had a little affair with a boy who worked at the gas station. Some simpleton mountain boy from out by Asheville, who didn't know his ass from his elbow. She only slept with him for a month, but after that, old Franklin wouldn't even touch her. She begged and cried and apologized, but he was hard as a rock. The kind of man who just can't live if everyone isn't obeying him every minute of his life. You should see how he ordered his children around. He had this big dream to send his boys to military school. He wouldn't leave them alone for a minute. Then when Faith would try to intervene, he'd shout her down or knock her from here to Tuesday, and act even stricter with the boys. He told her he had to protect them from her influence. He used to talk bad about her right in front of the children. I once heard him say, 'Boys, your mama is a dirty old lady. A dirty, slutty, creepy old lady.' Well, right about then, you know, I'm sure you never guessed this, but my marriage has its ups and downs, and me and Roland weren't getting along for a while. Faith and I would spend days at a time talking to each other."

Marjorie nodded, sipping her highball. She felt herself drifting away as she got tipsier. How was it possible that she'd known Faith all these years but didn't know what Helen knew? Maybe Marjorie didn't know Faith at all. Maybe they weren't real friends.

"Well, one day Faith and I were out in her yard with her three boys. They were racing around, pretending to be horses, jumping over piles of bottles and clumps of grass. So Frankie Budd comes out of the house, and the oldest boy sees a particularly tall clump of grass and says, 'Permission to jump, sir.' And Frankie looks at him and says, 'Permission denied.' Permission denied to jump over a little hump of grass!

"That night I said to Faith, 'Let's you and me run off together. I've got some friends and relations in Lake Charles, Louisiana, and we'd get along somehow. We could start new lives together. We could even get jobs,' I said, 'and then after a while we'll find us some better husbands.'

"She was scared to do it. She said she'd never be able to divorce Frankie, because if he found out where she was, he'd take the boys away, and she couldn't leave them alone with him.

"After that, I just felt sorry for her and we stopped seeing each other. She could have left. She was simply afraid to be on her own."

Marjorie wanted to say something to defend Faith. But why hadn't Faith ever told her about all this? Marjorie had never seen Mr. Budd hit his boys, but then by the time Marjorie met the Budds, the boys were all too big to beat.

"You know, Faith was a very strange woman anyway," said Helen. "She used to collect travel brochures and pretend she was going to take trips. To Yellowstone Park and Carlsbad Caverns and places like that. But Frankie wouldn't give her a dime. Except once! He told her to buy the family cemetery plots, and she put all the money in an account in her name and just pretended to buy the plots. But then she was afraid to spend the money. It was a whole heap of money. Frankie Budd had this paranoia about not being buried right, but he had a superstitious fear of undertakers. When he used to see that undertaker Mintor who lives down his way, Frankie would almost run in the other direction. Those Budds are real backwoodsy."

Something in the highball made Marjorie sneeze. Before she could think of an answer, Helen got up and went to the kitchen to refill the drinks. Marjorie felt as if she were betraying Faith somehow by listening to Helen. But then, hadn't Faith betrayed Marjorie? Faith had just pretended to share things. And hadn't Faith gone off to Florida and left Marjorie alone?

After Helen came back in with more drinks, Marjorie stayed and talked for an hour more. Helen spent the entire time gossiping about other women in the neighborhood. She told Marjorie that Mrs. Booth had had a nervous breakdown once and run out in the street with only her girdle on, and that the Mansons' oldest boy had been arrested for peddling heroin, and that Sally Ann Ruby had been picked up for soliciting. Mrs. Katerwaller had this information straight from a county court judge. "There's a lot of trash in this neighborhood, Marjorie. I don't see how you put up with it," Helen concluded.

Once Marjorie was home, she wondered why Helen didn't think the LeBlancs were trash. Their house was the ugliest, most run-down building on the road, and most of the time Ruth and Sam and Carla ran around acting like wild things. Karen wore too much makeup. Marjorie wondered if she had given the impression of being more sophisticated than she actually was, by not acting shocked at the things Helen did. But it wasn't as if Marjorie had been pretending to be someone else. People were always sizing her up and making her out to be something she wasn't at all. Just because she didn't criticize and act disagreeable.

She hadn't even argued when Helen had been bad-mouthing Faith.

After Marjorie got back to the house, she realized that she had not enjoyed the visit. It occurred to Marjorie that Helen had never learned how to gossip properly. There was too much real venom, and no laughter, in how she said things.

* * * *

On Sunday, Marjorie stayed home and defrosted the freezer, while Lorna and Sam sat at the kitchen table looking through a picture book on Alaska, and Dace watched the television Sam had plugged in on the kitchen counter. There was an antismoking commercial on that showed a cigarette dressed up like a cowboy riding a horse over a plantation. A narrator said, "He rose up out of the tobacco field . . ." and a chorus sang "JOHNNY SMOKE! JOHNNY SMOKE!" in a melodramatic tone, punctuating the story of the outlaw killer Johnny Smoke. Dace sang along with the chorus.

Lorna told Marjorie, "Jeanette's moving to Alaska with my friend Allison Paley. The one who got fired from the country club. Jeanette bought a VW bus, and now she and Allison are making these bead earrings and selling them to stores in Chapel Hill to raise money for gas and stuff. Jeanette's gonna put bunks in the bus and paint a sunset on the back. Jeanette says you can make about ten times as much in Alaska and that I'd be stupid not to go with her."

"Anything would be better than working for minimum wage at a country club," said Sam.

"You're not going anywhere until you finish high school, Mr. Big," Marjorie told him, smacking a block of ice from the back of the freezer.

"If I left for Alaska," said Sam, "I could earn enough to build a little house for me and Lorna and Dace. If I finish high school in Durham, all I'll be able to do is wear a dumb organ-grinder monkey's jacket and work as a busboy."

"You're not going to Alaska!" said Marjorie, surprising herself by losing her temper. "You're not going anywhere."

"And I'm not living with no man," said Lorna. "I been there and back. I'm on my own from here on out."

Marjorie slammed an ice tray against the sink. She hadn't even known she was in a bad mood. It was that Helen Katerwaller. Really, she was an out-and-out snob. It was just a matter of time before she talked bad about Marjorie.

Marjorie turned back from the sink and yelled, "Dace, get your fingers out of the butter!"

Dace dropped the whole stick of butter on the floor and stood looking at it, not daring to raise his head to Marjorie.

"And don't you talk about Alaska again!" Marjorie told Sam. "And clean up your room! It's a pigpen. First you grow up enough to clean your room, and then you talk about running off to raise a family!"

Marjorie ran out of the kitchen.

"Jesus fucking Christ!" said Lorna. She watched Sam pick up the stick of butter, and then added, "Maybe your mama's afraid I'm going after you to get you to support me or something." Lorna frowned. "Well, that's a pile of shit."

It was the first time Lorna had even hinted that she'd given a moment's thought to such a thing. Sam felt flattered and light-headed. "Nah," he answered. "That's just Mama. You never know what sets her off. All you can ever be sure of is it doesn't have anything to do with what she says she's mad about."

Lorna nodded, as if the explanation were perfectly sensible. "My mama's the same way. She once threw a whole plate of macaroni at Jeanette just because Jeanette said she wasn't hungry. But all along what was bothering Mama was her aunt getting operated for a tumor."

* * * *

Almost a week passed, and Marjorie did not call Helen. But Helen called on Friday and invited Marjorie to go to a Saturday rock concert in Chapel Hill. As soon as she heard Helen's voice on the phone, Helen felt elated. She saw that she had missed Helen. And then, Marjorie had never been to a rock concert. The truth was, Helen was expanding Marjorie's horizons. She decided to go.

Marjorie felt wonderful when she climbed into the Lincoln on Saturday afternoon. Helen was in high spirits. She had just talked to her poorer relations in Lake Charles on the phone, and her cousin Katie had told her all about another ridiculous cousin of theirs who had bought a five-hundred-dollar stereo for her baby daughter, aged two. The cousin said that they wanted the baby to have music in her blood, and every night at bedtime they put on *Porgy and Bess* or Glenn Miller. Then Helen talked about a friend of hers from Charlotte, who had bought a hundred dollars' worth of roses every week and who never wore the same dress twice in the same year. She had a closet big enough to park a Cadillac in.

At the entrance to the rock concert was a girl dressed in a peasant blouse, a blue-jean skirt, cowboy boots, and a beaded headband. She handed Marjorie a yellow paper that listed the musicians who were singing. Someone named B.B. and a band called Country Joe and the Fish.

Marjorie was wearing her nice dress, and she knew she stuck out like a sore thumb, even though everyone else there wasn't exactly her idea of a church. There were boys painting flowers on each other with watercolors, and a girl without a shirt on sitting on top of a van. There was a young man lying under one of the spectators' benches, smiling up at the sky and saying *"Great!"* and a white girl with a blond Afro, who sold Helen a button that said "Newcomb X" on it. Marjorie heard a black girl yelling across a row of seats, "Go to hell, white boy!" and saw two girls making out with one another under a tree. There was a high-school boy with his head shaved, wearing a sandwich board that said: "I'm burning my draft card, what about you?" and he really was holding a match to his draft card and catching it on fire, while people gathered around him. Marjorie also saw her daughter Ruth with a boy who had a two-foot ponytail, but Marjorie stopped herself before she called out to them. She liked the strangeness of the situation. She didn't want to make it seem ordinary and familiar.

She bought a T-shirt for Dace from a girl who was selling macramé and shirts and carrot cake. Helen shook out a chenille bedspread on the grass floor of the stadium, and she and Marjorie lay down to watch the concert, just like everyone else. And that's when the thought struck Marjorie that she was the strangest person there. It was as if she were an alien in one of those science fiction movies, who comes down to earth and doesn't know a thing about it. She felt as if she had lost contact with her own planet.

After the concert, Helen drove the Lincoln along a back road outside Chapel Hill and parked in front of an old house with a bearded, hippyish-looking man sitting in a rocking chair on the front porch. Helen talked to the man for a minute and then ran back to the car with a bag of what she told Marjorie were hashish brownies. Marjorie had never known such a thing existed. Helen and Marjorie sat in the Lincoln after turning the car radio on as loud as it would go, and they each ate two brownies.

By the time Helen started the car, Marjorie was seeing purple neon borders around stationary objects. She also felt as if she had become more sensitized to changes in things. She noticed a picket line outside a department store, and saw that Eckerd's drugs looked as if it hadn't had a coat of paint in years. There was a whole section of pine forest that had been knocked down as you came off the highway. Helen parked the car and Marjorie followed her into a bookstore, where Helen bought *The Bull from the Sea,* and then they went to a store that sold posters and cigarette papers, inflatable replicas of Cutty Sark and Jim Beam bottles, 7-Up cans with flashing purple lights on top, protest buttons, sew-on patches, and surplus army jackets. Helen got herself some cigarette papers and bought Marjorie a pair of dark glasses with red rims. Marjorie put them on and looked at herself in her compact mirror and thought she looked like a ladybug. She noticed that the sales clerks and customers had started saying "Thank *you*" instead of "*Thank* you," as if there had been some agreement among everybody that people were going to talk like that from now on. The world had been changing out from under her.

When the Lincoln pulled into Marjorie's neighborhood, she watched the houses, darkened by her glasses, spinning by and noticed that Blue Henry's house was missing. When had it been torn down, and who had done it? How could a whole house have been knocked apart without her noticing?

"Margie, you're really something," Helen said, stopping the car in front of the LeBlancs'. "I swear nothing fazes you. You're *cosmopolitan.*"

Marjorie shut the door, only half listening. When she walked into her house, her daughter Karen was sitting in the living room, watching a late-night movie.

"Where have you been?" Karen asked in an accusatory tone. She couldn't believe the glasses.

"Oh, here and there," said Marjorie. "Up, down, and around." Marjorie walked down the hall to her bedroom, and by the time she undressed, she was seeing blue angels dangling over her bed, their hands and dresses flowing into one another and joining like paper dolls.

*   *   *   *

All along, Marjorie had sensed that Mr. Katerwaller did not like her, but she never let it bother her, and he was easy enough to avoid. He was practically never home. One of the things Geraldine LeBlanc had taught her daughters was that two lady friends always had to respect each other's marriages; when the man came home from work, it was time for you to get back to your own kitchen and start cooking supper. Another rule was: It was all right for a woman to complain about her husband to a close friend, but the friend must never join in and criticize the husband. Marjorie saw this rule as both moral and practical. The moral side was that it was wrong to do anything to divide husband and wife. The practical side was that as soon as the wife started getting along with her husband again and he found out you'd criticized him, you'd never see your lady friend again. Marjorie had always stuck to this rule. Perhaps that was why she had never led Faith into a discussion about Franklin Delano Budd. Marjorie had always felt deep down that Franklin Delano was a skunk, and she didn't want to ask for trouble.

Marjorie was thinking of this as she walked around to the patio behind the Katerwallers' to join Helen for some iced tea. Stepping onto the patio, Marjorie saw that Helen was drinking a mint julep and not tea. She was staring off into space and had not put on any makeup. Her book, *The Bull from the Sea,* was face down on the glass table, and when Marjorie seated herself, Helen forgot to offer her a mint julep.

Helen reached out for Marjorie's hand and said, "Margie, I called you over because I need to talk to you about something serious. Tell me straight out—I want to know your opinion: What do you think of Roland?"

Marjorie recalled how Roland Katerwaller had frowned at her in the door, and what Lorna had said about his bringing women to the club. Marjorie believed Sam had told her that Roland Katerwaller had gotten a girl fired from the country club just because she sassed him. Marjorie had a pretty low opinion of Mr. Katerwaller, but she said, "Oh, I can't say, Helen. I hardly know him."

Helen appeared almost feverish. Marjorie had to check an impulse to lay her hand on her friend's forehead. Helen leaned forward and said, "You don't know how he treats me, Marjorie, do you? Oh, I know I put up a front, but I realize I just can't stand for this anymore." Helen stared into her mint julep. "Yesterday my cousin Katie told me point-blank: She said, 'Helen, you leave that maniac and come live with me here in Louisiana. You've already put up with more than any human being can bear.' I could scarcely answer, I was crying so hard, but I finally told her she was right.

"What would you do, Marjorie? I went into Belk's the other day to buy a red-and-white silk scarf, and as I was coming out I saw a man across the street who I thought might be Roland, but then I saw there was a young girl, barely a teenager, with him, so I just looked the other way, thinking: Well, that wasn't him after all. But just as I was getting into my Lincoln, I heard him laugh. He has this way of opening his mouth wide and throwing back his head, and I could tell that laugh from the devil if I had to. I just sat in the car with my head on the steering wheel until I heard Roland's laugh walk away down the street.

"What would you do, Marjorie? This isn't the first time; oh, no. I've seen him coming out of the Little Colonel Hotel with a red-haired lady in a chinchilla coat, and another time I caught him pushing some friend of a friend's into the back hall closet at a political convention. I've even had a woman I'd never met come up to me on the street and tell me that Roland had forced her, and that the three-year-old boy with her was my own husband's son! I don't to this day know for certain if she wasn't lying, although the boy didn't look a thing like a Katerwaller. He was dark and pointy-faced, like a little weasel.

"And that isn't the half of it. Roland is so jealous of me. He won't let me step out the door without him if he thinks

I'm going somewhere where there'll be men around. However, he almost never goes to parties. Sometimes he brings me to the Whiteside Manor Country Club or the Carolina Inn, but we hardly ever go out. And if I just want to drive to the grocery store, he won't let me go if he thinks my dress is too high at the bottom or low at the top. Oh, I know I dress up well enough, but I've lived to see him rip a new silk evening gown in two just because it was shoulderless. He's always been jealous of me. I'm like a little canary bird in a cage. What would you do, Marjorie?" Helen stopped talking and looked at Marjorie.

Marjorie thought for a minute, but Helen did not start up again. "Well, it's hard to judge, Helen," said Marjorie. "I've never been in that position."

"If you were, would you put up with it? Would you?" Helen said. She stood up and went to the kitchen and came back with two mint juleps. She handed one to Marjorie and said, "Would you go to Lake Charles? My cousin isn't as well off as I'm used to, but I could even get a job. I could be an independent woman! Would you put up with it?"

Marjorie sipped her mint julep and finally answered. "No, Helen, I don't think I would put up with that kind of thing. If I was in that kind of position."

Helen told her that settled it. She had already called the Raleigh airport and there was a flight out to New Orleans at seven o'clock Monday, and all she needed was for Marjorie to drive her there. Helen would have her bags packed and her reservation ready.

* * * *

Marjorie argued with the hospital administrators to get out early from work, and at five o'clock on Monday she parked the Oldsmobile in front of the Katerwallers' and rang their doorbell. She rang it three times, and finally Mr. Katerwaller came to the door and asked Marjorie what she wanted.

"Who is that?" Helen called. Marjorie could hear other people's voices in the living room, and when she walked past

Mr. Katerwaller, she saw Mr. and Mrs. George sitting around the coffee table, sipping champagne. There were several other important-looking men and their wives talking together behind the sofa.

"Marjorie LeBlanc!" said Hope George. "Come on over here and join us; I haven't seen you in ages. Mr. Katerwaller and Mr. George just pulled off the biggest business deal in the history of Durham!"

Marjorie sat down in the straight-backed chair and accepted a goblet of champagne. She looked up at Helen, but Helen averted her eyes. She avoided talking to Marjorie the whole hour that Marjorie stayed at the Katerwallers'. At six o'clock, Mrs. George invited Marjorie to join them at the Whiteside Manor country club for a celebration dinner, but Marjorie knew the invitation was not in earnest: She was still in her nurse's uniform, and Mrs. George was wearing an off-white linen dress and two rows of pearls. Helen had dressed in a blue formal that set off the color of her eyes, and black stockings with lacy roses in them. Marjorie excused herself, saying she had to cook dinner.

It was no surprise to Marjorie that Helen never visited or called once during the next three weeks.

At the end of July, Marjorie ran into Helen on the street, near Belk's. Marjorie had become so stir crazy knocking around the house by herself that Sam and Lorna had invited her to go with them and Dace to a matinee.

"Well, Margie LeBlanc," said Helen. "I hope you're doing well." Helen gave Marjorie an embarrassed smile and almost ran down the sidewalk into Belk's.

REBELLION AT THE
WHITESIDE MANOR COUNTRY CLUB

Watch out, here comes Faith Budd, Faith thought to herself as she barreled down her yard and across the street and up the steep hill leading to Marjorie's house. Faith did not even knock; she threw open the LeBlancs' door and called out: "It's me, Marjorie. I'm home!"

Marjorie dropped her steel wool pad on the stove and came running out of the kitchen, wiping her hands on her apron.

Faith caught Marjorie by the shoulders, to study her face for a minute before giving her a hug. "Oh, I was just pining away for you!" she told her. "How are you four doing?" she called over Marjorie's shoulder.

Marjorie turned around and saw all her children standing in the hallway, watching with such expressions of relief that Marjorie realized she must have been a terrible burden to them all summer.

Sam and Carla made popcorn in the kitchen, and Ruth looked through the *TV Guide* for a good movie, and they all settled on a suspense thriller about life after the nuclear war. Even Karen LeBlanc, who really had never approved of Faith Budd, sat next to Faith on the living room couch and watched the movie from start to finish.

* * * *

That Saturday, Marjorie drove Faith to the corner drugstore to pick up some rubbing alcohol, because Faith had decided she wanted to pierce her ears. "It's a fad in Florida City," Faith told Marjorie, "and it's just the kind of zany thing I'm in the mood for."

Marjorie was thinking about whether she should have her own ears pierced, when a truck carrying hundreds of chickens in cages pulled in front of the Oldsmobile. Feathers drifted like snow from the back of the truck.

"Oh, Lord Almighty," said Faith Budd. "It seems like every time I ever turn onto this road, that chicken truck is smack in front of me."

Marjorie switched on the windshield wipers, and Faith hooted.

"It must be the Winn Dixie," Faith said. "It must be the truck that runs to the meat department."

A few feathers were still stuck in the windshield wipers

when Marjorie turned them off. Marjorie pulled the Oldsmobile into the left lane and then steered quickly back into her own lane when she saw an oncoming car. "Carla just tuned up the motor, and I'm dying to try out the accelerator," said Marjorie. "You know, there's nothing she can't fix on a car. She's even working on some boy's truck down the street. Pretty soon she'll start charging. She's fiddled with the Oldsmobile so many times I don't think there's a part left in it that isn't new."

"My little boys' Chevrolet is just like that," said Faith.

The Oldsmobile passed the 7 Eleven. And there, walking out of the doorway with an Icee, was Helen Katerwaller.

Marjorie thought of something that had always irritated her about Helen Katerwaller: the way she never said "What?" but had to say *"Excuse me?"* or *"Pardon?"* and never said "No" but had to say *"Not to my knowledge."* Marjorie felt she should notice Helen in some way but was afraid to honk her horn. "There's that Helen Katerwaller," Marjorie told Faith, sweeping past the 7 Eleven, then decelerating to keep from getting too close to the chicken truck.

"I used to be friendly with her," said Faith. "She was kind of nice, but she's one of those people who can't help how they were raised. She was raised to be kind of hooty-tooty, I mean." Faith fell silent and watched a cage on the top of the chicken truck teeter and then fall back into place. "Did I ever tell you, once she asked me to run off with her to some lake in Louisiana? I was having trouble with Franklin Delano, and Mr. Katerwaller had seduced a black girl, a little slip of a thing not more than sixteen, who came to work in their house, and her parents had got some Yankee lawyer to slap a paternity suit on him. Oh, that was way back before you moved here. It was the talk of the town, a maid suing an important white man for support and all, but I don't think they won, it was an unheard-of kind of thing, and then the family moved off to Detroit or somewhere. It was all hard on Helen too. It told on her looks.

"One day Helen came over and said to me, 'Faith, I'll kill

myself if I have to live here anymore. Why don't you come with me and we'll help each other out and keep each other company until we get our feet back on the ground.'

"I might have seriously gone and done it, but she kept right on talking, and said, 'Of course, I'll have my circle of friends, and you'll have your friends, but I can help you with money things.' I didn't know just what she was proposing. Did she want to live in one place and me stay in some boardinghouse on a back street? And maybe sneak out to eat lunch with her? I couldn't make heads or tails of it. But it wasn't until that moment that I realized she thought she was better than me. She thought I looked up to her, so she looked down on me. Well, of course that wasn't all. I was afraid to have to raise my little boys and work too. Just like she was afraid to run off all by herself. I hadn't held a job since I met Franklin Delano, he wouldn't let me work, and I never had finished school or learned anything worth knowing. I don't know how you done it, Marjorie. I've always admired you so, how you make it on your own. And I was afraid Franklin Delano could take the boys away. Oh, I was afraid of lots of things. But I guess at that moment the thing that scared me most was old Helen Katerwaller herself. Her saying that to me took away the last little bit of self-respect I had at the time.

"Marjorie? You know I never told about that to anyone? It was such a hard time in my life when the boys were little, I can't even bring myself to think about it. I thought things would just go on and on getting worse, and I never invited people over, I was so ashamed of my home life. Well, finally I made it through. You know what finally changed, what got me out of that house and started me talking to people again? You know what changed things?"

"What, Faith?" Marjorie asked.

"I met you," said Faith.

Marjorie stepped on the accelerator and sped around the chicken truck.

"I thought you were such a live wire, the way you went to nursing school and worked full time and raised up four children all by yourself. I thought you were so brave and strong. I wanted to be just like Marjorie LeBlanc."

* * * *

Marjorie's thirty-eighth birthday came at the end of August, and when Sam forgot to ask her what she wanted, she told him that what she'd like most was to eat a fancy dinner with Faith Budd at the Whiteside Manor Country Club dining room.

Sam was still thinking of an answer when Marjorie dropped him off at work.

"They won't let her in without a husband or a boyfriend or a father or *something*," Lorna said over the pickle dishes. She was eating the black olives faster than she was putting them down.

"And even then, he'd have to be some kind of asshole—a bank president or a real estate man," Lorna added. "Or a lawyer." Lorna handed Sam a bunch of carrot sticks, and he passed them through the dish-disinfecting solution. Lorna had had to wash the goblets since Mrs. Rollins fired Allison Paley. On some days, Lorna washed all the carrots and goblets together, in one load.

"We could pretend she was somebody important," Sam volunteered. Lorna seemed to consider the suggestion. "She could let on she was somebody's mother. Somebody important's mother."

In a high, needling sort of voice, necessary for imitating Mrs. Rollins, Lorna said, "No woman has ever set foot into Whiteside Manor Country Club unassisted," and pulled up a plate of radishes to begin scalloping them.

Sam said, "We'd have to create some kind of commotion at the door so Mrs. John T. won't see Mama coming in."

"We could rob the cash register or set fire to something," said Lorna.

* * * *

Marjorie LeBlanc said she couldn't imagine a little rule
being so important, but Faith Budd sat up for a week plotting and replotting, while trying on her wildest dresses to
find the right one for the dinner. In the end, Lorna had
agreed to Faith's plan for distracting Mrs. Rollins at the
door.

Instead of using the back entrance, Lorna walked past the
dining room cash register, heading in a beeline for the
kitchen. She sashayed in her cutoff shorts and yellow bandanna halter top, which showed off her stretch marks. As she
reached the far edge of the cash register, she knocked the
dish of green and white anisette mints onto the carpet.

"Well, Christ in a bucket," she said, stooping down and
scooping the mints back into the crystal dish.

Mrs. John T. Rollins watched for a full minute before
speaking, for the simple reason that she could not believe her
eyes: Mrs. Rollins was seeing a half naked kitchen girl bobbing her rear end up and down in the exit doorway, picking
after-dinner mints off the carpet and mixing them in with the
mints already in the dish.

Mrs. Rollins left her post at the entrance and said in a low
voice, "You can leave those right there, thank *you!* Right
there! Don't put them back in that dish, thank *you!*"

Lorna laughed as if she were sharing a private joke with
Mrs. Rollins. "Well, I can't hardly blame you," Lorna said.
"These things taste like kerosene mixed with sugar anyhow."
Lorna handed Mrs. Rollins the dish and ducked out the exit.
Mrs. Rollins did not hold immediate power to hire and fire,
and Lorna figured that by the time the restaurant closed for
the night, Mrs. Rollins would come to her senses and tell herself she didn't want to waste another week teaching some
trashy girl how to do the pickle plates.

When the exit door swung closed behind Lorna, Marjorie
LeBlanc and Faith Budd were seated at a booth for four at

the back of the restaurant, near the kitchen door. A solitary candle in a red glass container flickered between them. On the table were two pickle dishes stacked high with black olives, and two butter plates holding five pats of butter apiece, each stamped with a crown.

Faith and Marjorie ordered the filet mignon because Sam had counseled them that it was the only dish on the menu that was any good. Marjorie and Faith had shrimp cocktails and a raw oyster platter, drank four Bloody Marys with extra pepper, and were halfway through green salads topped with purple cabbage and the filet mignons, well done, when Mrs. Rollins noticed the two women. Faith Budd said she thought the oysters tasted the way slugs would taste, if you ate slugs, but that the Bloody Marys were special.

Mrs. Rollins had gone all the way to the back storeroom for a new bag of anisette mints and refilled the dish herself after throwing out the old mints. When she returned to the dining room and spotted Faith and Marjorie, Mrs. Rollins did not note immediately that anything was out of the ordinary. This was because Faith Budd had thought to bring two men's suit jackets from the coatroom behind the cloakroom, and she had draped the jackets ostentatiously over the backs of the imitation-leather seat backs. But once Mrs. Rollins recognized the coats, she kept her eye on the two women, fearing that they might have brought some lowlifes with them to the club. Or just as likely, given the clothes the women were wearing, some college boys had brought them. Mrs. Rollins had had trouble with college boys before.

Marjorie LeBlanc was wearing a purplish satin dress the exact shade of the lipstick she had borrowed from Karen. Both she and Faith had gold stud earrings in their newly pierced ears and Faith was dressed in what she called her "slinky and sleazy gown," one thousand, four hundred and twenty-five red sequins sewed onto black backing. "I look stunning," she had told Marjorie when they climbed into the Oldsmobile. "And you look fit to kill." Marjorie thought she

looked pretty good. The only thing out of place was her nursing shoes, but Marjorie's ankles were too swollen from standing all day to fit into her high heels. Now the two women
stared at each other across the table, admiring their costumes. They looked almost as if they were on a date with each
other.

Mrs. Rollins was distracted by a disturbance at the bar.
Some of the men had become tipsy and were singing "Don't
give a damn about Duke University" and the Tar Heel song,
and the state senator had fallen off his stool.

* * * *

When Sam came out of the kitchen to water, butter, and
roll the new party of eight, he saw that the last people in the
world he would have wanted near his mother—the state senator and Bobby Sanford—had taken the table next to Faith
Budd.

At this very moment, Bobby was crouching on the floor beside his table, demonstrating to Faith Budd that he could lift
up his heavy oak chair by one leg while keeping all four chair
legs parallel to the ground.

"Go to it, Bobby boy!" The state senator egged him on.

"That's real impressive," Marjorie told Bobby Sanford,
trying to be nice. "Now you just sit back down and get some
dinner in you."

Sam saw Mrs. Rollins peering toward the state senator and
frowning.

"You have to be real strong to do this," said Bobby
Sanford. "It takes a lot more strength than you need to pick
up a chair from above."

Marjorie and Faith looked politely away and concentrated
on eating the last bites of their filets.

"That isn't all I can do," said Bobby Sanford, steadying
himself by holding on to his table and the edge of the
women's booth.

Mrs. Rollins arrived at Faith's elbow. To Faith and

Marjorie and the state senator and Bobby, it seemed as if Mrs. Rollins had appeared from nowhere, like a police car pulling out of a clump of bushes on the highway.

"Are you ladies here with someone?" Mrs. Rollins asked.

"Mrs. Helms and I were escorted here by Jesse," said Faith Budd. "I guess he must be talking with one of the men out front. You know Jesse: Once he gets started talking about politics, can't nothing keep him quiet." At this time in history, Jesse Helms was a two-bit editorialist on the evening news, but everyone knew who he was and respected him. However, he was not a member of Whiteside Manor.

"Ladies aren't allowed here unassisted," said Mrs. Rollins.

A waiter appeared at the women's table and set down two plates of chocolate éclairs and a chocolate mousse. "I'm going to bust in two if I eat another bite!" said Faith, scooping up a forkful of mousse.

"A lady has never entered the Whiteside Manor Country Club restaurant unescorted," said Mrs. Rollins.

"I should hope not!" said Faith Budd.

"These girls are with us," the state senator said, standing up, the picture of chivalry, a tall man with steel-gray sideburns and piercing green eyes, the monogrammed tablecloth tucked into the front of his pants. When he turned, the pickle dish and the cocktails on his table began crowding together like cattle running through a chute, and the senator's bourbon fell to the floor. He pulled the tablecloth out of his belt in a deft motion, balancing with his left hand on the table. But Bobby Sanford was still clutching the table edge to hold himself upright while he lifted the chair up and down by its one leg, and so the table tipped over. Bobby Sanford fell sideways and the pickle plate leapt through the air and caught Mrs. Rollins in the knee.

Faith and Marjorie excused themselves, after wrapping their éclairs in blue cloth napkins to take home. On the way out the door, Faith Budd laid down a twenty-dollar bill and scooped up a handful of anisette mints.

* * * *

The next day was a slow day at the Whiteside Manor dining room. There were a few men from the Rotary Club at the bar, but no one sat down to order a meal. Mrs. Rollins had taken an afternoon off. Sam swished a few celery sticks in a goblet full of disinfecting solution, and Lorna stepped outside with Dace, cutting catercorner across the parking lot to buy some cigarettes at the drugstore. Dace walked a few yards behind, weaving in and out of the cars and pretending to shadow Lorna, while she pretended not to notice him following her.

Just as Lorna passed two Cadillacs, Mr. Katerwaller threw open the door of a large yellow car in front of her and stood up. He was clutching a *U.S. News & World Report,* and he seemed to want to block Lorna's path. "You stop right there, little girl," he said. Then he lowered the magazine and held a pistol at Lorna's waist level. "You get in my car." He pointed inside the lush interior of a Chrysler New Yorker. "Don't yell don't scream don't talk just do as I say and you'll be fine."

Afterward, Lorna said that she had been so surprised she hadn't even had time to think; her mouth had reacted for her. "Like hell I will," Lorna told him. She felt Dace come up beside her, and she grabbed him by the shoulder and maneuvered him behind her. "But I'll tell you what you do. Don't yell don't scream just do what I say get in your car and drive it into a tree."

Lorna turned her back to the car and pushed Dace in front of her through the parking lot. Sam stepped outside to have a cigarette just in time to see Mr. Katerwaller slide the gun back inside the *U.S. News* and hold it shut in a clumsy way that reminded Sam of a man caught reading a pornographic magazine in public. Then Mr. Katerwaller ducked into his car and drove out the entrance side of the parking lot.

When Lorna reached the back steps of the country club,

her heart was pounding so ferociously she felt as if she couldn't breathe or speak. She sat down on the steps and pulled Dace into her lap until she steadied herself.

"He pulled a gun on me and tried to force me to go with him in his car," she told Sam.

"We have to call the police," Sam answered her. He ran to the pay phone on the corner.

"I don't know, Sam," Lorna called after him. "I don't think it'll be much use."

* * * *

That night, Sam told his mother and Faith Budd about how the police had refused to arrest Mr. Katerwaller. Sam and Lorna had walked out on their jobs and climbed into a police car, which had cruised around the area, and flagged down Mr. Katerwaller's big yellow Chrysler only a few blocks from the country club. The police had found three registered guns in Mr. Katerwaller's glove compartment. Then they had slapped him on the back and told Lorna it had been a little misunderstanding, with no harm meant. The whole time Sam and Lorna argued with the police, Dace stayed curled up in the back seat of the police car. He wet his pants, and when Lorna pulled him out of the car, he refused to walk. When he saw Mr. Katerwaller, Dace started screaming at the top of his lungs, and nothing Lorna did would make him fall quiet.

The police officer shook his head. There was Dace, his face streaked with dirt, hollering and wearing a thirdhand pair of overalls without a T-shirt; and Lorna in her cutoff shorts and bandanna, looking like a hitchhiker who had just stepped off a cattle truck; and Sam, in his ridiculous black cummerbund.

Now Sam lay on the living room couch, with Dace asleep on top of him, and listened to Lorna talking in the kitchen to Sam's mother and Faith Budd, as if talking could somehow change things.

Lorna told Marjorie and Faith, "I said to that officer, 'Your buddy Mr. Katerwaller there threatened me with his gun and tried to force me into his car.' And that pig just looked off over my shoulder like he was embarrassed to listen. Mr. Katerwaller was leaning against his big fat car and joking with the second officer while he sorta looked at one of the guns. Then Mr. Katerwaller took back his gun and got in his car and drove off."

Lorna didn't say that Mr. Katerwaller had winked at her as he started the car.

"And all that time, Dace was out there, screaming like he was scared to death and Mr. Katerwaller some kind of boogeyman."

Dace adjusted his position on top of Sam. Dace was sleeping on his side, with his thumb in his mouth, and nestling against Sam's chin. Sam could not even bend over to take off his shoes. He settled into the couch and closed his eyes.

He had stood there like an idiot the whole time, holding on to Dace's hand, and not thought of a thing to say. He should have leaned in Mr. Katerwaller's window and told him, "You're a dumb hick asshole who can't keep his own fly zipped." He should have grabbed the police officer by his belt loop and said, "You arrest this peckerhead. You take away his gun and lock him up." Sam should have thrown a rock through the Chrysler's windshield.

It was three o'clock in the morning, and Roland Katerwaller peered through the night air ahead of his car and saw a tall, gaunt figure backlit against the lights over the highway. There was something monstrous about the figure, which filled Roland Katerwaller with fear, and he put on his brakes. Sam LeBlanc walked around to the passenger window, stuck his hand through to the glove compartment, and pulled out a gun. Then he pointed the gun toward Mr. Katerwaller and said, "You get out this car, mister. You get out this car and take off your shoes and socks and necktie." Mr. Katerwaller got out of the car and looked around him. There was no one else on the highway. He took off his shoes and socks and necktie. "Drop them right there and turn around," said Sam.

"Drop your car keys." Mr. Katerwaller turned around and dropped his car keys. Sam tied up Roland Katerwaller's hands and feet with his shoelaces and silk socks, and he muffled him with his silk necktie. Then Sam rolled Mr. Katerwaller over into the gully dividing the two sides of the highway and sped away in the Chrysler. Mr. Katerwaller lay there all day, until a lady driving her little boy home from school spotted him. It was Gracie McPherson.

Gracie McPherson walked down into the gully and said, "Oh, it's you." She climbed back to her car and left him there.

Then two girls in a VW van drove up, and Allison Paley ran down the slope, saying, "Hey, you all right?" But then, when she recognized Mr. Katerwaller, she said, "You look kind of nice there." When she had climbed back to the top of the gully, she said, "You look even better from here, you ugly old ape."

All afternoon, people in station wagons and beat-up cars were stopping to stare down at Mr. Katerwaller. Finally, there were so many cars gathered on the edge of the highway that a state trooper parked and went down and got Mr. Katerwaller out of the gully.

The telephone rang in the hallway, and Dace opened his eyes for a moment, and then closed them again.

Sam's mother answered and told Lorna that it was her sister Jeanette. Lorna took the phone, and Sam heard her say, "I'll tell you what's funny. For just a split second, when I saw how fancy that car was inside, I thought: Man, I bet it'd be nice to sit in there! Sure, I'll sit in there."

By the time the police officer untied Roland Katerwaller, Dace and Lorna Winsted and Sam LeBlanc were over the Tennessee line and on their way to Alaska. They had painted the Chrysler Day-Glo orange to disguise it, and no one recognized them during the whole trip to the Canadian border. They were the first people to drive a Chrysler New Yorker into Alaska.

"Jeanette says she can't even get the legal men at the court to let us fill out a complaint," Lorna told Sam's mother, putting down the phone for a moment.

Lorna drew the phone back to her ear and said to Jeanette, "You know what gets me? I've been thinking, I might of just got in that car after he showed me that gun. Or some other lady he did that to would of just got in the car. And all along she wouldn't of known that he was such a scaredy-cat that he'd run away if you just told him off." Lorna continued talking on the phone for a while to her sister, and finally hung up.

"Jeanette says we should put ground glass in his dinner next time he comes into Whiteside Manor," Lorna told Marjorie LeBlanc. "Maybe I just might, except I'm quitting the end of this week. By the end of this week, Dace and me'll have enough money to start a new life in Alaska."

* * * *

It's too much, Marjorie LeBlanc thought as she lay in bed the next morning. It's really too much. Marjorie LeBlanc is not just going to sit still and watch the world go by. I'm going to walk over there and tell that Helen Katerwaller a thing or two. Marjorie LeBlanc is not going to live in a country where a man can wave a gun at a girl and try to abduct her and then joke about it with the police afterward.

It was six o'clock, and for all Marjorie knew, Helen Katerwaller was just getting in bed after a night of partying. Well, Marjorie had to be at work by seven forty-five, and Helen Katerwaller was going to have to get up.

Marjorie pulled on her milky nurse's stockings and her uniform and shoes, and bobby-pinned her silly white hat to her hair.

She did not even stop to make herself some coffee first. She walked across the vacant lot and over the road to the patio and banged on the back door of the Katerwallers' house. The back door was right next to Helen's bedroom, and she'd be sure to hear Marjorie.

Sam saw his mother step onto the patio. He had lain awake in bed all night, and at five-thirty he had walked over to the Katerwallers' yard and then around to the back of their house. He had stood on the patio in his T-shirt, waiter's pants, and wing tip shoes and looked at the glass table and the pots of geraniums, and decided that he was going to throw a geranium pot through the glass table. And the next day he would throw a pot at the Chrysler's windshield, and the next day he'd throw one at the Lincoln, and every day he'd come back until all the geraniums were gone and the Katerwallers got so nervous about just being alive that they would have to pack up and leave.

Sam had reached up to a planter and drawn out a large blue pot exploding with red geraniums. He was so tall that the distance of the pot's flight downward from his upraised arms was enough to shatter the table into a thousand pieces. Instead of splintering, the glass broke into little squares that looked like ice cubes. The cubes darted and ricocheted around the patio. He hid behind a fir tree, and waited for Mr. Katerwaller to come out. Sam lit a cigarette. He felt diabolical and criminal. His hair was unbrushed and dark whiskers shadowed the skin over his upper lip. Then Sam saw his mother. He pulled back farther behind the row of pines so that she would not spot him.

Barely a moment after Marjorie LeBlanc knocked, Helen Katerwaller opened the door. Marjorie stepped back in surprise, and Helen, who had been awakened by the sound of shattering glass five minutes before, looked over Marjorie's shoulder.

"The table!" she said. "I thought I heard one of the pots fall onto it! God, what a mess." Mrs. Katerwaller acted as if she thought Marjorie LeBlanc had heard the table break all the way across the vacant lot and come to notify her about it. Helen walked past Marjorie and picked up a pot shard.

The smell of the tobacco mulch enveloped Marjorie. She thought Helen looked terrible. Her hair stuck up in the back, and her face looked oily and creased. She had blue pockets under her eyes.

"I don't know about the table," said Marjorie. "I came to tell you about something else." Marjorie waited until Helen straightened up and looked at her. Then Marjorie spoke in such a loud, forceful way that Sam had no trouble hearing her from behind the pines. "I just want you to know that your husband threatened a girl at the country club with a gun and tried to force her to get into the car with him. I want you to know I think he was going to seduce her at gunpoint."

Marjorie saw Helen Katerwaller's mouth tremble. "I don't believe it," she said. She stuck out her bottom lip with a defiant expression.

"Well, you better believe it, because it's true," Marjorie answered, leaning forward so that Helen had to take a step back. Then Marjorie turned and walked off the patio.

"We could sue you for slander!" Helen called after her. "Roland could sue you for slander and libel for saying a thing like that!"

*　*　*　*

At the country club, Lorna told Sam, "I can't believe what your mother told her! I can't believe old Marjorie LeBlanc went over there and said that. I can't believe you broke her table! I can't believe it."

" 'Well, you better believe it, Mrs. Katerwaller,' Sam said over again, leaning against the pickle-plate table and looking toward Lorna. " 'You had just better believe it.' We could make his life miserable. Me and Mama could go there every morning, and Mama could yell things at them, and I could heave those pots through the windows. 'Well, you better believe it, because it's true,' " Sam repeated, picking up a tray full of pickle plates and backing against the kitchen door. He turned to walk into the dining room and saw the state senator and Bobby Sanford sitting next to Mr. Katerwaller. Sam walked backward into the kitchen and set down the trays.

"He's out there," Sam said. "He's sitting with the state senator and that idiot medical student."

Lorna stopped piling radishes onto the pickle plates and peered through the small window in the kitchen door. Then she took one of the dishes, scraped off all its olives and radishes, and submerged the whole plate, with the remaining celery and carrots, in the disinfecting sink. She buried two old carrot tops and some potato peels under the carrots, and, under the celery, a scrap of wet paper bag from the floor and a tuft of steel wool. She dabbed at the excess water on the plate with a dirty dishrag, and held the dish out to Sam. "Well, take him this little present from me, will you?" Sam carried the plate ceremoniously to Mr. Katerwaller's table and returned to the kitchen. Mr. Katerwaller pretended not to see Sam.

Hardly a minute later, Mrs. Rollins opened the kitchen door, holding the pickle plate, and demanded, "Why aren't there any olives and radishes on this tray?"

Sam looked over at Mr. Katerwaller's table. He had turned around and was frowning at Sam, as if Mrs. Rollins's presence had given Mr. Katerwaller extra courage.

"There was a whole heap of olives on that tray when I brought it out," Sam said loudly.

"Mr. Katerwaller tells me there wasn't an olive on it."

"Well, he's lying," Sam said in a loud voice. "He's just lying, and that's all there is to it."

Mrs. Rollins shook her head and put her finger to her lips. She brushed by Sam with a peeved expression and put down the pickle plate and picked up a new one, with black and green olives and radishes.

Sam pushed the kitchen door back open, and he and Lorna watched Mrs. Rollins set down the plate and say, "There you are, gentlemen. I hope everything's fine and dandy now." Mr. Katerwaller's back was turned to Sam and Lorna, and they heard him grumble something under his breath. Mrs. Rollins hurried to the entranceway to usher in a new party of diners. The state senator and Bobby Sanford and Mr. Katerwaller stuck their hands into the pickle dish at the same time and began wolfing down black olives.

The state senator leaned forward with a leer on his face, and Sam could hear him telling the end of a dirty joke over the noise of the dining room: "So then she sings out from behind the bed, 'I see your hinie, all nice and shiny. You better hide it, or I will bite it!' " The senator waggled his head as he sang, and Bobby Sanford giggled, and Mr. Katerwaller let out three loud guffawing laughs.

His wide shoulders jerked up and down as he guffawed, and then, suddenly, something was wrong. Bobby Sanford was peering at Roland Katerwaller and saying, "Hey, you OK? You all right?" and the state senator was jumping up from his seat. He ran around behind Mr. Katerwaller and thumped him on the back.

"Come on, Buddy. Come on, Buddy," the state senator said over and over as he pounded Mr. Katerwaller's back.

Mrs. Rollins rushed up to the table and said, "My God, my God, my God! He can't breathe!"

"Olive seems to have gone down his windpipe," said the state senator.

Mrs. Rollins joined the state senator in pounding and thumping. From where Lorna and Sam stood, it looked as if Mrs. Rollins and the state senator were beating Mr. Katerwaller to death. Bobby Sanford sat where he was, with his mouth slightly open, and offered no medical advice whatsoever. All the diners at the surrounding tables stood up and looked on with concern.

* * * *

It was the biggest funeral Durham had seen for some time. Marjorie LeBlanc and Faith Budd were not invited. When Hope George drove by in her black Coupe DeVille on the way to the services, Marjorie and Faith were sitting on the front steps drinking gin and tonics and talking about how sad Sam was that Lorna was leaving for Alaska.

"I had to put my foot down," said Marjorie. "I said, 'Sam, when you're done with school, you can go to the moon for all I care. But right now, you're just going to have to wait your turn.' It broke my heart to tell him."

"Lorna doesn't seem like the marrying kind anyway, but maybe Sam could go out and join her when he's older," Faith answered, just as Hope George's car turned the corner.

"I hear Helen Katerwaller's moving away and selling her house," Marjorie remarked.

Both women refrained from saying the nasty things they were thinking about Mr. Katerwaller, out of deference to the widow. They watched the front tire of the Coupe DeVille flatten a cardboard container lying in the road. Helen Katerwaller was sitting in the back seat, adjusting a smoky gray felt hat with a veil that hid the top of her face. She was wearing gray silk gloves that went all the way to her elbow.

6. Living Through

SADDLEBREDS

Marjorie sat on the living room couch, paging through Karen's fashion magazines, looking at the advertisements and any of the pieces on sex, and occasionally stopping to read an article from start to finish. There was an article on eyebrows and one called "Living Through Your Children." The one on eyebrows said that if you had blond or light-brown hair, you should use a black eye pencil to make your eyebrows look one shade darker than your hair. On the other hand, if you had medium-to-dark brown hair, you should use a weak peroxide solution to make your eyebrows a shade lighter than your hair. The other article talked about the danger of being an unfulfilled woman. Unfulfilled women tried to live through their children and husbands, pressuring them in terrible ways, forcing them to do things they had no interest in. Marjorie pondered the words "living through." There was a creepiness about them, something that made her think of a spirit operating through a living person. Like the dead lady in that horror movie *Rebecca,* who kept haunting her husband when he remarried on and tried to go about his normal life. The article urged homemakers to get out of the house, to start hobbies and join associations and do part-time or volunteer work.

Marjorie read the two articles with an equal degree of detachment. The first did not implicate her, since she had black hair, and the second did not because she had always worked and never pushed her children into feeling they had to be successful. All she wanted from her children was a little company. If she had her way, they could just stay at home with her forever, never making anything of themselves at all. She let them get away with murder.

Marjorie shifted into a more comfortable position on the couch, picked up a stack of *Cosmopolitan*s, and looked at all the covers, staring especially long at a model wearing metallic eye shadow that made her eyelids look like bottle caps. Marjorie's ankles were swollen and her feet were killing her, so Ruth had told her to spend Saturday lying down, with her legs propped on the sofa arm, and Karen had dragged piles of *Cosmopolitan, Mademoiselle,* and *Glamour* magazines into the living room. Sam and Carla had brought Marjorie a cup of coffee and a plate of sweet rolls. The children treated Marjorie this way once in a blue moon, and whenever they did, it was just like Mother's Day: They walked around congratulating themselves for spending one morning doing what she had done for them all their lives. And then Marjorie had to make a fuss and praise them for every little thing, so that by the end of it all she was exhausted.

This morning, after their half hour of spoiling her, Marjorie's children had vanished, drifting out of the living room one by one. Carla was learning how to drive Bubba Kearny's semitruck, Sam had wandered aimlessly up the street with his hands in his pockets, and Karen was at her friend Sally Ann Ruby's. They were probably pretending to study French and deciding what to do with their eyebrows. If Marjorie remembered correctly, Sally Ann didn't have any eyebrows; she plucked them off and drew new ones on. At the hospital, Marjorie had once gone into the maternity ward and been spooked by a strangely bald face: It was a girl who had just woken up after having a cesarean and had not had time to draw on the eyebrows she had plucked out. She had reminded Marjorie of the Phantom of the Opera. Marjorie tried not to think of her daughter Karen's face looking like that.

Ruth had stomped off into Sam's bedroom after Marjorie tried to have a friendly discussion with her. Now Marjorie's oldest daughter was looking through the course catalog for City College in New York, where she had been accepted before asking for a year's deferral. Ruth said she was afraid college would stunt her growth if she didn't spend some time in the real world first. Marjorie had been arguing with Ruth all fall to get her to take advantage of the year's deferral and apply to local schools. Ruth had told her mother there was no point in going away to college except the going away part. Marjorie had answered that if she felt that way, why study in college at all? Marjorie pointed out that Ruth did not even know what courses she wanted to take.

"I certainly don't want to be a nurse, that's for sure," Ruth had told Marjorie the next morning over breakfast.

Marjorie, who was looking at herself in the toaster and adjusting her nurse's hat, answered, "That's fine with me. Neither do I."

Ruth said that she might major in quantum mechanics, or maybe political science, which was one good reason not to go to a local school, where they wouldn't even have political science; they would call it government. Marjorie could hardly follow this argument. Ruth also declared that she would probably have to pretend to be a man to major in political science. She said she had noticed that if a man talked about human rights, everyone called him a communist, but if a woman talked about the same things, everyone called her a do-gooder or a social worker. A man who talked politics, he was dangerous. A woman, she was naive. Ruth said that whatever she did, she wanted it to keep her looking mean and dangerous. Marjorie said that would probably be easier in a small town than in New York. Ruth explained that she wasn't such a yokel as to think New York City was the end of the world; she hoped to find a way to study in Peking, and maybe Brazil as well.

Both Ruth and Carla bent over backward to find jobs that

offered danger and adventure, that would allow them to swagger around looking like Jesse James. At the beginning of the summer, Carla had found a job as a file clerk in a prison, and Ruth worked afternoons after school helping a veterinarian vaccinate large livestock. Ruth complained that her job was turning out to be a little more than "nursework for animals instead of people," and Carla quit at the prison in September because they discouraged her from talking with the inmates; the staff just sent her on errands for sandwiches and coffee and let her revamp the old bail records when she got bored. Then Ruth got a racehorse farm to hire her and Carla to muck out stalls and chauffeur rich people's horses to horse shows. For a while, Ruth had talked seriously about becoming a jockey, but her interest seemed to be flagging. Sooner or later, Marjorie mused, Ruth would come to see that there wasn't a job on earth worth having.

When Marjorie had been Ruth's age, all she had hoped for was to marry quickly so that her mother wouldn't send her to nursing school to land a doctor for a husband. Marjorie would have preferred never to work a day in her life. And she certainly had never wasted time as a girl wondering about what kind of job she wanted.

Marjorie thought she had never had any influence on her children at all. Ruth floated off into the world and came back with strange ideas about women's liberation and the President and good music and the right movies to see, and did everything under her power to influence her mother. Marjorie smirked at the "Living Through Your Children" article lying face open on the floor. It was Ruth who always had to test and weigh her ideas by running them through her mother. Marjorie never felt that she had to strain her thoughts through anybody.

Carla honked the horn of Bubba Kearny's semitruck and parked it in front of the LeBlancs'. When Marjorie waved, Carla jumped out of the driver's seat and Bubba Kearny climbed down from the right side of the cab. He was a bony boy with cinnamon-colored hair and large ears. He walked around the front of the truck with his hands buried deep in his pockets and looked at his shoes when Carla talked to him. He climbed into the driver's seat and drove the truck back down the road.

Carla banged the front door open against the wall. Her face was flushed and she was breathing hard. "I'm going to be a lady truckdriver!" she told Marjorie in tones of rapture.

"You be careful you're not leading Bubba on," said Marjorie. "He's sweet on you, and you don't want to hurt his feelings."

Carla looked at her mother with a shocked expression and said, "He's not that kind of guy!" as if Marjorie had somehow insulted Bubba. Then Carla turned and called down the hallway, "Hey, Ruth, let's get a move on. We gotta be going."

"Going where?" Marjorie asked.

"To work."

"Today? But it's Saturday."

Ruth stumbled into the room, pulling on some boots. "It's a horse show. We have to help this lady who owns this big fancy Saddlebred that cost twice as much as a Chrysler New Yorker. She doesn't know how to drive a horse trailer or anything."

"Weekends are the only time I have to spend with you all," Marjorie pouted.

Her daughters exchanged secretive smiles, like two accomplices. Except for their sallow coloring and dark hair, they didn't remind Marjorie of herself at all. But you could see from a mile away that Carla and Ruth were related to one another. They were both too tall for girls, and then there were those long, bony faces towering over their lantern jaws. Only Karen managed to look more conventional, copying her face every morning from those magazine articles showing how to apply makeup.

Carla rolled her eyes. "Evenings are the only time I have

to spend with my children!" she said in a melodramatic voice.

Ruth added, "Breakfast is the only meal where we all still see each other."

"Sundays are special family days," Carla intoned.

"Karen, you are not going away to any special summer camp for learning French. You'll be leaving home soon enough."

"Don't go to the grocery store. There's plenty of food here."

"Don't go to school. Watch educational television."

"Don't go out to buy clothes. If you stay home, you can walk around naked."

Marjorie had to laugh. "You two!" she told her daughters. "You make me feel like an old clutchy thing."

* * * *

Ruth talked Marjorie into driving to the horse show. This was Ruth's idea of a compromise, but Marjorie had not wanted to leave home at all. She had wanted to stay put on the couch. If she was lucky, she might have convinced one of the children to remain home with her. Somehow she always let herself be persuaded.

Marjorie stopped the Oldsmobile down the road to pick up Faith Budd. She had been cleaning up her sons' room, and when Ruth rang the bell, Faith sprang through her door wearing a psychedelic T-shirt that said "The Grateful Dead" on it, and her son Lou's sunglasses, which Marjorie said made Faith look like a horsefly.

"You better change those shoes," Ruth told her, pointing down to some Moroccan leather slippers Bertha had sent Faith for Christmas. "If a horse steps on your foot, he'll break your toe." Faith ran back in the house and came out a few minutes later in an old pair of boy's work boots, her hair tied back in a red bandanna. "I look like an escaped lunatic!" she proclaimed happily as she got into the Oldsmobile. "Boy, am I glad you all came and rescued me. I didn't have anything to keep me company but Johnnie Walker."

Marjorie parked the Oldsmobile at the stable, and she and Faith climbed into the cab of a horse trailer as Ruth and Carla loaded an enormous chestnut horse. Ruth got into the driver's seat, and Carla rode in the empty half of the trailer with an Irish setter from the farm. When they reached the showgrounds, Faith ran straight to the ring, but Marjorie stayed behind to watch her daughters unload the horse. Ruth tugged the animal by the head, while Carla pushed on its shoulders. The horse kicked against the sides of the trailer, and sprang backward in one sudden motion. Marjorie stepped sideways onto a rusted nail sticking out of a board.

Marjorie was so terrified of horses that she barely noticed. She leaned down, yanked the nail from the sole of her nurse's shoe, and threw the board into a clump of pines. Ordinarily, she would have checked to see that the nails were pointing downward, but all she could think of were the silvery U's glinting on the horse's feet. She kept her eye on the animal as Carla backed it out while cursing at it and saying, "Come on, Ugly Mug, move your fat behind."

"I hope Mrs. Fisk doesn't win any ribbons today on Udder Failure," Ruth told her mother, scratching the horse on the neck. Mrs. Fisk was the owner of Utter Valour, a delicate Saddlebred mare with nervous brown and violet eyes ringed by startled whites. Carla and Ruth bent down to unwrap what looked to Marjorie like green Ace bandages from the horse's legs.

"Don't worry, Mama," said Carla. "Udder Failure's too stupid to kick."

Marjorie nodded, remembering her own foot. She thought she should probably get a tetanus shot. She had her last one when? Five years ago, when she scraped herself on the barbwire Ruth had dragged home? Or had that been three years ago? It was before Ruth had cut the barbs off to keep in the box under her bed. Marjorie could not remember. Had she gotten a tetanus booster? There had been some controversy as to whether the booster shots were advisable anyway: Marjorie had learned in her nursing courses that some doctors believed the original shot should be good for over ten years. But had Marjorie ever been given a tetanus shot at all? The children had been vaccinated against measles, tetanus, polio, DPT, and smallpox, and Carla had gotten that horrible rabies series when she was four, after bringing home that mole in the coffee can, and the three girls probably would require German measles shots.

"Hey, Mama, you there?" Ruth asked, her face directly over Marjorie's. "Can you hold these a second?" Ruth handed her the pile of Ace bandages, smelling of liniment, and Carla led the horse over to a silver-haired woman dressed in a silk cowboy shirt, tight red pants, and a bowler derby. Carla helped Mrs. Fisk mount her horse, and the woman sat back in the saddle, pushing her pointy boots forward. Marjorie liked rich horsey people even less than horses. When horsey ladies appeared on television, they were often aristocratic girls who killed their mothers to get an inheritance sooner. Or they were oversexed women who encouraged men to accompany them on rides through lush green countrysides. Or they were well-preserved spinsters with unnatural attachments to their horses.

Marjorie put the Ace bandages in the cab of the trailer, walked over to the clump of pine trees, turned over the board she had stepped on, and then pushed on it to embed the nails well into the ground. She walked back toward her daughters and noted her foot was not hurting—although her legs were still killing her from standing up in the hospital all yesterday.

She watched Ruth raise Mrs. Fisk's stirrups. Mrs. Fisk was holding her leg up daintily and talking in a girly, aristocratic drawl. "Oh, Ruthie," she said, and Marjorie wondered. Ruthie? with the hostility mothers feel toward people who warp their children's given names. She suddenly thought of

Helen Katerwaller—where was she now? Helen had never even called Marjorie by her rightful name—it had always been "Margie".

"Ruthie, you're a wonder. I wish you had more free time to train good saddle horses instead of shoveling out those ole race horses' stalls and taking care of them. I don't know what I'll do now that I've lost Marla to exercise Utter Valour for me. U.V. has started cutting up something awful since that girl left. It's always a shame to see girls grow up and lose interest in horses. I told her she should have stayed down here and studied at Wake Forest, but she had to go off to Holy Oat up north. And now she's gone and dropped out to work on that *Angela Davis* to-do. I saw Marla at the stable last Christmas, and she had grown an Afro out to here." Mrs. Fisk dropped the reins and held her hands at arms' length like someone demonstrating the size of a fish that had escaped from a line. "When I knew her, she always just had simple braids," Mrs. Fisk added to indicate that she alone knew the real Marla. "She braided her hair in French braids, just like you do the tail of a horse."

"I'm going to City College in New York City," said Ruth. Out of pure spite toward Mrs. Fisk, and for the first time since Ruth had received news of her admission, Marjorie felt glad her daughter was leaving the state to go to school.

Mrs. Fisk gathered up her reins as if she were afraid Utter Valour might run off to a northern university as well. Carla slapped the horse on the rump and said, "There you go!" Utter Valour skipped forward with high, animated steps.

Carla and Ruth sat down together on the trailer ramp, and Marjorie wedged herself between them. The Irish setter whom Carla had brought in the trailer threw herself in front of Marjorie like a grain sack heaved from a truck. When the dog hit the ground, she said, "Whump!" and then wagged her tail and tilted back her head on Ruth's shoe.

"Mama, this job is the pits," said Carla.

"I can't take this anymore, anymore, anymore," Ruth moaned. "I like the animals fine, but the people—"

"The only fun thing," said Carla, "is when Ruth sneaks
out with Udder Failure in the woods behind the back pasture
and races her around until she breaks gait."

"We had a bet," said Ruth. "We didn't know if you could
get a fancy Saddlebred like that to trot and gallop around
like other horses, but you sure can. Udder Failure downright
enjoys it."

"Mrs. Fisk hasn't won a ribbon in weeks, because Udder
Failure has started doing some pretty strange things in the
ring," Carla confirmed.

Marjorie was not sure what her girls were talking about.
They were always wandering off into worlds completely un-
known to her, gathering peculiar scraps of knowledge. She
suspected that making a horse "break gait" was some form
of delinquency. "Well, if you all don't like working at that
stable, Karen always has more than enough baby-sitting re-
quests, and she could find you jobs in a minute to tide you
over. She says the Carmichaels offer her more work than she
can accept."

It occurred to Marjorie that "baby-sit" was an awfully
strange word. It made her picture someone setting up babies
in a row of high chairs. And then she pondered whether
"baby" referred to the person doing the sitting. Karen was
only sixteen, hardly more than a child herself. Just two years
ago, Mrs. Busybody George had told Marjorie that Karen
had gotten into trouble with the Carmichaels for trampling
down their flowers to make faces in their windows at night.
Now Karen spent three days a week tyrannizing the Carmichael boys into behaving.

"Last time," said Ruth, "I baby-sat for the Carmichaels,
Tommy peed on his brother Parks, and Parks dropped Mr.
Carmichael's toy soldier collection out the second story window, and then William Emory got into the bottom desk
drawer and found these dirty magazines and spread them all
over the floor—"

"Mr. Carmichael collects toy soldiers?" Carla interrupted.

"Lots of grown men do," said Marjorie.

"Boy, does he collect toy soldiers. He spends hours painting their Confederate flags and decorating their uniforms. He has little miniature cannons and rifles, and some of the soldiers come lying down so that you can't stand them up and they have to be dead, and he paints blood spots on those."

"It's perfectly natural for a grown man to have girlie magazines," Marjorie thought to add.

"Not these magazines," said Ruth. "There's one with this man tying up this poor donkey and—"

"Well!" Marjorie said. "If you don't like baby-sitting for the Carmichaels, there's always the Starkweathers."

"They shortchange you," said Carla.

"I wish we could of went to Iceland with Aunt Bertha," said Ruth, but she regretted the words as soon as they escaped from her mouth. Aunt Bertha had gone on another archaeological expedition for the summer and fall and had written Marjorie, offering to take Ruth and Sam along for a few weeks, but Marjorie had answered that her children were too young to travel that far. Ruth's mother had decided you had to be at least twenty-one before you could leave North America. Ruth had told her, "Plenty of guys are drafted overseas when they're younger than that. Old enough to fight, old enough to travel." Marjorie had just stared at Ruth's war protest T-shirt, which was the one that read: "Join the army, travel to exotic places, meet new exciting people and kill them," and then told her daughter: "Sam is *not* old enough to fight."

Now Marjorie turned toward Carla and said huffily, "Well, I'm not your Aunt Bertha. I'm just plain old Marjorie LeBlanc. I may not be the most exciting mother in the world, but I do my best."

"Aw, Mama." Carla tried to stop her.

"Why, Bertha hasn't even written me since she left. If you were with her now, I'd be worrying myself to death. I couldn't even get a hold of you in an emergency."

"Since when have the LeBlancs ever had an emergency?"

Ruth said. She picked up a rusted wire lying inside the trailer and began twisting it.

Marjorie noted to herself that Ruth had never learned to act the way you expected older daughters to. Even when she was little, Ruth had just been a ringleader for the other children, first with Sam and later with Carla, whenever there was some mischief to be done. And in junior high and grade school, Ruth had been just plain bad; Marjorie was the first to admit it. Karen was the one Marjorie would have picked for an older daughter—you didn't find her chasing snakes and swearing and getting thrown out of American Legion assemblies at school for refusing to say the pledge of allegiance. Karen didn't irritate all men in Marjorie's generation by saying the most outrageous thing anyone could think of, for the pure pleasure of it. But then, Karen wasn't exactly the kind of person you might want to trust a secret to, either. Oldest daughters were supposed to share their mothers' confidences. Not one of Marjorie's girls had come out the way daughters should. What had ever happened to that hardworking oldest daughter Marjorie used to see as a girl? The kind who was heavyset and unmarriageable, old beyond her years, who did the laundry for all the boys in the family and cooked dinner and solved domestic disputes? The kind of daughter who did not insist on talking back about every little thing?

"Mama," Carla said, "I'll bet you Aunt Bertha has written. It's just she's way out in the country somewhere, where the mail's extra slow."

"Humph!" Marjorie answered.

"If I were in some amazing place, I sure wouldn't waste time writing a letter," Ruth announced.

"Well," said Marjorie, who did not want to argue with two of her daughters at once, "no job is perfect." It took Ruth and Carla a moment to remember what their mother was referring to. "You just have to make the best bad choice." This had become one of Marjorie's favorite sayings, although she usually applied it to eligible men rather than jobs.

The dog lifted her head and gave a low whine, which rose to a bark. She rattled her tail against the chain connecting the ramp to the trailer. Ruth tickled the dog's neck, and then twisted the wire in her hand into a crude pair of spectacles and balanced them on the dog's nose.

"Look, Mama, she's indognito." Ruth removed the glasses and tossed them under the trailer.

"Now I've been putting up with Dr. Mooks and Dr. Leaks for a long time, biting my tongue every minute of every day to keep from complaining."

"Well, that must be awful hard on your poor old tongue," Ruth answered. She wished Marjorie LeBlanc would give the doctors a piece of her mind just once. For years, she had been telling her children that Dr. Mooks and Dr. Leaks, two of the highest-ranking surgeons in the hospital, had laid hundreds of perfectly healthy patients to rest. Dr. Leaks was "a tall, fine specimen of a Harvard man, with all his hair but nothing in his head," and his nickname among the nurses was "Hands." Carla and Ruth already knew that Dr. Mooks never waited for the painkiller to take effect before giving you stitches, and that a leg bone he set would grow out as crookedly as a tree branch around a boll. Marjorie always said she had never been sick a day in her life, but if she were, the first place she'd go was as far as possible from the hospital where she worked.

"Friday," said Marjorie, "Dr. Mooks received some kind of fancy-pancy award from the A.M.A., but Nurse Arrington saw him just that morning spill a cup of coffee on a stroke patient and not so much as say he was sorry. Well, I'm not bringing my work home with me. Aren't we going to watch this horse show?"

"Y'all go," said Carla. "I'm closing up the trailer." Carla stood and the dog sprang sideways from the ramp. For a moment, the dog looked as if she would land just as she started, ribs to the ground, but then she twisted into the air and landed on her feet.

Ruth and her mother wandered around other horse trailers toward a noisy area behind a stable. When they rounded the building, this is what they saw: women in sequined and silk cowboy blouses that matched the bridles of their horses; cigar-smoking men in three-piece suits and bowler derbies, perched heavily over their horses' kidneys; horses foaming at the mouth and sweating and plunging harum-scarum against each other in a way that made Marjorie think of a terrified crowd trying to escape from a burning movie theater. Around the ring were onlookers carrying toddlers and picnic baskets and red and blue and yellow ribbons. Certain portions of the crowd identified themselves as being related to a particular rider by catcalling and whistling when a horse went by. Marjorie squeezed by a man who was shouting into the ring, "You show 'em, sugar. You show those judges."

Ruth waved to Faith Budd, who was standing on the other side of the ring, her wild outfit looking almost commonplace in comparison with her surroundings. Faith disappeared for a moment behind a large rust-colored horse that seemed to be running in place and trying to throw its head off its shoulders and onto the judges.

"Ooooh, look at Udder Failure, Mama!" Ruth said.

Utter Valor ran across the middle of the ring, stopped dead, stumbled forward with springy steps, and headed toward Marjorie, turning jerkily at the last moment. Mrs. Fisk bounced up and down in the saddle, and Marjorie clearly heard her say, "Oh, fuck you, U.V.!" as seven or eight other horses rushed by.

"Ho ho!" Ruth cried behind Marjorie. The people on Marjorie's right made ratlike noises with their mouths, hooted, clicked their tongues, and yodeled.

* * * *

Faith had worked her way back around the ring to where Marjorie and Ruth stood. Faith's bandanna had come loose, and she had twisted her hair into an onion-shaped topknot.

She looked through her sunglasses at Marjorie and said, "I never thought a horse show would be like this. I thought they would be somehow, well, more high and mighty. I thought there would be a man with a pack of foxhounds in a red jacket, and ladies riding around in those big-bottom pants and black baseball hats."

"This is a different style of riding," Ruth told Faith. "This is saddle seat; this is the *South.*"

Marjorie though it was ridiculous the way Ruth liked to use the word "South" to suggest a bizarre, exotic world. Before Marjorie could think of an adequate response, Ruth leaned over the fence rail and said, "Hey, there's Carla driving up the road on the other side of the ring."

Marjorie looked over the horses and saw her youngest daughter beckoning her from the cab of the horse trailer. The dog's tongue flapped out the window, pinker than dogwoods.

What bothered Marjorie was that Ruth had driven the trailer to the show and was now jingling the trailer keys in her pocket.

"I think Carla must have hot-wired that thing," Marjorie told Faith.

"I bet," Faith hooted.

"She's waving at us," said Ruth. "She wants us to go over there."

Marjorie and Faith followed Ruth around a little girl who whined, "But I didn't want second place, I wanted first place," and past four men who reminded Marjorie of bullfrogs, all with big puffy necks, wearing derbies and croaking at the sweating, frenzied horses in the ring.

When Ruth, Faith, and Marjorie reached the trailer, Carla said, "I have an idea. I thought we could drive back to the stable and then take the car along that road toward Hillsborough and look for box turtles."

"How will Mrs. Fisk get back?" Marjorie inquired.

"Oh, she can ride," Ruth said.

Then she sputtered with laughter, making Marjorie feel

doubtful. Could a horse walk thirty miles in one afternoon? Marjorie looked behind her at the ring: fire-colored dust jumped up from the horses' heels. "We just got here, and already you want to barrel off to someplace else," she told Ruth.

But Faith Budd was climbing into the trailer cab and crying, "Don't look back, Marjorie—you'll turn into a pillar of salt!" and Marjorie allowed herself to be cajoled into the driver's seat. Carla slid out obligingly and climbed in the back of the trailer with the dog and Ruth. Marjorie drove the trailer the thirty miles to the stable, while Ruth and Carla pounded on the metal wall behind the driver's seat, making animals sounds.

"Mooo!" Ruth called. The dog and Carla howled.

"Wild things!" Marjorie shouted back. When they arrived at the stable, Marjorie parked the trailer behind a large structure full of hay bales, where the girls directed her between snickers.

"Don't think I don't know you all are up to no good," Marjorie told her daughters as she got out of the trailer and slid into the Oldsmobile. Ruth and Carla piled into the front seat between their mother and Faith.

"I know you're plotting some kind of mischief," Marjorie continued, but she unloosed a devil-may-care titter, which spun in the air behind the car, mingling with Faith Budd's loud, soaring laugh. Ruth imagined the laughs caught up into the wind and blowing over the pinewoods like two runaway kites.

THE BUDD HOUSE

Sam had strung a chicken-wire fence around the back garden and turned the box turtles loose inside. There were four, of varying shades of green, and all of them had refused to eat since Faith Budd and the LeBlancs had picked them up from the rainy road and brought them home in the Oldsmobile a month before. Ruth sat on the back steps, watching Sam as he bent over and held a piece of lettuce before the largest turtle, which had its neck and tail out but was ignoring him. Finally, the turtle pulled its head back into its shell until only the eyes and beak showed. The turtle gave Sam a stony look and Sam returned it.

Karen had perched herself on the sill of the bedroom window that faced the back yard. She was watching Sam and sewing a piece of needlepoint. The pattern was a small blue house with pink dogwoods blooming in front of it, and Karen was just starting on the dogwoods. "Maybe those turtles aren't eating because they belong in the woods. Maybe they don't like it here."

"I think they aren't eating out of spite," said Carla. "Well, you know how reptiles are, the way a snake can go a year without eating if he just swallows a mouse at Easter." Carla had taken apart the Oldsmobile's carburetor that morning and was cleaning the parts with a filthy red rag, and laying them out carefully on a piece of cardboard resting in the grass.

Mr. Mintor's new coon hound came around the corner of the house, dragging a leather strap attached to its choke chain. The dog snuffled along the edge of the chicken wire, bared its teeth at Carla, and then suddenly sank to the ground, its tail between its legs, as if it had taken a fright at all the LeBlancs penned inside the chicken wire.

Mr. Mintor's voice rose up from the road. "Buster! You git the hell down here."

Mr. Mintor climbed the hill and picked up his dog's leash. Buster groaned. Mr. Mintor was wearing one of his famous dirty ties. He was dressed formally, as if he had been on his way out the door to his undertaking business, but his sky-blue silk tie had a spot of mustard on it.

"Chained him to the flagpole out back and he snuck off on me," Mr. Mintor explained, looking embarrassed. He put both hands in his pockets, even the hand holding the leash. He asked Sam if the chicken-wire fence was for the turtles and then said it was a good idea, turning to point out all the squashed frogs and snakes on the road, lying flat and dried as pressed flowers.

"How's your mama doin'?" Mr. Mintor asked Sam.

"She's resting," Ruth called out.

Mr. Mintor nodded and then turned to leave, as if this were all he had come by to ask anyway.

Ruth thought of her mother, cheered on by Faith Budd, getting out of the car on the road into Hillsborough and calling, "I'll get him!" then darting into the woods lining the road shoulder, to emerge a minute later with a box turtle the size of a coin purse. The light rain was turning Marjorie Le-Blanc's lilac blouse to a royal purple, and she stopped in the middle of the road to waggle the box turtle at Faith Budd.

"We've done it," Ruth had said. "We've sent our mother over the deep end." But both she and Carla had been caught in a moment of perfect happiness, their jobs abandoned behind them, their mother forgetting in that absentminded way she had when confronted with her children's wickedness to inquire about Carla's hot-wiring the trailer. Carla and Ruth had sat pressed together, with yellow-and-green turtles scrabbling on their legs, and at that moment it had seemed as if anything was possible: They could have picked up their mother and Faith Budd and driven the car right off the top of the hill, upward toward the moon.

Now, as Ruth watched her brother and sisters, she felt restless. She got the strange sensation she sometimes did that she was never going to come to the end of her childhood. Here she had been on earth more than eighteen years, and not one of them spent on her own as an adult. This thought always filled her with a terrible impatience, or vanity at her amazing patience; if she could have bought a ticket and taken a bus out of her family into her womanhood, she would have. At the moment, Ruth felt cemented to the back steps, caught in a frame of time where Sam would always be stooped over, staring quietly at a box turtle, and Karen stitching a gloriously ugly needlepoint, balancing on the windowsill in her nylon hose and high-heeled sandals, set slightly apart from the other LeBlancs. Carla would be bent forever over a car motor, her lopsided ponytail angling over her shoulder. And Marjorie LeBlanc would be in the living room, stretched out on the couch, with her swollen ankles propped on a stack of magazines.

Karen got up from the windowsill, disappeared inside for a moment, and then stuck her head back out the window. "Hey, Ruth—Mama wants you."

Ruth opened the back door and then secured it against the wall with a rock, to cool off the kitchen. Her motions were measured, slow as possible, because she suspected her mother was going to ask her to make dinner. "Always the oldest child!" she said aloud to anyone who cared to hear.

"Honey," Ruth heard her mother say in a tone she had never used before. "I can't open my eye." Either the tone or the words pierced Ruth with such foreboding that she stopped dead under the lintel of the living room door before going forward.

Marjorie was sitting up on the couch, one eyelid drooping above her cheek like a half-moon. "I didn't think anything of it when I got up this morning," she told her daughter, "but I've started to feel a little numbness in my legs, and now I wonder what it could be. I showed my eye to Dr. Mooks yesterday at work, and he said I was just being nervous and high-strung and told me to take a tranquilizer. But now it's just gotten worse. I really don't think this is a nervous tic at all."

Marjorie studied her daughter, as if Ruth were the one who was ill. "I saw Carla's taken apart the Oldsmobile again. I think maybe I should get Faith Budd to drive me down to the hospital." Marjorie stood up and walked toward the hall closet, and her legs crumpled. She tilted against the wall and walked back to the couch, dragging her right foot.

"Mama!" Ruth cried. "Oh my God, Mama!" Ruth stood paralyzed for a moment, and then she ran to the hall and dialed Faith Budd's number. Ruth pictured her brother and sisters out in the backyard, unaware of anything, caught motionless in a different world. But as Ruth listened to the Budds' phone ring, Karen came into the hall.

"What's going on?" she asked in a quavery voice. Mrs. Budd picked up the phone before Ruth could answer Karen.

"This is Ruth! There's something wrong with Mama! I think she's having a stroke. She wants you to take her to the hospital."

"Don't you worry, Honey," Mrs. Budd said in the calmest voice Ruth had ever heard her use. "I'm coming directly."

Ruth hung up the phone and Karen followed her into the living room. Marjorie was lying down on the couch. She had folded her arms on her stomach, and her fingers were curling crazily, cross-eyed, Ruth thought, but that wasn't the right word.

"It's not a stroke, Ruth," Marjorie said evenly. "I heard what you told Faith, but the symptoms aren't right." Marjorie seemed to sink lower into the pillow, closing her eyes and scowling, as if she were pondering all the sick people she had tended, trying to call up the right one.

Karen rushed through the kitchen and into the backyard and said, "There's something wrong with Mama! Mrs. Budd's taking Mama to the hospital!" Sam and Karen and Carla came crowding into the living room, and the next time Marjorie opened her eyes she saw her four children straining over her with looks of apprehension. They seemed to be peering at her from a great height, as if she had fallen into a well or a mine shaft. She tried to move toward them, but the weight of her own body overpowered her.

"I'm right here!" Marjorie told them. She heard Faith Budd's car pull into the drive.

Faith, dressed in a boy's bathrobe and her red slippers, threw open the front door and called out, "Sam and Ruth, you help me with your mother." Faith and Ruth pulled

Marjorie up and she walked a few wobbling steps between them until her legs gave out.

"I'll carry her," said Sam. Of all the things that had happened to Ruth so far—hearing her mother first cry out, seeing her eye droop over her face, watching her legs weaken and her hands curl—what Ruth remembered later with terror was that moment when Sam, who suddenly looked so old and tall—why hadn't Ruth noticed?—lifted up their mother and carried her as if she were no more than a sleepy child.

"There isn't room for all of you in the Chevrolet," said Faith. "Carla and Karen, I want you to go over to my house and wait for me there. We're going to have to stretch Marjorie out in the back seat."

"No," said Marjorie. "They can come. I want to sit up."

"Not on your life!" Faith Budd told her.

"I want to sit because it hurts my back to lie down. Meningitis?" Marjorie asked, as Sam helped her into the back of the car. Karen and Ruth got in after her, and Carla sat on Sam's lap in the front seat.

"Franklin Delano took the pickup, so we'll just have to see what this Chevy can do," Faith Budd said, turning on the ignition and racing the Chevrolet out of the driveway. She sped by stop signs and a cement mixer and traffic signals onto the highway, where she passed every car or truck in front of her, from both the right and left lanes. No one noticed the Chevrolet. No one honked, no police sirens started up behind them, as always seemed to happen in the movies when taxicabs raced toward the hospital transporting women in labor. How funny, Ruth thought, as the Chevrolet finally skidded into the road to the hospital. It's as if there were a separate world in this car belonging to the LeBlancs, and the world out there doesn't have anything to do with us.

When Faith Budd stopped the Chevrolet in a doctor's parking space outside the hospital, Marjorie said, "I'm having trouble talking, but it's not a stroke. I can think of the words, but I can't move my jaw." Marjorie suddenly pictured a rust-colored horse with nervous violet eyes looking down at her. Two orderlies who called Marjorie by name rushed her through the double doors on a wheeled bed, with her four children and Mrs. Budd in her bathrobe and slippers running behind. Marjorie came to rest in the hospital foyer in front of Dr. Mooks and said, "Tetanus."

Dr. Mooks laid his hand on Marjorie's forehead. With a tranquillity that made Ruth want to grab him by his lapels and shake him, he said, "No fever. Can't be tetanus. No such thing as tetanus without a fever. Did you notice a fever earlier today?"

"No, but it's tetanus."

Then Dr. Mooks did an astonishing thing. He wandered away from the wheeled bed where Marjorie lay, and he walked to a vending machine and bought himself a Baby Ruth bar and then came back into the foyer.

"I can't move my jaw," Marjorie said in a close-lipped way that gave her a definite look of animosity. "My muscles don't work in my face, and my hands and spine hurt."

"Meningitis?" Dr. Mooks asked, as if he were offering Marjorie something to eat. "Nope. No fever, no meningitis."

"Marjorie!" Penny Arrington seemed to swirl into the foyer from nowhere. "What's this? Marjorie LeBlanc sick? What's going on?" She looked down at Marjorie.

"Tetanus," Marjorie said. Could she have had a fever earlier and simply not noticed? Marjorie could see Penny's hair crowning her face like a circle of silvery flower petals. She seemed to sway on her stalk and bend closer. Marjorie smelled a sweet, honeyish smell. But she could not lift her eyelids enough to see well, and the pain in her spine was unlike anything she had felt before. So this is what pain is! she thought, recalling times she had bent with concern but without empathy over cancer victims and patients newly emerged from the operating rooms.

"Can't be tetanus." She heard Dr. Mooks's voice receding, as if he were backing away. "No fever."

"Well, what's she doing in the foyer!" Penny Arrington cried over Marjorie. "You children sit down right in there. Marjorie, you're coming with me." Marjorie felt herself being wheeled along a hallway. A hand rested on her forehead, and she heard Penny Arrington's voice. "It's true, no fever. Well," Penny said under her breath, "it can't hurt to run an analysis for tetanus, and it's worth it just to spite that old Mooks. He never knows what's going on here anyway, does he, Marjorie?" Marjorie tried to laugh, but instead a feeling that was neither death nor sleep, but just a kind of stillness, took her over.

* * * *

For dinner, Mrs. Budd would cook meals complete with meat, a starch, three vegetables, and dessert, and for weekend lunches she would bring sandwiches with the crusts cut off to the LeBlancs' kitchen and leave the sandwiches for Marjorie's children to eat whenever they wanted. Faith Budd did not approve of children sleeping alone in their own house, and so at night Sam would stay on the Budds' living room couch, while Carla, Ruth, and Karen slept down the hall in the Budd boys' old room.

Faith took one LeBlanc at a time to the hospital, and would not allow any of them to accompany her more than once a week, because she said the hospital was too depressing a place for children. Even when Marjorie's son and daughters visited her, they could only stand over their mother, who lay sleeping or drugged.

Ruth would sit by her mother's bed, staring at her sleeping face, pale as salt, and think: How can you die when there's so many things you don't even know about me! For although Ruth had been aching for the day when she could set out alone in the world, she had always seen Marjorie LeBlanc as somehow standing in the distance behind her, marveling at Ruth's adventures.

Ruth imagined her mother surfacing to consciousness for

only ten minutes while no one else was in her hospital room. Before sickness lulled Marjorie LeBlanc back into wooziness and incomprehension, Ruth would make her listen to the things Ruth wanted to tell her mother but had never been able to. Ruth told about the time, kept secret from Marjorie LeBlanc all these years, that Ruth and Carla and Blue Henry had killed a cottonmouth snake with only bricks and a knife, and then hung the snake on a signpost. Ruth told how Karen used to walk around peering into people's windows and then other things that had happened as the children moved away from their childhoods. How Carla had a kind of genius for stealing, and how Karen secretly wrote letters to her father's address in New Jersey, and that Sam was putting aside money to go to Alaska as soon as he finished the school year. Ruth told how after a concert called "Jubilee," held in Chapel Hill, Truman Sharpless had driven her toward home, and stopped on a back road and pushed her down on the front seat; how she had fought him and then given in when he pinned her arms to her sides and shamed her by saying, "Hey, Baby, be cool, be cool, I thought you were cool"; and how since then Ruth had stopped sleeping with boys and hated Truman with such a piercing hatred Ruth herself could not make sense of it. Ruth finally told her mother there were lots more things she might like to know, and then, in Ruth's imagination, Marjorie LeBlanc would sit up in her hospital bed and lean forward, listening intently.

After two weeks, Marjorie's illness became more serious, and Faith and the children were not allowed in Marjorie's room. "She can't receive visitors right now," Ruth heard Faith tell a neighbor on the telephone. "She has tetanus all through her body. They say anything could kill her, just a ray of light creeping in under the curtain or a loud noise." Ruth had not slept through the night for a long time. Whenever she tried to fall asleep, she would catch herself because she was afraid that if she lost consciousness she would wake up in a different world, where her mother was no longer living. If Ruth could prevent something as inevitable as sleep, surely she could keep a loud noise from happening, or light from creeping under a shade, or her mother from dying.

Over Faith Budd's protests, Ruth started driving the Oldsmobile to the hospital almost every day. She was working unsteadily, baby-sitting nights and weekends, and she could not keep her mind on looking for a full-time job. She would set out early in the morning to inquire about jobs in restaurants and supermarkets, and find herself driving off alone on a state highway that brought her to Elizabeth City or Kitty Hawk. Or she would make it through the back door of a supermarket, but then stare with a glazed expression as the manager showed her the plastic wrap and hot press used for packaging pigs' feet. She would look up startled when he spoke to her about Slim Jims and Poor Boys, unable to answer his questions because she had not heard them. Or she would remember to put on a dress before she applied for a job as a salesclerk at Belk's, and halfway through the interview realize that the personnel supervisor had been staring at her left breast the entire time. She looked down and saw that she had absentmindedly slipped into her old army jacket in the car, the jacket with the two sew-on patches that said "Legalize marijuana" and "Make love, not war—fuck the draft."

Ruth would sit with Faith for hours at a time in the hospital foyer, listening to her talk with other hospital visitors or watching her page through *Natural History* magazines from the wall rack, or the Time-Life books she brought from home. Ruth had been surprised to find that Faith had hundreds of travel brochures, as well as the whole Time-Life series on the different countries of the world and various subjects such as *Oceans* or *The Desert.* They were the only books in the Budds' house, and dog-eared as someone's favorite romance novels. Ruth hadn't expected Faith to be the reading type—Ruth doubted that Faith had more than a grade-school education, and she certainly had never traveled anywhere except to Florida. She hardly left her house except to visit Ruth's mother. Sitting on Winston Budd's bed and paging through the Time-Life book on Brazil, Ruth suddenly had had a strange vision of the Budds' house: She had seen it cresting their hill of the neighborhood, with Faith at the helm, geography books and navigational maps on an oak table nailed to the floor behind her.

"Look at this!" Faith would say, holding up a *Natural History* picture of a cave, to distract Ruth from staring at the far wall of the hospital foyer. "Stalagmites and stalactites."

The woman sitting across from Faith said, "I've visited some big caves like that, called Carlsbad Caverns." She was an old woman, with a son in his twenties who never said anything. They both had the same square, plow yoke shoulders and oval faces peering through thick hair the color of wet loam. But the woman looked like a whittled-down version of her son: barely five feet tall, with spindly arms and legs, as if all her substance had been distilled out of her to make her son, a huge, neckless boy with a prominent brow bone.

"I'm Ida Bates," the woman told Faith. "We're not from here. Me and Eustace Junior and my husband drove out here in the Winnebago to see the Smoky Mountains, when Senior's heart broke down." The woman's eyes filled with water and her son stood up and walked to the window, then leaned over the sill, gazing down the road.

"Well, where do you come from?" Faith came to the rescue.

The woman wiped her eyes on her shirt sleeve and sat up straight in her chair. "We're from Idaho, but Eustace Senior sold the farm and retired a few years ago because he had blood pressure and arthritis and emphysema, and we moved out to a town in New Mexico, called Deming. We live next to a place called Rock Hound State Park. Eustace Junior collects geodes—you know those rocks that have ugly stuff on the outside but agate and crystals in the center?"

"I have a paperweight made of one of those that my little boys gave me one Christmas," said Faith Budd.

"He sells them to this wholesaler. Ooooh, it's pretty down

there. Desert. I thought we'd stay out there forever, cut off from everybody, it was so peaceful. But Eustace Senior started to get all restless and talking about buying a Winnebago and traveling around. He hardly looked up when we had a flash flood or dust devil out in Deming. So one day he up and bought a used trailer and drove us down to Carlsbad to see the caves, the stalaculites, or whatever. Never could remember which is up and which grows down."

"Stalagmites are up," said Faith. "And stalactites are down."

"How do you know that?"

"It's in this book I have. I won a subscription to this set of books five years ago in a contest. 'Ask an Intelligent Question' was the name of the contest. So I wrote in: 'When you say, "Your name is mud," are you throwing off on someone by saying they're dirt, or do you mean Dr. Mudd, the doctor who treated John Wilkes Booth?' "

Ruth leaned forward in her seat and looked at Faith Budd. How had she thought that up?

"It was the most intelligent question anyone sent in," Faith said.

"Well," Ida asked, "what was the answer?"

"They didn't know," said Faith.

Ida sat in silence for a minute as if trying to decide for herself. Then her shoulders hunched forward and her eyes began to water once more.

"So you all went to the caves?" Faith asked.

"Oh," said Ida, pulling herself up again in her seat. "Yes, we took this tour of the caves. There was this lady leading the tour who kept saying, 'Don't touch the stalaculites, because if you do, they'll stop growing and they've been growing in these caves now for thousands of years.' "

"I've read all about that," said Faith. "You see, the water drips down from the roof of the cave real slowly like, drip by drop, and builds up those things, and if you put your greasy finger on it, the grease gets in the way of the water and the things stop getting bigger."

"That's just it," Ida hurried on. "So this man keeps trying to touch them anyway, and the tour guide keeps squawking out at him, 'Now you stop that, or I'll have to send you back!' but he just kind of sneers at her and keeps on doing it. So finally we get to this real old stalaculite hanging twenty feet—stalacumite—and this man stretches out his big, greasy hand to feel it—"

"Oh, my!" said Faith Budd, as if she were personally in charge of protecting stalactites.

"And the tour guide smacks him right in the neck! 'I told you to keep your hands off!' she tells him. He fell backwards and got his pants all muddy. And the rest of the tour, he was just as pleasant as you could be. Now *there* was someone who took her work seriously."

The woman clamped her hands on her knees and leaned back, looking away, as if the importance of working hard were the point she had been leading up to all along. But then she stared straight in front of her and said, "Senior broke his back working for sixty straight years, and what did it get him? Not a thing. You tell me, how can a man work his whole life and only get two years to retire before his heart gives out? What kind of life is that, where you have to work all your life away?" She leaned forward and said in a loud whisper, "You can hardly blame Eustace Junior for just wanting to sit around sawing rocks open with a rock saw."

Eustace Junior leaned forward and pretended to look at something on the horizon.

* * * *

Another week passed, and Marjorie showed no signs of improvement. Faith looked through Marjorie's bedside drawer for her address book and called Bertha in Wisconsin, and then the college where she worked, and then a small town in Iceland, where no one who answered the phone spoke English. Afterward, Faith sent a telegram to Iceland, but weeks passed without any answer. Ruth felt relieved: Once Bertha came to take care of them, or they went to Wisconsin to stay with her, they would all be admitting that Marjorie LeBlanc was going to die. Ruth was glad that Bertha had found a place so far away that she could not be drawn into the strange world centered around Marjorie's illness that her children had come to inhabit. Ruth imagined Bertha walking across frozen terrain toward a glacier, oblivious of what was happening. Ruth took comfort in the image, but then thought: How did Iceland really look? Was it warm in the summer, with piney meadows, not that different from places she knew? When the image of Iceland changed in her mind to a familiar landscape, Ruth was irritated by the sense that she could not control the world outside her. Bertha would be back by Christmas, and already Mrs. Budd looked exhausted from taking care of Ruth and her brother and sisters.

The Budds' house was not a comfortable place. In the early morning, all the LeBlancs would eat breakfast as quickly as possible and slink out the door and run across the street to their own house. Before they escaped, Mrs. Budd would scurry around the kitchen, fixing enormous breakfasts of eggs fried in bacon grease, bacon, grits, frozen orange juice, buttermilk biscuits, and cinnamon toast, and Mr. Budd would sit at the table looking straight in front of him with a snarling expression, pretending that the LeBlancs were not there. When he was done eating, he would leave immediately for work, and in the evenings, when he returned, he would sit in the living room watching television, surrounded by portraits of his three sons in military uniforms. His sons looked like him: They had the same golden crew cuts and olive-drab eyes. They reminded Ruth of unfriendly bristling dogs from the same litter, Mr. Budd in front in the armchair as if leading the pack of his sons behind him. Lou and Joshua were in boot camp, and Winston had been in combat for months.

Ruth had found a letter to Winston started by Mrs. Budd. The letter had been left on the kitchen counter and was blurred by tears, and written in a shaky, drunken-looking

script. There was no date, and not even the greeting "Dear."
The letter said:

*Winston son, I think of you morning noon night. I am mailing
you a box of brownies, because that's what I always thought
mothers sent their sons in the army, but you know I can't make
brownies worth fiddlesticks!!! I confess I used a mix. I worry
about you and wish you would write. Your daddy is fine and very
proud of all you boys, I hear such awful stories about what it's
like over there and I worry about you and wish you would write.
I heard the Henry boy has been lost in action for some time. I
am confident he will be found. Do you remember the little
LeBlanc children from across the street you used to play with
when you were small? Your daddy and I are looking after them,
because their mother Marjorie took a turn and is in the hospital
with the lock jaw. She has been there some time now and it's
hard to visit her she is so bad off, I am worried as you know she
is my dearest friend. She is the one whose husband shot your car,
do you remember, right after you rebuilt the motor? Well, the
old Chevy did us all a service, I took Marjorie to the hospital in
it. The doctors can't understand why she won't respond to
treatment. A Nurse Arrington says she knows Marjorie will snap
out of it, that maybe it's partly mental just to spite the doctors
out of thinking they know everything. Well, I worry about her,
as without her I won't have a friend in this world, well you know
I'm just talking, I'm the happiest woman in the world with a
good provider for a husband and three strong boys. Your daddy is
proud of you all and I know he is eager for news, if you write
here, we'll send on your letters to Lou and Joshua. Take care, I
love you to death, your Mama.*

When Ruth read the letter, she stopped thinking about her
mother for a while and concentrated on Winston Budd. She
tried to feel sorry for him; nowadays everyone was talking
about how Vietnam was harder on soldiers than any earlier
war, and how only university students and married men were
finding legal ways to avoid the draft. But when Ruth thought
about Winston Budd in Vietnam and what might happen to

him, she just pictured him doing the same things to people *there*. She decided she felt sorrier for whomever Winston Budd ran across, thinking he would put his own twist of meanness into whatever she imagined. So then Ruth tried to worry about Mrs. Budd instead—it didn't seem as if any of her boys ever wrote, and Mr. Budd hardly spoke to his wife.

There was a tension in the Budd house that none of the LeBlanc children had ever felt in their own. It was as if there were a civil war going on between Mr. and Mrs. Budd, which was so subtle and unspoken, Ruth sometimes thought she was imagining things. When Carla took a helping of grits before Mr. Budd, he would look at her with a smile halfway to a leer and then turn his head and look at Mrs. Budd, dragging the expression over to her without changing his face for a moment.

One night when Sam cried out loud in his sleep, Ruth heard Mrs. Budd wake him up and then fetch him a glass of warm milk and sugar and say, "It'll settle your head and your stomach!" When Mrs. Budd walked back into the hallway, Ruth could see Mr. Budd's glimmering pale pajamas shuffle toward his wife, and Ruth heard him mutter something under his breath and then lean into the living room with a threatening pose. Mrs. Budd had walked by him into the kitchen and then brushed back down the hall past him, as if Ruth were merely seeing things and Mr. Budd were not there at all. But then Mr. Budd's shape walked under the lintel of the boys' bedroom door, stood motionless for a moment, and glided over to the bed where Karen lay sleeping. Mr. Budd's voice growled, "Prissy little thing!" Ruth had kept still under her sheets, watching as Mr. Budd's shape bent over Karen, putting its face close to hers. But then Mr. Budd had done nothing, just straightened back up and said, "Never seen a little girl paint herself up so much. Well, it don't do much good!" and chuckled to himself.

During the evenings, Mr. Budd had a singular manner of speaking to his wife, which Ruth noted with increasing frequency. He would say, "Where's my tobacco?" to Faith Budd in a way that implied it was her fault that the tobacco was lost, although he never actually uttered a word of blame and finally found what he was looking for in his jacket, hanging on his armchair. Or Mr. Budd would hold up a shoe with a hole in the sole and say, "What's this?" with a malignant expression on his face, to which his wife responded, "I took it down to Brickerman's, but they were closed for a death in the family." Sometimes Ruth was uncertain what exhausted her more—her mother's illness or the war between husband and wife that seemed to lurk everywhere in the Budds' house. Ruth began to wonder if growing up with a mother alone, despite all the burdens this laid on her as the oldest child, might not be a kind of luxury.

When Ruth lay down in Winston Budd's bed one night, she tried to pretend she was Winston, and she imagined a kind of cruelty worming into her from the atmosphere that Mr. Budd exhaled. She let herself feel a meanness traveling upward in her limbs like a hookworm and coming to rest in the center of her. Then she turned over onto her back, exhausted by the effort of being Winston Budd, and tried to imagine what it was like to be Ruth LeBlanc before her mother had fallen ill. Ruth felt such a pang of homesickness that she almost cried out loud, as Sam had in his sleep the week before.

After the LeBlancs had been living back and forth between their mother's in the day and the Budds' at night for four weeks, Mr. Budd sat down at breakfast one morning and said to Karen, "You sure eat a lot of good Budd food." Karen looked at him uncomprehendingly and then dropped her fork and ran out of the house.

"Just how long do y'all plan to keep sitting at my table and sleeping in my beds and running roughshod in my house?" Mr. Budd continued, ignoring what Karen had done and turning to Carla.

Carla peered back at him with a look of curiosity.

"Franklin Delano!" Mrs. Budd cried, her eye whites widening around her pupils in a way that made Ruth think of the chestnut Saddlebred that she and Carla had taken to the horse show eight weeks before.

Mr. Budd continued: "And now their mama don't have her job waiting for her—"

"The hospital had to let Marjorie go," Mrs. Budd rushed in, as if she could soften the news by speaking it before Mr. Budd did. "They're having to make cuts and lay people off, and Marjorie's been out of work so long and it doesn't look as if she's going to get well right away."

"But she's worked there for almost ten years," said Ruth.

"Little Miss, I'm doing the talking here," Mr. Budd said.

"They fired her!" Carla cried.

"They're laying Penny Arrington off too, even though she's got seniority," Faith said.

Sam's underbitten jaw slid forward into a frown, and he stared at the hands lying in his lap.

"What I'm trying to say," said Mr. Budd.

"Don't!" Faith pleaded.

"I said, What I'm trying to say is: I've had it!" Mr. Budd stood up and with a quick motion of his arm sent all the plates on his half of the table crashing to the floor. Then he pulled a blue Standard Oil cap off a wall peg and stalked from the room. Mrs. Budd and the four LeBlancs avoided looking at each other until they heard Mr. Budd's truck drive away from the house.

SHRINERS

Ruth was surprised by how easily the LeBlancs had been scattered apart. Aunt Bertha was coming to take her and Sam to Wisconsin, and Carla and Karen had already been sent to New Jersey. It was funny, Ruth thought, but she had never seen herself as having a second set of grandparents.

Only Mrs. Budd, in her easygoing, practical way, had thought to look in Karen's bureau drawers for the Coffins' address; Faith said Marjorie had once told her Karen still wrote to her father. Mrs. Budd found an envelope enclosing a letter with the name "Bertrand Byron Coffin," an address, and a telephone number, embossed in gold at the top. A gin bottle in one hand and a cigarette in another, cracking jokes about "Mr. Budd's fits and tantrums, anyone would think he was a madman," Faith dialed the number.

A high, birdy voice answered the telephone. "Mrs. Bertrand Coffin speaking."

"Hello, Mrs. Bertrand Coffin. This is Mrs. Franklin Delano Budd, and—"

"Is this another practical joke?" Mrs. Coffin asked. "I certainly don't know anyone named Franklin Delano."

"My given name is Faith and I'm from Durham, North Carolina," Faith said firmly.

"Durham, oh!" said Mrs. Coffin.

"I'm a friend of Marjorie LeBlanc's and I'm calling because she's in the hospital for I don't know how long. Just lies there with her eyes closed and her head turned to the wall and doesn't talk and—"

"Heavens! What's wrong with her?"

"Tetanus," Faith Budd answered, after a certain dramatic pause.

"Tetanus?" There was another pause. "Why, I didn't know people still got tetanus." Ruth could just see Mrs. Coffin picturing Marjorie LeBlanc lying on a straw tick inside a tobacco shack.

"I was wondering if you'd care for any of the children while Marjorie recuperates. I was going to send them all to their mother's relations, who can't be contacted right now, but then I thought—"

"You thought of us?" said Mrs. Bertrand Coffin. Ruth wondered how Mrs. Coffin would wriggle her way out.

"I'll have to talk to Bertrand when he gets home and then

call you back. You know, my son left New Jersey several years ago. He works for the federal government in Washington. Of course, he's miserable there. Well, maybe it's better that he's not here to inter—What did you say your number was?"

After supper, Ruth picked up the telephone in the kitchen as soon as she heard Mrs. Budd answer in the living room.

"This is Mrs. Beatrice Coffin. Bea. I've discussed the situation with Bertrand, and the fact is, I'd—we'd love to take the two younger girls. Bertrand doesn't think we can manage all four, but I do remember Byron once telling me about how sweet and pretty Carrie always was—"

"Karen," said Faith Budd.

"I already reserved the plane tickets!" said Bea Coffin. "And thank you, Faith Budd. Faith?" Mrs. Coffin asked in a feathery whisper.

"Humm?" asked Faith.

"Don't tell Byron!"

*   *   *   *

When Bertha arrived at Christmas, Ruth showed her a stack of unpaid bills; a letter from the landlord saying the rent was three months in arrears; insurance forms; and a check containing Marjorie's severance pay. "Peanuts," Bertha told Ruth. The hospital bill above insurance amounted to ten years of Marjorie's savings—"A good reason never to save," counseled Bertha, who had thirty-six dollars in her bank account after paying her plane fare to Raleigh. Bertha put aside her return ticket to Wisconsin for Marjorie to use when she was well enough to travel. "We'll sell all the furniture and rent a trailer," Bertha told Ruth in an offhand way, as if moving the LeBlancs to Wisconsin were as uneventful as opening a door.

Bertha's words made Ruth feel as though she had been kicked loose like a stone that had lain too long embedded in the ground. Aunt Bertha seemed oblivious of the atmosphere

of tragedy that had surrounded the LeBlancs since Ruth's
mother had entered the hospital. Bertha turned the radio on
loud in the living room while paging through anthropology
journals; she kept Ruth, Sam, and Faith up until long past
midnight, playing hearts and passing around a bottle of
bourbon; she taught Ruth and Faith old songs from Catholic
school, which Aunt Bertha bellowed out in a raucous voice
that made Ruth think of a pirate celebrating a looting spree:

> Eat my body,
> Drink my blood!
> Fa la la, fol de rol,
> Fa la la, la la LA!

Bertha directed the packing of the LeBlancs' house in a haphazard way, sometimes boxing up the belongings of an entire
room in a half hour, sometimes lingering for a day over a
Ray Bradbury book about life on Mars she had found in a
box full of Sam's old clothes.

Most of the LeBlancs' furniture was too run down to
bother keeping, but Bertha saved Sam's and Ruth's beds and
a nice pine rocking chair for taking to Wisconsin. Ruth,
Sam, and Bertha spent a morning loading all the other furniture—wobbly chairs, imitation-wood dressers, and a battered
kitchen table with dents in its metal legs—on top of and inside the Oldsmobile, which Ruth, accompanied by her aunt,
drove down to a used-furniture store with a peeling sign that
read "Herman's Antiques."

Mrs. Herman was a straight-backed woman, with spinster-
ish glasses hanging from a chain and heavy black shoes.
Whenever the LeBlancs picked up any merchandise, she
would approach them and say, "Please don't touch! Don't
touch!" Ruth wondered how anyone who was so jealous of
her belongings could sell household furniture.

Ruth noted to herself that most of the things in the store
failed to rise to the level of antiques. Inside, the store looked
like a graveyard for modern homes: There were torn imita-

tion-leather couches with cotton batting poking through the rents; sagging Posturepedic mattresses; a Formica-topped table with burn marks where someone carelessly had set down hot saucepans; an electric lazy Susan with a broken motor; an American eagle wall ornament; refrigerators with broken handles and shadeless floor lamps; plastic cups and plates, paperweights of all shapes and sizes, shag rugs, a beauty mirror circled with light bulbs, and a shelf full of old Shriners' outfits, including green satin parade uniforms, a gold-tasseled banner, and maroon fezzes. While Mrs. Herman engaged in conversation with Aunt Bertha, Ruth tried on one of the fezzes and looked at herself in the beauty mirror.

"I could give you a hundred and eighty bucks for the load," Mrs. Herman told Aunt Bertha. Ruth thought they should ask for more—her whole house sold for a song! Aunt Bertha looked toward Ruth, studied her for a moment, and said, "Well, that's a little less than I expected, but I'll admit, none of this furniture's made of the kind of material that will hold up. Throw in four of those maroon hats and you've got yourself a deal."

It was Ruth's idea to wear the fezzes to the hospital the day after Christmas, when Marjorie was first able to sit up and enjoy visitors. Faith said she thought the fezzes might raise everybody's spirits. During the holidays, Marjorie had been too ill with a secondary infection to see anyone, and Christmas had been a somber affair for her children, who had absentmindedly exchanged presents with Aunt Bertha and Faith Budd while sipping eggnog and watching Engelbert Humperdinck sing carols on television.

Bertha was carrying three of the fezzes in a paper bag, but Ruth was wearing hers when she stepped into the hospital elevator. A tall man slid through the closing doors behind Faith Budd and Sam and pressed "Mezzanine."

"Going up," Faith Budd announced.

"Take that off," the man said to Ruth. Ruth did not hear him, because she was thinking about Mr. Budd. Mr. Budd had gone hunting in the mountains; he had done so every Christmas for five years, Faith had told her. Ruth was afraid to ask what Faith had been doing all those Christmases. Did the boys come stay with her, or did they leave her alone by herself in the house? Really, it seemed an almost random event that Faith Budd was married to her husband. As Ruth felt the elevator jerk into motion, an unusual idea flashed through her head: She thought it was inexplicable how girls, after the age of sixteen, were expected to marry, and did marry, shucking off their lifelong selves to begin a family. When Ruth considered the possibility of throwing away the self-sufficient, free spirit that she was, she felt almost guilty, the way you might if you abandoned a friend on a street corner. Girls went out looking for boyfriends and husbands as if it were the most natural thing possible to tie yourself to some man, when really, Ruth thought, *it's the most bizarre thing in the world.* She allowed herself to assume a more modern, rational earth in the future, where you would look back and scoff at the idea of yoking up with men, the way girls laughed now at the very notion of wearing an eighteen-hour girdle.

"I said thank you very much, you can take that off, thank you very much," the man repeated. Ruth looked up uncomprehendingly, startled from her thoughts.

"That hat's not for girls to wear. To people who know better, that hat is sacred." Ruth had been wearing the fez for so long now, all during the drive to the hospital, and even before, as she sat at the breakfast table eating her grits, that it took her a moment to realize what the man was talking about.

"To people who know better, a young lady wearing that hat is like dragging the American flag on the ground." Ruth saw Bertha, who was standing behind the man, rustle in her paper bag and pull out the other three hats. She and Faith and Sam put them on.

Ruth tried to give the man an answer, but all she could think was: A Shriner, Jesus help me, it's a Shriner.

Faith, Sam, and Bertha looked over the man's shoulder

with knowledgeable, superior smiles under their tasseled hats, as if they were from some part of the world where people were well-traveled and sophisticated.

He did not see them behind him, and his voice took on a bullying tone. "Young lady, I expect you and any other young lady who comes in here to act in a manner that shows respect for all the people in this hospital." Even under ordinary circumstances, nothing got on Ruth's nerves like a grown man talking down to her in that fatherly sort of way. It was the very thing that had always made school principals and certain high school teachers and most of Ruth's past employers particularly hard for her to bear. It was, she realized at that moment, the very thing that had been driving her relentlessly toward shiftlessness her entire life: She would sooner quit a job or be suspended from school or even thrown in jail than be near someone who took on that king-of-the-castle look and called her "young lady."

In the split second after the Shriner made this mistake, Ruth pictured Mrs. Budd bending over a gin and tonic and writing a letter to Winston in Vietnam; Mr. Budd snarling from his armchair in front of his son's photographs; Ida Bates lamenting her husband's illness; Ruth's mother saying she thought she had more than a nervous twitch in her eye, and then crumpling against the wall; Aunt Bertha clucking "peanuts" over her sister's severance pay. Ruth felt a wild feeling rise inside her, which she thought might be the same impulse that drove people to murder, to smash shopwindows in riots, to load their children into battered station wagons and escape in the dead of night from houses in which their husbands lay drunkenly asleep with their shoes on.

Ruth took a step toward the Shriner and tapped a button on his shirt with her finger. She felt her lip tremble and curl involuntarily into a criminal sneer. "Who died and made you God?" she demanded of him.

As Faith would relate later to Marjorie, something in the words Ruth had chosen or the tone she used "set that Shriner off. He went right for her hat, he looked like he was diving on top of her, and then it was all a scramble in the elevator and the doors opening and closing on the mezzanine floor with the elevator rising onto your floor, and then suddenly he notices me and Sam and Bertha all have on our hats too and he begins to shout. I mean yell and holler. Things about holy brotherhoods and the last places on earth where men can be men and that sort of thing, and then he closes his mouth and starts following us down one hall and the next like those Frankenstein monsters in your dreams keep coming and coming until there he is in your doorway."

The Shriner pursued Ruth right into her mother's hospital room. Marjorie LeBlanc sat up in her bed with such a pure, melodramatic look of sickness that the man stopped, paralyzed, a few feet inside the door.

"May I ask you what you're doing?" Marjorie asked in a feeble voice, with the absolute authority of someone who has been enjoying ill health for a long time. "You should be ashamed to just march into the room of a sick woman. Who do you think you are?"

The man backed out of the room, and Marjorie sank into her cranked-up mattress.

*   *   *   *

On the way home in the car, Faith said, "I'm glad Marjorie got a little chuckle out of our hats. She certainly was in a sour mood." Faith had her hand on Ruth's knee as if Ruth still needed calming down. Faith, Ruth, and Bertha were sitting in the back seat with their fezzes on, but Sam had taken off his hat because he was too tall to wear it in the car. Sam was driving, and pretending to himself to be the chauffeur and bodyguard of three foreign diplomats from a mysterious, elegant city in northern Africa.

"Ha," said Bertha. "If looks could kill! The expression on Marjorie's face when she lit into that guy—that's the same look our mother used to use when she was sick." Bertha fell silent a moment and then added, "I keep thinking about the time when my mother had malaria. When I was about thirteen, and Marjorie would have been around eight; she might not even remember."

"Malaria!" said Faith Budd, leaning forward so that the tassel on her hat dangled crazily.

"Oh, Mama couldn't have gotten sick with anything less dramatic. My father borrowed a car and wanted to drive down to a little town on the Louisiana coast where he was born, and Mama refused to go. Too close to home for her. She never even wrote letters to her own family, and by then she had been pretending for years to be Texan. She thought Texans were more cultivated. She and Daddy had an argument, and for once we ended up traveling together. It was a long drive, and I think we even had to ride a ferry. Around nightfall, Daddy said, "It's mosquito hour; make sure the windows are shut," but Mama pretended not to hear him, and she rolled her window down just a little bit. By the end of the week, she had malaria. She was bright yellow for days on end, and for months she had a come-and-go fever she could coax out at the drop of a hat. She loved being sick. She'd ask Daddy to stay by her in the bedroom all evening after he came home from work, and all weekend. He'd get so stir crazy he was fit to be tied.

"It was the only time he ever paid attention to all her demands. Oh, was she demanding! Mama would call out to us in a sick-lady voice, 'Could somebody fetch me a hot compress?' Marjorie and I would sit on the back steps pretending not to hear. I had just started smoking, and I'd light up a cigarette. We had this joke about the smoke warding away Mama, because we'd nicknamed Mama 'Madame Malaria.' 'Oh oh, here comes Madame Malaria!' I'd say, and Marjorie would strike a match and hold it up to my cigarette.

"Then in a few minutes we'd hear Mama coming down the hall. Sneaking, because she'd smelled tobacco and wanted to catch me. There was this loose board near the kitchen door, and when Mama stepped on it, it gave off a whine, and I'd spit on the cigarette and throw it through a knothole in the front steps. Then she'd pop through the door with that face of hers, looking all yellow-green and monstery—"

"Mama's not like that," Ruth objected loudly, so that Faith patted her again on the knee. "She didn't ask to get sick. She can't wait to get better."

"Suit yourself," said Aunt Bertha. "I was just thinking of the look on her face when that Shriner came in the room."

* * * *

Marjorie kept waking to the same dream. She was lying in a wicker settee on a porch overlooking a field of sunflowers. All the sunflowers turned toward her, and then suddenly they did not look like flowers anymore. They had tricked her and become faces. There was Rita Lopez and Jeanie Yanulis, Faith Budd and Ellen Moody, Penny Arrington and a pack of nurses, Blue Henry of all people, Lorna Winsted, Marjorie's own sister, a number of women Marjorie didn't even recognize, and off to the side, her children. Of course, her children would be there in that jury of flowers, all those faces turned to her and judging her. The faces did not seem to be able to open their mouths, but they still communicated to her and scolded her: "Haven't our lives even made a dent in you, Marjorie LeBlanc?" "Don't they move you at all?" "Are you just going to lie there your whole life and watch us?" "Aren't you going to grow up?" That was one of the children's voices. Marjorie couldn't believe how treacherous they were being. "Marjorie Coffin, rise up!" someone called, melting into giggles. So now they were laughing at her, calling her by her awful married name. She was good and mad. She stood up from her wicker settee and gave everyone a mean look. It felt good, giving them all that look. "Get up, get up!" They goaded her on. She ran off the porch, throwing up her arms as if to scare away a flock of chickens.

"Well, it's about time, Lazy Lady!" Bertha and Ruth

stood over Marjorie. She remembered where she was: in her
own bedroom, stripped of all the furniture except the bed,
Faith Budd's television, and an old dresser.

Bertha bent down to roll up the braided rug on Marjorie's
floor, and sang:

> Lazy Susan, will you get up?
> Will you get up?
> Will you get up?
> Lazy Susan, will you get up
> So early in the morning.

Sam tied lengths of twine around the carpet. Bertha, Faith,
Ruth, and Sam had been packing the house for a week, and
holding noisy garage sales on the front lawn, trying to get rid
of the smaller things now that they'd sold every bit of Marjorie's furniture. They had taken Marjorie's home apart piece
by piece, and left her only the Oldsmobile and a little island
in the bedroom. Bertha was leaving with Ruth and Sam on
Friday, since Christmas vacation was almost over and school
was starting in Wisconsin on Monday. Marjorie could not recover from the fact that she had missed Christmas. How
could her children possibly celebrate without her buying the
presents?

Marjorie had pronounced that she was unfit for the long
journey northward by plane. Bertha had looked at her doubtfully and said, "Why, all you have to do is sit in your seat!"
but then relented and agreed to let Marjorie stay in North
Carolina convalescing for a week or so, while Ruth and Sam
settled in. Marjorie had wanted to stay longer in the hospital,
but when she complained that she was being discharged too
early, as Ruth pushed her in the wheelchair to the Oldsmobile, Bertha had said, "Marjorie, are you clean out of your
head? Whose money are you going to use?" Although it was
Bertha and the children who looked as if they'd escaped from
somewhere—wearing those ridiculous fezzes that had started
all the trouble with the poor Shriner.

Bertha picked up the broom and began sweeping years of dust from the floor where the carpet had been, and singing:

No, Grandmother, I won't get up,
I won't get up,
I won't get up,
No, Grandmother, I won't get up
So early in the morning.

Ruth held the dustpan and told her aunt, "That's the dumbest song ever written. Mama used to wake us up with that song, and Karen used to say that forever afterwards it got on her nerves in just exactly the same way an alarm clock does if it goes off in the middle of the day. Does that happen to you, Aunt Bertha? If I hear an alarm clock anytime at all, I get this awful sinking feeling like I used to on school mornings when I wanted to stay under the covers."

Marjorie thought of Karen staying in New Jersey. And Carla. You betrayed me! she thought, sending bad feelings toward Faith Budd, wherever she happened to be at the moment. Marjorie turned toward the wall. Bertha and Faith had left a stack of magazines slumped on the floor for Marjorie to look at, but they weren't the kind she was interested in: *Natural History* and *World Travel,* which were Faith's, and a stack of deathly dull anthropology publications and women's journals from Bertha. The one on top was called *No We Ain't! A Radical Feminist Magazine by and for Southern Women.* "That's the stupidest thing I've ever heard of. Who would read it?" Marjorie said.

"What?" asked Ruth.

"Nothing," Marjorie answered. On the cover of the magazine was a black-and-red woodcut of a cotton plant. Inside the cotton ball was an x-ray-like picture of a man curled up and sleeping. His legs and hands were stuck out in front of him and he had a long nose that Marjorie thought made him look purposely like a boll weevil.

Marjorie picked up a *Natural History* with an iceberg on

the cover and saw that someone had cut out a number of the pictures. That would be Sam, who she knew was counting the minutes until he could run off to Alaska.

Marjorie heard the phone ring, and then Faith Budd yodeled in the other room. A minute later, Faith poked her head in the door and said, "Penny Arrington's got some civil rights organization to go after the hospital for laying her off. She's going to sue their pants off. She's a real fireball!" Bertha toasted the room, raising a jelly glass full of Faith Budd's gin, and sat down on Marjorie's bed.

"That's wonderful," Marjorie mumbled, without turning over. It might have been the first nice thing she'd said in days, but she certainly didn't want her own job back. Her body still felt muscleless, like a dried-out floor rag. Her two youngest children were in New Jersey and her house was an empty shell and Bertha was dragging her to the edges of the earth. She closed her eyes and thought: This is it, this is the end of the line, this is the end of Marjorie LeBlanc. She pulled the sheets up to her neck and decided she might just spend the rest of her life in bed.

*　*　*　*

Sam was driving slowly, getting used to the feeling of the rented trailer attached to the back of the Oldsmobile. Even though most of the LeBlancs' furniture and household belongings had been sold, there were still so many boxes that Ruth had been afraid she wouldn't be able to close the trailer door. Aunt Bertha sat next to Sam, shouting directions like a navigator and glancing at a map in her lap.

Ruth had stretched out in the back seat, looking at a *Cosmopolitan* Marjorie had asked Ruth to buy and later given to her to read in the car. Ruth closed her eyes and saw Mrs. Budd holding Sam by the elbows and saying, "Don't you worry about your mama! You know she's going to get all her strength back and be just fine. Between me and afternoon television, she'll be better than new when we're done with her." After Sam and Ruth had got into the car, Ruth looked out the window and saw Faith Budd walking along the road behind them, trying to delay their departure by refusing to stand still. She was crying and twisting the front of her dress in her hands as if she could not bear to see them go. Boy, Ruth thought. I don't think I've ever said a nice thing to her in my life. Ruth wondered what Faith would do when Ruth's mother joined her family in Wisconsin. It was nice to leave, and terrible to be left behind. The only way to avoid being left behind was to always keep a move on yourself, like Aunt Bertha.

Ruth adjusted the fez she had put on early that morning, and looked at the *Cosmopolitan* cover. She doubted she would ever wear a dress or makeup in her life, but she certainly liked to see how cosmetics were put on, just like anyone else. And to look at the weird things women in New York were going to be wearing when Ruth got there. Ruth had once dressed up as a woman on Halloween. She had copied her outfit right out of a *Cosmopolitan* advertisement, including the ghoulish makeup and the shirt that opened all the way down to her navel. Ruth's mother had told her the costume was in bad taste, but let her go. She had been thirteen at the time and never listened to her mother anyway. Ruth felt a stab of loneliness when she thought of Marjorie LeBlanc: Ruth saw her standing on the back steps, a frail woman whose white nurse's shoes seemed to anchor her to the ground. She had her hands on her hips and a cross look on her face. She was telling Ruth something, but there was no sound to the memory, and Ruth could not make out what her mother was saying.

7. What, What, What Will Move Marjorie LeBlanc?

OSHKOSH

In 1943, when Bertha LeBlanc was thirteen years old, her father, Willie LeBlanc, borrowed a car and drove from Galveston to Freeport, Texas. Geraldine refused to go and convinced Marjorie to stay with her, so that only Bertha accompanied her father. Willie LeBlanc parked his car a little outside Freeport, behind a clump of beach grass and as close to the ocean as the road would allow. Then he took off his shirt and laid it on the hood of the car and sat on top of the shirt, leaning against the windshield and staring out into the ocean. Bertha threw a floor rug on the hood and perched next to him. Willie LeBlanc sat so long in silence that in the time Bertha waited beside him, she saw a shark wash up on the sand; four Portuguese man-of-war jellyfish bobbing in the waves; a small tornado, which dangled down from the sky until it formed a water spout; a girl galloping along the beach, riding sidesaddle; two men with rifles, pulled down to the shoreline by a pair of hounds, who sneezed when their noses hit salt water; and two cityish-looking ladies who decided to take off all their clothes and play in the breakers.

"Well, All be damned," said Willie LeBlanc.

Willie and Bertha stayed where they were, watching the women laugh at each other and dive under the whitecaps and run out of the waves. Bertha did not feel strange at all, sitting on the car hood, spying on two naked ladies. After all, she and her father had arrived first, and in a short while the women grew tired, dried themselves off, dressed, and continued down the beach.

After they left, Bertha counted three more men-of-war riding the waves, and then Willie LeBlanc said, without turning his head to look at her, "See that? That's the ocean off Freeport, not some piddly little locked-in Galveston Bay. A man looks off out there and knows he don't know what freedom is anymore. A man needs his freedom. A man who don't have to come home every night to his house and go out every day to work, he's a man. A man who always got to come home to the same faces every night and hear those faces say the same things and eat his meals at the same time, he's not a living man anymore. Once I looked inside a fat man and took his x-ray. You can't look any deeper inside a person than that. And when his x-ray came out, he had a house key in his stomach. Now just tell me, how did that key get in there? I think he swallowed it because he just didn't want to go home no more. His wife found him lying outside the front door, where he fell down and cracked open his head and busted his hip. I think his body made him fall; it just couldn't take another day walking into his house. A body wants to see things. A man needs to roam. A man can't take being born into a big wide world just to be locked into a tee tiny little house where he's got to tell his wife she's the best cook in Texas every living dinner of his life. It's a crime to tie a man down. When I was fighting in the war, people trying to kill me every waking moment and me trying to kill them, that's the most alive I ever been. Every morning I woke up, couldn't say where I'd be next. I crossed an ocean, I crossed from one country into the other, I crossed rivers, I wint through towns I couldn't even say the name of. Look here, a man was dying. Look there, a man was dead. But Willie LeBlanc, he waited to die. He waited until he got himself locked in a job sitting in a little booth taking pictures of people's bones so he could pay for an ugly wood house he had to go home to every day. Every single day. Each and every day of his life. If you was a boy, Bertha, I'd tell you: Don't you ever let no woman chain you down."

When he was done talking, Willie sat for another hour on the car hood, and then he and Bertha drove home. It was the first time Bertha's father had ever talked at length to her, and afterward she waited on the steps each night at seven o'clock, hoping he'd sit down next to her and talk with her again as he had that day in Freeport. But he never noticed Bertha as he trudged up the steps on his way back from work, and by the end of the year, Willie LeBlanc was dead. When his widow, Geraldine, realized that she could not pay off her house's mortgage with Willie LeBlanc's small pension and moved back to her home state of Louisiana, where none of her Galveston friends could delight in her reduced circumstances, Bertha continued to sit on the front steps of the family's new rented house. Geraldine would yell at her daughter to pull down her dress and stop sitting on the steps like some piece of trash, but Bertha never listened. She sat there every day, sometimes thinking about her father's words, or about escaping her mother, or just about escape in general.

She pondered all the different kinds of people who took up rambling lives: hoboes riding boxcars, and traveling salesmen; sailors sinking over the edge of the world in metal ships; truckdrivers and circuit judges; baseball players, cowboys, and famous explorers. It took Bertha years of thinking before it occurred to her one day that she did not know of any women who were professional drifters. But even then, in the way of girls, Bertha barely registered the fact, just as she had ignored her father's beginning his words of advice with "If you was a boy" and accepted what he said as a personal message to her. When Bertha sat on her steps and daydreamed about riding dog sleds to the Yukon and charting uninhabited rivers, these were her own daydreams, and she could do anything she wanted in them.

After Bertha ran away to school and got the first college

diploma in her family, she returned to New Orleans, not because it was her home, but because it was a port city where you could watch the largest river in the country setting loose barges into the sea. She got a job waiting tables. Customers asked her out, but as time passed she accepted their invitations less and less. Whenever she felt lonely and began spending time with a man, a terrible panic would engulf her when he began to sound serious, and she would think funny thoughts: She would see the man in her mind's eye, standing inside a house's doorframe, waiting for her to come home. He stood with his arms akimbo, wearing an apron and holding a wooden spoon. He would be smiling at her, and Bertha would be coming up the front walk, wearing a homburg hat and smoking a cigarette and carrying a newspaper. As soon as her foot touched the house's walkway, a wave of claustrophobia would overcome her. She'd drop the newspaper and run.

While Bertha was waitressing, she tried to think of better work, but unless you were Amelia Earhart, there were no women's jobs that would take you off to other places instead of making you stay behind, waiting for men to come and go. For seven years, Bertha waited on men who came and went in the bar where she worked. One day, she read an article in the newspaper on a woman named Margaret Mead. Before she knew what was happening, Bertha had entered the doctoral program in anthropology at Tulane. She spent the next twelve years fighting with men anthropologists and traveling around the world.

Even though she was now the best teacher at the college in Ripon, Wisconsin, and had more than enough publications, Bertha suspected she would be denied tenure, so she decided to stay in Wisconsin long enough to fight the college and make it give her tenure. Then she would look for a job somewhere else, maybe in California, maybe in Maine or Tennessee. For the time being, she enjoyed the outlandish Wisconsin landscape, with its snowdrifts that climbed to the tops of houses by midwinter. Ruth and Sam seemed happy enough:

Ruth had found a job at the cookie factory, and Sam, who had never been much of a student, already was cutting classes regularly and enjoying himself. He said his favorite subjects were agriculture and shop. But Bertha thought that Marjorie would probably hate Wisconsin; people were harder to get to know in the Midwest, and Bertha's little green house stood at the edge of a field, far from any neighborhood. Marjorie had been by herself in North Carolina for two weeks now, and would be coming to Bertha's house tomorrow.

* * * *

Bertha wondered if it was possible for an illness to paralyze a part of a person the doctors could not locate in their medical texts. If instead of deadening a nerve or crippling a muscle, a sickness could dry up some fiber of her inner being, to leave her distorted in an undefinable way. Bertha remembered a different Marjorie: one who ran to work with her hair flying out of her bobby pins, who hoed her children's back garden and threw meat loaves together and sang ridiculous songs over the ironing board, cried melodramatically and laughed at wry jokes she heard and told among the friends who were always gathered around her. The woman Bertha met at the airport seemed like an impostor. When Sam, Bertha, and Ruth drove to Oshkosh to pick up Marjorie Le-Blanc, a shriveled woman with a mustard complexion and a mouth pursed in a bitter expression waited for them in the cold outside the airport doors.

"Mama!" Ruth rushed forward, and Marjorie gave her a kiss that made a brittle sound in the winter air.

"You all are late," Marjorie said sullenly. "I've been standing here in the cold for half an hour."

"The ice on the roads held us up," said Ruth.

"Well, you could have waited inside, Marjorie!" Bertha cried, picking up her sister's suitcases. "Look at that windbreaker you're wearing. You'll freeze to death in that. We'll have to get you a parka."

"And where's Sam?" Marjorie demanded.

Sam waved to her from the front seat of the Falcon, only five feet away.

"He's keeping the car warm for you. Let's us get out of this cold!"

"Well," said Marjorie. "You think your own son would rush to greet you after so long!"

Sam got out of the car, leaving the motor running and quickly closing the door to keep the heat inside. He and Marjorie stared at each other as if they were distant relatives meeting for the first time and trying to make out a family resemblance. Sam seemed to have grown half a foot since Marjorie had fallen ill, and she saw that his thinness had turned to a gauntness, although he was dressed in a parka that gave him the appearance of bulk. When Sam hugged his mother, she sank her hands into his parka and said, "Why, Sam, you're starving to death! You're like one of those cats who are all fur!"

Bertha got into the driver's seat, and Sam and Ruth slid into the back on either side of Marjorie.

"There's a letter from Carla waiting for you at home," Bertha told her sister.

"What about Karen?" Marjorie asked.

"Karen hasn't written," said Bertha. "I think she's really busy with schoolwork. Her grandmother's got her in a very good school out there in New Jersey."

"I don't see why all my girls couldn't be here," said Marjorie.

"Oh, it wouldn't make sense to make them change schools twice in the same year," Bertha answered. "You said so yourself." The truth was, she didn't know if she could handle two more in addition to Marjorie. Bertha would have to wait and see how much attention her sister demanded.

Marjorie stared out the window, pretending not to hear. She rode in silence until they reached the gravel road to Bertha's house, a green structure whose north face warped outward, making Marjorie think of a sail.

Ruth pointed out the window and said, "The Oldsmobile gave up the ghost. Without Carla around, it didn't last a week after the long ride up." Next to Bertha's house Marjorie saw her yellow Oldsmobile, wheelless and on cinder blocks, its front end almost hidden by snow. It looked like a pale slab of melted butter.

When Marjorie said nothing about the car as the LeBlancs pulled in front of the house, Bertha told her, "You look like you need to put a little meat on your bones. You're as skinny as Sam. Tomorrow me and Sam and Ruth are cooking you a homecoming dinner. We already got a twenty-pound turkey and cranberries and sweet potatoes and turnips and started the pies and—"

"I don't think I'm up to it," said Marjorie. "I would really just like a place to lie down."

"Oh, this is *tomorrow,* Marjorie," Bertha said. "You'll have plenty of time to rest today."

"Thank you anyway," Marjorie answered, taking a bottle of medicine from her purse. "But I'll be resting tomorrow too."

* * * *

Marjorie's illness had progressed from one stage to another through a number of personal victories. When the doctors told her she had nothing serious, she produced a mortal illness; when they said her illness could not be tetanus, she humbled their cherished manuals by developing a form of tetanus they were too narrow-minded to predict; when they told her she would die immediately, she lingered, her locked jaw set in a position of chronic spitefulness; and when they said she would never fully recover, her muscles knit themselves as rapidly as a pair of socks. After they pronounced her well, she complained of continual pain and weakness.

In her illness, Marjorie had enjoyed such triumph over the doctors she had never been able to challenge in her good health that she refused to relinquish her state of infirmity.

As soon as Bertha showed her the rollaway couch in the living room where she would be sleeping, Marjorie rooted herself there. Each morning, she folded up the couch, put on her bathrobe, and then lay back down on the sofa's expanse of gaudy red and orange flowers, waiting for someone to bring her coffee. Now, if Bertha disagreed with her about anything, Marjorie complained of an ache in her jaw. If Ruth suggested that her mother wash the dishes, Marjorie rubbed her elbow and asked someone to fetch her an Ace bandage; she believed the tetanus had caused her wrist muscles to atrophy. If Sam stayed out too late, Marjorie would wait up for him in the living room, a shawl wrapped around her shoulders and her face growing pale as the lampshade that Sam could see glowing in the darkness a mile away from the house. Marjorie would open the door, her back bent as if it hurt her, and say, "My best friend sent two of my children away. My own daughters love strangers in New Jersey more than their mother. And now my son doesn't care if I sit up in the bitter cold, old lady that I am!" And she would let out a little moan of a laugh. In fact, Marjorie turned up the thermostat so high that the first thing Sam did when he came home was to open all the windows in the guest room he shared with Ruth.

Bertha suspected that her heating bill for February would be higher than her rent. She was uncertain how long she would be able to support four people. The cost of living in Ripon was low, but the Equal Pay Act was not yet at work, and Bertha's salary was half of what she could have earned as a waitress at the elegant Heidelberg House restaurant in Green Lake. She was also a little worried about her sister: Marjorie had never been adventurous, but at least she had been reasonably independent and uncomplaining.

After Marjorie had been in Wisconsin for three weeks, Bertha came home from work and sat down on one of the large red flowers on the sofa arm. "Marjorie," she asked, "just how long do you plan to lie here?"

Marjorie barely looked up from her *Good Housekeeping* magazine.

"You should get out and look around a little. If you walk down the road apiece, there's South Woods. There's a spring there. You can see deer."

"I think that's a bit far for me to walk right now," Marjorie said, looking at a picture of a kitchen that had been remodeled in early-colonial decor.

"You could send some letters of inquiry around to places that might want nurses. There probably aren't any jobs in Ripon, but there's lots of towns within driving distance: Fond du Lac, Green Lake, Oshkosh—"

"Oshkosh!" Marjorie said, letting out a titter. "Do you remember how when we were girls, Oshkosh was the end of the world? How if you didn't like someone, you'd say, 'Send him to Sing Sing!' or 'Send him to Oshkosh!' And how if someone talked to you like you didn't know anything, you'd say, 'Well, I'm not from Oshkosh!' " Marjorie looked up from her magazine and gave Bertha an infuriating, mincing sort of smile.

"Marjorie," said Bertha. "You know it wouldn't hurt to start thinking about work."

Marjorie closed the magazine over her finger to keep from losing her place and stared reproachfully at Bertha. "I never thought I'd live to hear my own sister call me a freeloader!"

"That's not the point," Bertha told her, sighing, and giving up for the time being when Marjorie opened her magazine and began reading. Bertha had a million and one other things on her mind, and sooner or later Marjorie would come to her senses.

* * * *

Marjorie continued to spend all day on the couch, where she sat propped against pillows, with several afghans piled over her legs and a quivery cup of tea in her hand. She would crochet or write short, contentless letters to Carla and Karen in New Jersey, Faith Budd back home, Ellen Moody in Wyoming, Rita and Jeanie in New York. Over the last ten years, Marjorie had almost never found time for crocheting and letter writing.

By March, Marjorie LeBlanc had everyone in the family waiting on her hand and foot, although she reached this state so gradually and her demands were so subtly expressed that no one seemed to notice. She got up early in the morning, before anyone else, resettled herself on the couch with a heating pad in plain sight, and gazed out the window, across the gravelly road in front of Bertha's tiny house. Although there was really nothing to look at, just the Oldsmobile embedded in a snowdrift near the road, and then a stretch of bluish-white snow climbing upward over an empty field in the direction of town. Bertha, Ruth, or Sam would make the big breakfasts Bertha always insisted on, and when someone came into the living room to ask Marjorie what she wanted, she would say, "Oh, don't you worry about me, I'll just have a cup of coffee and a piece of cinnamon toast." Sam would rush to make her the toast, which seemed such a meager request in comparison with the big meal everyone else was eating.

During the day, while Sam was at school and Ruth and Bertha were at work, Marjorie would clutter the table by the couch with *Reader's Digest*s and women's magazines and *TV Guide*s, junk mail, half-eaten plates of leftovers, and ostentatiously displayed Kleenex boxes and medicine bottles. When Ruth came home, she would clear away the plates without thinking, and the family simply ignored the rest of Marjorie's messes. Bertha and the children would sit on the floor or armchair to watch television together, but they never perched on the couch, which had taken on a private character, as if it were Marjorie's top dresser drawer.

*   *   *   *

In mid-March, as Ruth walked home from work, the cold bit through her hat, scarf, and wool face mask, through her parka and sweater and thermal underwear, through her two pairs of socks and mittens and her boots. Ruth still had not learned the quick pace of people who grow up in cold climates. Unless she concentrated on walking fast, she walked with a drawl. She ambled now, as she considered the possibility of quitting her job at the cookie company and looking for different work.

Ripon had three main places of employment: Speed Queen washers, the Jolly Green Giant company, and the Rippin' Good Cookie factory. Ruth loaded cookies into paper boxes. Every day, the thin, silent woman who worked on Ruth's left would battle the man who stood on the other side of the conveyor belt, a small man with sloping shoulders who loaded the cookies in a slow, methodical style. He always lagged slightly behind the conveyor belt, so that the cookies would gather in bunches behind him. The silent woman would give him piercing looks, and work so quickly Ruth could hardly watch the woman's hands. Beyond the woman, the cookies would pass in a perfectly spaced necklace of boxes. It was only her deft packaging that kept the man from destroying the rhythm of the cookie line. Sometimes the silent woman became furious and held her arms straight at her sides as the cookies sailed by her, spilling onto the floor. The man would pick the cookies off the floor one by one, setting them back on the belt. This extra effort would retard even more the progress of the cookies behind him on the line, and the sight of him moving so slowly—leaning over, straightening, plonking down a cookie, leaning over, straightening, plonking down a cookie—would jerk the silent woman into an even deeper state of fury, which set her back to work at a faster pace than before.

It had taken Ruth two weeks to learn their names: Susan Shekalio and Wayne Dmytryk. Ruth would try chattering at them in her twangy accent. The man generally only nodded back at her and smiled, or answered her briefly in a foreign-sounding accent with rounded vowels. Once, when Ruth had told him she was starting college in New York in the fall, the man had said, "My oldest boy, hey, he's a good worker, but the other one Michael's never liked to work. So I said to myself, 'I guess we better send him to college.' "

The woman ignored her. Sometimes Ruth felt as if she had intruded on a marriage, so engrossed was Susan Shekalio in her battle with Wayne Dmytryk. After three weeks, Ruth had decided that it probably wasn't true that work made you grow up and gave you a broader vision of life. She had been worried about going to college because she knew that it narrowed your view of things, but now she decided there probably wasn't a job on earth that didn't turn life into a tiny workaday world. In North Carolina, Ruth had cooked in a cafeteria kitchen and been shown how to make the same ten dishes over and over; the jobs she'd had with animals only taught her about animals. Carla had said that all she learned from that job in prison were the kinds of things you figured out as soon as you needed to know them: how to scratch serial numbers from stolen stereos, unlock a steering wheel without the ignition key, or smuggle cigarettes and stamps to prisoners. Baby-sitting hadn't taught Ruth anything. Being an older sister had already shown her enough about bossing around children to convince her that she was never going to raise a family. Her Ripon job was only teaching her how to load cookies into boxes.

Ruth rounded a hill above Aunt Bertha's house and stopped walking as a revelation coursed through her: *What I should probably do is to work as little as possible for the rest of my days.* She resumed walking across the field, thinking, college is a good place to start; slid down an icy embankment; and came to the igloo Sam had built across the street from Aunt Bertha's.

* * * *

Sam had told his aunt that he was going to Alaska as soon as he finished school. When he said that Lorna and Allison were living in Juneau to be near Allison's brother, who was hiding out near Whitehorse, Aunt Bertha had gotten a far-away look and answered dreamily, "That's in the Yukon." Then she had given Sam a pile of anthropology and geography magazines with articles about the Arctic in them, and shown Sam diagrams of ancient Alaskan houses in an *American Anthropologist.*

"I like these ice houses," she had said, pointing to some drawings, "because I like the idea of a house that comes and goes with the weather."

Sam had built himself a variation on one of the drawings. He dug a tunnel from the road, extending for twenty feet under the snow and surfacing in a domed structure made from ice bricks. There was a hole at the top of the house, where he could look up and see the sky, and another hole in the house's side, where he built fires. He would lie in the igloo hours at a time, until Ruth wondered why he wasn't getting hypothermia. He went there to be by himself or to skip school. Ruth thought that she and Karen would probably be the only LeBlancs to go to college. Sam already had two hundred and fifty-six hours of unserved detention for missing classes.

Ruth stuck her head through the tarp covering the hole in the side of the house. She saw Sam stretched out on a pallet made from dried grass.

"Sam, are you clean out of your mind?" Ruth asked her brother. "You're going to die of cold out here. You don't even have a fire built."

"I was just lying out here thinking," Sam told her. "It's warmer than you'd expect."

Ruth sat down inside the house and leaned against a wall. After a moment, she said, "Christ, Sam, my back and my butt are already frozen solid."

"I got a letter from Lorna," he told Ruth. "She sent me a calendar with pictures of Alaska on it and said I should come on up there and live. She could get me a job in June."

"That's great," said Ruth. "Now let's get the hell inside, where it's warm." She stood up and stooped down in the mouth of the tunnel.

Sam crawled after her, saying, "Mama's gonna kill me if she finds out I'm leaving after she took all the trouble to get here."

"Aw, I doubt Mama's gonna stick it out anyway," said Ruth. "She's so homesick for North Carolina, she must be thinking of moving back."

"Well, I dunno. The house won't be there," Sam answered. Faith Budd had written that the landlord had torn down the LeBlancs' right after Marjorie left. He wanted to build garden apartments. "And there's no work waiting for her."

"Well, I don't think Mama wants to work anyhow," said Ruth, emerging onto the street.

Sam and Ruth saw Aunt Bertha struggling out of her Falcon with two bags of groceries. She was swaying her hips and singing "Papa Was a Rolling Stone." She handed the bags to Sam and ducked back in the car for more groceries, her voice echoing loudly inside the Falcon: " . . . all he ever left us was alone-hone-home."

Ruth took the last grocery bags from the car, and Sam said, "Yeah, Mama's done with working. She's gonna stay on that couch until Mr. Right rides up to her door in an Eldorado and carries her away."

Aunt Bertha answered absentmindedly, "Oh, she'll come around."

"Jesus," Sam answered. "Here she has all this free time, and all she does is lie down."

As Bertha pushed open the front door, Ruth shouted, "What, what, what will move Marjorie LeBlanc?" loud enough for her mother to hear if she was listening, which she was not. Marjorie LeBlanc was asleep, with her head buried under a pile of afghans.

*   *   *   *

Sometimes during the day, when Marjorie sat alone on the couch, she would grow restless and make brief sorties into other rooms. She still never stayed off the couch very long, as proof to herself that her aches and weaknesses were just as real when she was alone as when there were others around to hear her complaints. She would sometimes rifle through Bertha's closet and try on the strange clothes in there—caftans and lederhosen and embroidered Mexican shirts and a rawhide-smelling jacket from Iceland, saris, and a square-dancing skirt that twirled out into a circle if you spun around. Once Marjorie went through the unpacked boxes that Bertha had driven from North Carolina and stored in her basement. Marjorie found a pile of her old nurse's uniforms and nurse's shoes, white stockings, and finally the hat that fit over her hair like a horseshoe.

She put on the clothes and walked upstairs to the full-length mirror in Bertha's bedroom. A haggard lady with black hair molding to gray scowled back at Marjorie. Her white stockings bagged at the thighs, and her uniform fit loosely, as if it belonged to someone else. Or as if it were a costume the lady had dressed up in for a masquerade party. Marjorie took off the clothes and stuffed them into the back of Bertha's closet, and then put on a bright-blue kimono Bertha used as a bathrobe.

Marjorie would also while away moments of restlessness snooping in Ruth's drawers to see if Ruth kept a diary or had any secrets tucked away somewhere, but Marjorie never found anything of interest. Finally, however, in late April, when the postman delivered two letters from Carla, one to Marjorie and the other to Ruth and Sam, Marjorie thought to steam open the second letter after reading her own. Once a week, Carla wrote her mother short letters lacking in news. When Marjorie opened the newest letter, she read:

Dear Momma,
I miss you. I'm in history right now and not paying attention to sneak you this letter. The school here is more ok than it was in Durham, but you know me, I still don't like it and am just keeping my head above water gradewise. I'll be glad when school's out and I can be reunited with my family. I know taking

*on another LeBlanc right now is too much for Aunt Bertha. I
hope you get to feel better.*

xxxooo Carla

Marjorie read the letter over once, without much interest.
It was as dull as the newsless notes Marjorie had been sending Faith Budd. Well, it wasn't as if Faith needed Marjorie,
the way Faith had goaded and prodded her during the two
weeks Marjorie had been convalescing in North Carolina. It
was almost as if Faith had been eager to get rid of her: Faith
would bend over the bed, with her hair pulled up into a bun
as tight as a garlic head, and say, "I see *roses* in your
cheeks." "You look like the cat's pajamas." "In another
week, you'll be out hunting possum." As if she were dying
for Marjorie to get up and clear out.

Marjorie picked up the envelope addressed to Ruth and
Sam, noting that it was thicker, that there were perhaps
three sheets of paper in it. Carla almost never wrote long letters, and Marjorie was pricked by curiosity. It was four o'-
clock, and Ruth and Sam would be home any minute, so
Marjorie would have to be careful and act fast. She went to
the kitchen and put on the teakettle, to make herself a pot of
Bertha's strange Morning Thunder herb tea and to steam
open the letter over the kettle. Marjorie sat down on the
couch and peeled open the envelope, tucking the letter inside
an open magazine so that she could hide it quickly if necessary.

Dear Ruthabega and Samule,
*I'm sorry to hear Mama is being so weird, I guess all those
years of taking care of sick people finally got to her. I can't
believe I got to stay here with the Coffins who are let me tell you
two dried up old fish face snobs. You can't drink milk at the
table unless you put it in a pitcher first, and then after dinner
you pour it back into the carton and lose half of it spilling it.
Nobody eats dinner in the kitchen you eat it in the dining room.*

*And nobody comes and visits and chats on the porch. They don't
even know the names of their neighbors.*

*They call their neighborhood UPPER Montclair, but as far as I
can tell there's no such thing at all as Upper Montclair, there's
only Montclair in the phonebook and the one Montclair High.
It's just that the people who live up on one end think they're
above everybody else.*

*And get this: they tried to send me to a PRIVATE school called
Montclair Kimberly Academy. I kept them from doing it but you
know Karen, she's there and studying French. I know Mama
would say we all have to stick together and love each other, but
GAWD AWMIGHTY I am being sorely tried.*

*Karen sure is turning into a case. You know she lost her
North Carolina accent the first week she was here. First she
played it up, but get this: Mr. and Mrs. Coffin have a MAID. The
first day Mrs. Gilpin gets here, Karen says in this Scarlett
O'Hara voice that would make chills go up your spine, Hi Miz
Gilpin, I hear your from North Carolina too, Oh I MISS it down
there, don't you? And Mrs. Gilpin said, I don't remember it
down there so I sure don't miss it. My parents left when I was
little, they had to run away in the middle of the night, because
the big white family in the town didn't want them to go away
looking for work. My parents had to have a friend take their
suitcases to another town and buy train tickets there, and then
they snuck away in the dead of night with just us kids to the
other town's train station. Naturally, they did not take us kids
back to visit. Ruth you should have seen the gyrations Karen
made to come out looking good after that but Mrs. Gilpin didn't
give her a chance to answer, she just took the vacuum cleaner out
to the porch. The porch has a carpet on it, and a bookcase. This
is the gospel truth. It's glassed in.*

*Now I don't know how she did it so fast, you know Karen, but
she's already talking in this high and mighty voice without any
accent at all, not North Carolina, not New Jersey. She tells
everyone she wants to be a lawyer, and she pretends she's always
lived with the Coffins. Mama would throw a conniption fit if she
saw. Still no sign of Mr. Big, I think Grandma Coffin is scared to
tell him we're here. She wouldn't be an awful lady if she wasn't*

so hooty tooty. She feels bad I don't like it here and she gave me money to go bowling if I promised not to tell Grandpa Coffin, who thinks bowling is roughneck. Karen says Grandfather and Grandmother, like she was some dumb English lady in a book.

A while back, I thought to call up Rita & Jeanie, member them, Mama's old friends who ran out on her. I hitchhike into New York City a lot to see them and this is the only thing I like about being here. They are wild. They are into all kinds of different politics. You would like them.

I love you once, I love you twice, I love you more than beans and rice, Love love love, Carla. Tell Aunt Bertha I miss her but am too tired from writing this letter to write her one. You can show it to her but of course don't show it to MAMA.

Marjorie read the letter twice and the last line ten times, and then put the pages back into their envelope and glued the envelope shut with rubber cement. With an icy look, she stared out the window at the icy landscape. The yard was lined with high ridges of snow, and the Oldsmobile had disappeared into a drift. Marjorie took in the starkness of the outside world, the gray sky that pulled down over it like a window shade, until she saw her daughter and son appear on the edge of the field, headed toward the house. They walked in step, with identical careless movements, as if together they had come to the decision that they were going to be driftless and irresponsible as long as life lasted. They had always had more influence on each other than she ever had on them. As Ruth and Sam passed the tallest snowdrift, where the Oldsmobile lay buried, Marjorie suddenly imagined them to be two strangers—two hoboes coming to the house to ask for dinner, or traveling salesmen or religious workers who would talk idly at the door, trying to get her to let them in.

Marjorie picked up her hot-water bottle, filled it from the teapot in the kitchen, and sat back on the couch. She arranged two afghans over her legs and placed the bottle over her ankles, only half covering it with a sweater. She picked

up a *Reader's Digest* and looked at a "Humor in Uniform"
she already had read several times without finding any of the
jokes funny. She waited for Sam and Ruth to come through
the front door, but then heard their bootsteps in the snow
veer off toward the other side of the house and come through
the back way into the kitchen.

"Well, I'm glad you're so pleased to see your own mama!"
Marjorie muttered to the closed kitchen door. She got up and
stood over the heating vent, which let in all the sound from
the kitchen. At first, all she heard was Sam and Ruth rattling
around in the refrigerator, but when they came over and sat
down at the kitchen table, Marjorie distinctly heard her
daughter bad-mouth her.

"Sam, I wish we could tell her about it, but you know
Mama is *not all there.* Let Aunt Bertha handle it."

"Mama's never been all there."

"Well, now she's even less there than she used to be."

Marjorie held herself absolutely motionless over the heating vent, but then all Ruth said was: "We better go in there
and say hi or we'll never hear the end of it."

Marjorie ran back to the sofa and rearranged the afghan
and *Reader's Digest* and hot-water bottle in her lap. She
pushed Ruth's letter to the far end of the table.

"Close that door!" Marjorie warned, as soon as Ruth
and Sam came in. "Don't bring that kitchen cold in behind
you."

Marjorie LeBlanc's children said hello, sat down on the
floor, and turned on the television, as if they had not been
talking about her the minute before.

At dinner that night, they ate and joked with their Aunt
Bertha and addressed questions to Marjorie in a unctuously
friendly manner. At the end of the meal, when it seemed to
Marjorie as if no one was going to tell her anything, she put
down her fork and looked pointedly at Bertha. At that moment, Karen's face flashed before Marjorie: Karen, with her
styled hair pulled back with a narrow blue ribbon. Karen,

who never wrote, and had forgotten about her own mother altogether.

"Bertha," said Marjorie. "You don't happen to have any news from Karen, do you?" Ruth and Sam looked at their plates with guilty expressions. They were powerless to hide things from their mother.

Bertha laid her hand on Marjorie's arm and said, "It seems Karen wants to go to the same school next year. She called and said she'd have a better chance of getting into a good college from there. It seems she wants to stay on with the Coffins."

AN UNEXPECTED DIVIDEND

The bus to Upper Montclair fled down the highway, bypassing the industrial wastelands of Jersey City and the sulfur-smelling meadowlands, where yellow reeds crowded outward from Newark. The bus hurtled past the melting snowdrifts on the flat roofs of business districts, turned off the highway, and deposited its first passenger in front of a brick house with an unblemished lawn of snow. In order to avoid Karen and the Coffins, Carla had chosen a window seat next to a red-haired woman with a daisy over her ear. Beatrice Coffin sat by herself two seats behind Carla and was knitting a pair of argyle socks, a nest of wool coiled in her lap. Mrs. Coffin was a frail woman, whose wrists and ankles were shaped as delicately as bird bones. She was wearing a yellow cashmere scarf and a light-blue wool coat with wide winglike sleeves, and whenever Carla looked down the aisle at her, Carla thought of a parakeet. Karen had sat down next to her grandfather. Mr. Coffin, who was still not comfortable around his grandchildren, was leaning across the aisle and talking to an oldish man who was wearing the same blue tie as Bertrand Coffin, with infinitely fine red stripes. The man had identified himself as a stockbroker named Tom Hinckley, and the two men were now trading anecdotes about the Port Authority, race riots, the tax code, the De Camp bus line which ran between Manhattan and Upper Montclair, and shoe shining.

"I used to get my shoes done in Port Authority every morning last year when I was still taking the buses in regularly. Now I'm switching over to the Erie Lackawanna," Mr. Hinckley said at the end of a long anecdote about the time a mugger had taken not only Mr. Hinckley's wallet and briefcase but also his newly shined shoes.

"Problem with shoeshining," said Mr. Coffin, "is those fellows expect too much in tips with things changing the way they are. I had my shoes shined last week, and why at the end, I reached into my pocket, took out a quarter, handed it to the fellow, and do you know what he did? He flipped the quarter back at me and said, 'You keep it, Buddy, you must need it more than I do.'"

"Really!" said Mr. Hinckley.

Carla leaned forward and saw that Karen was listening politely to the anecdote; Mrs. Coffin had looked up from her knitting, and a smile tugged at the corners of her mouth as she studied the seat back before her. But the woman beside Carla, with the daisy over her ear, let out a loud guffaw and said, "Holy shit!"

After this, Mr. Hinckley brought the conversation back to race riots, and he and Mr. Coffin exchanged the fact that each of their grandfathers had fought in the Union Army during the Civil War. They violently agreed with one another that certain recently made movies were unfit for children to see, because the films glorified outlawry and made common criminals seem like heroes. When the bus reached Mr. Hinckley's stop, he stood up to put on his overcoat, held out his hand to Mr. Coffin, and said, "Well, it really has been a pleasure meeting someone like you on this bus."

Mr. Coffin stood up and shook hands. "Don't I feel the same. This has been an unexpected dividend."

The red-haired woman leaned into the aisle to watch Mr. Hinckley get off the bus. Then she turned to Carla and said, "Jesus, what a pair of stiffs! Did you hear that?"

" 'You keep it, Buddy; you need it more than I do!' " Carla said back, and the woman put her hands to her face and let through a muffled laugh. "You must be from someplace strange?" she asked Carla. "You got a real accent."

"I'm just staying here awhile," Carla said.

"I'm visiting my sister in Montclair. She just ran off with her husband's girlfriend. Sally that's my sister found out one day this louse she married was sleeping around on her. So Sally goes to the louse's girlfriend Tina's apartment to scare her, but then they ended up hitting it off, and Sally decided she liked Tina better than her own husband. They ditched him and ran off together. Now the louse comes by and harasses them, yelling outside their door, that kind of thing, so they're moving back to Jersey City, where we grew up. He calls out from his car for the whole neighborhood to hear, 'You two bitches are really fucked up!' And Sally calls out at him, 'The problem's on you,' and then Tina says, 'Yeah, the problem's on you, ya jerk.' Sally wants to move back to Jersey City because the air's better there. Too much pollen out in the suburbs, she says. In Jersey City you don't have to worry with that stuff. Oh, here's my stop! Nice talking with you. My name's Sophie, Sophie DeFex."

Carla imagined herself following Sophie DeFex off the bus and watching the bus disappear down the street. Carla realized she had not even said her name. She turned to the window and pressed her nose to the glass so that her reflection would not block the view. Rows of houses ran away from the bus as it passed. A light snow was falling. Carla heard Karen talking about the fancy restaurant where the Coffins had taken her to for her birthday. Carla, Karen, and Bea had met Mr. Coffin at eight o'clock, when he got off from work. Carla had come along for the free ride, but once in New York she persuaded Bea to let her visit Jeanie and Rita instead of going to the restaurant, which Carla certainly had not dressed for, in any case. She had not changed her Country Joe and the Fish T-shirt and blue jeans for weeks. Bea Coffin, who thought that Jeanie and Rita were some kind of relatives to the LeBlancs, made Carla promise to be back at the Port Authority at eleven o'clock and handed her four dollars to take a taxi. The Coffins could not even imagine the kind of person who rode the subways after dark.

Carla had taken the IRT express to Fourteenth Street and then walked to Rita and Jeanie's apartment. They had given Carla her own key, and Carla had begun to spend almost every weekend with them. When she opened the door to the apartment that day, Rita and Jeanie were watching the news about Watergate on television and whooping and laughing. Their hall was cluttered with picket signs, literature on South Africa and Vietnam veterans, books on macramé, a horse halter suspended from a nail, piles of cake pans left over from bake sales, a clump of bananas someone had left on a makeshift bookshelf, and a mound of dirty laundry.

"Hey, it's Carla," Jeanie called out. "Show her what her mom sent us, Rita."

"I sure will," said Rita, standing up and clearing a place on the couch for Carla. The first time Carla had visited, she was amazed by how little Rita and Jeanie had changed since they left North Carolina. Even now, Rita was wearing a cotton shift, as if oblivious of the winter, and Jeanie was dressed in hiking boots and had the same lopsided ponytail she had since time immemorial.

"Sit down, Hun," Rita told Carla, and disappeared into the small room with a mattress on the floor, where Carla stayed when she slept over. Rita came back with a box and threw off the lid. Jeanie turned around in her armchair, leaned over the back, and lifted a layer of white tissue paper. Rita pulled out an orange-and-red afghan and held her arms up, stretching the afghan out as far as she could.

"It's king-sized," said Jeanie.

"Mama hasn't made one of those in years," said Carla, touching a red square of wool. "I guess she has more free time now." She felt a swirl of homesickness wrap around her.

"It was nice of her to think of us," said Rita.

"I wrote home about you all," said Carla.

"We really fell out of contact in the last couple years or so," Jeanie said. "It was nice to get a present."

"I got to leave New Jersey," Carla said abruptly. She sat down on a low couch, next to a half-eaten slice of carrot cake lying on a paper plate. She stared at the floor. "I want to know if you could lend me money for a bus ticket." Carla saw Jeanie glance over at Rita.

"Hun," said Rita. "Maybe your Aunt Bertha has enough on her hands right now. Your mama will send for you as soon as she can."

Carla knew she was putting Rita and Jeanie in a difficult position. "Oh, forget it," she said. "I shouldn't of asked. It's just those Coffins." Carla had already told Rita and Jeanie how Mr. Coffin put shoe trees in his shoes and how he had *Wall Street Journal*s in his basement going back to three years before Carla was born. She had told them there was a desk in his den where everything had a special place: he had a tray for paper clips, and another one for pencils, and special, color-coded file drawers where he kept newspaper clippings about golf tournaments. He had his own stationery, which said "Bertrand Byron Coffin" in gold-embossed letters at the top, and matching envelopes that did not have glue on the flaps because he said it was better not to trust preglued envelopes and to glue all envelopes closed yourself. He had once lectured Carla for thirty minutes on how Nixon possessed all the qualities of a tragic hero, because like Hamlet he was a great man but too ambitious. Bertrand Coffin had finished his lecture by saying, "Don't roll your eyes at me, young lady!"

"The thing about the Coffins," said Carla, "is they think

they have the right to be sizing you up all the time and condemning everybody. Mama never does that. She lets us get away with murder."

Rita laughed and pushed her glasses up on her nose. She looked at Carla's ponytail cocked over her back, her leather boots with their gnarled laces, the way she sat with her square hands braced against her knees, and wondered to herself for the hundredth time if Jeanie had exercised some mysterious influence on Carla. Rita had often wondered whether parents were misled in thinking that they shaped their children more than outsiders did. Try as she might, Rita couldn't find the ghost of Marjorie LeBlanc in her daughter.

"Besides," said Carla, "Upper Montclair is some weird place. I'll tell you something really strange about Upper Montclair. There's a red semitruck parked in a lot behind a store about two blocks down from the Coffins'. It's a beautiful truck, brand new paint, with a flying horse hood ornament and sixteen wheels and plates for twelve states on it. Now here's the strange thing: It's been there for three months and nobody seems to be using it or even taking care of it. It just sits there, collecting snow. That's the kind of place Upper Montclair is. It's the kind of place that can waste a whole beautiful semitruck."

"Man, oh, man," Jeanie answered.

"I swear," Rita said, "I swear Carla's learning to talk politics directly from you, Jeanie. That's exactly the kind of crazy speech you would give."

"Montclair is a hellhole," Carla continued. "And worst of all, those Coffins are there, always having to let you know what's wrong with you. I'm up to here with it. I gave Grandpa Coffin a bottle of Johnnie Walker Red Label for his birthday, and all he did was hint that the gift was inappropriate because it was a cheap brand of whiskey. 'It's more pleasure in drinking cheap whiskey,' I told him. 'There's tradition behind it.'"

"What about Mrs. Coffin?" Rita said. "Isn't she any better than him?"

"I've never seen her disagree with him," Carla answered. "She's the one puts the shoe trees in his shoes."

"Well, we'll keep you sane," said Jeanie. She went into the kitchen and came back with a fresh slice of carrot cake. "You can stay here every weekend until you're an old lady, if you want. We like having you here."

Carla ate the carrot cake and then fell asleep on the couch and had a dream about Richard Nixon that ended with a startling image of a nurse's uniform, which wavered, unoccupied but with a human form, in front of the stove in the LeBlancs' kitchen in North Carolina. Ruth was standing next to the stove and telling the uniform in an exasperated tone: "You've never even known the name of one vice-president since the day I was born!" When Carla woke up, the late evening news was on and reviewing Watergate, and it was time to meet back with the Coffins. Jeanie or Rita had wrapped the afghan around Carla.

* * * *

The bus began to empty quickly, dropping off passengers in front of houses so big they reminded Carla of hospitals. The Coffins and Carla disembarked. She heard Bertrand Coffin saying something about the tax code to Karen, and Karen answered with a sentence that had the word "loophole" in it. She was beginning to sound exactly like Bertrand Coffin, who talked like people in family shows on television. He would say, "You've got a good head on your shoulders" and "You bet your life." Carla had never known there were people who actually talked that way. "You've got a good head on your shoulders, Karen," Bertrand Coffin was saying now, as he and Karen stepped through the front door of the Coffins' house and he hung up his coat. "You already know what you want to do with your life. Byron was the same way: He wanted to be a lawyer or a stockbroker or a banker from the time he was grade-school age. He wasn't like those people who are never sure of themselves, always lazing around to find out what life might just drop in their laps." Bertrand Coffin closed the closet and looked pointedly at Carla, who was standing in the front doorway, pulling off her boots.

Carla returned his look, and as she unlaced her boots, she thought: Don't you worry, I know what I want to be. I'm going to be a burglar for the movement. I'm going to rob banks and give the money to underground political organizations in countries around the world.

Carla saw her life roll out before her: Karen would be working as a federal prosecutor under Byron Coffin in a conspiracy case against Sheila Christmas. Sam and Ruth Le-Blanc would visit Karen in her law office; at first, Karen wouldn't recognize them, because she had been avoiding the LeBlancs for years. Sam and Ruth would tell Karen that the real name of Sheila Christmas was Carla LeBlanc. Ruth would tell Karen she had to choose sides: Would she help her sister by going to visit her in jail and, when the guards weren't looking, trade clothes with her and then let her escape? For Carla and Karen LeBlanc, with their minky-black hair and lantern jaws, looked almost identical underneath their opposing clothes and Karen's makeup and Carla's dirt. So that she wouldn't be implicated in the first-degree escape, Karen could later tell her colleagues that she had been forced at gunpoint to exchange clothes.

Karen would go visit the jail. She would sit down in the counsel room of the federal prison, feeling self-conscious in her elegant suit of dark red. In the Wall Street firm where she had begun her legal training, wearing a suit that was neither gray nor navy blue was an act that bordered on revolution. When the guards brought in Carla, Karen would ask her sister if she was satisfied with her legal representative from the public defender's office. Carla would answer: "I'll tell you the two biggest lies in the world: 'The South will rise again' and 'If you can't afford a legal representative, the court will appoint you one.' " Karen's heart would unharden, and she would change places with Carla. After the escape became known, Karen would return safely to her job as federal prosecutor under her father, the chief prosecutor. But she would begin to wonder about the rightness of her work.

One day, she would walk into court and say something sassy to the judge.

The judge would say back: "You be careful, young lady, or you're going to step over the line."

"Don't you young-lady me," Karen would hear Marjorie LeBlanc say to a salesman in Eckerd's drugs who had caught Carla shoplifting years ago. But when Karen looked around her, she would see a herd of men's heads, some still furry, others balding or already smooth, turning toward her and seeming to lean forward and close in on her. She would suck in her breath, still warm from her own talk. "Don't"—she felt the words coming back toward her a second time, as easily as inhaling—"young-lady me, mister, and as for that line I'm supposed to cross, I awready crossed it." Suddenly Karen saw Marjorie LeBlanc standing in front of her, nagging her brother and sisters about a lost shirt, her mother's speech swelling around them like a wind, and she thought: All along I was paying attention to the wrong thing. I was listening to what she was saying instead of how she said it! I should have just been hearing her rage and her sharp tongue and I didn't even know it; all I heard was how none of the words made sense.

Carla threw her boots into the hall closet and then stood still, looking into the darkness there. She felt such a terrible surge of longing for the LeBlancs that her legs began to shake. Behind her in the living room, the murmurs of Karen and Bertrand Coffin mingled, grave and indistinct. Carla thought she heard Karen say, "my Harvard application," but Carla did not even have the heart to sneer at the words. She looked under the curtain on the front window and saw the red semitruck glittering under the streetlight. Snow swirled around it restlessly, and the truck also looked restless, as if, like Carla, it longed for escape.

* * * *

Three days later, Carla wrote a letter on Bertrand Coffin's gold-embossed stationary. The letter said:

Dear Ruth and Sam:
I am borrowing a red semitruck and driving to Ripon. I will call you when I get to Oshkosh.

> *Love,*
> *Bonnie and Clyde*

Carla put the letter in a gold-embossed envelope and dropped it onto a stack of mail that Mr. Coffin intended to mail "first thing in the morning, while all the slugabeds are still asleep." Early that evening, after supper in the dining room, Carla climbed out of her bedroom window and crept around to the Coffins' garage. She picked up a cardboard box containing four days' supply of food, a hammock, a Gulf credit card, a false ID, and a man's khaki work uniform. With her short hair, reasonably small chest and tall build, and her natural intuition for crime, she knew that no one would suspect she was a girl and question her on her route to Wisconsin. The semitruck was constructed in such a way that it was impossible to hot-wire, so Carla had fashioned a key from a particularly malleable substance that had not been easy to obtain. When Carla left the garage, she could already feel the stick shift moving through its multiple gears as smoothly as a hand playing scales on an oboe.

Carla thought she heard somebody following her, and she ducked for a moment behind a tree and walked thirty feet in the opposite direction to see if she passed anyone. But nobody was there. She turned around, backtracked down the street and around the corner, and got in the semitruck. She put the key in the ignition, and the truck made a low, happy purr. The needle on the dashboard indicated that the tank was three-fourths full.

The engine began to make a slight clicking sound, so Carla idled the truck for a moment. Then she realized the tapping was coming from the side window, and she looked down, startled. She saw a sharp nose sticking out under the hood of a windbreaker. Carla's first impulse was to put the truck in reverse and step on the accelerator. But then she saw the person in the jacket hood pass around the front of the truck in springy, birdlike steps. Carla turned off the ignition and unlocked the door by the passenger's seat. Mrs. Coffin grabbed the seat and pulled herself up. She sat down and looked out the windshield, and then crossed her arms as if she were waiting for Carla to talk.

"Oh, Jesus," said Carla. She could not believe she had been caught, and by Bea Coffin, of all people.

"I read your letter. It fell out of the envelope."

Carla sighed. "I sealed that envelope."

"You only thought you sealed it. Bertrand buys the kind of envelopes without glue on the flaps," Bea Coffin answered. "I know you aren't happy here. You think we're stuffed shirts. You think Bertrand's a snob."

Carla coughed.

"Well, you're certainly right. He's an old stuffed sofa." Mrs. Coffin pulled her hood down farther over her face, and Carla was startled by how much her grandmother looked like a villain. A *conspirator* was the word that came to mind. "If I had it to do over, I wouldn't have been Mrs. Bertrand Coffin. I'd have been a war correspondent. I'd have liked that. Oh, I know what you think of me—"

"I don't really—" Carla began.

"But you're wrong. I wasn't always Mrs. Bertrand Coffin." She pulled down her hood. Her silver hair gleamed in the streetlight and her eyes were whorls of darkness. "How do you think I feel being married to a man who never once in forty-five years has drunk his milk straight out of the bottle?

Who buys envelopes with no glue on them and has his shoes polished every Tuesday and Thursday? How do you think I felt when my own son bought his first federal bond when he was fifteen and wore a necktie every day in college because he felt comfortable that way? Who never visited his own children and married a little snippet named Cindy Meeks, who sets a table with special butter knives? You should have seen how Bertrand's family treated me when I first married him. They thought I was a communist. Of course,"—Bea Coffin giggled—"I didn't know the first thing about communism, except that it bothered them. I argued with them at every election, and they'd turn their noses up at me, the undertaker's daughter. My father was an undertaker, you know. In Amesbury, Massachusetts. Why, can you guess what I did when Kennedy was shot? I called Bertrand's parents on the telephone. They were *ancient* then. Even then they hadn't accepted me. I called them up and I said, 'You killed Kennedy! You killed Kennedy!' I said that to old ossified Horace Bertrand Coffin. And do you know what he said back? He said, 'Who? Who?' By then he pretended to be hard of hearing so that he didn't have to listen to anything he didn't say." Bea Coffin slid closer to Carla, bumping against the stick shift. "Where were *you* when Kennedy was shot?" she demanded. "Probably crawling on your knees under a kitchen table!" She leaned back in her seat and folded her arms.

Carla tried to think of an answer.

"I know you're not happy here," Bea Coffin began again. "And I know there's nothing I can do to make you happy. You don't even notice that I put extra mushrooms in your salad and dried flowers in your bedroom, do you?"

Carla had not noticed.

"That's why I came to a decision yesterday. I called those two friends of yours in New York. Oh, I know they're not your relatives. Karen told me long ago, but I would have known anyway. I spoke to a very fine lady named Jeanie, and she told me she was an old friend of your mother's, and how nice it was to have you around. I asked her if they'd let you live with them. I said I'd cover room and board. Why, what they pay on that apartment is highway robbery! It's rent-controlled."

Carla's heart began to pound, and she reached into her pocket for a cigarette. She pulled out a joint and put it quickly back. "What did they say?" she asked.

"They said they'd love to have you."

"They did?"

"You can go to one of those New York schools, I guess. Of course, they'll have to talk it over with your mother. Now I want you to do some things for me."

"You name it."

"I want to know who owns this truck."

"A creditor. He lives two miles away and he's been trying to sell it. He never comes to look at it and he doesn't even wash it."

"I want you to drive me in this truck to New York to see a horse race. I've never seen a horse race. I've got two hundred dollars in my pocket. I want to bet. I've never bet before. And finally, while you drive, I want you to let me smoke that marijuana cigar in your pocket. That's something else I've never done."

When Bea and Carla got home at 6 A.M. the next morning, Bertrand Coffin was standing silhouetted against his window-panes. Bea told Carla he reminded her of one of those cutout people you find in houses snipped from black paper that she used to see in New England as a girl. The marijuana had not had any noticeable effect on Bea, but her mouth had a nice, timothy-hay taste to it. Bea Coffin and Carla had thrown away all their money betting on a horse called Flyaway Jane.

OMRO

Sam LeBlanc had constructed the largest ice-built geodesic dome in the history of the world. It was taller than the dome in St. Paul's Cathedral and fifty yards across. Overhead,

Sam had inserted slabs of ice, which sunlight poured through but miraculously did not melt. The sun glinted on solar panels made of a spongy material that Sam had fashioned from lichen, and the panels warmed the floor of the dome. On the floor, gardens flourished and rabbits grazed. Sam LeBlanc's gigantic igloo was the only structure in use after the post-nuclear-war ice age in which human beings could plant food sources. He had begun constructing his igloos near White-horse, Canada, when he had been unable or unwilling to find steady work in Alaska. When people asked him over the ham radio service through which global communication was now conducted what he felt had been the greatest contributor to his research, he replied, "Unemployment."

Sam turned up the flame in his gas lamp, and the inside of his snow house danced with light. He blew on the fire in its alcove and threw in some twigs and lichen-covered bark until the flames snapped and crackled. It was almost April, and the igloo wouldn't last much longer. School would finally end, and he would be on his way to Alaska. He wondered whether work would be as easy to find as Lorna said in her letters. Sam had saved three hundred dollars from odd jobs, which would only pay for a one-way bus ticket and upkeep for a few weeks. Lorna said she had a friend who might be able to find Sam a part-time job putting up wallboard and aluminum siding. Sam knew just enough about carpentry and construction to keep a job if his boss liked him. He was willing to work if that was what Lorna wanted, but not for any other reason: His heart, when he searched it, was unsoiled by any unfounded attraction to work, clean and blank as one of his mother's uniforms.

The igloo was almost hot inside. Sam lifted the wooden hatch in the roof and felt a rush of cool air. It was midnight, but when Sam looked down the hill, he saw a reading lamp flicker from inside Aunt Bertha's living room. His mother was still awake, lying on the sofa and stirring a cup of tea. Marjorie LeBlanc and her flowered sofa and hot-water bottles and tea. Sam closed the hatch. She'd fall asleep in a while. He wouldn't go in just yet.

*   *   *   *

Marjorie rested in her cocoon of afghans. She wasn't even bothering to pull out the rollaway bed these days; she'd just stretch out on the sofa cushions. It was late, but she could not sleep. She had been drinking Morning Thunder tea all day, and her nerves were jangling and her brain humming. When she closed her eyes, she could feel herself falling, and when she jerked herself awake she had the same sense of not having her feet on the ground, of being a free-floating thing. Really, she had nothing left. They had torn down her house and taken her job, and now all her children were abandoning her at the same time. Sam thought about nothing but running off to Alaska; Ruth insisted on going to college. Karen had disowned them all. And now Carla was choosing to move into New York City and go to school there. There wasn't a chance of her leaving New York City to stay in Ripon, especially with her brother and sister gone. Certainly Marjorie LeBlanc alone was not enough to tempt anybody anywhere.

Marjorie turned onto her stomach and buried her face in the crack between the cushions and the sofa back. When she closed her eyes, she saw the Budds' house, and so she opened them. If it hadn't been for Faith, Marjorie might still be safe at home in North Carolina, all her children with her. Well, that wasn't really fair. What else could Faith have done? But Marjorie knew one thing for certain: She never would have packed Faith in a plane and sent her away. Never. Marjorie LeBlanc hadn't even meant much to her own best friend.

Marjorie sat up and looked out the window. The field across from Bertha's house was perfectly flat, except for Sam's igloo, which looked almost luminous under the moonlight. Marjorie could make out the depression that ran up from the road over the tunnel he had built. The tunnel was beginning to sag, and probably was not safe. Both it and the house would melt in the next month. All that work for nothing.

Marjorie decided to see the igloo for herself before it caved in. She put on two sweaters and a parka, two pairs of socks, boots, gloves, mittens, two hats, and a scarf. She took the flashlight from the closet and opened the front door. The cold knocked the wind out of her. She stood still for a moment, gathering her breath, and then walked across the gravel road and lifted the burlap bag covering the tunnel entrance. She aimed the flashlight up the tunnel. Sam had reinforced it with boards, and it reminded Marjorie of a mine shaft. She doubled over and crept along the tunnel until she reached the tarp covering the end. She lifted up the tarp and a wave of warm air rushed to meet her.

"Oh!" she said. There was her son, squatting next to the gas lamp, with his black head of hair bending over a small fire he had built. He looked narrow as a burnt matchstick. He seemed to be unnaturally thin and twice her height. None of her children looked a thing like her. She felt cheated somehow; it seemed only fair after all the years of raising them that she might have left at least a physical mark on them, letting the world know they were hers.

"Mama!" said Sam. After a moment of hesitation, he added, "Well, come on in."

Marjorie ducked under the tarp and looked around her. She could almost stand up straight in the igloo. Sam had tacked calendar pictures of Alaskan landscapes to the walls, and he had an apple crate on one side, which Marjorie could see was filled with magazines. The magazine on top was cast into shadow, but when the fire flickered, Marjorie noticed a herd of caribou walking across the cover. She sat down on the crate.

"It's nice to see you up and around, Mama."

"Just when do you plan to leave for Alaska?" Marjorie answered.

"Not till after school's out."

"Humph," Marjorie said.

Sam didn't try to say anything else. He busied himself blowing on the fire and poking at it.

"Other mothers lose their children bit by bit. Not Marjorie LeBlanc. Mine jump out of the nest all at the same time. I'd just like to know why. I'd just like to know why my children can't wait to get away from me. Just what kind of horrible thing did I do to make all my children run away from me the first chance they could?"

"Aw, Mama," Sam answered. "We're not running away from you. Didn't you ever want to run off *to* somebody when you were growing up?"

"No."

"You ran off with Byron Coffin to North Carolina."

"I didn't have anybody anymore where I was. And besides, look what that got me."

Sam ventured to say, "If I was to have four children, I think I'd be glad to be left in peace after all the years it took to raise them."

"You wait until you have children!" Marjorie exclaimed.

Marjorie reached into the crate and pulled out some magazines. She was amazed by how much light the gas lamp gave off. It seemed stronger than an electric lamp. She opened a magazine, and a large aquatic mammal looked up at her. The strong light made the animal appear real, swimming up out of the picture. "Manatee or Sea Cow," it said underneath. The caption explained that early sailors had mistaken manatees for mermaids.

"Faith Budd gave me those magazines when we were staying with her. She found me all the ones she had with articles on Alaska."

Marjorie sat so long looking through the magazines that Sam's fire burned down to a black circle and grew cool. She had found an anthropology journal with an article called "Early Viking Keels," written by Bertha. Marjorie paged through drawings of monstery-looking boats that curled up in the back like dragon tails.

"Hey, Mama? Hey, Mama?"

Marjorie was imagining what it would be like to sail across the Atlantic in a scary boat like that, and she didn't hear her son.

"Mama? It's getting kind of cold." Sam picked up the gas lamp. Marjorie held on to the journal and followed him out the tunnel.

* * * *

Ruth stayed at The Spot until late, drinking bourbon and ignoring the college boys in the corner of the bar. The bartender had told her he needed a new waitress, and Ruth was deciding to quit her job at the cookie factory and move on to The Spot. It was the only real bar in town. After her first bourbon, a man in a motorcycle jacket that said "Zodiacs" on the back offered to buy Ruth another drink, but she refused and moved to the end of the bar. There were two motorcycle gangs in town: the Masters and the Zodiacs. They were mostly paunchy, balding men in their mid-twenties, who wore jackets with psychedelic designs on the back. They drove Harley-Davidsons and rumbled on a hill outside the town, or rode in a motorcade down the main street and circled back around when they reached the police station. "Shooting the loop," they called it.

"Hey, you," a woman said, pushing up against Ruth's elbow. "My husband offer to buy you a drink?" The woman had on a Piggly Wiggly supermarket uniform. She was thinner than Ruth and about her age, with lanky brown hair pulled back into a braid.

"The motorcycle guy?" Ruth asked.

"Yeah, him."

When Ruth did not say anything else, the woman sat on the next stool and said, "You can have him if you want him."

"No place to put him," Ruth answered.

"Goddamn," said the woman. She poked at a pinkish drink with a plastic cocktail stirrer and asked Ruth, "You a student at the college?"

"No," said Ruth.

"Oh. I thought you were, because I didn't recognize you from high school. I know everyone in Ripon. God damn. You can't pass a face on the street you haven't seen one hundred times already."

"I'm from Durham, in North Carolina."

"That's nice. That's real nice. I spent my whole life in Ripoff, Wisconzin. Every morning I get up and I say, 'Nancy, you aren't going to make it. You aren't going to be able to stand another day in this dumb stinking town.' I get by doing little things, hey. I look for strangers passing through and I talk to them. Goddamn. If I wasn't married, with four kids, I'd leave tomorrow. You got a boyfriend or husband?"

Ruth shook her head.

"You have a romance going?"

Ruth shook her head again.

"Well, don't even bother to look for any. There aren't any men worth your time in Ripoff. You think I would of married who I did if there were? See that guy over there in the corner?"

Ruth turned around.

"That's Wesley Page. He fucks chickens. See that guy in the red hunting vest laughing it up with my husband and the other guy?"

Ruth turned around again.

"What he does for fun is he drives down to Green Lake when the ice is real thick and rides around on the ice. He says it's better than Jesus Christ, because Jesus only walked on water, but he can drive on it. His name's Dale. I went out with him in high school, but he never did anything except dry-hump me.

"See that girl sitting across from us? She got real fat at

the beginning of tenth grade and then disappeared for seven months and came back skinny as a rail. Nobody knows who took the baby or anything. That guy next to her used to have a twin brother, but he was killed by a city man out here hunting deer. And that guy over there, he got his leg messed up in Vietnam and couldn't find a job anywhere. That bleach blonde, she's his wife. She works as a chiropractor's assistant. There isn't a person in this town I don't know something about. God damn."

The woman laid her head sideways on the counter. "I feel like a pig in a poke," she concluded, and then closed her eyes.

Ruth waited a minute to see if the woman was going to keep talking, but she seemed to be falling asleep on her stool. Ruth got up quietly and paid her bill. When she stepped outside, she walked slowly. It was the end of March, and the cold was almost tolerable. She looked up at the bank sign that flashed the time and temperature, and saw that it was two o'clock and sixteen degrees. Almost warm. When she had first come to Ripon, Ruth had felt cold all the time, but now, after experiencing weeks at fifty below with the wind chill factor, she hardly noticed the spring cold. She thought she could accustom herself to living anywhere, as long as she didn't have to stay anywhere very long.

Ruth climbed into Aunt Bertha's Ford Falcon and raced it down Main Street, shooting the loop. She tore back in the direction of Aunt Bertha's, flying past houses and the high school, more houses and then barren fields that looked blue in the moonlight. She turned toward the highway, and Bertha's square green house sailed toward Ruth over its expanse of blue snow. Ruth parked the car and walked around to the back door, to keep from waking her mother in the living room.

Ruth's heart almost stopped when a giant shadow sprang up on the kitchen wall like a jack-in-the-box. She heard an eerie low roar.

It was only Marjorie LeBlanc, holding Sam's gas lamp. She had turned the lamp up so high that it hurt Ruth's eyes to look at the mantle.

"Oh," said Marjorie. "I heard a noise, and I was worried it was a burglar. I got up to get a bite of something. I was just fooling around with the lamp." Ruth turned down the gas until the strange roaring sound quieted.

Marjorie took a kettle of boiling water from the stove and made a pot of Aunt Bertha's Red Zinger tea. "You should try this. It's made from rose hips," Marjorie said. She opened the refrigerator and cut herself a hunk of Wisconsin Colby cheese.

Ruth was dead tired, but she took off her jacket, sat down at the table, and poured herself a cup of Red Zinger from Aunt Bertha's green ceramic teapot. Her mother looked wired.

"I didn't feel like sleeping," Marjorie said. "I've been on the couch all day today anyhow." She tittered in what Ruth thought was a mindless sort of way.

"Mama, just how long do you plan to stay on that couch? Until doomsday?" Ruth dared to ask. "Don't you even want to walk around a little and see things? Just to air out your head?"

Marjorie put down her hunk of cheese. "You don't need to get high and mighty with your mother. Everybody wants me to change. Bertha and Sam and you. You all want me to just give everything up without so much as a Job's swear. Well, just let me tell you something—"

Ruth groaned. She didn't feel like listening to any more talking that night, least of all from her mother.

But Marjorie ignored her. "You want me to change, but all you children, you've been exactly the same from the time you were little. I could of told from the time you were babies how each and every one of you was going to turn out. You're the ones who never change. You don't even remember how you were when you were small. I remember, I know. You were always bent on leading the others astray, in any direction but the one I pointed them to. Karen was a little dressed-up thing, and Sam was quiet and daydreaming to escape from the given moment, and Carla was always looking for trouble. You think you know everything, but there's whole long stretches of your own life that you can't even recollect. But I know, I was there."

Ruth's mother looked down at the green teapot as if it were a crystal ball.

"Do you remember the time I decided to take you to Mass? Of course you don't, you were little. It was in Fayetteville, right after Mr. Big left. I tried to dress you all up, I'd made you red smocks with white aprons and Sam had a miniature blue suit with suspenders. I got a ride into town, and then walked with you down to the church. On the way, you ripped your dress and then cried when I lost my temper at you, because you said it was an accident. Of course, you'd done it on purpose. I saw you. You pushed up against a wire fence with a snaggle of rosebushes poking out all the way along it. You leaned against the fence and walked that way, with your feet way out to the left of you and your whole weight against the rosebushes.

"And there you were anyway in your down-at-the-heel Mary Janes, with socks that didn't match. Karen used to go through all the drawers and find the socks that matched and then put all the ones that didn't in your drawer. And you never noticed! Never! And when we rounded the corner by the church, Carla sat right down on an oil stain on the ground. She must have been about four, and Karen started yelling, 'Mama, Mama, Carla's sitting in a puddle. Look! Look!' So I turned around to pull her up, and Sam, who was off in the clouds somewhere, tripped on the curb and fell backwards and cracked his head on the pavement. Karen started shrieking, and then all the families walking into the church turned around and stared down the street at us. A skinny lady in an ugly yellow hat even walked back out to get a better look. There you and Carla were, poker-faced, looking like this kind of violent thing happened every day of your lives and hardly mattered to you. No one came down the steps to help, they all just stood there and looked at us, the way people look at someone they don't think is enough like them to be really human. The way you see people look at some drunk sleeping with his mouth open in a parking lot on a freezing cold night, or a fancy lady being stopped by the police, or the way rich people drive by a raggedy family sitting on a porch. Like there's nothing you can do to help them, because they're too far beyond the pale. That's how they looked at us. Even the priest walked by like we weren't there. And I never went to Mass again after that, never. So I picked up Sam and laid him out on a bench and wadded a handkerchief behind his head. And finally some old guy in a car stopped and loaded Sam into the back seat and drove us to the hospital. I looked in the rearview mirror and saw I had a smudge of dirt down my cheek and my hair was all flying loose and my lipstick on crooked. I looked like I'd escaped from somewhere."

Ruth was amazed she had never heard this story before. It was just the kind of memory mothers liked to dwell on. She had no idea what Marjorie LeBlanc was driving at.

"There are a whole lot of things I haven't told you. I went through years and years of you that you hardly know about." Marjorie opened another box of tea, pulled out a tea bag, and poured a cup of already brewed Red Zinger over the bag. Morning Thunder, Ruth saw on the tea box.

"That's got caffeine in it," said Ruth. "You'll never get to sleep if—"

Marjorie took a gulp from the tea. "I just don't understand how you can go on year after year, staying the same, and then one day you just run off, and I'm the one who's supposed to adjust. I'm supposed to sit back and watch my world crashing down and still keep on being Marjorie LeBlanc."

*   *   *   *

The next day, Marjorie folded up the couch early in the morning and went for a walk in South Woods. She surprised two teenagers kissing in a car beside the dirt path running down to the woods, she almost missed stepping in some kind of animal trap, and she fell through a layer of ice over a stream bed and wet her leg up to the knee. By the time she got back to the house, her foot was completely numb. But then she went out again in the afternoon and climbed to the top of a hill in Kiwanis Park. She looked down on a group of men wearing red jackets and carrying rifles, perhaps on their way back from the rifle club up the road. One of them pointed his gun barrel at her, pretended to pull the trigger, and laughed. Marjorie ignored him. She walked out of the park and along the road, and shocked herself on an electric fence, trying to pet a horse.

That night, she went to an Alfred Hitchcock film showing at the college and walked back home through the town cemetery. The following morning, she drove Bertha to work and then took the Ford Falcon to Oshkosh and drove up and down the side streets looking at houses. She spent the next two weeks traveling between Ripon, Green Lake, Fond du Lac, and Berlin. The towns were far apart, tiny islands separated by expanses of snow, and even the farms between them were far from each other, sunk in the middles of icy fields. Marjorie thought she would rather die than live in one of those solitary, neighborhoodless houses, but there was something appealing about the spareness of the landscapes. They were bleached clean, just like her. Empty.

One afternoon when she was out in the Falcon, Marjorie got caught in a blizzard and barely made it through the swirling snow to a little eating place—what Marjorie had always called a coffeehouse, but who knew what they called it here—in a town called Omro. *Omro,* Marjorie thought, was the kind of sound you might be tempted to yell into a well or a mine shaft. When Marjorie walked into the coffeehouse, a lady in an electric-orange vest was trying to place a call to Milwaukee. The only other person inside was a cityish-looking man in hunting clothes: He had on those brown and green mottled pants that army men wore for camouflage, and he was balancing an expensive leather rifle case on his knees. Marjorie sat on the other side of the room from him, close to the window. She watched the wind pick up piles of snow and heave them at the coffeehouse.

"Looks like you made it just in time," the woman in the electric orange vest said, coming to the edge of the table with an order pad. "Can I bring you something hot to warm your bones? Some tea or soup?"

Marjorie ordered some beef consommé. When the woman brought the soup, she asked Marjorie for her telephone number and offered to try and place a call to Ripon for her. Marjorie was tempted to give a false number; she didn't feel like being reached by anyone just yet. But then she changed her mind and wrote down Bertha's number when the wind tossed another wave of snow at the window. The lines probably wouldn't be back up for some time. Marjorie moved her chair over slightly to see out the window better, broke some crackers into her bowl, and ate slowly, bending over the steam to warm her face. Marjorie had never eaten consommé before: She had always considered it too fine and elegant-sounding to be real food. But then, it was just canned Campbell's soup, nothing out of the ordinary at all.

The man in the hunting suit rose and walked to the window. Marjorie saw him staring at a gray Lincoln Continental. The snow was building up so fast that the car seemed to be burrowing earthward. It reminded Marjorie of a sand crab.

"Get a load of that snow," the man said, whistling to himself and then turning to Marjorie. "Baby, what were you doing riding around in a snowstorm? You could have frozen to death out there."

Marjorie put down her soup spoon and narrowed her eyes

at the man. "The name's not Baby," she said in a gruff, cow-boyish voice that surprised her. She wished she had a nonfiltered cigarette; she would blow out a puff of smoke and glare at him with a dangerous expression.

"Say what?" the man asked.

"I'm forty years old," Marjorie answered. "I have four grown-up and practically gone children. What's a blizzard to me? And what I said to you is: My name's not Baby." Marjorie went back to her soup. She opened another cracker package and watched a flurry of crumbs snow down into the consommé.

"Well, excuse me for living," the man answered. "So what *is* your name?"

"Sirhan Sirhan," Marjorie LeBlanc told him.

The waitress laughed loudly into the telephone, and the man, who thought she might be laughing at him, wandered back to his table and pretended to inspect his rifle. She hung up the phone and walked over to Marjorie's table and said, "The local operator thinks it's going to be a while before the telephone company even remembers there's a town called Omro buried out here in the snow somewhere. Hey, my name's Trudy. I don't suppose you want to waste a few hours playing spit?" She held up two decks of cards. A black queen looked at Marjorie with raised eyebrows, as if daring her to do something.

"That's one card game I've never heard of," Marjorie answered.

"I'll show you," said Trudy, looping her electric orange vest over a chair and sitting down.

* * * *

In between rounds of spit, Marjorie and Trudy tried for five hours to get through to Ripon. When the snow finally stopped and the roads were plowed, telephone lines were still down. When Marjorie reluctantly stopped playing cards and drove home, everyone was standing at Bertha's living room window, worried to death. They made such a fuss over Marjorie that she really felt she had been on an adventure.

She got up early the next day, before anyone else was awake, so that she could have a little of the morning to herself. She felt impatient, and dressed hurriedly, pulling on her pants and boots over her long johns and not bothering to find a shirt. Marjorie took Sam's parka from the closet and decided to wear it. It fell past her knees, and the sleeves extended twice the length of her arms. Deciding not to waste time looking for her mittens, she threw open the front door and waded through the snowdrifts to Sam's tunnel and lifted the flap. Marjorie tried yelling "OOOOmrooo" through the tunnel to see what it sounded like. It made a nice double echo. She walked up the tunnel, wondering how long it and the igloo would hold up; she remembered how her mother used to make Bertha fill in the holes to China she dug in the backyard. Marjorie lifted the flap at the end of the tunnel and walked inside the igloo. She stretched out on Sam's grass mattress.

Then the roof caved in. It happened without warning; the ceiling seemed to leap down onto her, covering her in icy rubble. A brick of ice landed on her chest and a carpet of snow thudded on top of her. She lifted her arm to protect her face from the section of wall that caved in above her head.

She was completely buried, except for her left arm and the left side of her face. However, she suspected she would be able to push off all the rubble by kicking and thrashing, so she lay still for a moment. She imagined she was a prospector lying inside a collapsed mine in one of those movies about the American frontier where the miner's friends stand outside, calling to him and trying to dig their way through.

*   *   *   *

"Mama! Mama, are you OK? Mama!" There was Sam, bending over her with a dramatic expression and lifting chunks of ice off of her.

"No bones broken," Marjorie answered. She sat up and pulled her foot from under a pile of ice. She stood. "Sorry about your ice house."

"I thought you were a goner," said Sam, brushing the snow from his mother's hat. "Well. Must have been the weight of all that snow yesterday." He bent down and began heaving chunks of ice off the apple crate full of magazines. Sam straightened the magazines and picked up the crate, while Marjorie fished around in the rubble for as many calendar pages as she could find. She and Sam struggled through the powdery snow covering the field, back to the house.

At breakfast, Marjorie talked a blue streak about how the game spit was played. When everyone had left for school and work, she shoveled trenches through the snow that covered the yard in a thick mattress.

After that, she cleared the walks every morning, until the layer of feathery snow turned into a hard crust on the yard. In early April, there was another heavy snowfall, and Marjorie got up early to dig the Ford Falcon out of the driveway and to push the snow off the car with a broom. When Bertha drove Ruth and Sam away, Marjorie started to work on the walkway.

She huffed and puffed as she hefted shovelfuls of snow off the walks into the yard. She had come to enjoy the early morning right after everyone went out and she was left alone to brave the elements. The wind bit at her face, and she chopped at the ice on the walk with a pick. After she finished, she stood on the front steps and admired the wiggly path running away from the house toward the field.

Over the crest of the hill at the end of the field, a head rose, hatless, and under it a person impossibly clothed for the weather: a woman in a rose-colored sweater and black pants, without a coat or a scarf. Marjorie watched the woman's knees rise and fall over the snow, and she seemed to be wearing only navy-blue tennis shoes, without any kind of overboot. Her arms were crossed under her breasts, and red, gloveless hands stuck out at her sides. Marjorie wondered why the woman would be walking toward the gravel road, of all the deserted places. As she got closer, Marjorie speculated that the woman might be drunk: Her brown hair flew out in wisps and her onion-shaped bun had already slid far down the right side of her head.

Marjorie dropped the shovel. "Faith!" she yelled across the road, and then hurried along the walk, sliding the last yard on a runway of ice.

Faith turned into the yard and walked with high-kneed steps across the snow. She and Marjorie hugged over a mound of snow dividing the path from the yard.

"I've run away!" Faith said breathlessly. "I left the car at the top of the hill. I don't have any chains on my tires."

"Come inside, you'll die of cold," Marjorie told her, guiding Faith around to the walkway and over the ice.

When they got in the house, Faith said, "My toes feel like lead sinkers."

"Take your shoes off and stand over here on the heating vent." The two women took off their boots and shoes and huddled over the vent. Their faces were barely six inches apart, and raw from the cold.

"What do you mean, you ran away?"

"Oh, Marjorie, I felt so lonesome and nothing-to-doish after you left. I'd sit in my living room staring across the street, watching them knock down your house and wondering if my life was over. I thought it would be different when Winston came home, but it wasn't—he keeps to himself just like he always did. I got so I felt like the house was my own grave. I just sat in my window and wondered if my life was over." Faith stopped and looked down at her feet.

"The cold makes your feet tingle when they start to thaw," Marjorie told her. "Let's sit over there on the couch."

The two women plunked down onto a pile of afghans.

Faith drew her hands to the sides of her head. "Oh, Marjorie, I've done an evil thing!"

Marjorie felt a flurry of wickedness inside her.

"I've stolen my boys' Chevrolet and five thousand dollars from a savings account full of Franklin Delano's money."

"You didn't!"

"I did."

* * * *

When Sam, Ruth, and Bertha stepped out of the Ford Falcon, they were met by the smell of black-eyed peas and collards cooked with ham bone, smothered pork chops, and a peach cobbler with too much cinnamon in it.

"You don't think Mama's cooking, do you?" said Ruth.

Sam looked down the gravel road and saw a Chevrolet with snow chains but no snow tires. "That car," he told his Aunt Bertha, but she looked back at him uncomprehendingly.

When Bertha opened the front door, there was a strange woman sitting on the flowered couch, looking through a United States road atlas.

"Mrs. Budd!" Ruth called over Bertha's shoulder.

"Faith Budd!" Bertha cried.

"You call me Faith LeBlanc. I'm traveling incognito." Faith winked at Sam.

Marjorie came out of the kitchen, wiping her hands on one of Sam's long-sleeved shirts, which she had tied around her waist to use as an apron. "Faith's left home. We're making a celebration dinner."

"We were hoping and praying we'd get done before you all came home. We spent half the day at the station putting chains on my car. I hate the idea of chaining up a car."

"We're planning a trip," said Marjorie.

"Is that so?" Bertha asked. She was still standing in her parka and scarf, trying to take things in. Ruth and Sam were shucking off their clothes behind her, and Sam leaned over and pulled off his aunt's hat: Her hair lay flat on her head like a field trampled by a straying animal. "Faith, you're a sight for sore eyes," Bertha proclaimed. Then she dropped her book bag, threw her coat onto the couch, walked over to Marjorie, smacked her on the cheek with a loud kiss and then snorted in her ear, and slipped beside her into the kitchen to lift up the pot lids.

"A Mr. Mintor kiss!" Faith called from the living room.

Ruth and Sam followed Bertha into the kitchen, and Sam poked his nose inside the oven door to smell the peach cobbler better. When dinner was ready, Faith and Marjorie piled bowls and plates on the table.

"I've run away from home," Faith explained again for everyone's benefit. "I have five thousand dollars tucked in my bra, minus the cost of gas and chains for the tires." Faith ate a spoonful of black-eyed peas. "Small payment for raising those boys. I left Franklin Delano a note saying, 'Sweetheart, I've fallen in love with another.' "

"You didn't," said Ruth.

Faith nodded. "He won't guess in a million years where I've escaped to. Marjorie and I are going to travel together."

"I think that's wonderful," Bertha said, spearing a black-eyed pea. "Just where are you going, and how long are you going for?"

"For a year!" Marjorie said in an uproarious voice.

"Until the money runs out," Faith joined her.

"We thought Sam would stay here with you, to finish out the school year," Marjorie said with her old worried tone, seeming to back down a little. She stood up to clear away the pork chop plate, and Sam saw she had forgotten to take off her makeshift apron. The sleeves of his shirt had slid down and were clinging to her hips.

"I'd love to have him," said Bertha. "Ruth too, until you go away to school," she told Ruth.

Ruth and Sam looked across the table at each other. Ruth wanted to say, "And just abandon us here!" but then she caught herself.

"After a while, we're going to hook around to New York and visit you and Carla and Karen in the fall," Marjorie said, reaching across the table and putting her hand over Ruth's.

"But first we're going to Beaver Island," said Faith Le-Blanc. "I read about it in a magazine. It's in the middle of Lake Michigan. You have to take a ferry to get there, and rose hips just grow along the side of the road."

"Then we're going to swing up and visit Ellen Moody in Wyoming, and then cut down to see some caves in New Mexico," Marjorie said with greater enthusiasm. "After that, Faith wants to see New Orleans, and maybe we'll drive way down to where they make Tabasco sauce."

"We're still planning," Faith said modestly. "Those were just the ideas we came up with today."

"How about Alaska?" Sam asked.

Faith seemed to study the idea with interest. "They had a thriller of an earthquake there. Might be interesting."

"Don't you worry, Sam," Marjorie told her son. "When we're done, I'll look for a new job."

"Why work?" Ruth told her.

"We're going to stay in the place we like best and look for bad jobs there," Faith said. "You know Franklin Delano Budd," she began, pronouncing the name slowly, in a way that made it seem as if she had never heard it. "He never let me work, so it's not as if I think I can be choosy. I know how to be practical. Well, I can learn to be," she added.

Ruth stared at her mother and thought she looked different. Marjorie LeBlanc's dark hair threw back the light from the overhead lampshade, and her cheeks were windburned, as if she'd spent several hours outside. "Why, Mama's happy," Ruth pronounced, and everyone at the table turned to stare at Marjorie. Marjorie LeBlanc raised a pork chop on the end of her fork and exclaimed, "Hoop-de-lah!"

* * * *

During the next three weeks, Marjorie and Faith huddled on the living room floor, spreading maps and magazines around them. In May, the snow began to draw back from the fields and icy water filled the depressions between hills. Small animals ran from their flooded holes, and one morning an apparently rabid vole made a beeline for Marjorie, and she had to fight it off with a broom. Gradually, the roads blackened with rain and the tree trunks shone red and yellow along fields of stubble. Tornado-shaped swarms of mosquitoes twirled high in Kiwanis Park. Faith Budd and Marjorie LeBlanc took the chains off the Chevrolet's tires and piled two coolers packed with food, four large suitcases, travel brochures, a road atlas, and several state maps into the Chevrolet's back seat.

Bertha had dressed in a blue caftan with gold embroidery and a Panama hat for the leavetaking. It was still too cold without a jacket, but Ruth wore only a T-shirt, flip-flops, and jeans cut off so short that the front pockets poked out under raggedy hems. She was also wearing a Panama hat, and had tilted it at the same angle as Aunt Bertha's. It occurred to Marjorie that Ruth looked more like Bertha's daughter than her own. Sam had on a bright-orange flannel shirt, which Faith said it hurt her eyes to look at.

"You're going to catch your death of cold standing out here dressed like North Carolina," Faith told Ruth.

Hugs were given all around, and Faith got into the driver's seat, turned on the ignition, and raced the motor. Marjorie slid into the car beside her, and spread open a map with Lake Michigan at its center.

"You wild women take care of each other and stay out of trouble," Bertha said, banging the door closed behind Marjorie.

Faith and Marjorie LeBlanc backed out of the driveway and took the gravel road around to the highway. The Chevrolet sped down the black asphalt. Marjorie turned in her seat and saw Bertha's green house perching by itself on the side of the field, with all that was left of Marjorie's family standing beside it. Then the Chevrolet flew around a corner behind a hill ridged with new plow rows, and the house leapt from sight.